THE CANINA THORN

THE UNCHOSEN SERIES BOOK ONE

K. J. DAWSON

Developmental and line edit by M.K. Martin, copyedit by Katheen Gooch, proofread by Dawn Yacovetta, and by Sue-Ellen Welfonder.

Cover art by Dar Albert at Wicked Smart Designs.

Published by Oliver-Heber Books

0 9 8 7 6 5 4 3 2 1

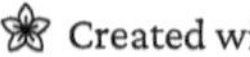 Created with Vellum

To
Those who choose
to be Chosen
to be the hero
to take the hard path,

When battles are done
and your Bones Are Weary,
put down your sword,
your shield.

Seek peace, and rest, and Joy.

THE UNCHOSEN SERIES

The Lilac Plague
The Rose Court
The Canina Thorn

MAP OF CORNARA

CHARACTER LIST

Dacia:

Empress Nicoleta Aurelian, "Nikka": Empress of Dacia

Calvus Aurelian, "Papa": Azure daisy scholar, Nicoleta's father, and adviser to the throne

Lord Marcus Constantin: Lily, Agricultural Emissary

Lady Katalin Vulpe: Rose noble, eastern ambassador

Rubia Bythesea: Getaen Healer, Nicoleta's mother's closest friend

Jamil Redvalley: Thorn, Head of the Empress' Own, the Empress' most trusted, elite guards

Irena Redvalley: Protector, Jamil's daughter

Thadeus: Thorn, Empress' Own

Liviana Constantin: Thorn, soldier recruit

Ziba: Getaen Protector, adviser to the throne

Pari: Getaen Healer, adviser to the throne

Rufus: Getaen: Getaen Ghoster, adviser to the throne

Cyrus Thushtra: Red Valley Clan Leader

Yutab Behar: Red Valley Clan Leader's wife

Auripo:
Dyana Coatys: Future Queen Consort, married to Eusebes II

Prince Asander Coatys: Second born child of King Eusebes

Prince Petre Coatys: Third born child of King Eusebes

Theracia:
Emperor Saam Oeagrus: Emperor of Theracia

Captain Kekad Dardan: Illyrian Captain, colony state of Theracia

Norte:
Borsea: Norte warrior, Illuminator

CORNARA CLASS SYSTEM

Rose: Upper noble with a title. Often in an influential position of authority in the kingdom. Often oversee an estate, at behest of the crown.

Lily: Lower noble with a lesser title. Often in a lesser position of authority in the kingdom.

Thorns: All military, including: city watch, Imperial Guard, and Emperor's Own.

Azure Daisy: Scholars and artisans, including: astronomers, philosophers, painters, sculptors, and historians. No title. Often have small inheritance and dwelling.

Clover: Skilled workers, including: farmers, merchants, and craftsmen. No title. Sometimes own land or property.

Poppy: Laborers, including: miners and servants. No title, no property.

Lilacs: Desolate, poor, diseased, and slaves.

Reeds: The Getaens, magical and non-magical. A class unto themselves. Although technically may marry into other classes, own
land, or have wealth, always considered Reeds.

*Individuals can move up the class system by marriage, by gaining
wealth, or by doing something extraordinary; and conversely, they
can be demoted.

TYPES OF MAGIC

Healer: Heals using herbs infused with magic. Can also use incantations alone or to strengthen the healing properties. Employed after someone is unwell. Negative use: poisoning.

Protector: Builds strength and resilience to injury or sickness. Three types of protection: mind, flesh and sinew, and/or blood and bone. Negative use: weakens bodies.

Illuminator: Infuses light into objects, primarily luminary orbs. Negative use: pulls light away.

Sonus: Modifies sound — dampens or amplifies.

Sensitive: Senses emotions. Also known as "the truth teller." Negative use: manipulates other's emotions and beliefs.

Clarifier: Heightens experiences, or clarifies memories. Negative use: forces someone to relive painful memories, manipulates memories, and/or erases memories.

Mirror (also known as a "Ghoster"): Records messages, feelings, or memories for others. Embodied as a "ghost."

Bonder: Bonds people or objects with magic. Negative use: creates a curse and attaches spell to person or object.

Seer: Can see possible futures.

Rippers: Can take essence, magic, or traits from others.

ONE

RODNIC VALLEY

An early winter wind bit at my cheeks, and acid burned up my throat. In the northern Rodnic Valley, I delivered the first speech on my tour of the kingdom.

"War is coming, and we will fight for honor." I lifted my chin, projecting firm confidence, though inside I roiled. My call to arms would determine our kingdom's success or demise.

The morning sky was dark with bloated clouds, but the threatening storm hadn't deterred the people. The Sonus repeated my words, her magically-enhanced voice carrying over the crowd that pressed together, filling the entire cobblestone road and beyond. Blank faces peered up at me. I swallowed, my stomach curdling.

"We will be victorious against the magic of the north and the tyrant of the south. We fight for Dacia." Only my rote memorization of each syllable enabled me to utter each practiced word. Though the Crown of Lore was heavy, I was determined to shoulder the responsibilities and had prepared myself well.

The Poppies and Clovers, mostly farmers and laborers, clapped, but there were no cheers. Most were glassy-eyed — seemingly disconnected from the urgency. I needed to strip away any hope they harbored that the invasion was a distant rumor. They needed to know. To act. And quickly.

With any luck, I would inspire enough recruits. Twelve hundred. We needed twelve hundred.

My betrothed, Prince Asander of Auripo, stood behind me. More than just a token of his country's support, he'd put his military experience to use, training my army in strategy and tactics over the last two moons.

As my eyes swept the crowd, a familiar face caught my gaze. Otho, Marcus' father, stood with his arms folded and stern lines furrowed across his brow. I couldn't be sure if his wife or children were with him in the crowd. It was pure folly, but I scanned around him for Marcus.

He wasn't there. Of course.

Since I'd arrived in the valley where Marcus grew up, walking on cobblestones his feet could have touched, dining in an inn he may have frequented, I couldn't help but see him around every corner. Was it possible to be haunted by the ghost of a living man?

As I stepped off the rough platform, Asander gripped my elbow, helping me manage the wobbly bottom step in a graceful manner. His perfect timing maintained the appearance of support and cohesion.

"Well done, Empress," Asander said loud enough for my guards to hear as he ushered me toward the inn.

"It wasn't well done," I muttered, stepping over a puddle.

He lowered his voice. "It was your first attempt. You simply need more practice."

I practiced until my tongue was sore.

Something was wrong with my address, I just didn't know what, nor how to fix it. But the solution definitely wasn't more practice.

We followed Jamil, the head of my Own, my trusted personal guard. He cut through the crowd, his glower enough to send even the boldest scurrying out of our way.

Though my message to the people fell flat, surely once they considered my ominous warning, they'd realize their desperate situation and volunteer to fight. They had to. The alternatives were the overtaking of the lands we stood on, forcing these same villagers into Theracian wars in distant lands, or direct subjugation to the magical Norte, whose cold cruelty sent a shiver down my spine.

As we entered the inn, I shook out my hands, redirecting my focus. Regardless of how vital it had been to keep the nobles happy and engaged, I had despised every barbed dinner with the Rose Court. But those occasions paled in comparison to the importance of this humble meal.

The northern guild representatives I would be dining with were critical to the success of the looming war. The next few hours would be my only chance to spur them to increase production before the fighting began. My words would have to dance the fine line between inspiring them and frightening them. Furthermore, the Agricultural Guild needed to immediately change course. And I'd already been informed who had come to report on their behalf — Otho Constantin.

~

IMPERIAL GUARDS SEARCHED each representative before allowing them entrance. Inside the inn, half a dozen of the Empress' Own lurked, alert for assassins.

I stood near the crackling fireplace and received each representative before we dined, stressing the importance of their guild's aid to the cause along with my gratitude. If my earlier speech failed to find purchase, at least the guilds could spur the local craftsfolk, setting them to long hours sweating over boots and gloves, arrows and swords, saddles and tents, and a myriad of other supplies. Even if I gathered enough troops, they would die exposed and hungry if I didn't spark a flurry of production.

Otho approached me and bowed. "Empress, I come on behalf of my father, the representative for the Agricultural Guild of the Rodnic Valley, who is too ill to travel."

Face to face, waves of conflicting emotions rolled through me.

Otho had provided transportation when Rubia and I fled our homes in Moesia, even lying to help us escape. But he'd also treated our desperation as a game, cruelly overcharging us. On top of the flood of memories, seeing Otho made me ravenous for news. Had he received letters from Marcus? I had not.

"Congratulations are in order. It was my pleasure to recognize your son as the new Agricultural Emissary," I said. With Marcus' new title, his family was elevated — a rarity — to the Lily noble status.

Those waiting behind Otho leaned closer, like vultures, ready to pick apart every word. Otho shrunk under their gaze, then he drew himself up. "It is a great honor, one Marcus has worked toward since childhood. All agricultural representatives, including my father, support our new emissary."

If the gossip was as widespread as my advisers hoped, everyone believed I had jilted Marcus in favor of Asander. The truth wasn't nearly so simple.

My official engagement to King Eusebes Coatys' second son brought Dacia a desperately needed ally. Protecting my kingdom was my primary concern. I had put aside my heart's desire and wouldn't allow myself the luxury of brooding over the past.

I understood why Marcus had left. I'd been mistaken to allow myself to become entangled with someone with whom I could never have a future. If my subjects ever realized how foolish I'd been in my personal life, would they trust me with more weighty decisions? Trust me with their lives?

As the representatives' attention intensified, I dismissed Otho, feigning disinterest for both our sakes. However, I planned to see Otho later that afternoon, though he didn't know it, yet.

Once I'd dealt with the northern representatives, we sat to feast. While we supped, the already muted voices in the room were drowned out by rain as it began pounding on the roof. A few wary glances were cast at Pari, my Healer, and Ziba, my Protector, who squirmed in their chairs. There was distrust and even outright prejudice against those who practiced magic, especially in the north. Asander sat on my right, demonstrating his perfect etiquette. On my left, Papa seemed oblivious to the tension, giving my hand a pat between bites.

Jamil stood at one end of the head table, deep in conversation with a man I didn't recognize. Possibly a local contact of the late Valentin. Jamil had predicted it would be near impossible to find anyone with Valentin's skill or background. From Jamil's scowl, it appeared he'd been correct. Still, we had to find *someone* who could learn to fulfill the role my trusted spy had left behind.

"I'll work with you on your forms tonight," Asander interrupted my thoughts.

"Thank you." I appreciated his vigilance.

"Once your technique improves, you should join the exercises with the recruits as we travel throughout the kingdom. It's an opportunity to showcase your strength and skill, bolstering the recruit's confidence in your wartime leadership abilities.

After our engagement, Asander had turned his full attention to my army. He'd suggested we wait until after I turned eighteen to wed, and I had agreed. When my advisers balked at the delay of well over a year, I reminded them that in Asander's kingdom, it was customary not to wed until after twenty years old — after the completion of their five years of mandatory military service.

Initially, I'd flattered myself that Asander was thoughtfully allowing me to grow accustomed to the idea of marriage. However, over our two moons of engagement, he acted content with our united, public appearances, all while privately keeping his distance. Perhaps he was waiting for me to show I was ready for a more affectionate relationship. But was I?

I'd always assumed my marriage would be like my parents. They seemed drawn to each other whether in public or in private. Instead of cold proprietary touches, my parents' affections were frequent and unforced. They would often caress a hand or whisper in an ear, as passionate about each other as they were about the work they shared. Papa had often looked at Mama like he'd just hiked through the desert, and she was life-giving water.

If I couldn't have passion, I could still hope for an affectionate relationship with Asander. Though I would likely never be as interested in armor and weapons as he was, we could find common ground. When he walked into a room, I wanted him to seek me out. Or at least think I was more important than any weapons that might be on display.

Even under the best circumstances, I wasn't sure how to go about creating a spark, never mind trying to do so while preparing for war. But Asander had flirted with me a bit before our engagement; I just had to signal to him that I was ready to reciprocate. Now was as good a time as any.

I held my breath and slipped my hand into his.

He gripped my hand tighter, and my heart fluttered. He lifted our clutched hands and placed them on the table, in full view of the room. My heart sunk.

Another hollow display — further public assurance that Auripo and Dacia were united.

Pari had been watching us, and she gave me a sympathetic look. She had advised me to be patient, reminding me that many arranged marriages turned to love.

Though, it was no wonder the prince and I weren't able to fall in love under pressure. With a public alliance between kingdoms in the balance, the expectation was a too-tight cord around my neck.

"Well done with the guild representatives," Asander said. "I probably would have shouted more about the horrors of the battlefield. But your people are so soft, it probably would have sent them into fits."

The prince's non-compliments were getting tiresome. I bit my tongue and reminded myself that Asander's background was starkly different from mine. At least this meal was almost behind us, and my brief meetings with the representatives had gone well. The northern territory tour was nearly done, then on to the central and southern territories.

"Don't you ever wish that you weren't a prince?" I asked. "Perhaps an innkeeper? Or a guard or adviser? Someone who could participate in the life of the kingdom, but not carry the mantle of responsibility?"

Asander's grip loosened. "It's a waste of my time to be wistful about things that cannot be."

I bit back my reply. I'd spent many days hoping for the impossible. I'd set out to end a curse, to find Papa, and discover the location of the True Heir, something no mere Azure should dream of. Wouldn't it be far easier for a prince to imagine becoming a basket weaver or a spy?

Lady Katalin Vulpe approached my seat. "May I have a word?"

Asander kissed my knuckles, shifting the angle of his body for maximum visibility for onlookers before marching over to Jamil. He rose with an easy and powerful grace that likely set more than one heart aflutter, even as I rejoiced at his walking away.

Katalin slid into the seat next to me. She had forgone her usual fuchsia and opted for a deeper red dress, which could almost be mistaken for black, a better match for her shrewd heart. The Rose noble had volunteered to fill the void as an adviser until I found a suitable replacement for Mystic Marianna. After Vasile's betrayal, I hesitated to trust Katalin. She'd been one of the High Judge's closest allies, and her priority had always been herself. Still, she too had been betrayed by Vasile. And she believed that securing me on the throne was her best chance for survival. So, for now, we were aligned.

Katalin splayed a dainty lace fan, obscuring her lips. "Otho's daughter has requested an audience."

I sat up straighter. How had one of Marcus' sisters, a Clover farmer until three moons ago, dared approach Katalin, a prickly Rose? I simply nodded. "I will see her. Tell her she may approach the table."

Before I could alert Jamil, Katalin interjected, "She wants to meet in private." I frowned, but Katalin continued. "She's harmless. Trust me, it's better to meet away from her father. His face alone could sour candied pears."

I started to search the room for Otho.

"Don't look at him! Could you be more obvious?" Katalin hissed. "Also, your speech was abysmal. You were as stiff as a corpse. Where's the passion you spew at the castle? Can't you regurgitate some of that?"

Asander approached the table, and Katalin snapped her fan shut and laughed lightly at some imagined joke.

"You are too clever, Empress." She beamed. "And, of course, I would love to ride in your carriage when we return home."

I fought to keep my face impassive. Before my stuttering tongue could clarify she *wasn't* invited, she flounced away.

It was only after Asander rejoined me that I realized Katalin hadn't said which of Marcus' six sisters wanted an audience, the reason for the request, nor the location of our rendezvous.

Asander lifted a goblet but didn't drink, just stared into the crowd.

Something was wrong.

"How many?" I asked, dreading the answer.

"Barely four hundred volunteers."

I rolled my lips together. Asander had suggested that service should be compulsory if we didn't get the minimum twelve hundred volunteers. I dreaded forcing my subjects into military service, but saying so would only cause an argument. Given that everyone in his kingdom, man or woman, was required to serve, Asander's view on a levy was very different from mine.

"Any luck with finding someone to replace Valentin? Anyone with the needed skills and knowledge of the Norte language?" I asked, changing the subject.

Asander glanced at Jamil before shaking his head.

"So, by all measures, our trip here was a f-failure."

"When we learn, our efforts are not wasted," Asander said. "We can adjust your speech until it has the maximum impact."

"We d-don't have t-time for adjustments," I fumed. "I d-doubt I'll be able to recruit enough volunteers b-before the Norte attack."

"Winter is the time for preparing, waiting out the storms.

Spring is for planting. This summer is the very earliest we'll see any attacks. Even then, it's unlikely. In all my studies, I've never heard of a kingdom mustering together an army and strategy in less than six moons. We won't see the true fight until the following summer."

I couldn't ignore the wriggling in my gut. Tatiana and her guard, Borsea, had been well prepared for their visit to Rupea Castle. They had possessed astounding knowledge of the castle's secrets, such as the tunnels frequented by nobles a century ago. The Norte had used their insights to execute an elaborate scheme involving deception and magic. They nearly overtook Rupea Castle from the inside and dispatched me and all my supporters in the process. I shuddered at the thought of how close the Norte came to controlling Dacia.

"This is merely our first visit, and we will return for a second tour of the kingdom in the spring," Asander said. "It will be to our benefit to have people join the army in waves rather than all at once."

"I trust what experience has taught you. But p-please listen to what my instincts are saying, too." I dropped my voice, willing Asander to finally understand what I'd been trying to tell him for weeks. "The Norte are clever. If they had a p-primary plan of striking at Dacia from inside Rupea Castle, they surely have a secondary one. I fear they've been preparing since long before Vasile ever sent his traitorous letter. And if I was right, our northern neighbors could have been priming for this conquest for years. We don't have a year or longer to prepare. We have moons."

I dreamed of tall, slender cloud-people with ice-eyes and hair the color of sun-bleached bones. They all had strange magic.

Every single person.

I was woken by my sisters' giggles. Mama tickled them awake and sang her silly morning songs.

As a servant brushed my hair, my mind drifted back to my dream. I wonder if the cloud-people ever existed. Probably not — it's impossible for everyone to have magic.

Even in my family, magic is thick in my parents' veins, but not all of us have magic. Of my three elder siblings, my eldest brother has none.

And I don't, either.

The children at school whisper that we should show signs before we turn eight. I think that's why the servants made me an extra special cake on my ninth birthday last week. I know Mama will call me to her room soon and give me compliments so I don't feel bad.

But I don't want to be like my brother.

—— ESME

TWO

WHAT LIVIANA KNEW

Ice-capped, jagged Norte Mountains formed a rugged backdrop beyond the city of Arcidava. The Rodnic Valley included many towns nestled in fertile pockets between rolling hills scattered across northern Dacia. However, Arcidava was the largest settlement nearest the preferred canyon pass to the Norte lands as well as where Valentin was stationed, so we'd chosen this location for my speech and all our weighty meetings.

Earlier, bone-chilling rain had dumped buckets of water, knocking the last stubborn autumn leaves to the ground. Fortunately, only a sporadic misting continued into the afternoon. Heat steamed from the Imperial Guards' bodies as they handed the recruits wooden practice swords in a field on the outskirts of town.

A white dot of Sonus powder on Asander's lip amplified his voice across the muddy, improvised training field outside the city, guiding the recruits through basic stances.

Jamil and I worked alongside the guards, walking down the lines of soldiers, moving arms and guiding feet into the proper positions. Most of the volunteers were farmers, Poppies and Clovers, and wore plain but well-constructed clothing. Their hands were lined with dirt, but they were not thin or sickly like the Lilacs who clustered near the Capidava's city gates, seeking alms.

Despite the recruits' good stature and willingness to learn, I would wager the True Key around my neck that most of our newest soldiers had never held a blade, let alone wielded one in an actual battle.

After the guards evaluated the recruits, they assigned each person to a unit. Jamil led me through the organized chaos to my open tent, which was flanked by soaked emerald green flags marked with the silhouette of the black wolf, the symbol of Dacia.

Under the cover, I voiced my inner fears as I gripped the hilt of my sword, the Canina Thorn. "We're dooming them to early graves."

"When the invasion comes, do you think they'll fare better without training?" Jamil asked. "The Rodnic Valley borders the Norte. It would be foolish to think this land will not see battle. Frankly, I'm disappointed more did not volunteer to protect their homes and families."

I tensed. My speech should have inspired more recruits. Asander's goal was a minimum — our northern border protection would be stretched thin even with the full twelve hundred, to say nothing of the inadequate mere four hundred; we would have to make do with what we had.

"We have six moons to prepare before summer," Jamil said. "Three moons for recruiting and basic training. And three more for more complex battle skills and full integration of battalions. Besides, we have trained city and Imperial guards."

I remembered what the black-clad members of the Imperial Guard had been trained to do all too well. "There's a big difference between raiding undefended cities laid low after the plague and having an army willing and capable of standing up to not only experienced soldiers but magical weapons. The Imperial Guard would benefit from additional training as well."

I cut short my oft-repeated concerns. We still had to cross several hurdles before we would be able to clothe, house, and feed more troops than we've ever fielded before. Every nearby town would be strained until the weak supply chains were shored up.

A group of female recruits clustered on the edge of the field until Asander assigned them to different units. Some of the women looked uncertain, but the Imperial Guards shouted and pointed until they took their places among the men. When they joined their groups, most of the men ignored them. It was progress of a sort, but tenuous.

I marched onto the field to discuss the evolving situation with Asander and my guards. We needed seamless, full integration. As I passed a woman, she fell into the muck. Whether she was pushed or slipped, I didn't know. Ignoring the mud, I held my hand out. She hesitated before reaching back. We gripped each other's forearms, and I pulled her to her feet.

She blinked, staring at me. She had striking gray eyes. Her other features bore the stamp of Otho, clearly her father. But she had her brother's eyes.

"You'll n-need to sew t-trousers." I managed to stammer as I released my grip.

"I have them," she blurted, massaging her arms before quickly dropping them both to her sides. "We all do. We didn't have time to change as we wanted to be sorted into our units with everyone else."

I gave a curt nod, not trusting my tongue. I marched to one of my Imperial Guards and held out my hand, signaling for him to hand me his blade. The last thing I needed was to clumsily cut Asander with the Canina Thorn. The guard pulled his sword from his scabbard and passed it to me.

"I will d-demonstrate some of the techniques you'll learn in the army," I said to the recruits.

Asander repeated my words, the Sonus dot amplifying my message for all. I considered putting on a dot of Sonus powder myself, but many of my conversations had to remain private. Asander got into a basic stance and waited for me to strike. We went through our standard routine. Asander simply met my strikes or neatly pivoted away, verbally explaining the movements to the onlookers as we went. I wasn't an excellent fighter — the only formidable thing about me was the sword still in my scabbard.

No one knew for certain if the Canina Thorn still caused the plague. I hadn't cut anyone with it since the Battle of the Rose Court. Moments after the battle, I'd named the sword in order to stabilize it as Marianna had implored me to do. Though I'd felt a shift in the magic, Marianna was no longer alive to behold and interpret the sword's aura. However, the blade still warmed in my hand and seemed like an extension of me. Or maybe I deluded myself that the powerful curse I'd wielded that had saved our people from the strange magic of the Norte still existed within my grasp.

In this moment, it didn't matter. I needed to sway the minds of my people. I gambled that the simple farmers of the valley wouldn't recognize if my technique was imperfect, nor if I was an expert fighter. All they needed to see was their empress, a woman, sparring with the fabled Warrior of the East.

Across the field, a page approached my tent with Otho behind him. I finished the exercises and returned the borrowed sword. Asander complimented my excellent swordsmanship, which was hollow praise, but at least he was going along with my gambit.

Imperial Guards continued integrating the women into their units. The women were bolder with their approach, and while the men didn't loudly welcome them, at least they moved to make room. Somewhat satisfied with the improvement, I strode past the recruits and rejoined Jamil under the tent. Otho bowed, pulling his cap from his head.

"Thank you for meeting me, Otho." I'd dreaded this conversation, so I got right to the point. "The Agricultural Emissary is the voice of the guild, but I have come to learn that, for d-decades, the farmers have looked to your father for practical guidance."

Marcus' grandfather had been a young man when his valley had been decimated by the plague. With too few laborers, they should have starved after two years of partial harvests. Otho's father foresaw that drastic measures were needed. He convinced the survivors to ration their food — to the point of weakness — for two winters. But most of them lived.

"While other guilds are beginning their preparations now, the Agricultural Guild doesn't have that luxury." Most guilds could work during any season, but not farmers. Even if I couldn't convince Asander the Norte could attack this spring, in merely four moons, I was determined to prepare for the worst. Asander had cited examples from hundreds of years' worth of battles that demonstrated the length of time needed to prepare for, and conduct war during its "proper season" — the summer.

My conversation with Otho would mean ignoring Asander's advice on methodical, steady production. Which meant I was crossing over the line my battle-worn betrothed had drawn in the desert sand. "We cannot assume we'll have a full planting season. We need to save what was already reaped this year and store it."

Otho worried the edge of his cap. "My father is ailing. He could not sway a dog to gnaw a bone."

"I pity his ill health. Truly, I do. But he knows better than most how critical it is that we prepare for too few laborers... or trampled fields." I thought about other options. "Can he dictate a letter to be copied and distributed to every representative, reminding them of his story?"

Otho glanced at the field, his gaze settling on his daughter. One thing I knew about Otho — he loved his family. And when he left Arcidava, he'd be saying goodbye to his daughter, possibly forever. When I'd traveled with him, he'd cut his merchant travels short to return to his family sooner. Otho worked so his children could have opportunities he hadn't. But seeing his daughter train to be a soldier was so much more than having his son travel to foreign lands in the relative comfort afforded to an emissary. I could only imagine what it was for a parent to watch their child march into danger.

The wrinkles around Otho's eyes and mouth were more pronounced as he stared unblinking at the field. "I will ride directly after I... say goodbye."

"Of course."

Otho wiped his reddening nose and shuffled away. My rising emotions turned to impotent frustration with our cruel god whose attention was clearly focused on Cornara. How many daughters and sons would Zalmoxis greedily snatch from the battlefield? Despite the rumors, I was merely a mortal, but I would do all I could to thwart him.

"Prepare yourself, Empress. This tour will not be easy," Jamil said as the Imperial Guards finished the initial instruction. "Some of the villages are small, and depending on their condition after the plague, they may not have healthy volunteers."

"This valley is the first the Norte must cross to attack Dacia. The single, Imperial-trained contingency we'd planned to send as a support will not be enough." My muscles tightened across my shoulders. "The Theracians have shown no sign of preparation for war, unlike the Norte. We need to relocate our southern city's armies to the north."

"Are you willing to risk the Getaen cities in the south? Moesia?" Jamil asked. "Your neighbors? Your uncle?"

I wanted to rip the flagpole from the ground and snap it in half. But I couldn't lose control in front of my fledgling recruits. My neck muscles tightened further, pinching at the base of my skull. "Curse the irresponsible, dead emperors who came before me. Instead of keeping their armies strong, they depended on the plague as a protection from invasion. Their laziness could be our undoing. We don't have the army we need to stave off attacks in the north and the south."

"We can be creative. It's not all about numbers. Asander has more battle experience than the entire Norte Council," Jamil said, his voice calm. "Don't lose hope."

But what about Theracia? Their many colony states, like Illyria on our southwest border, could be deployed with a snap of the emperor's fingers. I pictured an army of shiny beetles marching over a Dacian map, smothering it. "Auripo had better have brilliant strategic plans."

On the field, Marcus' sister tucked her assigned wooden sword into her belt. The recruits would have an hour to say their good-byes to their families. Many would only be a day's walk from home, but they wouldn't be returning any time soon.

I pulled my fur-lined cloak tighter. "What is the next step for finding a northern spy?"

"Lucius and I are still assessing the candidates. It will take some time."

The recruits began streaming toward the town, giving my tent a wide berth. Marcus' sister lingered, re-lacing her boots.

"We need to build from a dozen spies to ten times that number," I said. "They need to be watching enemy movements *now*, not starting after the first strike."

Jamil adjusted his gloves. "Better to select wisely, not quickly."

Marcus' sister was the last remaining recruit on the field. She eyed me from afar. I jolted, remembering Katalin's words.

I signaled to Marcus' sister. She jogged forward and gave a deep bow. She glanced at Jamil, uncertainty on her face.

"Which of Otho's daughters are you?" I asked.

"Liviana Constantin," she said, straightening. "Your Majesty."

"You wish to speak with me?"

"If I may. Firstly, we are deeply appreciative of Lord Philo's work in securing our family an estate." She paused. "We were heartbroken at his death."

I pictured Philo wiping his ever-watering eyes before his arthritic fingers curled around a pen to ink the records of the estate in Marcus' name — shortly before Philo's heart gave out in fright when he was captured by the Norte Mirrors. I cleared my throat, still angry with myself for not protecting him.

"The estate he transferred is an old one with a regal history. My little sisters have delighted in planning its restoration."

Tulia, my trusted personal servant, had gossiped about how many had coveted the vacant estate. It sat at the top edge of the Lily nobles' section on the Capidavan Mountain, but few could afford the extensive repairs.

"Papa said they'll begin repairs this spring," Liviana said. "That's when he expects Marcus to return to reside in Capidava."

I clasped my hands behind my back, trying not to look flustered at the mere mention of Marcus. "How is your brother?"

Liviana shrugged. "He spends a lot of time with the ship merchant Papa was always so keen on."

Was this merchant the person Marcus had calculated would help secure the best alliance for Dacia? I assumed he would focus his efforts on power-wielding judges. I had trusted him to negotiate alliances without the throne's oversight, but I was curious. "What is the merchant's business? What does he ship? Ore, weapons, silks, food?"

Liviana tilted her head, confusion on her face. "*Ships* are his business. He owns the boats the merchants hire to deliver their goods. But I think his fortune comes from a secret wax recipe he invented for sails."

That wasn't what I expected. I wanted to ask about every detail of Marcus' letters. Even more, I wanted to hear mischievous stories of his childhood, and of what he was like to have as a brother. But I didn't ask. I couldn't. Asander was my future. Across the field, the prince worked with my guards, the Sonus powder wiped from his lips.

Besides, for all Liviana knew, her brother and I had a strained relationship, which meant she was all the bolder to approach me.

Liviana continued, "More importantly, I —"

Hooves pounded the wet ground. We spun to see five Auripoans riding toward us. Asander rushed to my side as his kinsmen stopped and dismounted. Every horse was heavily laden with weapons strapped to their flanks. The Auripoans wore caps low over their ears and scarves up over their noses, which they pulled down to reveal their faces before lifting their arms in the traditional Auripoan salute.

Behind us, my Imperial Guards circled closer. I quickly dismissed Liviana. Before she left, she uttered something to Jamil and hurried away.

I signaled for the Auripoans to approach, scanning their faces, disappointed that Dyana Coatys, the future queen of Auripo, was not among them. Their heavy cloaks didn't drag along the ground, yet the hems were coated in mud. The visitors bowed to me and then to their prince.

"What brings you to the Rodnic Valley?" I asked the newcomers.

An Auripoan with a thick beard and scarred face stepped forward. "We observed movement at the mouth of the Curat River. Early scouts. The Norte are preparing for their next move. Prince Eusebes dispatched us to send word immediately."

Asander nodded, staying at my side. While he didn't have a close relationship with his older, half-brother, knowing Auripo's crown prince had kept up his agreement to patrol the Curat River was heartening. The river divided our lands, running from the snow-capped mountains in the north, down through the Curat Mountains that straddled both our lands and out to the Getaen Sea. With Norte spotted near the Curat, our aggressors could be preparing to strike either kingdom.

The bearded Auripoan continued, "King Eusebes believes the Norte seek to make their stronghold at the mouth of the river, cutting the Dacian and Auripoan armies off from each other. That would hamper our communications and increase the chances of inadvertently striking each other."

If Eusebes was correct, we needed to move our small army east, toward the river, leaving most of the Rodnic Valley exposed. A ball of knots squeezed at the base of my skull.

"Thank you for coming so quickly. You must be hungry after your travel." I signaled to one of my servants. "My servant will escort you to the local inn where you may eat and rest."

"Much appreciated." The bearded man bowed. "We will return to Auripo before first light."

"Of course." I guessed at what the contingency feared. If the Norte marched on the Curat river, the Auripoans could find themselves trapped in Dacia, away from the rest of their army on the other side.

"We bring good news as well," he said. "If I may, Eusebes asked us to deliver a package."

One of his companions grabbed a bundle from the back of her horse and brought the parcel to Asander. The prince unwrapped it to reveal several dark arrowheads.

"Black metal." Asander clutched the gift closer.

"A wedding gift from the King of Auripo," the bearded man said.

My mouth was too dry to speak. Besides, what could I say? It was a generous, if deadly, gift.

Another Auripoan spoke up. "They're strong enough to take down a snow leopard."

I whipped my attention to the man. Snow leopards were not real; they were from children's tales. But upon seeing his stern expression, my argument died on my lips.

KATALIN FLOUNCED past my room at the inn on her way to my carriage, reminding me that she would help me re-write my speech on the way to the next city. I inwardly groaned; Findava was three days away.

"I suddenly want to sit with Madame Palanka." Tulia pursed her lips.

"Palanka is riding with the hired Sensitive who makes your skin crawl," I reminded her.

"I'd rather be scrutinized by a Sensitive for days than sit near Lady Katalin for an hour," Tulia said, directing a page to transport our bags outside. "Though, tell me as soon as Katalin returns to her carriage. You know I do enjoy listening to Asander knit. It's quite calming."

I suppressed a grin as Jamil entered my room, signaling my carriage was ready. It was second nature to fall a step behind the head of my Own in public, him in the Shield position. After three days of organizing the new troops of the northern valleys, it was time for us to travel south.

"It's probably for the best that Tulia didn't join you." Jamil signaled to my Own, and four of them took up positions around my carriage. "There's someone you need to speak with."

Jamil took an overly long step toward the door. At his feet, I caught a hint of a shimmer. Black Sonus powder had been spread around my carriage, nearly invisible in the mud. The dampening circle would trap the sound inside the ring — keeping conversations private.

Before I entered the carriage, Jamil slid my Sonus stone into my hand. "An extra precaution."

He must have snatched the stone from my bags. I gripped it and stepped into the carriage. Inside, a cloaked woman waited. She pulled back her hood enough for me to see her face: Liviana.

The Auripoans had arrived before we'd finished our conversation, but I hadn't expected her to approach me again. What was so important that she convinced Jamil to arrange for this meeting?

"I knew Valentin Rekine," Liviana blurted.

My stomach dropped. Valentin's death had been shocking, swift, and violent. In the moments before my coronation ceremony, he had encouraged me, telling me he had faith in my ability to rule. Yet before the crown was placed on my head, Tatiana murdered him. He died attempting to protect me. The brutality of his death still tormented me, even during the daylight hours.

I held out the Sonus stone for Liviana. At her touch, the familiar, faint pulse of magic signaled our conversation was silenced.

"Valentin occasionally came into town to purchase supplies. No one knew he was one of the Emperor's Own until we heard of his murder. We assumed he was a merchant because he traveled about and spoke multiple languages. When Valentin visited our town, he was always kind to me. To our family."

The guilt I'd buried in a shallow grave arose within me.

"I may be an unlearned Clover, but I'm not dim," Liviana said.

"With Valentin dead, you'll need to replace him. And I want my valley protected. If your Own want a probable list of Valentin's contacts, I have a few. It's a place to start, to help your spies re-establish here. You can probably even track down Valentin's hide-out."

I nodded, understanding her urgency. "We were interrupted before you could relay them yesterday."

"True, but I also wanted to get your promise that you'll treat the names I give you with care. I'm willing to risk my life to protect my kingdom, but the people on this list... they might be just names to you, but they're friends, neighbors, and even distant relations. Most are just regular townsfolk. Some might be criminals." She seemed to search me for judgment. "Others, I suspect, Valentin had developed into something more."

"I swear to you that I will put my most judicious, level-headed guard in charge of questioning all these individuals."

"I never would have trusted a Caracalla — selfish men, the lot of them. But because of your Azure upbringing and things my brother wrote about you, I have hope in you, the Golden Protector."

I pulled the stone away, hoping to hide the flush rising in my cheeks by fetching parchment and ink from the satchel by the door. I wrote down the names as Liviana relayed them. Valentin's expertise was unmatched, and the late emperor never encouraged him to pass on his knowledge.

The list gave me another idea.

"Thank you for trusting me." I didn't hold back my sincerity.

"I trust that the same fierce Golden Protector who saved us from the Lilac Plague can also be victorious in battle." Liviana tugged her cowl into place.

With a swish of her cloak, she was gone, returning to the recruits' tents. Jamil slid into her vacant seat, his brow raised. I pressed the parchment into his hand.

"*One* person can't replace Valentin. But multiple scouts might. Start your interviews with these names. Track them down."

Mama listens to me recount my dreams in the morning as the servants dress me and comb my hair. Though sometimes she rushes me to the end, I know she likes my stories.

This morning she sent the servants and my sisters away and asked me for more details. I love getting time alone with Mama so I dragged out every detail. She didn't hurry me.

I told her about a small golden ball. It must have been crushed because it was flat on one side. A Dacian woman was clutching the sphere tight as she ran through brambles, her thick, velvet dress ripping. I remember it so clearly, even the gold stitching in the sleeve.

She wasn't alone. Another woman ran with her. They looked like sisters, though all Dacians look alike to me.

Afterward, Mama didn't join us for breakfast. Neither did Papa. I don't ever remember eating breakfast without one of them with us.

— ESME

THREE

THE MIRROR

A foot of snow covered Capidava's mountainside, except where workers had cleared the cobblestone roads and sprinkled a layer of sand. After the lackluster response from the people of Findava and the long days of travel, I was happy to be on my gelding and back to work at the capital.

Tulia and I traveled with a small contingency to the tannery on the edge of the city. As we drew closer, it was clear why the structure was placed in the poorest area.

Tulia made a dramatic face of disgust. "Why are we here again? The smell will kill me. You will come back to find me dead in the middle of the road. Murdered by stink."

The pungent smells curled the hair in my nose. I pulled out the small jar Pari had given me and wiped a layer of lilac-infused oil above my lip. I handed it to Tulia who generously coated the inside of her nose.

"There's not enough of this lilac potion in the kingdom to save me." Tulia's eyes watered.

"If you like, you can run errands while I'm inside."

Tulia brightened. Then she glanced back over her shoulder past the Imperial Guards behind us, shooting a glare at an unwelcome addition to our party. "Are you sure you don't want me to send Jovian away? That high hat is a leech amongst the Rose Court. You'll only be at Rupea Castle for a few days, so why make time for him?"

Jovian had made my life difficult from the moment we'd met. From unwelcome flirtations, to boisterous behavior, to exposing me as a fraud when I'd infiltrated the Rose Court, well before I'd ended the curse.

Jovian had practically groveled in his letter, which requested an audience. Humility wasn't like him.

"He was held by the Norte, just as the other nobles," I said. "The least I can do is meet with him."

"Of those kidnapped, he was given, by far, the most freedom. I heard so directly from his servants."

"Jovian has a knack for self-preservation," I said, dryly. "If he'll meet at the tannery, he is truly desperate."

More importantly, Jovian's father's family were merchants who were no strangers to leather goods. Jovian was more than capable of evaluating the quality and advising me on the uses. Asander had warned that not all leather was created equal; by merely showing up and asking questions, I'd know a lot more about what protected my soldiers. And the craftsmen were more likely to do their best work.

Tulia made a gagging sound, which caused me to reflexively gag, too. "You may go now, Tulia."

"Thank you," Tulia said, her gloved hand covering her mouth. She tugged the reins, and her horse trotted toward the main shops of the city.

We were on the main road next to the enormous city wall around Capidava. Ahead, the tannery was pressed between where the stone wall met the base of the mountain. I dismounted and handed my reins to one of my Own. Two green-cloaked Imperial Guards flanked the entrance to the structure, and Jamil whispered to one with blond hair peeping from beneath his black fur cap.

Historically, very few Getaens were accepted into the ranks of the Imperial Guard, so I'd immediately noticed the new Thorn when he'd been promoted three weeks earlier.

Jovian approached, flanked by two more green-cloaked guards, before dipping into a low bow. "Empress, thank you for meeting with me."

I nodded. Jovian's face was drawn, and his lips were practically blue from cold. He must have waited in the snowy courtyard for some time, careful not to miss his appointment. I took pity on him. "Shall we inspect the leather?"

"Whatever the Empress' whim, I shall endeavor to fulfill."

With Jovian at my side, we started toward the door. The newly-appointed Getaen guard led the way in Jamil's usual Shield position. The smell of rot, urine, and dung grew even stronger inside the tannery. Several workers stopped to gawk as Jovian instructed the guard to continue through the building and out the back door. We passed piles of soiled skins and vats of boiling water in varying shades of blue and green.

Jovian looked down at a pile of fur waiting to be scraped off a hide. "I apologize for the roughness."

"No need. This work is vital." I was less offended by the smells than the treatment I'd received when I'd infiltrated the Rose Court.

We exited through the back of the tannery and found ourselves in a small, open courtyard between two structures. It felt almost surreal; the blue sky and bright snow were a stark contrast to the caustic smells and the old ropes strung between the structures heavy with drying hides.

The Getaen Shield signaled for us to wait while two guards ducked into the next structure, verifying the security. He scanned the area, tensing when a shadow crossed the wall above. One of my archers perched nearby. I wasn't surprised — of course, Jamil would have extra Thorns though this was a quiet excursion.

The Getaen seemed to have a keen eye, and I'd heard he was from Moesia, like me. Unlike me, he'd adapted quickly to the colder climate; he wasn't even shivering.

Jovian pulled his fur-lined cloak tighter."I hope your trip to the Rodnic Valley was productive?"

Any servant could relay the events of the valley. "Jovian, why did you request an audience?"

"I wanted to apologize in person and beg your forgiveness." Jovian's ragged tone verged on desperation. "I was angry when my title was ripped from me after you became empress, and I made foolish decisions."

"The former high judge followed the law when he stripped you of privileges that had been bestowed by the crown. None of your family's personal wealth was taken."

"The judge was fair; I was a blind imbecile. Any previous emperor would have forgone a trial and had me stoned... or gutted like my uncle... without a thought. When the Norte held me captive in my home, I realized their sugared words were fetid lies. More worrisome was that they didn't hate me, personally. They regarded me as a nuisance — filth they intended to sweep away. When they touched me, it was... unsettling."

The guard marched through the snow toward the next building, and we followed on his heels.

"Touched you?" I wasn't sure I wanted to know more, but I had to ask.

"The person who questioned me, he was like Essa... *Lady* Essa, I mean. The Norte knew when I was lying. I tried saying as little as possible. It didn't take the Norte long to figure out that I was withholding information. At that point, they realized they'd lost my trust, and things got much more... difficult for me." He lifted his bare hands in front of him, almost as if he feared his own body. "When the interrogator came after that, he would grip my wrist, ask questions, and then nod with satisfaction, even without me saying a thing."

The guard entered the next building, ending our semi-private conversation. He led us deeper into the structure before my eyes could adjust to the relative darkness.

"Please wait for Jovian's instructions," I said to my guard. I blinked, hearing the smack of blades against wood-block tables.

"To the right, past the next three cutting stations," Jovian commanded.

The guard pivoted and strode past several tables of Clover craftsmen with massive knives, cutting each hide with precision.

"I vowed to myself that if I survived, I would strive to make amends," Jovian continued. "I pledge my personal, undying fealty to you, Empress Nicoleta Aurelian, for as long as I live and breathe. I have no right to beg for your mercy after what occurred in the Battle of the Rose Court, though I will ask it."

"Your friendship with the Norte resulted in the death of my Own, among many others. Ask their families for forgiveness, not me."

"I will. I will do whatever you ask in hopes of one day making amends for my wrongs." I could feel the noble's gaze on me, but I focused on my guard's pressed cloak ahead of me as Jovian spoke. "I allowed myself to be deceived by the Norte. I realize now I was prideful. But the things I saw... the blind determination within the Norte... Empress, they are hungry for our kingdom."

Jovian stopped and rubbed the edge of uncut hides in a tall, clean stack. My guard paused, then returned to stand right next to me. He was closer than protocol demanded, but my Own constantly increased security measures.

I hadn't forgiven Jovian for his folly, nor was I sure he understood the gravity of the situation. But if I could open his eyes, perhaps others in the Rose Court would rally to their kingdom.

"If the Norte had been victorious, everyone and everything you care about would have been killed. Every relation, every child, every servant, and even p-pets." I paused, not wanting to stutter. "It's not all about *your* life."

Jovian turned away from the hides, a sheen of sweat on his brow. "Those of us who were blind before, we are now your most ardent supporters. All the misguided Roses and Lilies of the court have returned. We are anxious to prove ourselves to you, our Empress. We will do whatever you ask to preserve the kingdom."

His sincerity gave me a glimmer of hope.

"Jovian, the nobles' ancestors were once strong wielders of the sword, completely devoted to an emperor, probably even to the Blood Conqueror himself as he carved out an empire." Some of those ruthless soldiers' children must have been black-hearted backstabbers in order to keep their power, but I left that part out. "We are on the brink of war. Your ancestors were responsible for protecting lands outside the capital. You say the nobles have returned? I need them to go back to their estates. But instead of slinking away to hide, I need them to prepare for battle. If you aspire to regain your ancestral title, you must earn it. Last time, you lost the battle before it began. This time, rally to your flag to defend Dacia, and inspire the other nobles to do the same."

"Y-yes. You just inspired a clever idea." He tapped his ornate dagger, similar in fashion to others in the Rose Court.

He turned, almost absently, back to the hides he'd separated, explaining how some were thinner and better for protection against the armor chaffing. I compared the thicknesses for myself as Jovian continued sharing his knowledge and insights.

"Furthermore, I and all those who were kidnapped, we all gladly submit to your requisition of our slaves into your Imperial care."

I slowly set the hide down. *Slaves into my Imperial care?*

"R-requisition?" I asked.

"This pile would make better rawhides," he mused to himself before continuing. "Yes, the Imperial Slave Requisition. Lady Katalin Vulpe delivered it to every household that had been involved with the Norte. Even your treasury adviser, Lord Philo's son has been requested to comply."

Zalmoxis, what has Lady Katalin done? "How m-many households? How many slaves?"

"I believe there were eight households involved, for a total of two hundred slaves, as Lady Katalin included the slaves on our estates outside of Capidava as well." A look of confusion crossed Jovian's face. "We were surprised, of course. But the payment Lady Katalin promised was fair. Especially, as the slaves are to be conscripted into the army. Rumor is that you have need of soldiers."

I started to feel light-headed. I needed to sit but couldn't look weak in front of Jovian.

"Thank you for your apology. I will consider your words. Will you bring me samples of finished, tanned leather?"

Lord Jovian dipped into a deep bow and scurried away. As soon as he was out of sight, I slumped against the table piled high with raw animal skins.

My guard rushed to my side.

"I'm all right." I waved him off.

He didn't slow, a menacing determination in his eyes.

My instincts screamed. A surge of energy coursed through me. I lunged forward, closing the distance, the heel of my hand jamming up into his nose. Warm liquid gushed onto my fingers. I slammed my knee into his groin, and yanked his hair, pulling his head down with him, knocking over a pile of leather.

He stumbled back, recovering, blood running down his face. I clutched my necklace, horrified at what I'd done; my instincts had taken over without rational thought. As I started to stutter an apology, he lifted his arm, the tip of a dagger between his fingers. I felt it, a sense of wrongness.

A Mirror!

A silver-handled dagger whirled through the air and sunk into my attacker's neck. The blade dropped from the Mirror's fingers and fell onto the scattered animal skins, his face a mixture of shock and anger. Jamil leapt over the mess to the falling guard, kicking away the attacker's weapon.

"Ask me a question. Ask me something only I would know," Jamil demanded.

"What was I wearing when we f-first m-met?" My pulse raced

as I started putting the pieces together. How long ago had the Mirror disposed of the Moesian recruit?

"Anyone could know that. Ask something *only I would know*."

"Who d-did you think I w-was at first?"

"A scholar there to help Calvus in the interpretation of the scrolls." He spoke quickly, and I nodded, relieved. He grabbed my shoulders again, squeezing so I couldn't budge. "My turn. What was the real reason you sent Marcus away?"

I flushed. "I d-didn't."

SWEAT RAN DOWN MY BACK. My arm shook, holding the pose as Asander counted aloud. After this morning's attack by the unknown Mirror, I refused to sit and fret. Instead, I poured all my anxious nerves into my exercises. Dyana, Asander's sister-in-law, had said training would drill the movements into my body, turning them to automatic reactions. Before, I'd had faith in her words. But now I *knew* they were true. My instincts saved my life this morning or at least gave Jamil enough time to act.

"Instincts are informed by what you see in the periphery," Asander continued a lecture he'd started earlier. "Your mind processed more than you realized before you reacted to your attacker."

"All my sword training and I didn't even have time to reach for my blade." I stretched my cramping arms over my head as Asander and I ended our exercises. The prince had moved our training into the Hall of the Emperors, in the room where the Crown of Lore was stored. Though the room was only large enough to run through drills, it was infinitely more appropriate than practicing in my chambers. "I think I'll join the soldiers for training tomorrow morning. The exercise will help me stay focused the rest of the day."

"That's ill-advised after your attack today," Asander said,

rolling his shoulders. "What are you going to do? Question every guard on the field?"

"There has to be a better way than interrogating everyone, every single time we speak. It's exhausting."

"The Norte have struck a blow, even without laying a finger on you," Asander said. "They've stirred paranoia. Fear."

"I wish we could just use a secret code word, but a Sensitive would extract that information with ease. We must think up dozens of distinct, random memories. And I never even left Moesia before last summer. I don't have a wealth of history with the people here." I yearned for a hot bath and my clean bed. Tomorrow I could start with fresh ideas.

Asander paused. "You and I have rarely spent time alone together. There's little about me you know that others don't."

Asander gave me a flirtatious smile, the like of which I hadn't seen in moons.

He stepped toward me, close enough for me to pick up every note of his scent — musky sweat and steel. He ran a hand down my arm, shifting even closer.

I began sweating more than I had when we were practicing. My gaze was torn between his green eyes and his lips. Was this *it*? I was breathless, but not in the way I'd dreamt, but rather like a dog who'd run too long. I'd imagined from the way Asander spoke of his sacred stars, our first kiss would be under the night sky, not in a windowless, musty room.

"Why is it that you don't carry the dagger I gave you?" Asander said. I could barely process his words. "I don't understand the Dacian's ways. Do you find weapons to be inappropriate gifts?"

"W-weapons are fine gifts. Jamil has even given me a few d-dagger lessons. I-I just d-don't find it c-comfortable in my b-boot." I sounded like a whiny child, but it bruised my ankle.

Asander smiled. Instead of melting inside, I felt stiff and awkward. Should I smile back? Did I have a bit of dinner stuck between my teeth?

"Well, Nicoleta, I assumed someone would get you a calf scabbard to carry it. But I shall see that one is created — perfectly formed to the curve of your leg. It isn't an ornate toy, like most of your nobles' weapons, it's an efficient tool — Auripoan black steel. One day it could save your life."

I tried to say something but sputtered, my mouth half-open.

"Your safety is my primary concern. Without you, Dacia will crumble. We won't have an heir for at least three years." He entwined his fingers with my slick hand.

I whispered, knowing otherwise my tongue would struggle with each syllable. "Who are you?"

Asander leaned closer, barely a hand-width between us. "What do you mean?"

"How can you change yourself so completely — so stalwart for the crowds one moment, then charming the next?" Though this was a new level of attention he'd never paid me.

"You'll learn, as I have, that it's better to take all your disgust, concerns, hurt, and expectations and lock them away. Wear a mask, and put all your feelings in different trunks in your mind. Then when the time is right, you find the right key and open what you want."

I watched his lips move. What would they feel like on mine? I'd only ever kissed Marcus before. That day, I'd cried until my head pounded as I mourned in the stables; Marcus had provided the comfort I desperately needed. Marcus had waited for moons to kiss me, too, but we'd essentially had a chaperon or three.

On the other hand, Asander and I were often alone, and the prince had let every opportunity pass. So far. I'd wanted to see if a romantic connection could form between us; now I would find out.

I ran my stiff fingers through his hair at the nape of his neck. I nodded, though inside I was a nervous tangle. As he drew closer, I caught a whiff of dinner's fennel and onions right as he pressed his lips to mine.

I braced myself, waiting to be swept up with emotion. The prince was clearly well-practiced in the art of romance from the way his fingers danced against my back and pulled me closer. But it was as if Asander was going through rote movements. I felt nothing but a barren desert between us — as if his emotions were still locked away, and he was simply wearing a different mask.

He straightened, leaving a residue of salt on my lips. He looked as if he'd finished a long-dreaded chore.

"The black metal arrowheads from the king," Asander said as if nothing had happened. "What are your plans for them?"

Mama asks me about my dreams every morning. My little sisters are jealous because Mama spends her mornings with me now. With six brothers and sisters, and me in the very middle, I don't always get noticed. Mama repeats my dreams aloud, which is what we must do to memorize the words. I know this is a great honor, but mostly I like that it's just us.

—— ESME

FOUR

HISTORY FOR SALE

I awoke early the next morning, sweating, and wiped the tears from my cheeks. The terrors that plagued my sleep came and went at their leisure, and last night, they resurfaced with vengeance. I exercised in my personal gardens, the cold snapping away my nightmares along with any of my confusion about Asander.

Back in my chambers, Tulia bounced on her heels, and her fingers flew as if with a mind of their own as she prepped me. My lady's maid animatedly conveyed the gossip she'd gathered from servants from several Rose households.

"Lady Katalin is like a child flailing your Canina Thorn, yet I wouldn't trust her with a dinner knife," Tulia spat. "Several slaves have already been sent to report to Captain Lucius."

I dug my fingers into my fisted palms as Tulia confirmed what Jovian had unknowingly revealed. As soon as I was readied, I rushed with Jamil to the map room. I had to catch Papa alone before the meeting with all my advisers. Katalin's actions were out of line, and I needed help to repair the damage.

We passed by the alcove where children used to play. Marianna's granddaughter and Essa's son were both gone now. Annuska spent her time at home and school, preparing for a future apprenticeship. But the only memory I retained from the boy's relocation was of the room where I left him. Per my instructions, the Clarifier left Annuska's innocent recollections in place, but neither of us remembered the name of the small, quiet boy she used to play with.

"I've received word on the interviews with Valentin's old contacts," Jamil said. "Several were just town gossips, not a fit for our needs. However, a handful of stout-hearted individuals were resourceful, quiet informers, with a range of skills. We've already started putting them to good use."

"I needed good news today," I said as we neared the map room. Jamil opened the door, questioned Papa, and then allowed me entrance.

"Ah, my golden-eyed girl." Papa squeezed my hand as we met at the table. As I expected, he'd arrived hours early, taking advantage of the vacant room before meetings began. A large map of the Getaen Sea's coastline was on the table, along with several scrolls. "I hear you're coming along in your Norte studies. You are your mama's daughter — such a talent for language."

I had been learning more Norte ever since the Battle of the Rose Court. Dyana had taken the time to learn the language of her enemies, and I followed her example. It helped that I already had a rudimentary understanding of the Norte language. But Papa had found me a university expert to converse with, and my skill had improved immensely. Valentin would have been proud.

But I'd not come for the compliments.

"Rubia said you are planning a trip." I changed the subject. Rubia's recovery had progressed enough for her to create Healing remedies alongside Pari, and her short-term memory had improved. She still couldn't fully recall her torture at the hands of Oslid, a Clarifier who'd been loyal to past emperors. Or perhaps she just didn't want to.

Papa pointed to the map. "I am thinking of returning to the Antelope Hills Clan. I am an honorary member, due to their alliance with your mama's clan."

Mama's nearly extinct clan.

Rubia was the only one left besides me, and I wasn't sure I could be counted. I'd never even visited a Getaen city.

"The scribes are still pouring through ancient scrolls for any bits of information on the Norte magic. Everything points to what we've suspected: the Norte and Getaen magic are connected, or related."

"It makes sense. The Getaens are descendants of the Norte," I said.

"Along with the indigenous peoples of eastern Dacia." He shifted back to the map. "I plan to leave before war erupts. Prince Asander advised me to return to the castle before the summer, or what he calls "the season of war." He expects the Theracians will be another year because they must coordinate their colony states, which is quite a task. Still, I'll depart in the upcoming weeks. If I don't go now, who knows how long it will be before I can return to the clans again."

"I am glad to see you have your old spirit for adventure, Papa, but I was hoping to entreat you to stay at Rupea Castle a b-bit longer."

The excitement in his face dimmed. "If the clans allow me access to their archives, I could discover vital insights on the Norte magic."

"I need to have someone I can trust overseeing things in Capidava while I'm away."

"You have many excellent advisers." Papa dismissed my comment. "That Sorin fellow, the trade adviser, he is young but takes his position very seriously. Or the new High Judge, Isidro, is more than competent. With Captain Lucius staying to train the guards, and the proficient new steward, together they can run things very well, I am sure. I'll be of more service in my research afar. The scholars have theorized the basics of the Norte magic, but there is much we don't know."

"The throne is v-vulnerable when it is left empty for any p-period of time. Though I agree I have respectable advisers, you are wise, and I know you would never do anything... immoral with the p-power."

Papa paused. "What happened, Nikka?"

"Lady Katalin *happened*." I sucked in a breath. "She essentially b-bought slaves from several noble households and made them p-property of the crown."

"She used money from the treasury to buy human beings?" Papa blanched. "Is she in the flesh trade now? The depravity."

"Oh, there's more." I folded my arms. "She c-conscripted them all into the army. They had no say in the matter. Now I have to *un*conscript them and hope they'll agree to remain of their own free will. We need every recruit we can get."

Papa's lips moved, but no sound escaped.

"Repercussions from her act will affect everyone," I continued. Papa was one of the few who were aware of the kingdom's anemic treasury. "According to Tulia's sources, Lady Katalin offered enough per slave to divert a significant amount of resources. She promised coin that I'd intended to use to buy ore from Lazica for weapons. Not to mention the feeding of our armies."

"What will you do?"

"I have some ideas. But while I focus on the treasury and the war, I need someone to p-protect my interests here."

Papa ran a hand over his bald head, muttering. He sighed and cast a longing gaze at the map. He moved the weights holding down the corners before rolling up the map and silently putting it away. With a look of grim determination, he faced me.

"I'll write up a letter instructing Captain Lucius to inform the purchased slaves of their freedom. The freed citizens can enlist in the army or leave. I'll have it ready for you to sign tonight."

"I know this isn't what you wanted. Thank you, Papa."

"It is my honor to stay and oversee this and any other needs until you return," he said. "When will that be?"

"As soon as I get the recruits we need. Three thousand, at least."

Papa was quiet, but his eyes spoke volumes. Three thousand

wasn't enough. He'd calculated it. But even those inadequate numbers seemed impossible to recruit.

"There's another way to even the field with the Norte," Papa said. "Magic against magic. It might be the only way. *Someone* should visit the clans for more insights, even if it cannot be me."

After speaking with Papa, I buried my indignation long enough to coherently oversee the meeting with my ambassadors. Even so, I constantly had to quell my urge to shout about the blaring issue on my mind: coin.

But the lack of treasury funds was not their responsibility. They needed to focus on communication, guilds, trade, crime, and other regional matters. I held my tongue. In the end, they needed to see to their responsibilities and me to mine.

After the meeting, Jamil and I slipped away. Luminary lights flared to life as my Own led me down the Hall of the Emperors.

"How do you want to handle Lady Katalin?" Jamil asked.

"What I want to do doesn't matter — the kingdom's needs are all I care about."

"Dacia is in a dire state if you're considering this bold action — it's never been done."

"Fortunately, I was not raised a prideful noble of the court, so what we're about to do pains me little."

"But it still pains you."

I pressed my lips together as we entered the windowless room. Now deep in the mountain, Luminaries lined the narrow space. A pristine table dominated the room, but there were no chairs. On the far wall, motes of light floated from floor to ceiling, bobbing up and down, obscuring the treasures they protected.

I passed my hand through the motes from one wall to the other, causing them to fall away. Behind the motes, shelves of open, satin-lined boxes awaited. Gold shimmered and jewels sparkled in breathtaking hues of emerald green, sapphire blue, and ruby red.

I pulled the Blood Ruby crown from the shelf and held it up. "This is both art and culture, as well as our history. Each piece tells a story, reminding us of where we came from and who we are. So, yes, it does cause me some amount of... pain. I am losing tangible connections to our past to preserve our future."

"It's the right decision."

I placed the ruby crown gently on the table, admiring it. The crown had been created at the behest of the first Dacian emperor, over two hundred years old. It was worn by the queen consort, Hanna Caracalla. There was no price I could put on it. Yet a figure needed to be named.

"I could go to the nobles and admit that Katalin had acted without my authority. But that undermines my influence."

"That would save you the coin, but your authority would suffer," Jamil agreed.

"I intended to free the slaves." I paced the floor. "Furthermore, my first choice was to purchase the Lilac slaves, but with an overall, consistent plan. Now I have some slaves who have been paid for and are momentarily conscripted. But the majority are still enslaved. With the status of the treasury as we prepare for war, I can't conceive of how to free them all, even if we sold all our treasured history."

Light footfalls sounded, right on time. Jamil exited, intercepting the visitor.

"What color do you never wear?" Jamil's stood outside the room with one of the questions Tulia had prepared. After the Mirror incident, Jamil had compiled a list of questions now kept under lock and key.

"It's not what color, it's what *colors*," Katalin replied. "Any dull, unfashionable color. And as I sway the tastes of the court, every color in fashion is a jewel-tone which enhances my complexion."

I snorted. That haughty tone was definitely Katalin.

"And why have you summoned me to this dreary, dusty hallway?" She sneered. "I should be asking *you* a question to verify your personage. You could be a Mirror luring me down to my death for all I know."

Jamil re-entered the room, with Katalin behind him. Her look of disdain melted away. Her eyes widened at the sight of the wall of treasures, but only for a flicker before she regained her calm composure.

She dropped into a deep curtsy. "What can I do for you, Empress?"

"Lady Katalin, I hear that we have grown our army by two hundred slaves." I kept my practiced words steady, though my impulse was to use my tongue as a knife, slashing her with the full force of my sharp frustration. "Tell me, why did you decide to personally visit every Rose estate involved with the Norte and demand their slaves? Why didn't you tell me your plan beforehand?"

"After the poor recruitment in the Rodnic Valley and again in Findava, I knew we needed to bolster the numbers," Katalin began, her tone practical. "And I know that you and I both would like to see slavery... changed. Most Roses have come to believe this labor system is a necessary practice for our survival. The requisition signals to the remaining noble households that slavery, as they know it, is at an end. And at the same time, we increased the number of recruits — an elegant solution to a complex problem. There was a hiccup with Lady Tyne, but I believe we will have that sorted soon enough."

"Lady Tyne?"

The older Rose noble had always been one of my only loyal supporters. From the time she laid eyes on the True Key to her abduction by the Norte, she had taken my words seriously. On the other hand, for some time, the Lady Tyne *I* thought was advising me, was a disguised Norte Mirror. The Norte had made the switch shortly after I'd been poisoned. Whether or not that Mirror died in the Battle of the Rose Court, I didn't know and probably never would.

"Lady Tyne refused to see me," Katalin complained. "Her dogs barked like mad. A vain attempt to keep her slaves, I presume. I sent her a requisition notice. I am your adviser, after all, and she should know I have jurisdiction for such things."

Temporary adviser.

I paused, my expression stern. "In the future, before you spend the treasury coin needed for food and weapons, you will confer with me."

Katalin stiffened, and the tips of her ears turned pink. "Of course, Empress. I wanted to help without bothering you. I overstepped. What would you have me do?"

For all Katalin knew, we had plenty of funds in the treasury. I didn't correct her misconception. The last thing I needed was a panic. Before his death, Philo had explained why the treasury didn't hold an excess. After I banned the raids and requisitioning of slaves, a primary source of imperial income evaporated. I'd stopped the rot hollowing our kingdom's core, but I'd created a financial bleed. And now I had a coming war, costly in both blood and coin.

"I recognize that you have unusual ways of solving problems." I put it as generously as I could. "When I freed all the slaves in the castle, my steward assisted them in finding whatever employment they wished to pursue."

The crown couldn't even afford to replace all the slaves who left. "It was never my intention for the crown to replace the freed slaves with new ones. When the crown buys contracts, we will give the slaves options. They may stay and work at their estates if the household stewards approve. Or they may seek employment elsewhere, roam the kingdom, or join the army and fight for Dacia. They will have choices as any free Dacian does."

"But that creates... creates an imbalance." Katalin stumbled through her words. "Some slaves are now completely free while the rest are still bound." A flash of concern crossed her face as she seemed to understand the unfairness of the situation.

"It's the best option," Jamil said.

Our only option.

"For now," I said. "But we will continue to buy slave contracts. These treasures will be sold. A historian has already begun research on each piece."

I studied Katalin's reaction. She was calm, but she couldn't hide her distaste, though a determination surfaced, too. I continued, "No one is as clever in the ways of the Rose Court as you. I want you to identify potential buyers. For example, Lady Tyne has a particular fondness for canary jewels. Evaluate the court and assess items that will bring the highest bids."

"If I might make a suggestion," Katalin said, her resolve strengthening. "Items that don't have significant historical value you might consider selling to foreign kingdoms."

"Auripo is our only ally," I said. "They're still a struggling nation. Who would we sell to?"

"Lazica, for one." She pressed her fingers into the table. "They are keenly interested in the affairs of other kingdoms, especially the mythical Golden Protector." She straightened, giving me a knowing look. I was no more mythical than she was. "The Lazicans sell their ore to all sides of a war, making a tidy profit while never getting entangled themselves. I'm guessing the right item could buy a small legion."

Lazica assumed they were safe because they always had been. But, I suspected the magical invaders' attention would eventually turn to the Lazicans' ore-filled mountains.

Katalin glided from one end of the treasures to the other, her gaze scrutinizing each rare item. Her attention fell on the massive musgravite necklace from Emperor Saam. "The Theracians would be another kingdom to consider. Of course, Emperor Saam wouldn't approve, so the sales would need to be on the black market — driving up the prices even further." She arched her eyebrow, smirking. "And his rumored unrequited love for you makes them all the more valuable. We could start by asking about potential buyers from our resident Theracian... *guests*. In fact, if it's our history you'd like to preserve, I have another idea."

I cocked my head to the side. "I'm listening."

"Everything the Golden Empress has worn, touched, or even admired, we should sell first. The items don't need to be of intrinsic value to be of worth." She snapped her fingers. "Like that shell you received from the Illyrians. It's worthless, except for the fact that you've touched it. Even the dress you're wearing right now could bring a fortune."

"What are your thoughts, Jamil?" I asked.

Jamil ran a hand down his clean-shaven face. "I think it would be best to keep the gifts given to you at hand, for now. But your clothing... I don't see how your dress or shoes will fetch a price, but I don't see the harm in trying, especially if it will save soldiers in the field."

Katalin's suggestion gave me another idea. Some gifts could be re-purposed in the castle. The material from Lazica could be used for any furnishings in need of repair rather than hoarding the items for my rooms. Even the Theracian's rugs should replace any needed in the castle and the governors' estates.

Only a few colony states had sent me gifts, but Illyria was one of them. I hadn't given the conch shell that sat on my writing desk much thought.

"Do you have any Illyrian contacts?" I asked

"What kind of contacts?" Katalin asked.

"The shell you mentioned, I'm curious... " I tapped my chin. "A shell collector from the Rose Court commented on it. Apparently, the rarer and more colorful, the higher the value. The one I received is a dull cream. It's pocked by what I can only presume is the normal course of a sea creature's life. The collector said it might be valuable due to its size, but his lip practically curled when evaluating it. Is there an Illyrian refugee somewhere in Dacia that we could ask about it?"

"I'll see what I can find out." Katalin dropped her gaze, looking at her fingers, rapping her nails on the table. "There is one item that will fetch an impressive price. Probably more than all the other items on that wall combined."

Based on her earlier comments, it was probably something I'd worn. What were my most valuable items? I gripped the sword at my hip. "Surely, you're not considering my sword or my crown. My sword could still carry a magical curse, and the crown's magic was never completely understood."

"I agree, it's a risk."

My temper flared. "This sword must be at my side for b-battle."

Jamil shifted his weight, silent.

"I was thinking of the crown," Katalin said. "We would warn the buyer that it could potentially kill them."

"You mean cause b-boils and inflame every fiber of their body in acute p-pain?" Katalin's disregard for others never ceased to surprise me.

She flitted her hand through the air. "I'm more concerned with the statement it makes to sell the *Crown of Lore* than the potential death." She paused and met my gaze. "How desperate are we for coin?"

I folded my arms, glaring at her.

"That bad," Katalin said, leaning against the table, her shoulders rounded.

I frowned, realizing she'd just manipulated me into telling her the treasury status. She'd never intended to sell the crown. "Nice ruse."

Clever fox.

"We're headed into a war," Katalin said. "Why not raise taxes? Everyone will expect it."

"I can't raise taxes on the commoners. I need them to volunteer to get into the fray. If they feel like they've fulfilled their duty, they're less likely to join, especially if they're already struggling after the plague. Nor can I ask the nobles for more taxes when I'm in the process of freeing their slaves. Even with a payment, the change will impact their lifestyles more than they'd like."

"It'll be a social reckoning," Katalin frowned. "The Roses will have our petals plucked."

"But what good will your gold and fine houses do when you're dead?" I asked. "Everything is going to change. And some of that is going to be ugly and imperfect. But it's what we must do to survive."

Katalin opened her mouth and then clamped it back shut. When she spoke again, she was subdued. "I only wanted to help you. That's all I've ever wanted. You know this, yet you shut the doors and don't let me in." She slumped further against the table, her hand brushing just below her ribs. "I wish you'd tell me what happened *that* day — the day Yasmine stabbed me."

I wasn't sure to what part of that horrible day she referred.

"What did you do?" Katalin asked. "When you chased after me, shouting, trying to stop me in the hallway. I saw you get thrown back. It wasn't natural." She slowly looked up at me again, her usual haughtiness stripped away. "It was like magic."

"I don't know what you're talking about. I don't have magic." But her words jarred the memory. Something strange *had* happened in the hallway. I'd been knocked backward, completely off my feet, though no one was nearby. I'd forgotten about it until now.

"You keep so many secrets from me." Katalin's voice had a strange rawness. "Because I don't know your goals nor the kingdom's true situation, I continue to blunder. What can I do to prove I'm trying to help you?"

"You've kept plenty of secrets from me, Lady Katalin. Trust must be earned." I stepped closer. "Your invitation to be my adviser is a chance to prove your loyalty. Don't go to the Roses again, instituting measures without my consent."

She nodded, her eyes cast down.

If I'd trusted her, I might have revealed my simmering curiosity. Something *had* happened that day. Something I was anxious to explore — with someone who hadn't lied to me as Katalin repeatedly did. If someone had intervened that day, I was determined to find them. And if I'd created the force on my own, I had to figure out how.

I wanted to do it again.

Of Mama's many servants, her most trusted is made of scorpion venom and snake bites. She pretends to like us, but I know she doesn't. When Mama is gone, she yells at us for splashing water outside of the bathing pool, or when we skip instead of walk, or when my three-year-old sister tips over a vase of flowers.

Yesterday, when I started to speak, the servant yanked my braid, hurting my neck. She said she doesn't want to know the thoughts of a ten-year-old whose mind is cursed by Zalmoxis. She told the servants I'm not to be trusted.

The worst part is that she seemed afraid of me.

I'm hiding under my blanket this morning. What did I do wrong? Mama is away from the city again; why has she abandoned us to this scorpion caretaker?

—— ESME

FIVE

MAGI BENEATH THE MOUNTAIN

The early morning air nipped at my nose as Asander and I rode down the snowy mountainside to greet Lady Tyne. The prince's mare lifted her hooves ridiculously high in the hoof-deep snow, but my gelding was well acquainted with mountain winters.

Tyne had not been seen in the Rose Court since the Norte attack. I'd given the noblewoman space to heal, but it was time for me to visit her, especially after Katalin's thoughtless attempt at coercion.

We were greeted by the few nobles out riding, heavy cloaks across their shoulders and brows mostly hidden under stiff fur hats. A servant girl scurried to the castle, a basket on her hip. For a moment, I thought it was Annuska, Marianna's granddaughter. But it wasn't her, of course. I keenly missed Marianna's advice. Without her sure guidance, I had feared I'd be a grain of sand in a windstorm. But she'd prepared me well. And in the end, she taught me to trust myself.

No one could ever be what Marianna was to me. I'd put off the task of finding another adviser, allowing Katalin to fill the void. But Katalin was juggling the ambassadorship, her diplomatic duties with Auripo, and now the adviser position. While I realized she'd never intended to dethrone me, Katalin still had trouble with boundaries. Why did she overstep even more with me than other leaders or past emperors?

Perhaps it wasn't that I needed to trust her but that she needed to trust me.

"Empress," Asander said, pulling me out of my thoughts. "About the dinner tonight..."

"Yes?" I braced for more grousing. In getting to know the prince, I realized that after his life of stern training and bloody battles, he had little patience for veiling his poor opinion of the decadence and indolence of the Rose Court.

"Would you show me the steps to one of the more common Getaen dances?"

I brightened. "Oh?"

"When we go to Moesia, I want to be able to dance with the commoners," Asander said. "Given the frivolity of your people, I wouldn't be surprised if a festival was orchestrated during our recruiting tour."

"Of course, I would enjoy teaching you," I said, though his words stung.

We fell silent as two servants trudged up the hill past us.

"I am glad I can share my honest thoughts with you, as a friend," Asander said. "I find myself stumbling because I've known one way of life, and suddenly, traditions and conventions have shifted."

I stared at Asander's profile. I'd been working on a friendship with the prince, but hearing him state our unromantic relationship aloud was like a slap. I'd hoped that somewhere inside him, he'd begun to think of me romantically. Furthermore, didn't he realize that I, too, was adrift from the life I'd known? My life had also suddenly shifted. The day I opened Mama's blue vision, my life changed. Yet, both our kingdom's survival depended on our actions in this unfamiliar landscape.

Around the mountain below appeared a robust woman in a tall fur hat, a long mustard coat, and two dogs on a leash. I blinked, making sure I was really seeing Tyne. The muscular dogs were fawn-colored with black markings on their faces, extending down onto their chests. Both of them had their noses out and ears perked, the tips of which hit near Tyne's waist. I dismounted, handing the reins to Asander.

"Let me prove my identity, if I may," Tyne called out before I could approach. "I rarely was able to talk to you alone, especially as your lady's maid was always lurking in your chambers. But I once advised you to smile more from the dais, as it would help ingratiate you with the Roses."

I'd been fooled by a Tyne-Mirror before, but this woman not only knew of a private conversation, but she had the true Tyne's bearing and inflection.

"Don't bother trying to prove who you are." Tyne's dogs sniffed the air between us. "The dogs will do the task. I took the liberty of borrowing one of your marama scarves from that helpful lady's maid of yours."

"That's quite enough; back your dogs away from the Empress." Asander stepped between me and the animals. The dogs growled, baring their teeth.

"You've already questioned your betrothed, I presume?" Tyne asked, leaving her menacing dogs between Asander and me.

"He was questioned this morning and has been at my side since."

Tyne gave a curt nod and commanded her dogs to retreat to her side as she approached Asander.

"If you don't mind." Tyne held out her hand for Asander's glove and then allowed the dogs to sniff the article. Then she commanded her dogs to find the owner — to teach the dogs Asander's scent, I assumed.

Asander's brow raised as he looked to me. It was all I could do to keep from laughing. Tyne was both exactly as I remembered and not at all what I expected. I'd pictured her cowering in her rooms, worried that everyone was a Mirror. But here she was, commanding the space around her, even a foreign prince.

"Now the dogs will know you, Prince Asander," she said before turning to me and curtsying. "I received the message that you wanted to speak with me after breakfast. I didn't realize you were coming to my home."

"I wanted to visit you while I was in the capital," I said, though my mind wandered. Clearly, something was missing from Katalin's story. The fearful woman I'd pictured was not the woman before me. Looking from the dogs to Asander, I asked. "What do you mean, the dogs will know the prince?"

"The prince will now be discernible from one of those pretenders — one of those *Mirrors*." She spat the word, her face darkening. We'd found out too late that the Norte Mirrors could change their appearance, even the clothing they wore, to disguise themselves. "When they captured me, I vowed to survive the ordeal and to devise a way to never be deceived by their false imitations again. I'd planned to enlighten you tonight after the noble's dinner at the castle, but let's not waste this opportunity now — I'll explain everything."

~

LADY TYNE ACCOMPANIED Asander and me to Rupea Castle, boasting about her trained dogs all the way. We passed the courtyard, snow piled in drifts along the edges, and strode through the main gates.

"And they ignore those they've been trained to recognize?" I clarified with Tyne.

"Yes, hence, why I needed the prince's scent." Tyne adjusted the leashes, her leather gloves squeaking. "Now the dogs will know him. Those who haven't been identified, the dogs will not allow close to me. And they'll attack a Mirror."

We walked the curved outer corridor, the ceiling open to the sky. Braziers marked every twenty steps, the blazing heat melting wide circles of snow.

"How would they know a Mirror?" Asander asked.

"Scent and training," Tyne explained. "The Imperial Guards'

dogs snarled and yapped when they came to question me — the canines smelled the Norte, not fooled by their disguises. They barked wildly at the Mirrors, those *pretenders*. The dogs knew the truth. Smelled it. But as the Mirrors *looked* like my staff and me, the guards never suspected the deception. But in reality, the Imperial Guards were speaking to Mirrors and mind-manipulated servants. After I was freed, I asked Captain Lucius about the dogs. There's more to it, but essentially these dogs are trained to alert their handlers when they encounter certain scents."

I grew excited at the notion. We could clear swaths of people quickly, using dogs, diminishing the threat of Mirrors to some degree. "Can they sense a Mirror we haven't identified?"

"That I doubt. But I figure if the Norte to infiltrate with a Mirror, it's likely one who's already been here and knows the area. How many Mirrors do you think survived the skirmish?"

Asander gave me a side-long look.

"Twenty Norte arrived at the castle, and half were killed. We don't know exactly how many survivors were Mirrors." Though I estimated that most of them were. And it was likely one of them who died trying to murder me in the tannery.

With Tyne's command, the dogs both sat, the snow crunching beneath them.

"Your dogs are well-trained," I said. "They respond to your every move."

"I purchased these two retired dogs and hired the royal dog trainer. Captain Lucius was not pleased and told me I wasn't to divert resources from the throne." Tyne's nostrils flared, and she adjusted the clasp at her neck. "As you know, I would never intentionally hurt the crown. So, I requested one of the trainer's previous apprentices to train the pups that I acquired a moon ago."

"How many pups?" Asander asked.

"Ten, though I plan to train more. I imagine many will request dogs when the animals' abilities are revealed, and I will be ready to help." Tyne lifted her chin. "We didn't understand the dangers before, and we can be excused for our foolhardy actions. But now we know the Mirrors' capabilities, and we must respond without frailty of heart. We cannot let the actions of those who've hurt us prevent us from moving forward with confidence. The Norte struck us down. But they did not defeat us."

A page hurried after us, handing Asander a note which he turned over to me. A dark blue wax seal — Lazica. My heart thrummed. Wedged between the Auripoans and the Theracians, Lazica must grasp their precarious situation. Dacia had sent Marcus to be a back-channel of communication. Had he been successful in gaining an ally?

"I'll take my leave," Tyne said, allowing me to privately review the letter. "But I shall see you again tonight at dinner, in case you have further questions."

After Tyne strode down the outer corridor, Asander and I moved to the nearest brazier, the flames heating my fingers. I cracked the seal.

Most Esteemed Empress Nicoleta Aurelian,

We have received word of the attack on the Rose Court last moon. We are relieved to hear that you are hale, and your court remains intact. We anticipate that your instinct will be to prepare for war. We are here in your time of need. We have discovered a new vein of ore, pure and of the finest quality for the tools of war. We are holding it and are ready to trade at your convenience.

Respectfully,
The Lazican Twelve

I reread the letter, my fingers shaking. The Lazicans were not pledging their allegiance to us. They could, and would, sell ore to all parties, including the Theracians and the Norte. No troops were coming. Nothing was pledged. It was trade, as usual.

Marcus failed.

"This was as expected. Still... " Asander growled. "We will find another way to succeed."

I crumpled the letter and threw it into the brazier, the fire devouring it. Our army was too small. The war could be long. What options did we have?

Magic. We need magic.

~

MY GETAEN ADVISERS worked in a large chamber deep in the mountain-side of the castle. The room was similar to the university where Papa studied with several long tables and a myriad of materials and supplies. Despite the stale air and rough-hewn walls, the windowless room felt inviting. Secreted away, my advisers and I were united in our determination to innovate magical tools and protections to counteract the Norte. I hung my hopes for success on the Getaens' work, far more than I preferred. But while my other options were withering, this one produced fruit.

Ziba and Pari accompanied the prince and me. Asander kissed my cheek, as he often did in public, before leaving to stand guard outside. My other advisers, Rufus, the Ghoster; Gul, the Clarifier; Hadrian, the Illuminator; and the new Bonder, Seneca, gathered closer.

"We can prepare against the Norte magic we've seen," Rufus began, "But we believe they revealed only a small portion of their capabilities. The scholars and scribes have been relaying their findings, but precious little insight has been uncovered." He glanced at the Illuminator, who was bouncing up and down on his heels, his attention flitted from the ceiling to the tables, back to the ceiling, then to his nails, never-ending. Rufus continued, "Hadrian reminded us that all magic has a light and dark side."

"A push and pull is more accurate," Ziba corrected. "All magic can be used for good or ill."

Rufus gave her a small nod but didn't look convinced. "Are we in agreement that the Norte magic is somewhat reflective of our own?"

Pari nodded. "They have Healers, but not quite like me. Somehow they produce Healing magic with a touch. Perhaps their sweat? Their power lives within them as we saw when Tatiana pulled the dagger from the Norte Healer; the blade was poisoned. The blade verified the Norte Healer's ability to both heal and poison, the light and dark, or push and pull, within them."

"And Illuminators," Ziba added, eying Hadrian as he wandered away. "Borsea is an Illuminator. She can produce bright light. Or darkness."

"I've also seen Borsea dim Luminaries without touching them," I added. "I saw Targen, a Sonus, mute sound as if he was surrounded by dampening powder, but I saw none. It would make sense that the ability came from inside him."

"And their Ghosters are true Mirrors, who can change their appearance in a heartbeat," Rufus said. "I can't do that, but here's what I *can* do."

Rufus guided me to his table and opened a marble box. Inside, water-like blue disks were organized in open, individual parchment containers. He selected one of the Ghoster disks labeled "Gully." Rufus slid it into my hand. It curled up into a marble-sized orb, and I spoke, knowing it would capture my words.

"Well done, Rufus. I know this will work." I gave him a smile as I placed the disk on the table. The ball flattened back to a disk though, this time, it was shiny.

"The disk's message should only work for Gul as that disk had a tiny snippet of her hair embedded inside," Rufus explained, handing the disk to Pari.

"Smaller than an eyelash," Gul added.

Pari snapped the disk. Instead of hearing my words repeated, the disk crumbled.

"Well done," I clasped my hands to my chest. "I had no doubt you could perfect it."

Rufus smiled modestly. "It was Seneca's idea. Each disk is

Bonded to the material embedded inside. That's what makes it crumble at the wrong touch."

The new Bonder stood behind Ziba and Gul. He was tall, even for a Getaen, and looked like a gust would knock him down.

"Thank you, Seneca." I gave the Bonder an approving nod.

Ziba had recommended Seneca, and I had invited him to officially join the ranks of the Getaens serving the crown. Unlike the other Getaens, I suspected that Seneca questioned his decision.

"I believe the disks themselves could be Bonded in advance, and you could add the material of the intended recipient yourself at any time." Seneca fiddled with his fingers. "It would be useful on the battlefield. I'm still testing."

"A worthy experiment," I said and turned to Ziba. "So, we have a good idea of what the Norte Healers, Illuminators, and Mirrors can do."

Ziba nodded. "And you've witnessed a bit of Sonus magic. We have some assumptions as to what the Protectors, Sensitives, and Clarifiers *could* do. But Seers, Bonders, and... Rippers," she struggled with saying the word. "We have no idea. Still, our knowledge is far greater than before the Battle of the Rose Court."

Hadrian paced along the far wall. Ziba and Pari had commented on how the Illuminator only worked for a couple of hours before rushing off, sometimes for days. He was erratic, to be certain. But he'd proven willing to bend the rules of magic, which was why I had become increasingly anxious to talk to him. During yesterday's discussion with Katalin, she'd reminded me of the strange occurrence when I'd chased her through the castle. I needed to discover what had happened that day with someone who viewed magic from a whole different perspective — someone like Hadrian.

Had someone performed unknown magic, interfering with my chase? Or was it something else? Keeping my swirling thoughts hidden, I turned to Hadrian, ready for the last demonstration.

The Illuminator jerked a thick scarf over his head, draping it like a short necklace. "Castle seamstresses have made these sample scarves." His words were clipped. "I got the idea from the Norte. I infused Illuminator magic into the fibers. The dark side protects against darkness. The light side against blinding light. Though I'm less concerned about darkness, as those effects quickly fade."

"How long until you have enough for my Own?"

"How quickly can the seamstresses sew?"

"Have you given them the measurements?" Ziba asked. "The specifications?"

Hadrian frowned. "They can figure it out."

The steward had relayed complaints from the seamstresses about Hadrian's half-baked sewing patterns. But the Illuminator seemed more inclined to climb the walls than give detailed instructions. I needed his mind sharp to discuss what happened with Katalin. While his quirky behavior was challenging at times, he was perfect for finding solutions no one else saw.

"Care to walk in my gardens, Hadrian?"

The Illuminator spun and dug through the piles on his desk. The desk just beyond Hadrian's belonged to the new Bonder. A large object caught my attention. A rolled-up pallet of blankets along with a large pack was propped against Seneca's desk. My stomach twisted. The Bonder had brought his personal things to this room. He slept here.

Seneca pivoted just enough to hide his face, his shoulders curling inward. I struggled to swallow the lump forming in my throat. Wherever he had been living, he was no longer welcome.

Because he served the crown.

With a triumphant flourish, Hadrian produced his gloves and cloak.

"Well done," I said, bringing attention to myself and away from Seneca. "Everyone believes we need more weapons, soldiers, and coin than our enemy to win. But this war will be different than the others. Magic will make all the difference. Thank you."

How much of what we're just learning have the Norte long ago mastered?

"Empress, may I join you as you return to our wing of the castle?" Ziba asked as Hadrian opened the door.

"Of course." I was anxious to speak with Hadrian alone, but I had planned to wait until we were outside, anyway.

As we started down the hall, Asander lectured Hadrian on staying within sight so he didn't have to vet the Illuminator again and again. Even so, we had to move quickly to keep up with him.

Ziba spoke to me in an urgent whisper. "Are there any viewing or listening stations in these halls?"

I raised my eyebrow and shook my head. "My Own's tunnels are not this deep in the castle."

"I've grappled with something for a long time. I've dreaded explaining it, but I must." Ziba grabbed my arm. "We know one of the Norte was a Ripper. It's time I explain what I know of this unspoken magic."

I stopped short, stunned that finally someone was speaking freely of this dark magic.

Ziba's grip tightened, pulling me ahead again. "Rippers are shunned in our Getaen culture, but what if the Norte accept and utilize their power? That could make the Norte formidable, indeed."

My hands shook. I'd asked Rubia about Rippers many times with little explanation. Ziba had only said they could "dull" Norte powers, perhaps. "What can a Ripper do, exactly?"

"People can give things to them, like their healthy bones, or their Sonus ability."

I wrenched my arm from Ziba and clutched at my orb pendant. "Push and pull. That's what you said. Can they transfer these "gifts" to others?"

Ziba shrugged. "Some people think Rippers are as rare as Seers. But I'm sure one was with the Norte. Whoever it was, they dulled the magic when we first met, likely so a Sensitive couldn't detect any lies. Without knowing it, the Norte confused your greatest asset, Marianna. Though she wouldn't have known their magical abilities anyway, she couldn't read them at all."

I followed Ziba's thoughts, and a few more things started to make sense. "When Tatiana fought Dyana on the practice field, and when the Mirrors began to use their magic to disguise themselves, the Ripper pulled back. That's why their auras seemed to fluctuate." The pendant's edge dug into my fingers. "What if the Ripper was taking Marianna's ability? Could they do that?"

Ziba shook her head with worry. "Who knows what a powerful Norte Ripper can do?"

Zalmoxis, we needed to find a Getaen Ripper to teach us more.

Mama asks about my dreams. I tell her only snippets.

I don't think Mama listened to me every morning over the last year out of love. She misses family breakfast often. If I tell her less, maybe she'll worry less.

After we were excused from dinner, Bijan told me he'd heard servants whispering about me. He wanted to know what was wrong, or what I'd done. Though Bijan is not my closest sibling in age, he's always been my best friend. He acted like he was trying to help me, but when I told him I didn't know what the servants were gossiping about, he didn't believe me. He tried to use his Sensitive magic to find out the truth. When I figured out what he was doing, I was so angry!

I'm never going to talk to him again. How could he do that to me? He should have believed me.

If I knew what I did to upset everyone in the household, I would try and fix it.

— ESME

SIX

HEARTBREAK AND MIDNIGHT

Hadrian brightened once we were shivering in my personal garden. Drifts of fresh snow had been shoveled to the side of the cobblestone pathway between the open grassy area, now blanketed in white. The ornamental trees and shrubs' naked branches coated in frosty crystalline shimmered in the afternoon light. I dismissed Ziba, and Asander stood near the doorway as I explained to Hadrian what had happened with Katalin when I'd chased after her in the castle.

"You were knocked back off your feet?" Hadrian mused. "Let's re-enact the whole event."

I tugged my gloves on tighter. "I was running after Lady Katalin —"

Hadrian jogged from the shoveled path to the fresh snow in the middle of the garden. "Was she further away than I'm standing right now?"

I hiked up my dress to my shins and followed him. The fresh snow barely covered my foot, but underneath, snow from earlier in the season had compacted and was a bit slick. "From where I'm standing, she was about ten paces."

Hadrian moved so he was ten paces away. "Where were her hands?"

"Down. Yes, she held them away from her side. She had turned and was looking right at me."

"How many people were around you?"

"Dozens."

"It's possible an onlooker performed some sort of magic, but I don't know of any magic capable of physically moving someone." He tapped his foot. "Did someone pull you?"

"No one was close enough." Everyone seemed frightened of my rage.

"What were you doing? Exactly."

I placed one foot in front of the other. "I put my hand out and commanded Lady Katalin to stop."

I cocked my head, inspecting my gloved fingers. I tugged off the gloves. There was something on my hand that day. My stomach clenched. Shortly before I found Marianna murdered, Marcus had told me he was leaving. The black Sonus powder from that dreadful conversation had stuck to my fingers all day.

My heartbeat quickened. I did have magic when I'd chased Katalin. I jerked my attention to Asander. "Please send a servant to fetch a bag of fresh, dampening Sonus powder."

I looked back at my hand and pulled my exposed, reddening fingers into a fist. Hadrian tromped closer as I lowered my voice. "I'd had Sonus powder stuck to my fingers."

That was the day my heart had broken a hundred times. Every word Marcus said cut me, shattering my hopes. Essa had died. Marianna was murdered. My world crumbled that day.

"Empress?" Asander pulled me out of my thoughts as he handed me a small bag.

I swallowed, my mouth dry. The past I'd buried for moons was crawling out. I dipped my fingertips into the bag, the black grains sticking to my flesh.

"This bag must be very fresh. Perfect." I feigned calm, as if visions of the past weren't pinging against my skull.

Asander retreated to the doorway as Hadrian counted ten paces away from me.

I inspected my stained fingertips. I sucked in a breath, my memories a flood, filling my senses. Instead of shoving them away, I let them spill over.

The grit under my nails. The sweat down my back. The abject fear of being hunted. The coppery smell of blood. Marianna was dead. Senseless. Pointless. Fury boiled in my veins. I had believed it was Katalin, and I was blind with hatred, determined to make her suffer.

"I'm Lady Katalin." Hadrian bolted toward the manicured shrubs on the far end of the garden.

I chased after him. "Lady Katalin! You are a wretched beast who will pay for what you've done."

Hadrian turned to face me, his hands down by an invisible dress.

I shot my hand up, tears in my eyes. I screamed, "Stop!"

A force pulsed against me. I was thrown back. I landed, snow flying, pain jarring up my spine. I couldn't breathe, the air knocked from my lungs.

Hadrian giggled like a maniac, and Asander slid down to my side.

"Stars, Nicoleta." His eyes were wide. "What just happened?"

I looked past him at the cold, clear sky, digging my fingers into the snow.

I just did magic.

I'D WORN a trench down to the dormant grass as I'd paced back and forth. Jamil stood near the doorway, but all Imperial Guards had been sent away.

"Again," I said to Asander.

He put his hand out, facing no one, his splayed fingers black with Sonus powder. "Stop!"

He coughed as his body was pushed back; his feet didn't slide far, but he moved.

"I can't believe this." I rubbed the heel of my hand against my forehead.

Hadrian danced around, practically singing, "It's working. It's working."

Asander stared at his hands, eyes wide.

"Rubia," Jamil said. "How can I help you?"

I spun to see Rubia under the archway, a long cloak wrapped around her. She looked from joyful Hadrian to Asander's blackened fingertips. I held my breath, waiting to see if this display would trigger an outburst. They'd been less frequent, but odd things sent her spinning. She released her cloak, and it fluttered open as she stepped a slippered foot into the snow.

"It's all about intention," Rubia said to Asander. Rubia had said those words to me a thousand times, but I'd never really understood them.

I did now.

Jamil signaled to my Own before striding to Rubia's side. He tried to guide her out of the snow, but her glare forced him a step back.

"Pari said I could find you here. This isn't what I expected to find." Rubia grabbed my hands, inspecting my blackened fingertips. "Did you try using the language of magic?"

I blinked, memories of Rubia's mutterings when she worked — the ancient words of the north, the language of magic. I sucked in a deep breath, and icy air reached its pointed claws down my throat.

She stepped back. "Try it against me."

I closed my eyes and pictured Tatiana as she murdered Valentin. My stomach twisted and bile bit at my throat. Tears welled beneath my lids and I cried out, the mourning of my soul welling inside me. My eyes flew open as I shot my hand toward her. "Palai!"

I flew back, slamming into Asander, sending us both sprawling. I groaned, wet snow down my sleeves and my back.

"Goddess of Earth!" Asander shifted, the snow crunching.

"Empress!" Jamil shouted, bounding to my side.

I blinked, my head throbbing.

Rubia hovered over me, a wicked smile on her face and her eyes sparkling, in her once-familiar expression. "Congratulations, my brilliant daughter, you can do magic. Now to harness it!" She reached out and grasped my hand, yanking me to my feet. "The Norte are in for a terrible surprise."

I danced late into the evening, carving out opportunities to speak with as many Roses and Lilies as I could. Lady Tyne had arranged to have her dogs at the entrance to the dining hall. She had collected scents from everyone who might be in attendance. The mood was lighter than it had been since the Battle of the Rose Court. I didn't know that I'd ever feel completely secure again, but the dogs took the jagged edge off my paranoia. It didn't hurt that Asander had given me a scabbard to wear on my calf for my dagger. Instead of pressing uncomfortably against my ankle, it rested securely along the muscle.

Madame Palanka had prepared my favorite meal: the least expensive food that the nobles would tolerate. That meant nothing from far-flung exotic locations. Instead, roasted venison, tubers with dried herbs, and barley rolls took center stage. Fortunately, the nobles had come to expect my "charming," simple tastes.

Past emperors rarely interacted with the nobles, preferring to stare down at them from the dais. I'd discovered that I was more comfortable dancing among them, letting them speak while I listened.

"With Capidava re-trials complete, I can be a steady resource for your father while you are away on your tour," the High Judge Isidro reassured me as we danced. "Though local judges from other cities still have much work to do; they'll be busy for several moons."

"I appreciate your constancy," I gave him a genuine smile. Isidro's work in righting past sins of the crown was nothing short of miraculous. After Vasile's behavior, I had a newfound appreciation for judges who not only understood the law but had compassion for the people.

With each change of partners, I received snippets of information and words of support.

"Creation of boots for the soldiers has already begun and all orders will be completed by the end of spring," the local leather guild representative assured me. "Having seen what a Mirror is capable of has spurred the local craftsmen into increased production."

"Would the beginning of spring be possible?" I would take an attack in the tannery if it meant getting supplies faster.

He blinked several times. "As the Empress commands, it will be done."

"Recruits are already training," I said as the song ended. "The sooner we can protect the feet of those who protect us all, the better."

"Of course," he said with a deep bow.

After speaking with every local guild representative, I was exhausted. I signaled to my Own and excused myself, looking forward to falling into my bed. Tomorrow night I would be at an inn, and after that, it could be weeks before I'd be back at Rupea. Outside the dining hall, I turned to gaze on the opulent gold throne across the room. The first time I'd stood here was less than a year ago, but so much had changed. I had been determined but felt as small as a mouse, not knowing a single person in the room. Now I was Empress, leading our kingdom to battle. After the upcoming bloody war, things would be different yet again.

Asander slipped out of the hall, joining me, a slight crease between his brows. My Own disappeared as the prince held out his arm, ready to escort me to my rooms. I rested my palm against his sleeve and paraded down the hall, feeling nobles and servants analyzing our movements.

Tyne was likely waiting near my rooms, so we'd only have a few moments of relative privacy. I wanted to discuss the prince's accommodations — a small matter. The prince's rooms were on the opposite side of my private wing, relegated to a distant corner.

"Asander, I prepared you a room nearer Rubia and myself. It's comfortable and closer to the map room and main corridor." With Essa's things cleared away, the space was larger than I'd expected. I didn't mention the tunnel that led directly to my sitting room as it seemed inappropriate.

"Why would you want me *closer* to your rooms?"

"I didn't want you to feel so removed," I struggled to find the right words as an unexpected strain grew between us. "We'll be sharing a room in two years, and I thought... " My voice trailed off seeing Asander's face, a mixture of confusion and, more alarmingly, revulsion.

Asander forced a light laugh, as we passed a servant. He dropped his voice to a whisper. "Nicoleta, no leader of any kingdom shares chambers with their spouse. Your steward already placed me in the rooms reserved for past queens. That's why they're on the opposite side of the secured wing."

My dinner turned to a stone in my stomach, and my feet slowed. Asander led me through the guarded doors to my private section of the castle. On the other side, I grabbed Asander's sleeve, stopping him.

"What kind of marriage do you envision?" I held my breath.

Asander cocked his head, studying me. "An honorable contracted union."

Sweat broke out along my hairline. That wasn't the answer I was hoping for. Where was the charismatic prince?

His face softened, and he pulled me away from the guarded doors and to the alcove near Essa's old room. "I swear I will never embarrass you the way my father has done to my mother. His affairs have hurt her deeply. Publicly, I will always support you."

I blinked, dissecting his words, hoping this was all a terrible misunderstanding.

"When Dyana arranged for me to marry you, I was relieved," Asander continued, his practical tone at odds with his startling admissions. "My father was considering some scrawny, sickly noblewoman. He knows I prefer strong, full-figured companions. Though you are not my ideal match, I will fulfill my obligation to produce an heir. I only ask that you wait to take a paramour until after we have a legitimate child."

Embarrassment coiled through me knowing my Own watched through the walls. Crawling into a dungeon cell was preferable to listening to Asander peel back the facade of our shiny relationship and reveal the emptiness beneath.

"Stars, Nikka, breathe. My duties to you are not a drudgery, and I assure you I will be a considerate bed companion. You're a lovely, intelligent woman." His words were sorry balm for his barbed explanation. "As royals, this is our duty. Our path."

The air thinned, the alcove shrinking. Asander's romantic attentions had been an act. Duty required he woo an empress. Attraction and love had never been part of the calculations for him; I was a resource, nothing more. When we kissed, he still wore a mask, doing what he thought would keep me... Keep me what? Satisfied?

"We are compatible rulers, you and I. I anticipate a jovial relationship and one of mutual respect. I hope you want that, too. I would hate for us not to be friends." He smiled encouragingly.

I wanted to slash the smug look off his handsome face with the very dagger he'd given me.

The best I could do was a slight, stiff nod before I turned blindly toward my room. When I saw a flutter of yellow material, I realized we'd walked all the way to my chambers. Tyne waited with one of her dogs near the two guards at my door.

"If you'll excuse us," I said to Asander. I ground my teeth as he kissed my cheek before leaving.

Tyne curtsied. "Any further questions after you've seen the dogs' performances at dinner tonight, Empress?"

I blinked, trying to focus.

The kingdom. I do what is best for the kingdom.

"I've been thinking... there m-must be a way to identify the Norte," I struggled through my words.

My marriage arrangement is best for everyone. Except me.

"How so?" Tyne's short, direct response helped snap my attention.

"Perhaps something they eat," I gripped my hands together behind my back and pinched the skin between my fingers. I shoved the hurt and embarrassment deep inside and focused on the task at hand. "Something that could d-distinguish the Norte from Dacians; something the dogs can d-detect."

"Conceivably, the minerals in the mountains leech into their food and water," Tyne suggested. "Something that leaves a trace in their hair or sweat. Testing our theory will be difficult, if not impossible."

I gripped my hands tighter and tamped down the tangle of emotion threatening to burble to the surface.

"I will put my mind to the problem," Tyne said.

"Thank you for all you've d-done."

"The honor is mine. When I was a prisoner in my own home, silenced and restrained, I felt defeated. Then I thought of my son. He fought to the very last breath until the plague took him. He wouldn't want me to give up. I fought to survive then and still do, just like he did." She rolled her lips in and took a sharp breath. "If he were still alive, we would have done anything to protect each other."

From what I'd seen and heard, Tyne had adored her only child. My parents loved me too, but I had wanted more. I'd dared hope for a romantic love. The reality tore into me like a knife — it was a childish dream.

"We will crush those who seek our homes, our lives." Tyne's fierce words lifted me just enough to keep from collapsing into a puddle.

"And I've left a gift for you in your rooms," she added, her eyes sparkling. "I've already cleared it with the head of your Own."

"That is very thoughtful, but your friendship means more to me than any gift."

She gave me a wink, then with a rustling of silk and a flash of sparkle from her canary-jeweled comb, she strode away with her dog at her side.

My guard escorted me inside my chambers where Tulia stood with her arms folded, glowering at a Dacian boy sitting cross-legged on the floor. Something shifted next to him. A bundle of fur. An ashy black dog.

My guard stiffened just as the dog raised its head, staring at me. Wait, it wasn't a dog. I froze.

It was a wolf.

"Empress," the boy scrambled to his feet. "My mistress, Lady Tyne, asked me to deliver this dire wolf pup, Midnight."

Tulia huffed as the beast stood. It was no mere pup. The wolf's back reached the boy's waist, and her broad skull only served to draw attention to her long muzzle and squared jowls.

"Lady Tyne gave her your scent earlier, but caution is still—"

The wolf moved toward me, and my guard laid a hand on his sword. The wolf growled, revealing black gums and large teeth. The boy's eyes went wide, his hands up, warning the guard.

"It's all right," I soothed. I took a step closer and immediately the wolf relaxed. I held out my hand, and she sniffed before pressing her nose and then head against my palm.

"She's two years old and was a challenge to train," the boy said. "But that's to be expected for a dire wolf. When Midnight responded favorably to your scent, we knew you were a match. Lady Tyne was so pleased I thought she might kiss us all."

A sense of warmth, comfort, and belonging passed between me and the wolf, in a way I hadn't expected. Inside, my walls crumbled, vulnerable. Everything I'd been holding in — not just my fears about the war but Asander's jagged words — bubbled, hot and fast like a pot boiling over.

"Leave us," I commanded as unfettered turmoil rose within me. "All of you."

The guard yanked open the door and shuffled Tulia away, but the boy lingered. "It's quite normal to have a rush of emotion when meeting a dire wolf. It's a sign of a strong b—"

The guard grabbed the boy by the shirt and dragged him away as he blurted something about a special connection. The moment my door slammed shut, I collapsed to the ground, my arms wrapped around the wolf, sobbing into her fur. Let my Own think it was a Bonded connection or whatever they liked. But the truth was my heart had never healed from Mama's death, or Marianna's, or Valentin's, or so many others, not to mention my failure to gain recruits Dacia needed in order to survive. Asander's cavalier dismissal of even a chance for love in our union trampled on my already tender heart, leaving it crushed in the road to be pulverized by every dirty foot, wagon wheel, and hoof.

Bijan apologized many times last week. My brother promised to never try and read my emotions with his Sensitive magic, ever again. I forgave him — I'm happy to have my best friend back. Though my older sister is closer to my age, she thinks she's too grown-up for me. Too mature for all of us, I guess. She moved into her own room years ago, and it's almost as big as the one I share with my three little sisters.

Our scorpion caretaker still avoids me, hissing if I even look at her. She must think I'm cursed by Zalmoxis. If Mama believes the scorpion, perhaps that's why she asks about my dreams. I haven't figured out what sickness might be tied to dreams.

My brother said that when people die, they can take a message from the living to Zalmoxis. Perhaps Zalmoxis is using my dreams to send a message back?

I don't think that's true. I don't feel cursed.

But am I?

— ESME

CHAPTER

SEVEN

PATRIDAVAN EVENINGS

In Patridava, the sky split, sleet swallowing my voice as I addressed the people. The Sonus repeated my words omitting my ever-increasing stutter. Even with my cloak, I couldn't shake the chill. But it wasn't from the pelting storm.

Dyana's messenger had found my caravan on the road, and her missive rattled me. The Auripoan patrol we met in the Rodnic Valley had never returned to their unit. After delivering word that the Norte had been spotted at the Curat River, they disappeared. Had they been forced another way? An impediment on the road, or an accident? Or had they been attacked?

Despite Dyana's bleak news, I spoke with conviction, urging the people to arms. Patridavans huddled under awnings and held their cloaks over their heads to no avail, their hair and clothing dripping. Yet, the people seemed to shrink away from my carefully crafted speech, extolling the citizens to fulfill their duty and protect the honor of their nation.

The onlookers tugged at their children and wiped water from their faces, distracted. Distant. As I'd spent most of my life as a commoner, I put myself in their shoes. Many of these people had moved here in search of opportunity. Many probably had the misfortune of experiencing a raid at the hands of the kingdom's guards. The feeling of violation haunted one for years. And now they were expected to fight alongside those same Thorns? To defend a crown that had attacked them?

"Ignoring the Norte isn't an option. The plague is gone, and we now have a tangible enemy we must face. We must work together or risk becoming subject to a kingdom that cares nothing for us."

I had always been in awe of Patridava — the wide, green fields, the diverse people, the prosperous vendors. But their tepid applause at the end of my speech didn't reflect back the veneration I felt for them.

My facade faltered. Asander held his cloak over my head and escorted me to the waiting, covered carriage. As the carriage *sloshed* through the stormy street to the governor's estate, Jamil was tense, keeping a watchful eye out the window. The prince acted more relaxed, as if our conversation three days ago about our marriage lifted a burden off his shoulders. My heart and ego were still bruised.

Between my people and Asander, I'd been scooped out, put on display, and found wanting.

As my unease grew, Midnight, my dire wolf, leaned against me. I shook off my petty grievances and self-doubt. Wallowing would not help me rally the kingdom. My heartbreak paled in comparison to the possible fates of the five missing Auripoans.

Across from me, Jamil ground his teeth as he stared out the window. He'd already voiced his concern about potential Norte Mirrors lying in wait, blending in with the crowds. I sat back, out of view, doing what I could to make Jamil's job easier. We all knew a clever attack could send all three of us to Zalmoxis.

I touched Jamil's shoulder. "I won't address the people openly in Moesia. Borsea and the Norte Council know that's my hometown. If they want to make a statement, that's where they will attack."

Jamil gave me a curt nod, not taking his eyes off the road.

Asander scanned out the opposite window, his back to me. The prince seemed oblivious to how deeply his words had wounded me. After three fitful nights, I foresaw three paths ahead of me: I could accept Asander, try to change him, or change myself to become the kind of partner he would want.

Even if I could change myself to be more appealing, it felt like a betrayal — a bridge I couldn't cross. And expecting Asander to change wasn't fair, either.

That left one option.

I'd already accepted the crown and the accompanying responsibility. Marrying someone who didn't love me in the way I'd wanted was a small price to pay in exchange for Auripo's allegiance. So, I would focus on the kingdom, not my unfulfilled yearnings for hearth, heart, and home. I took my hurt and tried to fold it up and put it away into yet another box.

"Is it possible that the Auripoan horses struggled in the snow, and their unit turned south toward the sea to cross the Curat?" Jamil asked, not turning his focus from the crowd.

"Dyana would have checked before alerting us," Asander said. "Is it possible bandits would have attacked them?"

"It's unlikely," I said. "The bandit leaders have been enforcing my rules thus far."

"And they're milking the crown for their efforts," Jamil grumbled, still focused on the city streets.

"They are asking for work and resources. We're able to help, so we are." Though I wouldn't be able to divert food or coin for much longer.

Neither Jamil nor I mentioned the other possibility — Getaens. The Roe Deer clan was several days south of the Curat, but their smaller, allied clans extended near where the Auripoans could have traveled. Fifty years ago, when the Theracians had crossed into the Red Valley clan's territory, the trespassers were slaughtered. The Roe Deer clan might have jumped to conclusions about the Auripoans.

Perhaps I'd rather it was my own people, in error, over the alternative. If the Norte had captured or killed Auripoan warriors, then our enemy's next move had already been made.

The drizzling rain slowed as did the carriage, near the entrance to the Patridavan governor's home. The sprawling estate was perched atop a rolling hill overlooking the expansive, bustling streets. While Rupea Castle was apart from every other Rose estate, high in the mountain, the governor's mansion was barely elevated, a short walk from noble homes and lavish shops.

"I'll hand off your dire wolf to the trainer," Jamil said. "Midnight can get started on learning everyone's scents in the estate."

Asander moved to follow, but I grabbed his cloak. I swallowed my pride, desperate to talk to someone about my failure, which would impact us all.

"My speech... it wasn't good. Lady Katalin helped me re-write it. But... " I struggled to articulate my thoughts. "What am I going to d-do?"

"Everyone has to find their voice. Their connection to their people. My troops hail from a lineage of warriors, and I know what words stir my army. Your people respond to a more... delicate touch."

"Why? Can't you just talk it through with me?" I hated to beg. But I was stuck, and I needed him.

"When you're ready, you will find the right things to say within yourself. And when you do, you'll know it." He gave me a patronizing pat on the hand.

Part of me still had a sliver of hope that Asander would pull me into his arms and tell me everything would be fine. How nice it would be, just for a moment, to let down my guard and just feel safe and cared for. Instead, he turned and strode outside where my Own had created a large perimeter around my carriage.

I stared at the back of Asander's head, my fingers digging into the edges of the cushion. He was probably right, but still, it wasn't *helpful*. Was this to be my life?

It could have been worse.

If events had worked out differently, I'd be promised to Emperor Saam, the man who had coldly dissected me. I shuddered.

Asander held out his hand for me. I released the cushion and set my hand on top of his, putting on a mask of calm, and stepped out of the carriage. Once on solid ground, he released me.

My heart is black steel. My heart is the hardest black steel ever forged.

Jamil gave the signal, and I nodded slightly to Asander as I stepped forward.

My Own tightened the perimeter around us as we moved. I was surrounded by guards sworn to lay down their lives for me, yet I felt utterly alone.

Above the entrance, we were greeted by a detailed, overhead fresco of a man with a bundle of barley in one hand and a star hovering above the other. I swallowed a gasp, realizing the frieze was a depiction of Zalmoxis, our god — a rarity. He'd been carved in a generous and inviting manner, also strange. In the hallway, the intricate sculptures and wide tapestries were a blur, only glimpsed between my Own as we strode by. Fresh flowers adorned a shrine to Zalmoxis, and I jerked my attention away, feigning to brush back a non-existent stray strand of hair. I kept my hand up until we passed the shrine, hiding my face. Apparently, the governor was as misguided as others I'd met in Patridava, begging for tragedy by attracting the attention of our vengeful god.

Asander didn't seem impressed nor concerned by anything in the hallway. However, he stared at the open-air, interior courtyard. With the break in the storm, Asander turned onto the pathway and poked a finger at the brown stubs of the clipped plants. "Extraordinary."

Dormant vegetation was by far the dullest thing I'd seen since arriving. "The estate is fascinating."

"No, I was just wondering what kind of vegetables or herbs were so precious as to be grown within the governor's residence."

One of my Own cleared his throat behind us. His dark hair was tied at the nape of his neck, his forehead framed by a deep widow's peak. "Those aren't vegetables or herbs, your highness. I grew up here. I can name most of these for you, if you'd like. My father was quite obsessed with ornamental plants."

"And this is a typical garden, in your experience, Thadeus?" Asander asked, pulling out a half-buried twig from the flower bed. I winced inwardly. After Valentin's death, I'd resolved to keep my distance from my Own, even avoiding their names. Asander had no such qualms.

"For nobles, yes," Thadeus replied. "And many Thorn families, Azures, and even wealthy Clovers have ornamental gardens like this within Patridava's city walls."

Asander snapped the stick between his fingers. A servant at the perimeter paused, seeing Asander's obvious agitation. I took Asander's arm, leading him a few steps away. Auripoans prided themselves on practicality, but I hadn't expected Asander to be so upset with a few flowers.

"This city is the wealthiest in Dacia. I didn't grow up with such finery. This is a strange place for me, too." I spoke with a forced calm and a note of warning.

Asander gripped my hand. "I expected Rupea might have impractical gardens, but this... " he stared at the empty flower beds. "I'm torn, worried your kingdom is too soft to be of any use. Auripoan fields were in constant danger of trampling hooves. Auripoans practice fighting techniques until they're too old to move. Half of the Dacian people either lounge in taverns or gardens for half their lives."

I took in a slow breath, steadying us both. Asander hadn't admitted he was jealous or fearful, but I guessed his feelings were deeper than the anger in his voice expressed. He was wrong about us in some ways, but lately, we'd been surrounded by nobles. These elaborate spaces were strange to me, too. Being in the governor's house was like wearing shoes that pinched too tight.

Though my instinct was to protect my wounded heart, I had sympathy for Asander. He was in a foreign land, and I was his only connection — his only friend. I could bitterly leave him out in the cold. Or I could provide warmth. He had been honest and was following his own code of honor. And he'd be at my side for these official events we both found excruciating.

I squeezed Asander's arm and lifted my chin, feigning nonchalance, as we entered a breathtaking reception room. Art lined the walls, sculptures dotted the room, and two massive fireplaces with raging fires were anchored on either side of the doorway. Katalin rushed to my side, a sincere smile on her face, which was even stranger than a flowered shrine dedicated to Zalmoxis.

Asander moved his hand to my back, returning to the rigid, doll-like escort he'd been for moons. If he was disgruntled by the frivolous courtyard, no one would ever guess. But I didn't begrudge his façade. Growing up as the son of a king, he must have learned from hard experience the importance of appearances.

Katalin introduced me to the governor's three adult children. They all had deep copper-toned skin, aquiline noses, and thick brows. She thoughtfully inquired about recent events in their lives: art they'd commissioned, horses they bred, and the youngest had just given birth to a baby.

"Thank you for the myrrh. We've already put it to good use in helping with colic," the youngest daughter said, brushing a dark, wayward curl away from her eyes.

"I look forward to meeting the baby soon." Katalin beamed as she gripped the noblewoman's hand. "Oh, I have a splendid idea. If the myrrh doesn't do the trick, perhaps a Getaen Healer might have a remedy."

The woman flushed. "Oh, Lady Katalin, I don't know where I'd even find a Getaen, let alone dare employ one."

My brilliant Healer is steps away, under this roof.

"Oh, it does seem rather a wild idea, but I've seen them work wonders." Katalin patted the new mother's hand. "I can get a Healer arranged for you, if you'd like. It would be no trouble."

Katalin smoothly transitioned from one person to the other, introducing me to each: a Patridavan judge, several local guild representatives, and other nobles. She had a knack for making them feel like the most important person in the kingdom. I was impressed. Was this part of standard childhood training for nobles?

"This is Governor Aelius Silvanus, and his wife, Lady Fausta." Katalin's smile widened as she introduced the governor's wife.

"It is an honor to meet you," Fausta said with a deep curtsy. She projected humility with just the right tilt of her head; however, from her elegant jewelry, posture, and plump, hourglass figure, I got the impression she was accustomed to the finer things in life. "Thank you, Empress, for the lovely rugs. They just arrived yesterday, and I had one put in your room."

"Very kind. They shall remind me of home." I nearly startled at my own words. When had I started to think of Rupea Castle as 'home'? Moesia would always be special to me, holding the memories of Mama and my youth. But Rupea was where I intended to stay.

"Horrid day for public speaking," the governor said. He was surprisingly fit for an older noble. His prominent nose and bushy brows framed his dull eyes. "Ghastly weather."

"Though we hope you will stay until the weather improves so you may speak again," the governor's wife quickly added.

Two servants entered the room with long, narrow boxes. Katalin clapped her hands together and looked at Asander. "You are in for a treat."

"I thought we might enjoy a bit of sport before dinner," the governor said.

"And after, I imagine," Fausta said, flatly.

There was a moment of tension, but Katalin eased it with a quick smile. "Empress, would you like to see your rooms now? They're quite lovely."

"I don't mind staying," I lied, realizing the servants were carrying sword cases. Staying was likely the more socially acceptable choice as only the governor's daughter excused herself, but I had no desire to watch men bloody each other, nor to listen while Asander talked about blades for the next hour.

"How kind of you, Empress. But you'll want to freshen up."

Katalin laughed a little higher than usual, giving me an easy excuse. I fiddled with my ring, signaling to Jamil and my Own strode toward us with Midnight at his side.

"Ah, yes, an escort." Katalin's shoulders relaxed a bit.

I glanced at Asander to be sure he would be fine without me. But, of course, he could barely take his eyes off the slender cases long enough to give me a slight nod.

I followed Jamil out of the room with Midnight at my side, Katalin and Fausta joining us. In the hallway, Fausta curtsied to me.

"If you don't mind, I must attend to a small matter." She turned to Jamil. "I arranged for the Empress to be in the royal guest suite with the added security measures requested."

"Shall we see you this evening?" Katalin asked Fausta. "I have been looking forward to your kitchen staff's creations. You always request the most amusing desserts."

"You are very kind, Lady Katalin. Of course, I will be joining you. I always enjoy your company," Fausta said before departing.

Katalin took my arm in hers. "Let's get you prepared for tonight."

"Why didn't you want me to stay for the fight?" I asked as Jamil led us down the hall toward the bedrooms.

Katalin's smile faded, and her eyes narrowed. "You have done great things, Empress. I think you can do almost anything. But give rigid rules time to flex. If you smash traditions all at once, you'll only harden the governor against you. We need his family's support." Katalin shook her head. "My goal is to demolish these traditions, too. But we must be clever about it."

"And nobles dueling is a tradition?"

"I'm talking about the traditions of men. Of emperors who pass their crowns to their sons and —" Katalin put a hand to her mouth. "Oh dear, I need to talk to Lady Fausta before dinner. I'll meet you in your chambers. We have much to discuss."

I waved Katalin off and followed Jamil down the hall. I paused at a windowless alcove to let Midnight sniff the heavy, decorative curtain. I knelt and scratched behind Midnight's ears, comfortable in our silence.

I had never known Katalin to dote, so her attentions to Fausta and her daughters were curious. She hadn't acted half as genuinely interested in anyone at the Rose Court.

"Is that Lady Katalin Vulpe scurrying down thataway?" a woman's voice carried from the hallway beyond. I shot up, but Jamil and I stayed silent, partially hidden by the alcove and curtain. "Horrid woman."

"She's a tragic tale. Be kind," another woman replied.

"Your heart bleeds for a woman who never acknowledges your existence. Pah!" the first woman snapped. "That fancy Rose come down from her fancy mountain. The way she butters Lady Fausta. Pah! Pretendin' she's one of the family, but she ain't. Never will be."

I strained to hear the softer voice. " 'Tis a strange kind of pining."

"You're too soft." The footfalls grew louder. "You be blind if you think that Rose's hurt was an excuse for what she did. Poor Lord Felix."

" 'Tis just 'Felix,' now."

I glanced at Jamil, and he shrugged. I held my breath as the women passed. Insolent servant gossip was the least of my concerns, but it wasn't very empress-like to be caught eaves-dropping.

Fortunately, they were lost in conversation though, with a mere glance over their shoulders, they'd see us awkwardly half-hidden behind the curve of the curtain. I could only imagine the wild rumors that would begin.

A stooped woman with gray, braided hair clutched an armload of towels, and a younger, broad-shouldered woman carried a bucket of sloshing water.

"It better not be a bloody mess like last time. Zalmoxis, it stunk," the younger servant said.

The older woman tried to hush her, but the younger woman

continued. "I'm not hopeful, though, I hear that Auripoan Prince is a butcher."

If there was a retort, it was too soft to hear as they turned into the room where I'd left the prince.

AFTER TWO DAYS of meetings and unending rain, the clouds finally parted. I was anxious for fresh air. After dinner, I slipped away, Midnight at my side. I'd heard all about the drunken bets placed each night after dinner. These traditions made little sense to me, but I'd decided to take Katalin's advice and let them be ridiculous without the Empress as an audience. At least Asander was almost content for the moment. Based on last night, I suspected all influential nobles, emissaries, or representatives would be engaged all evening, and I planned on taking advantage of their distraction to do some exploring in peace.

In my rooms, I grabbed my wool cloak and returned to the door where two guards were posted. They were both black-clad, but the green stripe on the sleeve of the one marked him as an Imperial Guard. The other was one of my Own, the same guard I'd spoken with yesterday in the courtyard with the pronounced widow's peak.

"You are from Patridava, correct? Do you know this estate?" I asked.

My Own hesitated before giving me a quick nod. The Imperial Guard couldn't conceal the brief flaring of his nostrils. I hadn't given much thought to Thorns when I was younger, other than to avoid them. But logically, some Thorns were born with more privilege, giving them an advantage in garnering an invitation to the most elite guard unit, the Empress' Own.

"Please, take me on a tour," I said to my Own, my wolf at my side. I considered sending for Pari or Rufus to join me, but Pari, Ziba, and Gul planned to sneak down to the Getaen district, and Rufus grew irritable if he didn't get regular time to himself.

Once we left the main hall, I was glad I'd requested a guide. It was a maze. I stared at the back of my Own, trying to remember his name — Thadeus. Outside the house, I was better able to orient myself by the stars through the lingering wisps of clouds. Thadeus led me across extensive, multi-tiered balconies connected by curving steps and stately walkways. Thorns were stationed along the route as well as mingling Lilies, who bowed as I passed.

The nobles who hadn't warranted an invitation to the after-dinner entertainment had little influence, but I nodded, giving them the same courtesy as the highest Roses.

I cleared my throat, and Thadeus glanced at me. "I've had a trying day. Is there a place where I can quietly think?"

"I have just the spot." The guard led me down a short flight of stairs and across another walkway. "It's the private courtyard of the governor's family. But, as you know, they will be busy until later this evening. However, the entire estate is owned by the crown, so technically, it's *your* courtyard."

My Own led me around a corner, and the walkway narrowed. A Patridavan guard in a heavy cloak and fur hat stood near a half-domed entrance. He stood taller as we passed through the doorway onto the narrow balcony that ringed the estate.

"How did you know about this place?"

"My father was a high-ranking Patridavan officer, so I've been here many times, though not since my official training began."

Between the ivy-covered wall on our left and the flickering lights of the city on our right, the idyllic space exuded a sense of wonder. The bright dots of blue Luminaries and warm candlelight mingled in the distance; seeing Getaen magic amongst the natural flames warmed me even though the night air stung my nose.

The long balcony opened to a terrace larger than my map room, surrounded by walls on three sides. The closest wall had dim, blue Luminaries lighting the space just enough to avoid walking blindly into the unlit brazier placed in the center.

"There is a gap in the ivy just there, your majesty." My Own pointed to the far wall. "There's a passage mostly hidden by vines and shadows, which affords the solitude you requested. The only access is the way we came or from the governor's private balcony. I will check the adjoining governor's rooms."

"It's fine." I stopped him and signaled for Midnight to do a check of the terrace. "Like you said, Governor Aelius and Lady Fausta are entertaining, and guards are stationed at their doors inside the mansion."

I intended to stay on the quiet terrace, anyway, having no desire to invade on the governor's personal space. Midnight paused and sniffed at the gap in the far wall, and her tail wagged. She finished her check of the balcony before backtracking to my side. Obviously, my dire wolf approved.

I waved, dismissing my Own. "Wait for me back by the archway. Naturally, if my advisers need me, please escort them here. Midnight will verify identities."

Thadeus nodded and returned to the entrance, and Midnight sat at the corner of the walkway and the open terrace, keeping watch. With my Luminary orb, I explored the area further, noting unlit torches on the walls, well-oiled and ready. Amusing that the governor's daughter acted as if a Healer was a breach of etiquette when magical Luminaries lit her family's private balcony.

Though Moesia wasn't far, Patridava seemed like a different kingdom. In Moesia, magic was part of our daily lives, especially in the Commons where I grew up. Though I'd learned from harsh experience that Moesian nobles in the Golden Lily quarter considered Getaens as *lesser*. Perhaps Moesia wasn't different, but my childhood as an Azure scholar's daughter raised by Getaen women made my experiences different.

From the passageway that led to the governor's balcony, I heard muted voices. I gripped the Luminary tighter. Had the governor or his wife returned? Perhaps the evening had gone poorly. Not wanting to intrude, I turned to leave. Someone shouted, an angry retort bouncing off the walls of the tunnel. I recognized the voice — Katalin.

I shoved my Luminary into my pocket. Katalin would never

miss an opportunity to mingle with high hats. What was she up to? She hadn't told me about a meeting tonight — I couldn't afford another costly mistake. I curled my hands into fists and stepped into the tunnel.

"I thought you would appreciate me coming to you privately," a man huffed. I edged closer to the private balcony, keeping to the shadows.

"I would have appreciated a conversation long before now," Katalin said, her voice taut.

I peeked around the corner, catching a glimpse of Katalin and a handsome man in the center of the intimate balcony. He had the same aquiline nose, bushy brows, and build of the governor, but I hadn't seen him earlier.

"It is my desire to put our past grievances behind us, Katalin," he said.

"*Lady* Katalin," she growled. "You never wanted to apologize before, *Felix*. Have you finally realized the cost of losing your noble title?"

I held my breath as they both fell silent. I had no idea what they were talking about. I considered approaching them when Felix spoke.

"I never meant to hurt you. I only realized the damage I'd done after it was too late."

"You didn't think marrying a weak, pitiful child from a recreant family would hurt me?" Katalin's voice rose.

"She'd lost everything. I couldn't let her be exposed to the hardships of commoner life and the derision of the gossiping tongues of the Rose Court."

"Do you have any idea what your *selfless* decision did to me?" Katalin's voice cracked. Underneath her anger resonated a rawness I'd never have guessed festered inside her.

"You recovered just fine."

"We were engaged, Felix. You told me you loved me," Katalin shouted, her voice trembling. "I believed you."

I shrunk against the blocks behind me, clutching my hand to

the pendant at my chest. This had nothing to do with machinations and everything to do with Katalin's heart, which clearly this man had broken. I edged away, ashamed at my eavesdropping.

"And I believed you'd be a proper wife," Felix said. "I had no idea what you were really like. You charmed those who you needed into your bedroom and blackmailed the rest. I count myself lucky I didn't marry you."

I braced a hand against the wall, unable to make my feet move. His haughty, cruel tone meant to cut Katalin to the quick.

"I don't know why I came to you, expecting a drop of compassion," Felix continued. "You've never shown it to anyone else. I am grateful I traded my title and my parents' admiration for an honorable wife."

I hoped Katalin would slap him. Twice.

Not wanting to invade further, I pushed away from the wall, taking a step toward the empty terrace, when the entrance darkened. The scent of mint and hay filled the tunnel.

I gasped.

I didn't need my Luminary orb to know Marcus Constantin stood before me. Heartache flooded through me, my knees weakening.

He breathed a whispered word, "Nic—"

I smacked my hand over his lips and pushed him back several steps to the deserted terrace.

Bijan caught me dreaming during my waking hours. He promised not to tell.

He must be as frightened as I am because he agreed to help me meet with the Historians. Like everyone else, they have refused to interact with me for the last two years.

I must somehow get information on my illness without alerting Mama that my symptoms are escalating.

— ESME

CHAPTER

EIGHT

NEW PATHS

I shoved the Luminary between us. Though Marcus' hand merely brushed over mine, it warmed every point of contact. My mind buzzed. His fingers pressed the Sonus stone next to mine, emanating a soft pulse, silencing our conversation.

"Nice dire wolf," Marcus said as Midnight moved to sit next to me. "Explains why Jamil asked to borrow my cloak."

"What are you d-doing here?" I could barely spit out my words, heat rising to my cheeks.

"I've been here for three days. The agricultural representatives have traveled from across the kingdom to discuss crops." Marcus went on about his meetings and plans, but I couldn't process anything beyond the fact that he was physically there, next to me.

The last time we'd been this close, I'd lost myself in his embrace. Marcus seemed to have tempered his emotions, but I ached to touch his face, his arms, to make sure he was real. I wanted to unburden all my worries like I used to do. To confide everything. To pull him close and allow myself to truly *feel* every frightening, ugly, horrible emotion roiling through me. Unbidden, the memory of the heat from Marcus' body when he'd wrapped his arms around me flooded my mind, of how I didn't feel the ground beneath my feet. My breathing quickened. In the stable, the pocket of time we'd stolen for ourselves had been seared into my memory, not as completely buried as I'd thought.

"Why d-didn't you come sooner?" I quickly added, "To report your findings?"

My heart beat like a bird's wing against my ribs. I was grateful for the low light, hiding the flush that was unfurling from my chest to my ears. I had an overwhelming urge to step closer, but I forced myself to be still.

"I'd hoped to speak with you tomorrow morning before my meeting. However, Tulia said you have an engagement with several eastern guild representatives. I should have known I'd need to wait in line," Marcus said with the half-grin I'd never seen him share with anyone else. "Tulia suggested I might be able to catch you tonight."

As an emissary, he would have been welcomed to the entertainment after dinner. But he had come to find me instead. I searched his face, still stunned to see him. I caught myself staring at his lips. I stepped back. If I could have slapped myself without looking like I'd gone completely mad, I would have. I was acting like a naïve child. Marcus was reporting to the crown. Not to *me*. I needed a moment to temper my emotions. "This is not a g-good time."

Marcus' gaze shifted to the narrow corridor where he'd found me. I let him suspect whatever he wanted about what I was doing in the tunnel. Anything was better than admitting that seeing him made my mind turn to soup.

I jerked the orb from his grip and marched to the ivy wall, putting much needed physical distance between myself and the farmer from my past. I signaled to my Own, who dutifully waited around the corner.

"P-please take me to my room."

I didn't look back.

As I strode across the terraces, I barely noticed the guards and nobles paying deference. With every step, I grabbed each of my exploding emotions, wrangling them and putting them away. Deeper this time, where they could wither and die properly.

In my rooms, Tulia waited, a bath drawn and prepared.

My dire wolf pressed against my legs as I sat rigidly on the vanity stool. Tulia removed my crown and the pins that held my braids and curls in place. She didn't meet my eyes, and I was sure she wondered how my conversation with Marcus had gone.

"I have everything lined out for the rest of your tour of the kingdom," Tulia said quietly. "Lady Fausta personally recommended one of her own lady's maids to accompany you for your tour while I visit my family."

"Tulia," I paused. "You've prepared me well. There's no need to wait until I leave Patridava in two days to return to your family. You can go tonight, and I can manage with another lady's maid."

The pins in Tulia's hand slipped into the bowl, clattering against each other. "I can't leave you. Not like this."

Though we hadn't discussed Marcus since he left, she knew encountering him would rip open old wounds. I would have preferred to keep Tulia close right now; it was true. But I was determined to do what was best for her. She hadn't been home in years.

I grasped her hand in mine, as Papa and Mama had so often done with me. I would have given everything — my crown, the comforts of the castle, anything — to see Mama again. I couldn't let my heartache prevent Tulia from returning home by even an hour. Besides, it was simply the shock of seeing Marcus. It was a silly reaction, and I'd be recovered by morning.

"My offer stands," I said. "If you decide to stay in Patridava, you have my support. You'll be near your family, and every Rose household will vie for your services."

It was the right decision, but that didn't mean it wouldn't hurt to lose her. Though Tulia was only fourteen, she'd been an enormous help. After losing so many people in my life, I dreaded leaving her behind. Seeing Marcus only served to remind me that

I'd lost him, too, in a way. He wasn't an integral part of my life anymore.

After my bath, Tulia fussed over nonexistent wrinkles in the cantrinta aprons she'd set out for me. Finally, she blew out all but one of the candelabras.

"Don't let anyone dress you in light green," she said. "I know it's a *shade* of Dacia's colors, but it looks putrid on you. Promise me you'll wear emerald or olive green. Nothing else."

I grinned, but my throat was tight. Saying goodbye should get easier, but it tugged at my heartstrings harder. Though Tulia hadn't admitted to wanting to stay with her family, I suspected she would remain in Patridava. I took her hand. "Thank you for everything, Tulia."

Tulia sniffed her reddening nose. "Serving you brought me the greatest rewards: most importantly, your friendship."

She gave me a quick hug before scurrying to the door. But before she closed it, she poked her head back into the room.

"My birthday is in the spring. I would like a horse. A white one, and it can have gray markings. I mean, if you're wondering." She half-laughed and half-cried her blurted request. Then, she clicked the door shut.

I flopped onto the bed, already missing Tulia's chatter. My dire wolf jumped onto the bed and lay down, rolling up next to me. I leaned against her, soon lost in thought. I fiddled with my pendant, and my thumb brushed against the leather strap. My stomach twisted. Marcus had given me the leather thong after the chain had been violently snapped. A hot tear defied my command and burned a trail down my cheek.

I determined to have another chain made to replace it at my earliest convenience.

$\sim$

A SOFT RAP came at my door, startling me awake. Before I realized I was on the edge of my bed, I rolled off, crashing to the floor. I rubbed my throbbing elbow and glanced back up at Midnight on my bed, sprawled out from corner to corner.

"Bed hog," I muttered.

Jamil entered, seeing me on the floor. His gaze moved to my bed. I'd obviously not even gotten under the covers and had somehow allowed my dire wolf to push me out of bed. "Lady Katalin has requested an audience. I'll send her away."

Katalin's name rang a warning in the back of my mind. Her argument on the balcony. Did she know I'd overheard it?

"No, I'll see her." *I'd rather get this conversation over with.*

I forced myself to my feet and tied on my robe, bracing myself for confrontation.

Katalin entered, her elegant posture and smooth gait almost enough to cover the fading blotches on her face, evidence of her altercation with a past love.

My dire wolf dutifully met Katalin at the door and licked her hand. Jamil shut the door, giving us the semblance of privacy. I invited Katalin to join me on the couches in front of the low-burning fireplace.

She didn't move. "Do you trust me?"

I winced. "No."

Her whole body curved in on itself. Her shoulders shook as she collapsed onto the couch like crumpling ashes of a burned parchment. I rushed to her side, unsure what to do.

"I want to trust you," I said, "But you keep d-doing things that are... " How could I phrase it? Reprehensible? Immoral? "Objectionable."

"I've always had my own rules. I told myself if I didn't cross certain boundaries, I was still a good person. That the things I did were in service of the kingdom." Katalin rubbed a hand across her abdomen where Yasmin had stabbed her. "I assumed my actions would make me more trustworthy to the crown. I thought my approach worked for Cassus VII, but he never appointed me as an adviser. He stunted my influence; he never fully trusted me."

For once, I understood Cassus' reasoning. Katalin had dug her claws into every crevice of the castle's affairs. He definitely would have viewed Katalin as a possible threat.

"Power is either growing or shrinking, never stagnant," Katalin said. "If you're not leveraging power to gain more, you're wasting it. Others will greedily rip away influence held by a loose grip."

"What use is p-power if you can't use it for g-good?" I placed my hand on her shoulder. "You've had to work so hard to keep your status on the mountain. You haven't been looking at the horizon, and you've lost your internal d-direction. P-power is using *you*, not the other way around."

Katalin's face scrunched in confusion. "What I did, I did to protect you. And you repay me by keeping me out, the same as Cassus."

I knew how Tulia had come into Katalin's employment — by blackmailing Tulia's master. Katalin was well practiced at convincing Roses to do as she pleased. "Your protection comes from leveraging dark secrets and vile manipulations."

She shook her head, her eyes narrowing. "You treat my work as beneath you. Or worse, as a petty annoyance. You don't know me. But, perhaps you should."

Katalin confessed her engagement and subsequent heartbreak and humiliation. With only distant relations, she'd had a glimpse of what could have been with the Silvanus family.

"When the life I'd wanted crumbled away, everything changed. I was so angry." Katalin stood and rapped her thumbs against her sides, on the edge between crying and screaming. "I went to Vasile when he was still a lower judge. He helped sway the High Judge into having Felix's title revoked. I realized how good I was at manipulating people — skills my parents had taught me, but I'd never fully appreciated until that moment. After that, it was easy, even enjoyable to arrange complex situations to my advantage. And I did it all without ever betraying the crown."

I closed my eyes, a headache forming. Whatever Katalin's motivations, her methods were bogged in a mire of questionable ethics. How could I possibly teach her? If I threw her a rope, would she take it?

Katalin wouldn't have come to me, asking difficult questions and ripping out her heart for me to dissect if she wasn't ready to hear what I had to say. She knew I wouldn't condone her actions. Even if she didn't completely know it, she wanted my true advice. Though I would never really understand Katalin, she deserved a chance.

"Look at the fire," I said. "What do you see? Describe it in two words."

"Heat. Destruction."

"Warmth. Comfort," I countered.

She raised a brow.

"Fire is powerful," I said. "But it can be used in different ways. Is it better to use fire for d-destruction? Or to warm all those in the kingdom."

Her face dropped, and her arm wrapped around her abdomen.

"We only live once," I said. "I've done all I can to protect Dacians, not to hurt them. I don't know what I could have done d-differently, but I know it began with the intention to end the plague. Now my only thought is to save our p-people. I must lead through a valley of b-blood and fire and hope we emerge on the other side. On my d-deathbed, if I'm satisfied with my efforts, then perhaps I won't fear Zalmoxis' torture. I'll have grown too strong for him to fight."

Katalin pressed her fingers to her temple. "You're not making any sense."

"You have been p-protecting me, but not out of kindness. You are securing me as a shield to keep your position." I paused, giving Katalin time to recover from the sting in my words. "When you act out of compassion for those who cannot do anything for you in return, you are on the right path."

Katalin lowered back down onto the couch, her back straight, the flames reflecting in the pools of her eyes. We sat in contemplation, Midnight squished between us, her head on Katalin's lap. After what felt like an hour, Katalin finally spoke.

"Some of the things I did, I don't regret. But other things," she let out a long breath and then squared her shoulders and lifted her chin, "I need to set to right. I just don't know how."

The Katalin I'd heard on the balcony sounded like a wounded soul, her pain laid bare. It conflicted with the biting woman I knew her to be. She was more nuanced than I had realized, a complicated woman who wanted to redefine herself in her own way.

"Jealously guarding your heart makes you a prisoner in your own life," I said. "Yes, it's frightening to trust. Yes, you are vulnerable, your weakness exposed, but you are also showing your true character and not letting fear govern you. That takes more strength than any Rose Court manipulation."

Katalin slowly nodded, her gaze unfocused. She stood and leaned against the mantle before turning to face me. "May I have permission to remain in Patridava and then travel to Capidava to attend to some personal affairs? I need to put things in order."

"I'll leave two Imperial Guards to oversee your work here. Then, I'd like you to join my tour as we travel south." I couldn't afford to have Katalin on a crusade in the capitol without me there to clean up her mess.

"Thank you," Katalin said. "I appreciate your offer of protection, but I have my Vulpe guards."

"I insist." I added a smile, to take off the edge of my thinly-veiled command.

She gave a halting nod. "I understand. Thank you for letting me continue to serve you and giving me a chance to prove myself worthy of your trust." She tilted her head to the side, considering me. "I've long pitied you for your naïve and trusting nature, yet time and again, your trust bears fruit. All my life, I've been schooled to seek power to secure my family's position and my safety. I can compel obedience, but never earn the adoration that commoners bestow upon you. Marcus tried to tell me similar things, but he was never as direct." She gave me a wry smile. "I may disappoint you, in the end, but I don't want to end up in the same situation again and again. I am determined to try an unknown path."

"Lady Katalin, I don't think anyone who has met you would believe that anything can stop you from reaching your goals." *You're as stubborn as a mule.*

Katalin blinked and quickly wiped her eyes, but her lip turned up in a weary smile. As she moved to the door, she bid me good-night. Before she could leave, I blurted a question.

"How do you know Marcus' sisters?" I inwardly chastised myself for cutting deeper into my still-bleeding torment.

Katalin rested a hand on her hip, her previous broken edges swept away as she studied me. "Before Marcus left for Lazica, he asked me to help his sisters prepare for their arrival in the Rose Court. He didn't demand it, attempt to manipulate me, or make me any promises." She shook her head. "Honestly, I could barely understand the concept at the time — a friend asking for help. In the end, I sent a letter to his sisters, introducing myself. And that's how our correspondence began."

"And that's everything?"

Katalin snorted. "Sometimes all it takes is one friendship to change your whole outlook on life. I admit, when I first met Marcus, I saw him as a means to an end. An attractive means. But he was smitten with someone else." She gave me a pointed look and brushed back her hair. "I'm not the kind of woman who needs to beg for any man's attention. I couldn't figure out Marcus' game, at first. He was kind and helpful and didn't ask me for anything in return. Then, something happened that I never expected, never experienced: we became friends."

"How long ago d-did he return to Dacia?" Why couldn't I hide the desperation in my voice?

"He was only in Lazica for a moon."

I shouldn't have felt wounded, but my heart squeezed. I'd sent Marcus to Lazica in the first place. I'd trusted him on a mission, to do something no one else had done: bring Lazica to our side of the coming battle. He'd failed. But he'd done exactly what I'd asked of him — he'd acted just like any other emissary, no special treatment, no unnecessary communication. No one could suspect that Marcus was essentially my spy in Lazica. He had probably come to find me to report, but I'd refused him.

"What has he been doing since he's returned?" I rubbed my sternum, trying to ease the pain building in my chest.

"Gathering information on grain storage, blight map tracking, and other dull agricultural things. Though he does have an interesting project he's announcing tomorrow. The rumor is there hasn't been an agricultural meeting with this many representatives attending in decades. As far as the majority vote, I think —"

Someone pounded on the door; Katalin and I both jumped.

Jamil appeared, his face pensive. "Excuse me, Empress. This just arrived."

He held out a missive with a red wax seal, the griffin stamp of Auripo. My palms began to sweat.

"Lady Katalin, you may leave my service for five days to see to your personal business in Patridava," I said quickly. "I expect you to return to my side in Moesia."

Katalin curtsied and hurried away. Jamil shut the door, and I snatched the letter out of his hand, inspecting it closer.

"Jamil, send for Asander. He should be here when I open this."

The scholar who teaches my siblings and me is about three decades old. Yet today, while I stared at him, he grew younger... shorter with rounded cheeks. Then he grew very old, his skin spotted and wrinkled. Then young again. Then older, but this time was different — he had a big scar across his nose and cheek.

When I blinked, suddenly Papa was next to me, talking to my teacher. My siblings were gone. How long was I daydreaming?

Papa escorted me to my room. I've been excused from my lessons with my siblings. Papa said I will have private instruction from now on — it's for the best.

I feel like my older brothers and sister are leaving me behind. Between their classes and responsibilities, I rarely see them. I like sharing a room with my little sisters, but they're so young. Their games and stories are too simple.

I wish I had someone to play with. To talk with. No one understands me.

— ESME

CHAPTER

NINE

UNHAPPY COMPROMISES

A Patridavan servant woke me at dawn. My eyes burned; I'd stayed up late the night before, discussing the missive from Auripo with Jamil and Asander.

"Please send for breakfast and my Protector," I said, excusing her.

From under my pillow, I retrieved the letter. Shuffling to the fireplace, I re-read it.

Empress Nicoleta Aurelian,

One horse was recovered from the missing messenger party. The horse didn't have a scratch on her, including all the Auripoan symbols in perfect order. However, in her saddlebag were five left hands. Due to the number, and the signet ring on one, we believe they are the hands of the missing party. What this means for certain, we cannot say, only that they were likely captured.

This type of deviousness and needless cruelty is unlike the Scythians, who are direct in their hostilities. We assume this is the work of the Norte.

Be warned, crossing the Curat River is no longer safe. The security of our letters is at risk. Henceforth, these letters will be basic updates to help secure our communication.

106

Regards,
King Eusebes Coatys

I shut my aching lids and pressed my forehead to the ink. Were the captured Auripoans alive? Awaiting rescue? Not knowing for certain if they were alive or dead was a torment.

The Auripoan king's dispassionate abandonment of his soldiers was disconcerting. And Asander's disapproval at my emotional response unnerved me even more. I despised the ugliness of war and the hard-hearted decisions that fell to me. I feared becoming like Asander — distant and removed. He was protecting his mind and his heart, of course. But at what cost?

I was already careening in the same direction. How many of my feelings had I already shoved down inside, compartmentalizing so as not to *feel?* Disturbing letters like this one only pushed me further down Asander's same path.

I crumpled the letter in my trembling hand and stared at the flames, lost in my ever-darkening thoughts.

Ziba and Pari entered, and I threw the letter in the fire. Ziba pursed her lips as the parchment burst into flames, but said nothing as they plied me with Protections and Healer teas.

When I was finally prepared for my last day in Patridava, I threw myself into the work and bottled away my worry for the missing Auripoans. I spoke to a large crowd of commoners near the southern gates before lunch, not getting a much better reaction despite the clear skies.

Fortunately, my meeting with the eastern guild representatives went smoothly and left me invigorated. As the eastern ambassador, Katalin had joined us. Afterward, Katalin accompanied me to my meeting with Governor Aelius, my last appointment before dinner, with Midnight between us. In this wing of the estate, the hallways were mostly empty except for the Thorns stationed at every doorway.

"Empress, I have been giving thought to what you advised me when we last spoke. I used undue influence and... " Katalin fumbled with her words. "I advise you to reinstate Felix Silvanus' title."

After overhearing his conversation with Katalin, I had no love for the man. The vindictive part of me was glad she'd found a way to strip his title. Still, it wasn't justice. It was revenge.

I raised my brow, "Are you sure?"

Katalin sucked in a breath. Midnight nuzzled her hand, and her shoulders relaxed. "As much as I hate to admit it, yes, I'm sure it's the right thing to do."

As we passed one of the meeting chambers, I noticed the banner on the door: a wagon wheel with a scythe: the Agricultural Guild. I nearly stumbled over my own feet.

Katalin looked over at the symbol and then at me with a conspiratorial smirk. I wanted to roll my eyes, but I excused her instead, instructing her to visit the judge and direct him to elevate Felix to a lord once again.

She only just stepped away when a man with gray-streaked hair and a prominent chin burst from the room, practically running into us. Midnight's hackles rose, but she didn't attack. The man gasped and dipped into a bow.

"Please forgive me, Empress," he said as the door shut behind him, silencing the arguments within.

I gave him a gracious nod. "Is the agricultural guild meeting here?" I assumed Marcus was overseeing the meeting.

"Yes. I apologize for the noise. We are debating a third planting this year."

"It's not the first time I've heard an argument, I assure you. My ears are not that delicate." Emperors in the past left the guilds to manage themselves, allowing them the illusion of control over their areas of influence. "I am sure your Emissary is open to hearing all ideas."

"Ah, well, he's the one advocating for a third planting. Furthermore, he's convinced every major city to hold back a portion of the grain that they'd normally be consuming this very winter."

I swallowed. I'd requested that Otho's father send that very message to the representatives because they'd respected his opinions in the past. "Didn't the representative of Rodnic Valley make such a request?"

He cocked his head. "The representative of the north is too weak for such a thing. But it would make sense that his grandfather would task Marcus to present the request on his behalf. Outside of the northern representative, there's no one else the guild would have listened to except Marcus. The Constantins have a nose for survival. And for business. But on top of all the Emissary's requests, he's also proposed a risky new venture."

Had Marcus come to find me to tell me about this venture? If I'd been able to keep myself from devolving into an emotional mess, Marcus might have told me all about his plans.

"He's over-eager, rushing everything," the representative griped.

We're preparing for war! I forced my voice to steady. "Is that why you're leaving?"

The man frowned. "Young Constantin is asking us to invest in a costly experiment that unquestionably won't benefit my city of Findava."

Guilds amended their rules by a majority vote, which was notoriously difficult. With the distance across Dacia, a majority of any guild in one location was a rarity. Katalin had mentioned that Marcus had orchestrated a massive meeting. Did he have enough voters in one location to take action? Whoever this man was, Marcus likely needed him back at the table.

I'd sent Marcus away when he came to talk to me, but a true friend would have listened. I should be supportive of this agricultural event, at the very least. He was my emissary after all.

I gestured toward the doors. "Will you join me?"

The Findavan representative gave me a firm nod. Jamil's nostrils flared, but he opened the door to the agricultural meeting.

I swept into the room, and the voices stilled. The older Findavan representative strode in at my side. Several gazes roved from him to Marcus. Seeing him, my heart quickened. I ripped my gaze away, purposefully looking at every man, including Otho, Marcus' father.

"Carry on, Emissary." I felt out of place, but that wasn't unusual.

Jamil moved to the chair furthest from Marcus, and the representative sitting there quickly vacated it. As I settled myself at the long table, the crushing weight of my presence further pressed down on the room.

"I am requesting support for a third planting." Marcus looked around the room, and as his eyes met mine, they seemed to linger just a moment longer.

The mood was stiff, stalling conversation. Finally, the Findavan representative who'd bumped into me spoke up. "The prices were already low this summer and fall. Additional planting will profit us nothing."

"It isn't about profits," Marcus responded, holding everyone's attention in the room. "It's about feeding the army and our people."

"It's more than just driving down the prices of food. The crops may or may not grow at all." A timid man with protruding ears and wisps of hair clinging to his head fidgeted with his hat. "This venture is too risky."

"We're going to war!" A man near Marcus spoke up, his hand drawn into a fist on the table. "The emissary has come up with a solution so we can extend our crop growing to nearly year-round."

What is this venture that could extend the crop season?

"It's never been done!" another man snapped, his cheeks red.

"Our craftsmen have created similar structures for generations, just not for this purpose." Marcus rose to his feet. "Rupea Castle's throne room has a ceiling made of glass, not to mention an entire wall. Several nobles' homes have copied this style. Why not use glass for a practical purpose?"

The Findavan next to me ran his hands down his face before slamming them into the table. "You are proposing entire buildings made of nothing but lead and glass. They won't stand."

"I assure you, they will stand." Marcus lifted his chin, calm yet confident.

"Even if we wanted to, the cost of the glass alone would deplete our guild funds completely!" another man argued. "If this expense is truly for Dacians, perhaps we could entreat the crown to fund the expense from their treasury."

A flush crawled up my neck as the representative's gazes burned through me. I stared at Marcus' chest. Very few knew our financial situation, but Marcus did: the kingdom's treasury had no funds to give. I glanced up at Marcus long enough to see a flash of sympathy on his face.

Marcus' voice became loud and demanding, redirecting the uncomfortable scrutiny back to himself. "These glass houses will be owned by the Agricultural Guild with profits for the guild."

"Even if we approve the expense, we still lack the sunlight needed," the red-faced man retorted.

"We could build them in strategic locations." The man next to Marcus reined in his shouting, though his hand was still fisted. "Must the structures all be in this valley? No. We could build further south, assuming we can find an underground vein of water."

Several people nodded in agreement. They were coming around to Marcus' proposal.

"If we are going to attempt this venture, successfully, we must do all we can," Marcus said, aiming to bring cohesion to those who still wavered. "Our guild will depend on it."

The Findavan next to me fisted and unfisted his hand. "Lord Constantin, I request we start with just one glass structure to evaluate. If concerns arise, I vote we drop this entire scheme."

I startled at hearing Marcus' title. He was a lord now, of course, but this was the first time I'd heard anyone refer to him as such.

"Agreed," Marcus let his chin drop in half a nod.

I sat stiffly as murmurs traveled around the room. Marcus pressed his fingers into the table, his back hunched and his attention down as he considered his options, my gaze roamed over him, taking in the details. Without his cloak, when his arm flexed, it was visible through his fitted camasa. His skin was tanned and a bit weathered from his travels. He looked up at me from under his dark curls, an intensity in his gaze. I pressed my hand against my stomach to stop the feelings that swirled every time our eyes met. Even in a room full of agitated men and at a distance from Marcus, I feared my heart was starting to feel things it shouldn't.

"Let's vote," Marcus' voice cut through the din.

All but two representatives raised their hands in favor, and I felt a twinge of pride at seeing the Findavan vote for Marcus' plan. Marcus looked pleased but modest while the man next to him exuberantly clasped his arm in congratulations.

Though I wasn't surprised that he fought hard for the commoners, it was strange to see him in this setting. Commanding. Insistent. In the castle, he'd allowed me to run meetings the way I saw fit. But as the emissary, this was his domain.

Jamil guided me to the door. Before I slipped through, I glanced back at Marcus. He was already looking at me over the shoulder of one of the representatives.

Friends. I can be friends with Marcus.

I followed Jamil out the door into the hallway, letting the tension drain from my fingertips.

"Empress." Marcus' spoke from behind me. His use of the formal title was another indicator of the trench that had been dug between us. How I longed to hear him say my name again.

I paused to let Marcus catch up.

"You brought the Findavan representative back into the meeting." He gently touched my arm. I feared he would hear my heart drumming as it pounded so hard. "Thank you."

My throat grew too dry to speak, so I mutely nodded.

"What do you think about the glass houses?" He let his hand slide down and away from my arm, leaving a trail of heat that our 'friendship' couldn't explain.

I swallowed the lump in my throat and tried to *not* admire his lips. "I-I thought you handled the m-meeting well."

I wanted to smack my forehead. That wasn't what he asked. I fisted my hands behind my back but didn't even attempt to feign a smile. Marcus would see right through my mask.

I can do this. I can keep my feelings separate. This man is my emissary. Nothing more.

"I appreciate your support. I am grateful we are still a team." Marcus looked like he wanted to say more as he took a step closer. I wanted to close my eyes and inhale him.

Jamil cleared his throat. I pulled myself out of my daze long enough to realize that representatives were filing past us, and a servant was waiting to get my attention.

"The governor sent the page to see if there was anything you needed before your meeting," Jamil said. It was a polite way of telling me the governor had sent someone to verify I was safe and report back. I was very late for our meeting.

I turned back to Marcus. "We haven't had an official meeting since your return. I will have my advisers arrange it."

"Perhaps in Moesia," Marcus said. "I may head there next to scout for sites for the glass house."

My fingers itched to reach out and touch him, but I held them against my sides. Marcus was an emissary. I supported all of my emissaries. And I would be working with all of them for the rest of my life, in a strictly professional manner.

Marcus bowed, and as he turned away, he brushed my hip, sending my heart racing all over again.

BEFORE THE SUN ROSE, my caravan waited outside the governor's estate. Despite the hour, the governor and his household stood outside to see us off, puffs of air appearing as they breathed in the brisk air.

"May I have the honor of escorting you to your carriage?" the Governor's wife asked. "I know it's unusual, but in these strange times, I hope you will not mind."

"Of course," I said, stepping to the side, Midnight moving with me.

"Thank you for reinstating my son's noble title," she said when we were out of earshot of her guards and servants.

I tensed. I hadn't realized the decision had been announced.

"His past actions were rash," Fausta continued. "He embarrassed our family with his hurried engagement and marriage into a disgraced family. We supported the emperor. It was difficult having a child reduced to a... Clover," she whispered the last word. "Lady Katalin informed me that you are officially reversing the ruling when you return to Capidava."

Katalin had asked me to trust her, yet she'd not only discussed the situation with the Patridavan judge but had proceeded much further and had notified the family before she'd updated me on her progress.

"It is no secret that my son's separation from our family has pained me." Fausta's eyes fluttered, and she looked up at the gray sky. When she wiped a tear from her eye, I slowed.

Perhaps I was looking at this situation all wrong. Katalin hadn't given herself any credit for Felix's reversal of fortune. She wanted me to benefit from the Silvanus' family's gratitude, and right away. While I was still here, perhaps? Was she being... humble?

"You are truly as gracious as Lady Katalin has said," Fausta continued. "You are the leader that Dacia needs. I see Lady Katalin was right."

Fausta's face shone with admiration. It was not an expression I was used to seeing from anyone.

"Lady Katalin has been so gracious to our family. I wish she would stay with us for the remainder of her time here, but she insists on staying at an inn."

I kept a blank face as I put together the scattered pieces of information. Katalin had been behind Felix's fall from grace, but she was trying to rectify it as best she could. And she was leaving the estate so the governor's son felt welcome to come and go.

She'd actually distanced herself from her most powerful Patridavan ally, Fausta, in the process.

The governor's wife stepped back. "Thank you again. Know that while my husband is getting used to the new way of things, you have his support. Change is difficult, but I already see the fruits of your labor beginning to grow. Lady Katalin trusts that you can save us. She has asked Aelius and me to put our faith in you." Fausta's pressed her hand against her heart. "Our entire family is eager to give whatever you ask. You have returned our son to our lives and have our deepest gratitude and loyalty."

I rocked back on my heels. Katalin had won *me* the governor's entire family's support. I hoped Fausta and her husband would feel as willing when I called upon them to divert food and clothing to feed a hungry, cold army.

"I appreciate you pledging your loyalty," I said. "All I ask is that you prepare your people for sacrifices in the upcoming moons."

"Of course." She dipped into a gracious bow before returning to the portico.

Asander opened the carriage door and whispered just loud enough for me to hear. "Dacia needs to prepare for years of war, not moons. This war may not end in their lifetime. We've battled the Scythians for over forty years. The bones of our friends and family are scattered across our eastern border."

Asander's words chilled me. I settled myself inside the carriage, stroking Midnight's shaggy head. Across from me was not the Patridavan lady's maid I was expecting.

"Tulia?" I blurted as the carriage lurched forward. "I expected you'd be visiting with your parents! I'm delighted to see you, but what of your plan to stay?"

"Your resounding speech yesterday forced me to reconsider. I couldn't help myself but join the noble fight against our enemies," Tulia said with her usual sarcasm, but her smile faltered.

After my Patridavan speeches, barely a thousand men and women volunteered to fight, less than a third of what Asander had projected. As Patridava was the largest city in the kingdom, the wealthiest, and in the shadow of the castle, we'd had much higher hopes.

I wanted to shrink and scream at the same time, but there was nothing to be done. The only thing within my power at the moment was to help the troubled young woman in front of me.

"How is your family?" I asked gently.

"Very well. My little brother is so much taller." Tulia handed over a letter. "From Lady Katalin's servant. I believe it arrived late last night."

Tulia gazed out the window, her hands clutched together. She was silent as Asander knitted. The clacking of his wooden needles blended with the patter of rain that started to fall. I knew Tulia would talk to me about her troubles when she was ready.

I cracked the seal on the deep orange edged letter, the Vulpe's signature color. Katalin *had* sent a full update on Felix. The note had been delayed in the transition between my temporary lady's maid and Tulia. I folded the letter and tucked it away, chagrined that I'd jumped to conclusions about Katalin. Perhaps she was changing.

When Tulia dozed off, Asander and I sat in silence apart from his needles' soft chatter.

"Are you looking forward to going back home?" Asander asked.

We'd arranged to stop at villages as we traveled south, but we planned to stay several nights in Moesia.

"The life I had before feels so distant."

"Like it's someone else's life?"

"I've never thought about it like that, but... yes. I'm not that same girl anymore even though it's only been six moons."

Asander grinned. He pushed up his sleeves and resumed knitting.

"You haven't filled in the sixth section of your tattoo?" I ran a finger across the griffin on Asander's forearm. It was comprised of nine artful strokes, each stroke filled in with red ink when he finished a year of service. His sixth year in the military had been completed since he'd come to Dacia.

The prince shifted away, the clacking of the needles quickening. "I can't fill it in until I've fulfilled the full year."

"You once said you blew into the military with the first winter storm." We were well into the cold winter weather. "Or did I remember that wrong?"

The tapping of the needles stopped. "You remember correctly."

I clutched my hands together, not sure what to say. I waited for Asander to explain, but he remained steadfastly focused on his knitting as if the simple task required all of his concentration. I stared out the window, ignoring the strain. My thoughts bounced between my childhood home, Asander, and Rupea Castle. Something Tyne had said kept coming to my mind. She'd been determined to live through her captivity. She was driven to survive, no matter the cost. How could I inspire my people the way Tyne inspired me?

"Nikka." Asander set his work in his lap, his green eyes meeting mine. "I cannot deny that I feel I've abandoned my unit. They're preparing for the season of war without me, scrounging for food and equipment as best they can without stealing from the very Auripoans they are trying to protect. I'm tormented by not being with my brothers and sisters. Instead, I'm here, safe and well fed in a luxurious carriage. They're sleeping in freezing mud or burnt-out estates. It doesn't feel right for me to count the days I've been lounging in ornamental Dacian courtyards toward my service."

I swallowed, unsure of what to say. How could I tell him his hours with me were not an extravagance? I'd felt much the same when I first met Katalin in her fancy carriage not far from here. I'd thought she was ridiculous, too, living in a cushioned world, blind to the realities of the commoners. Was that how Asander saw me? Was there truth to his perception?

"I didn't realize how hard it was for you to be away from your friends," I said.

"They are more than friends. When your life is in the hands of someone, when they save your life, they become your blood." He stared at his empty hands. "You wouldn't understand."

I wanted to console him, but I bit back my words. Realization shot like a quick blaze from my mind all the way to my toes.

I hold more power than a prince.

Asander was required to ask permission from Dyana, his sister by marriage, for permission to stay, to leave — for everything. But as the empress, I could send Asander wherever I chose. Dyana would understand, perhaps even be grateful if I sent Auripo's most famous warrior home until we wed. And it was what Asander wanted.

Something deep inside me cracked. The slightest fissure, but it reverberated inside me. I dropped my gaze to my lap. The prince regretted staying with me. I placed another stone at the base of my heart: a foundation for a wall.

I could not ignore the irony of advising Katalin to let her true heart show while I took steps to conceal and protect mine. But, as empress, I lacked the freedom to follow my desires; Katalin still had a chance at a life of personal fulfillment and happiness.

It pained me to keep from Asander his true desire, especially after he'd been honest with me about his wishes. But Dacia needed him. Our anemic army was floundering, and Asander was our single greatest resource. I couldn't let him leave, no matter how guilty either of us felt.

Asander's nostril's flared as he shoved his knitting into his bag. His sullen mood became my constant companion for the rest of the day.

I dreamed of the cloud-people again.

But this time, I was one of them.

We ran through a mountain pass. Bitter cold. Breathing hard. My lungs ached. I ran my finger across the white mountainside, leaving a streak of light. The man behind me shouted that I might get us all caught.

My dream shifted. The cloud-people hugged and cried. Snow-capped mountains loomed in the distance; relief. We split into a dozen groups. My friend was standing by me. Then she wasn't.

I was forlorn. Yet, somehow I could see her group. I could see all the groups — their lives folding in layers that I picked apart. I was more than a bird, overseeing everything; I was the air they breathed.

I studied one group; time reversed and the new course led to different endings. I looked again and again. So many stories.

Weddings. Births. Tears.

Life. Happiness. Death.

Fleeing. Fearful. Hunted.

I woke up sticky with sweat. I will not tell Mama my dream.

— ESME

CHAPTER

TEN

POLTAI DABAVESHI

The morning rays warmed my back in a Lily courtyard on Moesia's hilltop. A dog trainer gave me directions for Midnight while Rufus, Jamil, and Tulia watched, bemused by the trainer's complete lack of deference to my title and position.

"A dire wolf is not a friend. She is your protector." The trainer's voice grew shrill. "You must take control."

Jamil cleared his throat and rapped his fingertips along his pommel. The trainer clamped his mouth shut, but the edges of his patience had long frayed. If the trainer knew that Midnight had a pension for lazing on down-stuffed pillows in front of cozy fires, he would probably spontaneously burst from trying to hold in his reprimand.

"How are you feeling, being back home?" Rufus asked as I neared their side of the courtyard.

I passed another bed of bright flowers, droplets of water still glistening on the petals. When Mama was alive, most of our plants were hardy herbs that required little water. We did have a single pot of decorative azure globe daisies, and on particularly hot days, I'd resented them as I trudged up the hill with a sloshing jug on my hip.

"Though I enjoy the warmer weather, this place doesn't feel like Moesia to me." I looped around the perimeter again, the courtyard barely a quarter of the governor's garden in Patridava. "I'd never even stepped foot in the Golden Lily before three days ago."

"You can never go home," Tulia said wistfully.

"Honestly, I'm glad to be off the road, but I've done all I can here." It wasn't safe for me to roam the streets, so I'd been cooped up since I arrived, meeting the southern guild representatives and dignitaries. "I'm tired of smiling, nodding, and prodding people to p-prepare for war."

I felt like I was sinking in loose sand. Every town, every speech, with fewer recruits than we needed, I would eventually suffocate, buried beneath the desert.

"Moreover, the Sonus is giving my speech to the city. I'm not even allowed to watch," I complained.

Though I was sure the Sonus' delivery of my speech couldn't be any worse than the ones I'd given in the small towns we'd stopped in along the way. Governor Aelius and Captain Lucius had recommended I visit specific places, and I soon realized why. They had been untouched by the plague and had large populations of younger, healthy people to recruit. They had been spared by the plague, only to be threatened by war, but few volunteered to fight.

Midnight tapped her muzzle against me. I scratched behind her ears, and the tightness in my chest loosened.

The trainer mumbled to himself, but he forced a cheerful voice. "She's doing better."

"She's doing wonderfully," I said before I turned to Jamil. "At home, I have armies to organize, spies to coordinate, and a second tour to prepare for. Furthermore, I think my father is right about the Getaens. I should visit them."

Jamil stiffened, but before I started to argue with my Own's unsaid words, Rufus spoke up. "That might be a good idea. They're generally not welcoming of outsiders, but they may feel differently about you. They must be impressed by a Getaen on the throne."

Jamil grimaced.

"Whether I go to the Getaens or not," I said, "I'm determined to return to Capidava tomorrow morning. Please make the preparations to do so."

I dismissed Tulia and the trainer but asked Rufus to wait near the doorway while I spoke with Jamil. My Own approached me on my left, as that was one of the new safety rules: everyone had to pass by Midnight first before standing next to me.

"Should I be concerned by Auripo's silence?" I asked my Own. We'd heard nothing since our ally had confirmed the attack on their contingency.

"They did say that communication would be difficult, and you have been on the move. Still, I did expect something by now."

"Perhaps I should send them an update on the recruits? My news will not be welcome, but they should know the truth. Should I also tell them about our use of dogs to warn of Mirrors?"

"Only if you have hair or something from Dyana or the king that would secure a Ghoster message," Jamil said. "Do you have anything that would work?"

I shook my head and moved onto a related pressing issue.

"We must find a safe route to Auripo while we still have a chance," I said.

"It's a risk to send anyone across the Curat, but you're right. The sooner, the better."

"Jamil, it occurs to me that we should already have spies in place. We cannot and should not depend on the Auripoans for all our information. If they've been driven back, how would we even know?"

"Agreed. When we return to Capidava, we'll make tactical changes."

I shook my head. "Speaking of tactics, we have only managed to inspire two thousand recruits, barely half of what we need."

I tried not to blame myself and my dismal speeches, but as empress, the responsibility ultimately came to me, whether I liked it or not.

"Let us hope that Zalmoxis forgets our war this summer and waits until the next."

I bit the inside of my cheek and excused Jamil, who stationed himself by the entry.

"I received your message this morning," I said, approaching Rufus. "You have discovered something?"

"I've been thinking about our conversation at the castle, when we showed you our advancements with manipulating magic. Ziba mentioned a 'push and pull' in all magic; something clicked in my mind." He pulled out a bag and opened it, revealing white amplifying Sonus powder. "I've been working on something alone. Dip your fingers in."

Jamil hurried to rejoin me. "The empress isn't to be experimented with."

Rufus held up a hand. "I assure you, she will not be harmed."

"I think I know what you're testing," I said. "The amplifying powder should do the opposite of the dampening powder that we used before. Are you sure I should try this on you?" I looked around for something that wouldn't easily break.

"I've tried it many times. On feathers, a pillow, and even furniture. I barely created enough force to budge the chair."

"Perhaps if Jamil stands behind you?" I signaled to my Own, just to be safe, and Jamil stood several paces behind the Ghoster.

"What word should I use?" I asked. The Norte word, the language of magic, for 'stop' had strengthened the magic.

"Some words are stronger than others," Rufus said, his eyes lit with excitement. "Which one strikes a chord with you?"

I dipped both my hands in the Sonus powder, closed my eyes, and envisioned a battlefield. I'd only heard about them from stories the bards sung. No words came to my mind.

I refocused on Tatiana. Her sneers. Her deceit. Her baiting of my Own — and of Valentin who fell by her hand. In the space of a single heartbeat, she'd cut him down. I'd stood only steps away. Helpless. My heart thumped, anguish ripping through me as I pictured that fateful moment again. I was powerless to stop her from cleaving Valentin, my Own. My friend. A bubble started in the pit of my stomach, growing as it roiled up through my chest and begged for a release.

My eyes flew open, my arms flexing as I shoved my hands forward, and I expelled the anger from inside with a shout, "Polti dabaveshi!"

Energy pulsed away from my fingers, a force of wind sliding my feet back across the pebbles. Rufus and Jamil both flew away from me, landing with thuds. They skidded, sending rocks and dirt flying.

I punched my hands skyward, both thrilled and surprised.

The men I'd thrown didn't celebrate with me, though. They didn't move.

My momentary elation turned cold. Jamil groaned. I ran to Rufus' side. His skin was sickly white as he gasped for air.

"Rufus!" I grabbed his camasa. Jamil rolled to his side, clutching his chest.

"Zalmoxis, what have I done?" I grabbed the Ghoster's wrist. No pulse. I jabbed my fingers into his neck. Nothing. I hovered over the prone Getaen, trying to remember what Rubia had taught.

"Pari!" I screamed.

I laid my hands in the center of Rufus' chest. Pari wouldn't make it in time to help him. Desperate, I pressed the flat of my hand hard and fast against his ribs as Rubia had taught me. Down, release. Down, release. Down, release.

I whispered Getaen words over and over with every downward press, "Embalai dabaveshi, embalai dabaveshi, embalai dabaveshi."

Jamil crawled to me, coughing, his eyes watering. "What did you say?"

Bind your heart!

Why had I chosen something so dangerous? Why didn't I say something simple, like 'No?' Instead, I had picked words from my heart filled with fear and anger.

A popping sound came from Rufus' chest. Then a noise like

sticks snapping. Jamil winced but then grasped my wrist, pulling me away.

"He's gone, Nicoleta."

Jamil used my given name. I froze. Tears stung my eyes.

"No," I hissed. I ripped my hands away from my Own and returned to the Ghoster. I pressed against his chest again, the bones crunching. The horror of the situation crushed down on me. What I'd done. The damage I was doing even now.

I'd killed a kind soul.

Tears blurred my vision. I was cracking his ribs, possibly puncturing his lungs.

Rufus coughed. My hands stopped mid-air, over his chest. He coughed again.

"Rufus!" I gripped his hand.

A stifled cry sounded behind me. I glanced back. A servant had appeared, probably upon hearing my distress. I shouted, "Fetch Pari!"

The servant jumped and dashed away. I gripped the Ghoster's wrist. A pulse, faint and fluttering, but there. I could barely see for the tears. "Rufus, I'm so sorry!"

He wheezed. "Wind knocked out of me… is all."

I blinked, tears burning down my cheeks. What had I done? Between Jamil clutching his chest right after I'd thrown him back, and the words I'd used, I knew without a doubt what the magic was capable of. What *I* was capable of.

Whether Rufus had realized it yet or not, I'd stopped his heart if only for a short time. Possibly damaged it. My lip curled in disgust at myself.

The Ghoster had taken the full force of my magic. I hung my head over Rufus, my body creating a shameful cocoon over my adviser. I gently probed his ribs, repeating words of healing. The white grains of Sonus powder caught the light. I frantically tried to brush them off, but they stuck. Would the Sonus powder help or hurt the Healer magic I was performing? I didn't know. Rufus' breathing was shallow, his pulse still faint.

Where was Pari? Moments stretched on. I bit my lip, fumbling after Rufus' faint heartbeat. I pressed my palms on his chest, my fingers spread wide. Swallowing my threatening sobs, I chanted.

~

I'D BROKEN THREE OF RUFUS' ribs in restarting his heart and damaged tissue from the bottom rib up to the sternum. Pari assured me he could make a full recovery, but her smile was weak. And she didn't say how likely that would be, nor how long it might take.

Asander, my royal contingency, and many others from the Golden Lily left to listen to the speech made on my behalf. As rattled as I was, I would have been a stuttering mess for my speech. Still, I hated to be left behind.

I put my worries about Rufus and my weak army into the back of my mind, locking them away to examine later, a technique that was becoming easier every day. Midnight lay on my feet as I read the stack of letters from the castle. I finished writing a response to Papa and put the missive on the growing stack to be delivered to the castle.

"Is it possible for someone to change?" Tulia blurted.

"What do you mean?" I cracked the seal on a letter from the high judge.

Tulia placed folded marama scarves in a trunk. "Is it possible for someone with a dried husk of a heart and sludge in their veins to change? Can a fox decide not to be cunning? Or is it in their very nature?"

I set the letter down. Finally, it seemed Tulia was ready to talk.

"Lady Katalin privately approached my old master in Patri-dava, but of course I eavesdropped." Tulia's back was to me, her hands pressed against the top of the trunk. "Lady Katalin claimed my old master's misdeeds were forgotten and she was giving him a chance to begin fresh."

"She stopped b-blackmailing him?" I asked.

Tulia nodded. "They argued. He's been paying my wages all

this time, of course. He was upset that I've been offered positions at noble houses when he's invested in me. He wants me to return to his household."

I leaned closer. That's what Tulia had wanted for years: to be invited home, preferably with a recommendation from Katalin.

"My old master demanded that Lady Katalin influence my decision." Tulia's fingertips whitened against the trunk's lid. "She said it was presumptuous to assume I'd want to return and that I wasn't a chattel to bargain. My master called her a hypocrite and a dozen other names she deserved. In the end, Lady Katalin walked away without bending to his threats. The next day, my old master approached me with a generous offer."

Tulia spun around. The tip of her nose was bright red and her voice thick. "I thought the news would make me happy. Generous pay and my family. The ugly traps Katalin had set were gone. I hadn't realized how free I would feel. Yet, I was conflicted. On one hand, I have loved the pace and energy of the Rose Court. On the other hand, my family and home changed without me... I got left behind." Tulia sucked in a breath, blinking back tears. "The house seems to have shrunk. My brother barely remembers me. I thought I'd tell him stories as I once did, but he's more interested in playing with his friends. I realized my home was not just a place but a time. It's impossible to go back because the place I left no longer exists."

"That's why you decided to rejoin me instead of staying with your family?" I asked softly.

"Yes, but also because, though my old master is not cruel, he is weak. He lost my trust. I can't work for him again."

I stayed quiet, imagining what options twelve-year-old Tulia had at the time. If she'd quit, who would have offered her a position in their household? A Poppy with no recommendation would struggle to find decent work, especially a child. Even worse, if she'd made the unfortunate mistake of running into a merchant like Elek Moldva, she would have been sold as a slave and not a single person would have stopped it. I shuddered at the memory of

Elek's hands gripping mine, refusing to let go. Not all children had someone as fierce as Rubia to fight for them.

"What I cannot understand is why Lady Katalin would free my old master from his arrangement?" Tulia wiped her eyes. "I don't agree with most of her decisions, but they make logical sense."

"Could she be trying to make amends?" I asked.

"If she is, then that makes me even angrier. How can she even think she can simply erase her mistakes? Her actions ripped me away from my home. I can never forgive her for that. I'm a stranger to my family." Tears lined her eyes again, and she pressed her hand to her chest. "I don't know who she is anymore. I've changed — everything I thought I wanted has shifted."

Before I could respond, Ziba burst into the room. I held up my hand for my Protector to wait. "Another moment."

Ziba scowled at Tulia before retreating, shutting the door with a thud.

I took Tulia's hands in mine, wanting to comfort her, when I realized *I* was shaking. Tulia's account suggested that Katalin was again doing what I'd asked her. She was seeing people, not as tools but as living, breathing souls. But Tulia was right. What I'd done to Rufus would have lasting effects, and so would Katalin's past decisions. I could and would beg Rufus for forgiveness, but even so, I feared his heart tissue would be damaged forever.

"I'm sorry." I squeezed Tulia's hands.

"I'm glad I went home even though it was hard. What I had were rosy memories, and visiting was a dose of stark reality," Tulia said, her voice beginning to calm. "I'll fetch Ziba. You don't have much time for your Protections. Prince Asander will be back soon."

"At least, there won't be much preparation." Instead of dressing for a stuffy dinner, I'd be taking Asander on the long-promised tour of the Commons where I'd grown up. My old community was full of other Azures and prosperous Clovers, a mix of Dacian and Getaen families, and where magic was considered to be useful.

"I've arranged disguises for you both and the Empress' Own.

No simple task." Tulia smirked, looking and sounding more like herself than she had since we'd left Patridava.

I'd not given this personal tour much thought until now. But I was determined to journey to Capidava in the morning; I couldn't delay returning home any longer.

~

As THE TEMPERATURE DROPPED, I pulled the marama scarf over my head and waited for Asander near the servant's entrance. I'd already gotten word of the tepid response to the recruitment effort. But the prince had played his part, having stood on the pavilion near the Sonus during the speech.

"I hardly recognize you," Asander said as he approached, wearing plain merchant clothing.

Anonymity added a layer of protection, and I had stripped away the finery of the throne, including my crown and Midnight. Though I kept the Canina Thorn hidden in a stained, leather sheath under my cloak.

The prince's effort to be more affable since Patridava didn't go unnoticed. He was making peace with being stuck at my side just as I was learning to accept the fact that Asander's stomach would never flutter when he saw me.

At least he's politely curious about my past.

I led Asander along an inconspicuous route. I felt one of my Own watching us near the edge of the Golden Lily quarters. He was dressed in typical Moesian clothing, feigning interest in something in his satchel. He was the first of my Own on the hill, but six more were stationed along the way, four of whom I never spotted.

In the Commons, I slowed, overwhelmed with the familiar sights and sounds. My heart swelled with emotional memories and wistful longing for the time before the plague. Winter was my favorite season; the desert skies wept, and flowers bloomed. As the sun touched the horizon, the bright music grew louder. Before the plague, colorful streamers fluttered above rhythmic dancers.

Papa and Mama held hands, Rubia bantered, and everyone laughed.

"What was it like growing up here?" Asander asked.

"The summer days can cook an egg. But this time of year is glorious. Do you smell that?" I stopped on the street, lifted my arms as if I could embrace the air, and sucked in a deep breath. I practically tasted the jasmine, the exotic favorite flower of the Commons.

I opened my eyes to see Asander giving me a strange look. "Dacians and their flowers. I wonder at this kingdom."

I was too immersed in happy memories to take offense. I pulled the prince to my favorite spot where the houses were low and we could see the sunset painted in vibrant shades of vermilion. "I know we seem frivolous to you. But consider this — we never knew if or when everything would be stripped away by the plague. We strive to see the beauty and joy in everything. You will love Dacia when you learn to see everything as a gift, too."

Asander's face softened. A bit of the frost between us melted.

I guided Asander down a road I'd walked a thousand times. As we neared my home, my heart raced. It was smaller than I remembered with two pots of dried weeds out front and three dirty windows high in the wall. Asander's upbringing was strict, but he was still a prince.

We waited for the scheduled commotion down the street and then slipped across the threshold. Even if someone saw us and reported intruders, a Moesian Thorn would be sent to investigate, which was of little concern.

Near the hearth, I rolled my lips together, scrutinizing the prince's every glance. Asander stood in the center of everything I held most dear. A layer of dust softened the edges of the room and covered the table, stools, and shelves of plates and cups. Asander lifted a large bowl from the shelf, one Mama had used every day.

"That's a Moesian pattern painted on the side," I said. "I chipped the rim when I knocked it against the table. I was nine."

At the time, I had felt terrible. But now, the bowl drew me

closer. I ran my nail over the bumpy, broken spot, struggling with how to convey my thoughts. So many memories swirled around me, in every object and inch of the room. Comfortable, warm meals and interesting conversations late into the night.

Looking at my childhood home anew, I realized how melancholy the house had become. When Mama died, she took the joy with her. It was as if the hand of Zalmoxis had punched through the walls and ripped away the heart of our home.

I turned away from Asander and slipped to Papa's study door. I pictured my parents at his desk. The conversations I'd eavesdropped on. The dreams I'd had. Without anyone there, my home was just a shell.

I loved the Commons. I always would. But my path led me to a wider world. And wherever Papa or Rubia were, that was my home. It wasn't here.

My gaze slid over the tiles that concealed a cavern below. My uncle had been here to clean up the mess after the soldiers had kidnapped Papa, but there was little to indicate he'd been here since. I turned my attention to the wall where a piece of stone could be wriggled free, and a secret blue vision waited for a child: Essa's son.

I assumed I'd placed the boy with my uncle. Firstly, because he was a decent man. Secondly, he lived in a remote mining town, which offered a natural buffer between the child and anyone who might search for him. Few knew the child existed at all as Gul had taken their memories of him. Even Jamil and Irena's only recollection was of a young boy who used to roam the castle halls.

I had more memories than most, but even I'd subjected myself to a Clarifier's magic. I remembered visiting a Clarifier in Patridava, the child next to me. Then in a blink, the boy was gone, and two weeks had lapsed.

Only one brief memory of that time remained: seeing the blue vision in Papa's study — the same location where Papa once kept the master scroll of information on the True Key.

Asander touched my shoulder, and I jumped.

"My apologies," Asander said.

"No need. I was just lost in thought." I ran my thumb over the markings on the True Key around my neck.

Though I trusted Asander, I hadn't risked telling anyone about the boy's existence. And I trusted myself, too; I wouldn't have returned to Patridava until Essa's son was safe, as I'd promised. I would leave the blue vision and the past where it belonged.

"Tell me about your family," Asander requested.

"Before the plague, when Mama was alive?" I turned from the wall to face Asander. "Or after, with the raid and d-devastation?"

His face fell. "I'm sorry."

Three and a half years ago, when the plague raged around me, Asander was fighting for his life and kingdom. "You've had your own hardships."

"If I had been here, I would have helped you."

I snorted and then covered my mouth. "If you g-grew up here, you'd be at the top of the hill, focused on helping your own family's r-recovery after the p-plague. You wouldn't have had time for a girl in the Commons."

And you would've been taught to fear my cursed-tongue like everyone else.

He grew more serious. "I am sorry Dacia is drawn into battle. I truly am. But it is here. And we will face it together."

Asander clapped his hand on my shoulder and pulled me into an embrace. It wasn't a romantic gesture, but it was a kind one. Without thinking, I chuckled.

"What about this do you find humorous?"

"Nothing." As gradual and slow as a summer sunset, I had let go of my childhood romantic hopes and replaced them with what was real. "I've stood in this exact spot many times. If I'd have known then that I'd have you for a friend, I would have been overjoyed."

"Who wouldn't want a prince for a friend?" Asander gave me one of his most dazzling smiles, but this time I could see past his heart-stoppingly handsome features to the man behind the façade.

Despite his imperfections, I liked the real, unmasked Asander better.

"Truthfully, if you would have told me last year that we would be friends, I wouldn't have believed you. I mean... you're a *prince.* I would have been grateful for any friend."

Asander kept one arm around me and patted me on the head with the other. It was a gesture I might have used with Midnight, yet I didn't resent it. Instead, it solidified my resolve to navigate our relationship as friends — even with those boundaries, there was much room for growth.

Someone pounded on the door. Asander and I stepped apart, and he took the Shield position as we rushed to the door where we met two of my Imperial Guards, two unknown Auripoan soldiers, and a woman in muddy trousers, boots, and cloak: Dyana Coatys, the future queen of Auripo.

I wore my finest fota half-apron when I went to see the Historian of Culture and gave her a grand curtsy. She wasn't impressed. She made me peel the skin off all her grapes like a common servant while she spoke.

If I stopped peeling, even for a moment, she stopped talking.

But I did learn. I didn't realize that our Norte ancestors who arrived a thousand years ago were far taller than the Dacians and had skin the color of white marble — like the cloud-people of my dreams.

Before the Norte arrived here, other groups had already settled on the lands around the Getaen Sea. There were skirmishes between the groups, especially during times of famine.

The Red Valley clan was created when a water-loving people invited a group of Norte to join them. Though the Norte were small in numbers, they brought something to every group they joined: magic.

The Historian said that from the moment Zalmoxis saw fit to put humans on the land, there have always been changes. Cultures, civilization, people. With the rise of every kingdom, another burns in its wake.

— ESME

ELEVEN

NEW ENEMY, NEW TACTICS

Dyana appraised my old house with a wrinkled nose. The guards remained outside while the three of us convened at the hearth. "I see you're making yourself cozy while we are at war."

Asander stiffened, his shoulders tense.

"We have been on a tour of the kingdom, r-recruiting," I said in our defense.

"And how is that going?" Dyana raised a brow.

I clamped my mouth shut.

She let out a breath. "There is no time for pleasantries, I'm afraid. The Norte have attacked."

"What?" Asander gasped. "It's not the season of war."

"They live in perpetual winter, my prince," I said, fighting to keep calm though I'd spoken up about this possibility many times. "Snow and ice are not a concern for them as it is for Auripoans or the Scythians."

"There are rules to war!"

"Bah, Asander!" Dyana slammed a bandaged fist on the table and winced. "Listen to yourself. Rules change. This is a new enemy, with new tactics."

Fear trickled down my spine at her ominous tone. "What d-did they do?"

"They cut straight for the heart of Auripo. They attacked the castle," Dyana said, her voice grave.

"They wouldn't dare," Asander growled his denial.

"An Illuminator led them. I'm assuming it was our friend, Borsea. King Eusebes was able to thwart the attack, and he fought well." Dyana gave Asander a sympathetic look. "But your father was gravely injured."

Asander's lips pressed together as he gripped the side of the table.

We shouldn't be surprised by the Norte's move. I kept my thoughts to myself. After all, the Norte had attacked Rupea castle, too. They certainly seemed to believe no target, even a formidable castle, was beyond their reach.

"What we thought was a strength, they turned it against us," Dyana said. "The mountains have always been a protection, our castle nestled at the base. But the northern mountains, which we have used as a wall of icy protection, are now an open gate."

"Rupea castle isn't easily accessible from the north," I said. "Furthermore, Rupea was built into the mountain in such a way as to make it almost impossible to take by force. That's why they tried to take Dacia from *inside* our walls."

"Yes," Dyana agreed. "The Norte studied the weaknesses of both our kingdoms and dug their blades right between our ribs."

Asander turned to me. "They might hope you'll bring soldiers to the interior of the kingdom, to cities surrounding the castle, like Patridava and Findava."

"Why would the Norte Council believe you'd compromise the borders," Dyana asked.

I don't have enough soldiers at the borders as it is. Dacia will fall!

Asander looked from me to Dyana. "The volunteer recruiting is not going as well as we'd hoped. If the Norte know this, they might be manipulating us into tightening our circle within the kingdom."

Panic rose, and my lungs tightened. Dyana had once told me that the crown was only given bad options. It was true. But my people depended on me to make the lesser of the dreadful choices. I ran my hands over the dusty table near the hearth, picturing it burning to the ground — the walls around me engulfed in flames. If the Norte didn't immediately destroy us, the Theracians would raze the major cities, subduing the people as they had in Illyria. I couldn't let that happen.

But as much as the people needed me, they had to fight, too. How could I get them to rally?

I pressed my fingers into the table. Mama had chopped vegetables here, counseled me here. What would she advise me? Tulia and Lady Tyne's words tumbled through my mind again. Tulia's heartbreak over her brother and Tyne's determination to honor her son... I realized what they had in common: family. My breathing quickened as if I'd finally deciphered an ancient text; everything became clear.

I rushed to the entrance and addressed the Imperial Guards. "Knock on the doors. Tell everyone to go to the market square. There will be an important announcement."

Asander grabbed my shoulder. "What are you doing?"

"Asander, I know what I need to do, what I need to *say*." I hurried down the street, catching a miner coming home late. "T-tell your family, your neighbors — there will be a m-message from the crown in the market in one hour."

"On behalf of the crown," Asander corrected, giving me a warning look.

I didn't argue, but a Sonus would *not* be delivering this speech. I rushed further down the hill, knocking on doors, spreading word of the announcement myself. My Own thronged around me, but instead of letting them form an impenetrable wall, I sent one to take the message to the Golden Lily quarters and another to summon Jamil and a Sonus to meet me in the marketplace.

"This isn't wise," Asander warned. "You said yourself, if Borsea or the Council wanted to kill you, they'd do it here. With tens of thousands of people in Moesia, a Mirror could easily hide. And you have no clear successor. Dacia would have a civil war on their hands, which would make them completely vulnerable."

"I finally know what I need to say, and I will say it!" A fire had lit within me. "I've been thinking about protecting Dacia because that's what *I* care about. Foolishly, I was thinking about it from the perspective of the crown. Being here reminded me that our homes and loved ones are what matter."

Tyne had decided to surreptitiously fight against the Norte, not because she wanted to save Dacia but because she was thinking of her dead son. *He* inspired her. She lived for him. Not for Dacia.

The moonlit streets began to fill, Moesians chattering about the announcement. It wasn't long ago that Mystic Marianna had done a similar thing on my behalf, calling the town to the square. Now, I needed to advocate for the people, and I had to do it without her.

In the market, no one recognized me in the evening crowd, but my Own helped me push my way to the side of the podium. The area was being hastily lit by city officials by torches, which did little more than deepen shadows. No matter, the people didn't have to see me to hear my words.

Several Auripoans stood near the stage, including Dyana.

Asander shouted over the noise. "Are you sure about this?"

I nodded, grateful he'd come, despite his disapproval. I spotted Jamil scanning the crowd, and when he looked in my direction, I waved. The people jumped out of his way as he moved toward me. As he neared, I realized they were trying to avoid Midnight who was pacing away from Jamil to meet me.

"Is this your doing, Empress?" Jamil asked in my ear, trying to keep the frustration from his voice.

"It's a risk, I know. But I must. Trust me."

Jamil shoved something into my hands, and I realized it was the *Crown of Lore*. He draped one of my royal cloaks over my shoulders, covering my plainer one.

"Thank you." I didn't bother shouting over the growing noise but trusted that Jamil knew my gratitude.

I settled the crown on my braid, shoving it down a little lower than I normally would, securing it. Behind Jamil and Asander, Marcus' familiar silhouette shouldered through the crowd. He'd said he was going to scout south, but I hadn't seen him the entire time I'd been in Moesia. For a moment, I felt a pang of disappointment. He hadn't asked to meet with me. I quickly shrugged it off, reminding myself that an emissary would make an appointment when necessary, not before. And empress' time was precious.

I turned and tapped the Sonus' shoulder, gesturing for him to let me use his powder. After putting a dot of the white powder on my lips, he bowed and backed away.

I felt Asander and Jamil's gazes boring into my back as I ascended the steps, Midnight at my side. As I stepped onto the platform, the crowd hushed. Easily a thousand people were packed into the square with more crowded into the main streets that wound up the hillside. Midnight leaned her weight against me, her body tense and nose extended. The emotion of the crowd threatened to overwhelm me, and my head buzzed. But after all my speeches, I was prepared for the flood of energy.

"M-Moesians!" I struggled to form my unpracticed words but pressed forward. "This very hour, I learned of another t-treacherous Norte attack. They have now struck d-directly at the very heart of both Dacia and Auripo, taking many lives. They are p-powerful masters of magic who want your land for themselves. The very mines that are the life b-blood of Moesia, the Norte will use to finance their campaign to rule all of Cornara." I took a breath, taking in the excited whispers. Though I stuttered, the crowd leaned forward, hanging on my every word. "At this moment, the Theracians to the south are laying plans to invade, and the Norte are already closing in. Neither will stop until we stop them. Like the Lilac P-Plague, we do not know when or where they will strike. We could not fight the p-plague, but we can fight the Norte and anyone else who threatens us." I slammed my fist against my palm. "If we become a colony state, you, your friends, and your children will be conscripted into wars in foreign lands.

"Stop the Norte and the Theracians. Fight to keep your family from being ripped apart and sent away as they were after the raids."

The crowd silenced, and my heartbeat thrummed in my ears. "Stand with me to p-protect your homes, your children." I punched my fist into the dark sky. "And your families."

The crowd erupted in shouts and cheers. People grasped their neighbors in animated discourse and shouted their intention to fight.

Midnight growled. I felt the rumble of her body against my legs. I jerked my attention to my dire wolf just as she crouched, hackles raised.

Before I could grab her, Midnight launched into the crowd. It was like watching a tent collapse as the people crumpled, caught under her weight. Screams rang out. The atmosphere turned from excitement to fear. The Imperial and Moesian guards swarmed from the front of the podium, blocking anyone from jumping onto the stage. Asander leapt in front of the platform, drawing his sword as people pushed to get away.

I stepped back toward my Own. Jamil put a hand on my shoulder to guide me away, but I slowed as I caught the scent of mint.

"Keep your head down," Marcus shouted, placing himself between me and the crowd. He unclasped my heavy, royal cloak, dropping it to the ground, and pulled my plain hood over my head.

Behind us, the Imperial Guards were shouting instructions to the undulating throng. The last thing I saw before my Own tightened their protective circle around me was the main street of Moesia filled with a stampede of frightened people, desperate to escape.

~

"JUST LIKE OLD TIMES," Marcus whispered a half-hearted joke.

"Though it was easier to sneak around when it was just the two of us."

I flushed, tempted to punch him in the arm. No one was supposed to know about that horseback excursion to stop the Theracians on the night of the Harvest Fest, but of course, Jamil had figured it out. Probably all of my Own knew; an empress had few secrets from her personal guards.

We crept through the poorly lit, narrow alleys of the Fissure, Marcus at my side. It was if my senses were heightened. I was aware of the shrinking space between us. Every sound of the alley. The air he breathed. An arms-length would have been infinitely better, but it was impossible.

I'd read too much into what he'd said in Patridava. He hadn't come to see me; he was treating me as a proper emissary. As he should. But every time I was near him, my emotions bubbled to the surface.

The alley narrowed; we moved in single file. Four of my Own protected us from behind; two more scouted several paces ahead. Jamil acted as my shield, directly in front of me, and Marcus was close behind. I knew Moesia the best, so I chose the route.

We weren't alone. Others fleeing the market wove through the narrow alleys ahead and behind us. A few brave people leapt from roof to roof; they'd have to be well-practiced in exactly where to place their weight on the derelict structures.

"I've never been in this part of Moesia," Marcus said, tactfully not pointing out the squalor.

"This is the Fissure. I've been here, but not for several years," I said. "Rubia brought me sometimes when calling on the sick."

"Generous of her," Jamil said.

I nodded. Rubia's Fissure patients usually paid her in dried lizard meat or wild edibles from outside the city. Rubia seemed to think any payment would do. I think it was around the time that I chipped Mama's favorite bowl when I asked Rubia why she never got paid in coin. She had winked and said some people were too good for crown-stamped metal.

I later learned that Mama and Rubia had once lived in this dilapidated portion of the city. With the slightest change of fate, I could have been born here. I clutched at the orb around my neck, my fingers brushing against the leather strap Marcus had given me.

I couldn't help but glance back at him.

"Are you worried about the dire wolf?" Marcus asked, concerned.

"A little. But whoever she attacked likely got the worst of it."

Midnight had jumped into the crowd for a reason. The Imperial Guards and Asander would discover what they could. Without an heir, I couldn't risk staying.

Jamil hadn't given me a lecture on making myself an easy target. Yet. But I'd speak again if it meant I'd finally managed to convince Moesians to fight. I knew they were with me; I'd connected with my people. Unfortunately, Midnight's attack might have not merely stalled whatever momentum I'd gained but obliterated it.

"There's something you both should know," I said to Jamil and Marcus. "The Norte attacked the Auripoan castle."

"Bold," Marcus said. "But it makes sense."

"The Auripoans drove them back, but King Eusebes was injured," I said. "They're lucky the Norte didn't overtake them."

Jamil hadn't taken his hand off his hilt since we'd fled, and his eyes were constantly tracking every movement around us. "I agree. With the Auripoans focused on the Scythians, I'm surprised the Norte weren't victorious. A diversion, perhaps?"

"Who knows?" I balled my skirts into my fist, hiking my dress up to my shins so I could move faster.

"So, we're returning to Capidava?" Jamil asked.

"What reports do we have from the northern spies?" I was never more grateful for the list of names from Liviana, Marcus' sister. Several had already proven more than capable.

"As of the last report, they hadn't seen movement, nor anything strange in any of the valleys of the north," Jamil said.

"How deep are they spying in the mountains?" Marcus asked.

"That's not your business," Jamil said.

"So, not far." Marcus frowned.

My Own stopped at the next cluttered intersection. I jabbed my finger left, indicating which alley we should take.

"It might be best to begin my second tour of the kingdom, immediately." I'd finally figured out the missing element to my speeches so I wouldn't be dissuaded from another tour without good reason. "We can't wait until spring. The Norte certainly won't."

"What if Rupea is attacked while you're away?" Marcus asked.

"Rupea hasn't been overtaken in its three hundred years of existence," Jamil said.

What if Rupea falls for the first time while I wear the crown?

"Captain Lucius and the Imperial Guard have been trained in battle tactics," Jamil said. "They can fight without you overseeing their every move. However, you are critical for overseeing the war as a whole. The castle is the best location to coordinate strategy across the kingdom."

"Good point," I said. Jamil wanted me safely behind the Rupea walls, but I planned to be near the fight. "And not returning soon creates another complication. My papa may not be the right person to leave in charge in a time of war. His appointment was supposed to be a few weeks until I returned. Now, it'll be moons." I needed someone as trustworthy as Papa, as fierce as Rubia, but also possessed of a mind and quick and sharp as a blade; someone who knew the nobles and their duties to the throne.

"Your return to the throne will solve many problems," Jamil said.

"What about Judge Isidro?" Marcus suggested.

Jamil shot Marcus a scowl.

"He has proven to be reliable and strict in the law," I said. "He might be the best option. I will consider him for when I continue my tour. In the meantime, I'll return to the castle," I said, hoping to placate Jamil.

I wasn't surprised that Marcus understood my intention to leave the safety of the walls. I used to love that he knew what I needed without explanation. Instead of cowering to Jamil's unsubtle hints at wanting me to stay at Rupea castle, Marcus helped me. But his actions tore at me. I brushed off the unintended closeness between us and focused on silently directing my Own.

We crossed from the Fissure onto a street of quaint shops near Rubia's old home. Throngs of people were in the street. A few were crying, others running, elbowing their way forward, but most were loudly debating about what they'd witnessed. I heard "Golden Protector," and "war," and my head began to spin.

Marcus placed a hand on my back, and all my attention was on his light touch. I knew the area, but I appreciated the gesture. He kept me close to his side, protecting me from anyone who might slam into my shoulder as they pressed through the crowd.

"So, you'll be leaving first thing in the morning?" he asked as we followed Jamil through the crowded street.

"Yes. So, you'll be following me again?" I teased as I tugged my cowl lower, making it even harder to see.

Marcus snorted. "Is that what I'm doing? Well, perhaps I am. I finished assessing locations for glass structures today, so I'll go wherever I'm needed next. I was actually in the Golden Lily earlier to report to you directly."

"Why not send a servant to Tulia to make the arrangements." Most people knew I was unlikely to be available at a moment's notice.

"I was overly optimistic. Or perhaps just hopeful that I'd get to see you myself." Marcus' fingertips pressed around my waist. "I wanted to see you before I left the city."

I jerked my attention to him, looking at his shadowed profile. Surely I was interpreting more than what Marcus meant to convey. Wasn't I?

Marcus suddenly slid his hand from around my waist and grabbed my hand, pulling me to the side just in time for me to miss stepping into a hole where a cobblestone had broken away. His hand was warm and comfortable like my own hand was meant to fit into his. I melted inside, savoring a moment of true caring. Not for a crowd — there was no one to impress.

Marcus didn't let go of my hand as he led me through this part of town, one he likely visited as a merchant. And I let him.

"I'll be overseeing the agricultural supply routes personally, out to where you'll be stationing troops," Marcus said. "I hoped to catch you before you left Moesia as I don't know when you and I will be in the same town again. On my way back to the inn, I'd heard the rumor about a late-night royal speech. If I couldn't see you in person, at least I'd get to hear your words. I didn't expect to see you on the platform."

Any internal warnings inside me, I ignored. For just the length of this street, I would not be the empress. I would simply be that Moesian girl I once was — unencumbered by a crown.

And a fiance.

I slowed. There was no escaping my promise. Though Asander would never cherish me, we'd started to find a friendly under-standing.

"Marcus..." What could I say? We could never be together.

"You'll always be important to me," Marcus stepped closer, seeming to close us off from the rest of the urgent crowd. "As a Guardian or a fugitive, none of that ever mattered to me. But as an empress, I live to serve you." Marcus lifted my hand, and his lips brushed my knuckles.

Jamil shifted a few steps ahead of me. He'd warned me a hundred times to not be out in the open.

"We're not far from the G-golden Lily, but we need to keep moving," I said. "My Own will see me safely to my rooms."

Marcus acted completely at ease as he released my hand. But I knew him. I could practically feel the tension rising off of him.

I cocked my head to the side, considering the man before me. The chaos seemed to slow as I recollected Marcus and Asander the moment after Midnight had jumped into the audience. Asander had protected the crown. He would always be there to defend the empress because it meant Auripo's closest ally would be secure.

But Marcus didn't jump onto the platform, placing himself between me and possible danger, to protect his kingdom. He was like every other soldier who was driven to leap into danger to shield those they loved. He was there to protect *me*.

The realization took my breath away. I reached out to touch Marcus' face. He closed his eyes in anticipation. But I stopped, my fingertips yearning to graze his skin. I stepped back. If I opened that door, I knew putting those emotions back into their bottles would break me.

Break us both.

BACK IN MY room in the Golden Lily, I couldn't sleep. Though the initial spike of energy from the attack had worn off, I wanted to know what the Imperial Guards had discovered. And every time I lay down, the absence of my dire wolf's weight reminded me that she should have been returned by now. To focus my runaway imagination, I studied the map I'd requested.

I rested my head on my hands for only a moment when Jamil's voice suddenly boomed in my ears. I jerked awake, feeling my saliva on my cheek. As I wiped it away, I noticed a puddle of drool on the map.

Jamil had the decency not to smirk.

"Yes?" I acted like he hadn't wakened me. At my feet, Midnight stirred. My worry lifted, and I stroked the fur between her ears. "You're back! What did the Imperial Guard discover?"

"I planned to tell you in the carriage," Jamil said.

"Is it time to leave?" Why hadn't Tulia wakened me?

"Not quite. Lady Katalin insisted she speak with you before we leave," Jamil said. "But perhaps you should sleep. We don't plan to leave until sunrise, in two hours."

"Did you sleep?"

Jamil gave me a flat stare.

"We will both sleep in the carriage," I said. "It's a long road back to Patridava. Allow Lady Katalin in and tell us both what happened. It'll save me from having to update her later."

"Very well." Jamil ushered Katalin into the room.

I stood, brushing the wrinkles from my apron. Midnight gave me a look of annoyance but stood up, licked Katalin's hand, and settled back down next to my desk.

"I'm glad you're safe, Empress," Katalin said. "Though, you look terrible."

There's the Katalin I know.

"When did you return?" I asked.

"Just after dinner. I'd barely gotten settled in when some servant burst in, announcing your speech in the city square. Thank you so much for doing that after sunset. Getting trampled in a frenzy is not my idea of an enjoyable evening." She brushed a strand of hair behind her ear.

"They caught two Norte in the crowd," Jamil informed us both. "One was wearing make-up and a dark wig. The other was a Mirror."

"I almost feel bad about that Mirror." Katalin looked at Midnight and put a hand to her neck, grimacing.

"A few Moesians were injured in the scuffle but nothing serious," Jamil answered my next question before I could ask it. "It could have been worse as both Norte were armed. But Midnight stopped them both before they could act."

"It must have been one of the Mirrors who originally infiltrated the Rose Court," Katalin said. "But how did your beast know the other?"

"The trainer doesn't know for certain. His guess is scent transference. It's possible other undetected Norte are in the city. The dogs are searching as we speak." Jamil folded his arms, staring down at me.

"I knew it was a risk," I said. "But it was riskier *not* to speak to the people."

Katalin raised a brow but then brightened. "On a slightly different topic, I do have a bit of news."

I rubbed my bleary eyes. "Oh?"

"I found a buyer for both your golden dress and for a sapphire pin."

"If you'll excuse me," Jamil said, "I would like to check with the Own on the route we're taking out of the city."

Katalin shifted her marama scarf across her shoulders as she waited for Jamil to secure the door behind him.

I turned to Katalin. "Tell me about this buyer you found."

"Actually, I have several buyers."

"Multiple bidders, you mean?"

A mischievous grin played on Katalin's lips. "I realized I could bring in much more coin if I cut the gown into ribbons and sold it in pieces. If you approve, I'll have the royal seamstresses deconstruct the dress."

"Who would want a piece of my dress?"

"Who wouldn't? The best part is that I estimate there will be over a thousand strips. With a price that people in your Moesian Commons can even afford, it will bring a significant influx of coin. I can show you all my calculations, and I will run them by Sorin, too, if you like."

"And who is the buyer for the sapphire pin?" I asked.

"One of Marcus' contacts in Lazica. They especially like the pin because you've worn it." Katalin ran her hand across her scarf again, and I realized she had a massive blue sapphire set in elegant swirls of silver pinned near her collarbone.

"I've never worn that pin. I guarantee I would remember it." Tulia had exclusively dressed me in green or gold except for the musgravite necklace from Saam.

"Oh, but you have." Katalin unclasped it, rolling it between her fingers. "Just make sure as many people see it as possible as you leave today." Katalin secured the jewel prominently on my apron. "And you won't mind parting with it as it belonged to a distant Caracalla cousin who married below their station and was disinherited generations ago. A nobody that no one remembers. Anyway, are we still headed to surrounding southern towns?"

"Change of plans. Back to Patridava."

Her face crumbled a bit, but her voice was steady. "Perfect. I'll fetch the pin from you there and then make the arrangements to get it to Lazica."

I was impressed with all she'd accomplished since I'd seen her last. She was trying to make amends for her past mistakes and brokering deals as I'd requested. I leaned against my desk. "I'm impressed. Well done, Lady Katalin."

Jamil burst into my rooms, his face pale. "Empress."

I glanced at Katalin, ready to send her away.

"Everyone will know soon enough," Jamil said, shutting the door behind him. "There's been another Norte attack. But in Dacia. They struck a village on the edge of the Curat Mountains. The village isn't near a major pass. We can't figure out the strategic value, but we have reliable sources confirming it was a slaughter."

Katalin went rigid, her lips pressed together.

"Zalmoxis," I gasped.

"Soldiers in the Rodnic Valley were alerted to the incursion," Jamil said. "They arrived too late to save anyone that hadn't hidden in the fields. The eeriest part was the Norte were still there. Waiting. I can only imagine the sight. Our soldiers engaged. They were some of our more experienced Thorns and had been warned of the Mirrors and Illuminator capabilities, but they found themselves outmatched by unknown magic."

I leaned against the table, dizzy.

"According to the survivors, at least one Norte female was seen on the battlefield," Jamil said. "She did not wield any obvious weapons, but when she touched Dacian soldiers, they appeared to suffer either great pain or severe hallucinations or both. Several reported that the victim's eyes would roll back or widen, they would scream and contort their bodies, with wild claims of attackers, but nothing was near them except the woman. She immobilized soldiers, moving from one to the next, leaving the actual killing to other Norte soldiers.

I leaned over the table, my legs weak. "Sounds like they were seeing visions. Waking nightmares."

"That was my thought."

"What could cause that?" Katalin asked.

I gave Jamil a sidelong glance. Clarifiers — the Norte magic was a bit different from Getaens, but a signature skill was manipulating memory. Oslid, the warlock, had forced Rubia to see visions she couldn't distinguish from reality. I shuddered at how much more a Norte Clarifier could horrify their prey.

"Our soldiers retreated. The Norte didn't pursue them, but they didn't stay in the village, either. They disappeared, likely preparing another attack. We need scouts in the area, analyzing the attack, tracking where they retreated."

"Why didn't they pursue our soldiers?" Katalin whispered, mostly to herself.

"Change of plans," I said. "I want to see the location of the battle. I can coordinate strategy for the entire war from the Curat. We need to move east."

"I will join you," Katalin said. "I will immediately notify my servants of the destination."

"Not you, Lady Katalin," I said. "I have something much more important for you."

"Anything you wish, Empress."

I pulled a Ghoster messaging disk from my desk. It balled-up in my hand as I lifted it to my lips. "Judge Isidro, Calvus Aurelian, and other advisers to the crown at Rupea Castle. I, Empress Nicoleta Aurelian, officially install Lady Katalin Vulpe as the co-protector of Rupea Castle in my absence, along with my father, Calvus Aurelian. She will find temporary replacements to fulfill her other duties while she is overseeing the affairs of the castle. She will be a worthy leader in my absence, which I expect may be several moons."

I slid the ball onto my desk, and it flattened back into a disk.

Katalin's jaw slackened, her eyes widening before she regained composure. "And why do I deserve such an honor?"

"We both know you think of this as more of a scourge than an honor." I lifted the now shining disk into the air for her and Jamil to see — my decree — if Katalin agreed to it.

Katalin opened and closed her mouth like a fish, the most undignified thing I'd ever see her do.

I knew too well why Katalin abhorred the idea of visibly leading. "We don't always get what we want, but you are what we need. Do you accept?"

Katalin looked to Jamil as if expecting him to object. His face was blank, but he was likely as surprised as she was.

"It is an honor to do as you ask," Katalin said with a curtsy. Sweat glistened on her upper lip, and I was sure she was cursing me.

I pressed the disk into her hand and closed her fingers over the cool, blue glass. We would both be leaving the desert paradise for harsher climates. While I felt compassion for Katalin's new position, Jamil, Asander, and I would be stepping on frosted, hallowed grounds where blood was spilled and any pretense that the Norte were not converging on us had abruptly ended with blades, fire, and unknown magic.

In the square, a bard sang about a rare magic where people see visions of the future and the past — they fall into dreams that get harder and harder to wake from. My eldest brother, Cy, gave me a strange look. I ignored him, but the song sounded a lot like me.

What if I'm a Seer? To have no magic would be preferable to Seer magic.

No, I'm almost eleven. I'd know by now. And it wouldn't be fair for me to have it — I couldn't.

— ESME

TWELVE

SNOW LEOPARD

Before the wheels rolled to a complete stop at the edge of the Curat mountains, I jumped out of my carriage and snow crunched beneath my boots. Through the tiny slit of my cloak, bitter air sliced against my ribs. For most of the journey east, Asander's demeanor was colder than the ice on the windows. He was upset, and I sensed an argument coming but was in no mood to soothe him or try and sort out his feelings.

The Dacian commanders had decided which Curat mountain pass was the best place to set up camp. Apparently, a stream ran nearby, but I couldn't hear it. Jamil had prepared me to expect tension, but it was more like watching a swarm of wasps ready to sting.

The sound of axes chopping wood was nearly drowned out by the rustling of clothing and people shouting to each other. Most of the soldiers' tents were simply canvas flung across rope strung between tree trunks. Groups of tents circled fire pits, the backs of the tents pinned to the earth beneath the snow, the fronts open to the fire.

A man pushed through the soldiers and rushed to my carriage, breathing heavily. He looked younger than Jamil, in his thirtieth decade. Over his Thorn uniform, he wore a heavier cloak than standard issue and a stately clasp, indicating he was born to a proud Thorn family with resources.

"Empress." He bowed. "I am Ivan, the captain adjutant. We just received word yesterday that you'd be arriving. The captain is near the battlefield and sent me to give you provisions and an update."

"We have provisions," I said. Asander strode at my heels with Dyana and Jamil mere steps behind him. "A contingency from the castle met us en route with appropriate clothing for my party. But I would like an update, and I expected the captain to greet me himself."

"He planned to, but we were re-engaged in battle just this morning."

"What do you mean, *re*-engaged?" I asked. We'd come to analyze Norte tactics, nothing more.

"This morning?" Asander's eyes narrowed. "Where's the fighting?"

"I-I believe it's on the other side of this pass."

"You believe?" Dyana asked. "Please tell me communication hasn't broken down this quickly."

"Tell us what you *do* know," I demanded.

"This way, Empress," the captain's second in command led us forward on a muddy path.

Just ahead of our carriages on the rough road, several wagons were waiting to unload supplies. I recognized Marcus even before he turned around. I tripped over my own feet but caught myself. He said he'd be overseeing the supply line directly, so I suspected he'd be here. I just didn't think he'd beat us. Marcus gave me a respectful nod from across the field before turning back to his work. As he did, his cloak shifted, and something metal flashed on his chest.

"Some of our soldiers were also in the Battle of the Rose Court," Ivan said. "They believe that we're fighting primarily Mirrors though it's unconfirmed."

I imagined with the Norte's white uniforms, silvery hair, and bloodless skin that they'd be hard to distinguish from each other at a distance, especially considering how well the Norte would camouflage with the snow.

"We planned to camp on the other side of these mountains, nearer the river," Ivan spoke as we moved through the encampment. "Our scouts reported favorably. But by the time we arrived, the Norte had moved into the area. We had to retreat. Some of our best soldiers held the line to give us enough time to save our supplies. We set up a line of defense in the pass. The Norte pursued us but stopped at the edge of the valley. Then four days of quiet until the Norte struck again this morning."

Few actual soldiers were visible in the camp — most were civilians carrying wood or water. And I could smell broth cooking with the nutty scent of grains. We passed blankets thrown over another crudely constructed frame. Soldiers lay underneath on pine boughs, pairs of wool socks visible to passersby. I paused, staring, hearing a few snores.

Dyana rested a hand on my shoulder. "Even a soldier needs rest. Otherwise, who will take up the sword for the next battle?"

I swallowed and waved for Ivan to lead on.

"How many were killed?" I asked. "And injured?"

"Two hundred and forty-six didn't return," Ivan said. "Over five hundred injured."

We need Getaen Healers.

"There are over fifteen hundred soldiers gathered already, the majority of them from the Imperial Guard. Most of them are on the front. If we can bring back the injured to be treated, we do." Ivan pointed south, but the haphazard campsites and small copses of trees blocked our view of any infirmary.

"The new recruits?" I asked. "Have they received their wool cloaks and boots?"

"Not that I'm aware," Ivan said. We approached a cluster of tall, spacious tents properly constructed at square angles. We passed the largest tent and moved to the tallest with a green banner protruding from the top, rippling in the breeze. Two Imperial Guards at the entrance snapped to attention. The ground around the tent had been flattened, not a divot in sight, with a thick black band of Sonus powder laid on top.

"Your quarters." Ivan opened the canvas flap and led us inside. The Captain Adjutant, myself, Asander, Dyana, and Jamil easily fit around the center table. The ground was hard-packed dirt with a section cordoned off by a curtain. The captain adjutant swung back the curtain, revealing a narrow bed. Its twin resided on the opposite wall where I guessed Tulia would sleep. While not as spacious as the map room at the castle, it was efficient.

Ivan pointed to the roof. "This tent was waterproofed with a Lazican wax. It's the same treatment they use on some of their sails."

Dyana appraised the canvas. "A wise expense. I should like to find out more about this wax."

I could only guess who had access to this wax: Marcus. Even after I'd sent him across the sea, he was thinking of my comfort.

"In here, we can speak freely," Ivan said. "The captain instructed to hold this news until we were inside."

We leaned closer around the table.

"The captain believes some of our soldiers were captured. Alive. We received a bag of twenty hands. The surgeon says they were removed from living soldiers."

My stomach lurched. The Norte had done the same thing to the Auripoans they'd captured.

"What game is this?" Dyana gripped the hilt of her sword.

"Mind games, sister," Asander spat. "Unlike what we've ever seen before."

"The captains didn't say much, but I know they're disquieted," Ivan said.

"We need to send an update to the king," Dyana said.

"I have items that I'd like to send to King Eusebes as well," I said, speaking of the Ghoster disks. "Communication tools. I'll teach you how they work before the messenger leaves."

"Very good," Dyana said. "I'll prepare my message." She'd traveled with several Auripoan soldiers who were likely scouting out suitable sites for their tents. She gave Asander an expectant look, indicating she wanted a private, Auripoan-only meeting.

"I need to speak with the empress," Asander said.

Empress, not Nikka. Great.

"Jamil, inquire to see if a weaver, tanner, or cobbler is on site," I said. "Ask about the status of the cloaks and boots for the new soldiers."

Jamil nodded and followed Ivan and Dyana out of the tent, securing the flap behind him.

Asander unclenched his jaw, which must have been a significant effort as it had been like that all day. "I'm going to the front lines as soon as I gather my weapons."

"Soldiers can easily b-bring you updates." My irritation at his sulking behavior snapped. "Would that make you feel b-better? To see a f-fight? Or d-do you need to fight yourself?"

I regretted the words before they left my mouth. Meeting Asander's anger and frustration with my own would not help calm him or me. We were like two flames that would only ignite a bigger blaze if brought together.

Asander's nostrils flared, and he spun to face me. "To know what is happening — to know the situation so I can be of assistance — yes. Otherwise, I'm sitting like a useless lump, of no help to anyone."

"We've b-been over this. You've helped train my army. B-been at my side to support my b-bid for recruits."

"And how helpful has that been?"

His words stung. I ground my teeth.

"I shouldn't have said that. I'm sorry." He almost took a step forward as if to console me, but then he pulled back, his face hardening. "When my Auripoan contingency went missing... When my *home* was invaded, Dacia stood by. *I* stood by."

Part of me ached at hearing his pain. But mostly I was dumbfounded. He couldn't possibly have expected us to search for a missing group of Auripoans, or send a battalion to Auripo after we heard of the castle attack. Could he? We hadn't known about the attacks until the fight was over. Sending Dacians would have served no purpose and would have strained our already thin lines.

But, if I'd known in time to send reinforcements to Auripo, would I have sent troops to aid them?

Asander's shoulders slumped. "I know I'm failing horribly as your betrothed. I'm all twisted up in my endeavor to please you. I must start doing things that make sense to me. To find myself, and then I can pull myself out of this hole."

I pushed away from the table. "What are you saying?"

"Our agreement stands." Asander's voice softened. "But honestly, becoming a Dacian is more difficult, mentally, than I'd imagined. My commitment is with you, but my heart is still with Auripo."

I was sympathetic to his desire to be alone, but not enough to let him go to the front without me. I hadn't gotten this far to shrink inside my tent. Besides, if I was with him, he would take fewer risks. Dacia still needed his expertise to train soldiers. He had begun the work, but I wouldn't let him die in a self-sacrificial tantrum before he finished it.

"Very well, you may go to the front," I said. Asander's face broke into a beaming smile. I lay a finger on his arm. "But I'm going with you."

~

ASANDER'S MARE flung clods of churned up mud and snow behind her as she galloped past the edge of the camp. I followed on my gelding, thankful for his less exuberant pace. As we traversed up the canyon, we saw a line of weary soldiers trudging back to the camp. Some pulled stretchers bearing their injured comrades.

After an hour, I stopped trying to wipe my wind-abused, continually watering eyes. I was grateful for Katalin's foresight in sending a fur hat and an Illuminator scarf. The hat slid right over my favorite, simple crown, and the scarf clung above my nose, protecting my cheeks. Without the supplies Katalin gathered and rushed to us on the road, I'd either be stuck back at the camp or suffer frostbite.

The distinct clash of swords and thunk of arrows echoed through the pass, causing my entire body to thrum. Soon, a line of soldiers appeared ahead of us, behind what looked like a hastily built wall that stretched along the valley, between the mountains. Asander paused, scanning the rocky hillsides on either side, his gaze settling on a game trail left in the snow, trodden with human boot prints.

Asander dismounted, pulled a soldier aside and assigned him to watch our horses. The two of us hiked, crisscrossing up the mountain. We couldn't see the fighting, but we could hear it. My heart thumped with every cry, every reverberating hit. Finally, the trail wound around to give a view of the battlefield. Asander moved to my side as he lifted his shield, protecting us both now that we were visible.

Ahead, a man stood on a rocky outcropping, two other soldiers on either side of him, one of which was Ivan. Asander called out, and the man's eyes widened. He hurried to greet us, his captain's insignia flashing on his chest.

The captain bowed. "I didn't expect to see you in such a dangerous place, Empress."

I peered past Asander's shield at the fighting below. The floor of the valley was covered in a dissipating mist. The green cloaks of the Imperial soldiers stood out against the trampled snow. The Norte were more difficult to distinguish as they wore their usual white uniforms. Though, now they also wore fur-strapped boots, breastplates, and white fur bracers and cloaks.

"D-do you have a lens-scope?" My jaw was stiff with cold, and my gloves made fine movements difficult.

The captain pressed his scope into my hands. I put it to my eye, steeling myself. The magnification of the field was disorienting and unfamiliar. I scanned the valley slowly, letting my vision adjust. A Norte lay prone on the ground, the body at odd angles, a mist rising from it. I blinked and scanned a bit faster. The fog on the valley floor was actually dissipating Mirror's bodies, cut off from the primary Norte controller. But other bodies of flesh and bone, dressed in both Norte white or Dacia green, lay motionless on the rocks. I closed my eyes and swallowed, composing myself.

"Captain, when you see some of the soldiers move in the same way — not in a similar way but *exactly* the same way — you'll know those are Mirrors. They seem as real as you or me, but they're m-mindless. You could call them 'reflections' of their Mirror-creator. They generally cluster together. The real Mirror is p-probably in the back, further away from d-danger."

"Have you sent soldiers to flank the Norte?" Asander asked.

"We dispatched a small group with that goal over two hours ago. I just don't know if they can get into position in time," the Captain said. "The Norte press hard, so much that we think we will be forced to retreat, then they pull back, making flanking difficult."

"Their magic — they can only sustain it for short periods, I b-believe," I said. "Also, some of the Mirrors are more p-powerful than others. Some can control dozens of Reflection p-puppets while others might only be able to create one at a time."

Asander jerked his head as if he was a fish caught on a lure. He reached out without taking his focus off the valley. "Scope?"

I handed it over, and he leaned forward with the scope pressed to his eye. "Auripoans are on the battlefield?"

"Yes," the captain said. "They've been with us for the last two days."

A distant rumble sounded. A cloud of dark dust shot up from the mountainside across the valley.

"Rockslides," the captain explained. "Movement on the mountain dislodges loose rocks from the seasons of snow and rain. The small landslides tell us when and where the Norte are moving."

"He's not supposed to be here," Asander growled. He shoved the scope back into my hands and half-ran, half-slid down the face of the mountain, sending rocks cascading down below. Before I could ask any questions, Asander was halfway down to the valley.

He pulled the shield up just in time for a javelin to ricochet off the metal. The impact threw him against the rocks, but he quickly recovered.

What is he thinking? I shook my head, pulling the scope up to my eye, watching him.

"Empress, as you can see we are quite busy. Shall I arrange an escort to accompany you back to the main encampment?" The captain didn't hide his irritation. "The prince is lucky he didn't send rocks down onto our troops."

Asander rushed toward the Auripoan contingency, making his way through the group to one particular fighter. I lifted the scope. When the man turned around, I gasped.

"Petre!"

"Who?" The captain asked.

"The prince's brother, P-prince Petre Coatys, is down there." I handed the scope to the captain, keeping my face impassive. Inside, I reeled. Asander had forgone his own retirement in order to protect his brother from fighting. But clearly, Petre had cast aside that sacrifice.

"There's a new group joining from the rear of the Norte," the captain said. "That explains the dust-up."

"Fresh troops?" Ivan spoke up. "Perhaps this fight will go on longer than the last."

The captain handed me back the scope. "Do you recognize any of them?"

My hand trembled as I brought the scope to my eye. I took a deep breath, but I couldn't stop shaking.

The captain lowered his voice though there was little sympathy in his tone. "It is a shock for anyone to see battle the first time."

I clutched the scope to my chest with one hand, flexing my fingers with another. I imagined a desert stretched out in front of me and a warm breeze. Calm. Serene. Desert. I pulled the scope back to my eye. With a few calculations, I estimated the new group had a hundred fighters. I moved the scope to focus on those in the back. They were probably the Mirrors.

"I don't recognize any of them. Wait." I re-scanned the faces. There was one I'd seen before. She looked as focused as ever. "Borsea, Tatianna's p-personal guard, is there. An Illuminator. She's tucked in the back, likely with Mirrors."

"I've heard that special scarves are coming," the captain said.

"White on one side. B-black on the other." I tugged at mine, flipping it so he could see the white underneath.

"When are they arriving?"

"We didn't know there was fighting yet."

And I'd planned to give them to my Own and the castle guard first. I needed to re-think that strategy. All defenses were urgently needed by the soldiers fighting here.

"We have signals for the blinding light of the Illuminators. Our soldiers know what to do."

Memories of the Rose Court Battle pressed against my skull. My heart pounded. "Pull back now." I moved toward the trail that led up the mountain. "Even with their eyes closed, their vision will still be t-terribly impaired. Our soldiers will be no match for the Mirrors if they're half-b-blind."

"If we pull back to the line, they could press, and we'll lose ground. And our flanking troops will be alone if they attack." The rest of the captain's words were lost to the wind as I raced back down the animal track.

I didn't have time to discuss a strategy with the captain. I had to warn Asander and Petre. How would the Auripoans know the signals from my captains? They wouldn't! And even if my soldiers had a chance to warn them, the other Auripoans might not know our language.

My heart pounded in my ears as my feet slammed against the frost-lined path, blocking out sounds of the fighting.

Zalmoxis! I won't make it in time!

At the bottom of the mountain, I ignored the horses, instead running to a barricade constructed of stone and tree trunks. I yanked off my gloves, tossing them aside, and made sure my fur hat was secure. The last thing I needed was for my crown to make me a target.

"Let me through! Urgent message!" I push through the line of soldiers holding the pass. "P-prepare yourself for an Illuminator!"

As I squeezed past the soldiers, I emerged onto the battlefield. The smell of blood was a primitive knowledge — no one had to explain. Instinctively, all were born to recognize the ancient, dark scent of death. I slid my *Canina Thorn* from the scabbard, scanning the field for the Auripoans.

Petre's unit had stayed together at the front of the fray, on the right. A Norte growled as she attacked, and I parried instinctively. The strength of the blow against my sword sent a reverberating shock up my arm. I guessed the Norte in front of me was a Mirror's Reflection. Her white hair was pulled into braids from her forehead, tight against her scalp, to where they ended just below her earlobes.

I ducked and wove, dancing in deadly earnest as I waited for an opening. The Reflection's reach was longer, but with the *Canina Thorn,* I didn't need the typical mortal wound to defeat her. I rolled on the ground, rocks digging into my back. It surprised my opponent long enough for me to slice against her calf before I rolled back up to my knees.

The Reflection cried out, limping. The spark of life vanished from her eyes, and she collapsed.

Definitely a Reflection.

I pressed forward. Asander was fighting off two Norte, the shield in his left hand angled to protect his brother as well. Sweat ran down his face, and he cried out as if in pain himself when he sunk his sword through a Norte's abdomen.

I didn't dare call out for fear of distracting him. From the corner of my eye, I saw another Norte approaching me, a spear pulled back, ready to thrust. Before I could parry, the Norte tripped back, his face tilted to the sky. The spear dropped from his grip, the other hand reaching for his neck.

An ivory-hilted dagger protruded between the Norte's fingers, blood staining his hand. I spun, searching for Marcus, but saw only swarming chaos.

"Em—" Asander stopped short of identifying me aloud. "What are you doing?"

I ran to Asander, my lungs heaving. "B-Borsea. She's here."

I pointed to the fresh Norte troops who were engaged with the Dacian and Auripoans. "I can't see her from here, but I spotted her in the scope!"

"Tatianna's guard? She's here?"

"She could b-blind the whole army."

Asander whistled and changed direction, charging toward the fresh Norte troops.

Petre tried to force a smile, but it wasn't the same without his usual sarcastic joke, no attempt at easing the tension. Instead, he quickly reached up and pushed my fur hat back down. I hadn't realized that it'd come loose. This close, Petre's eyes announced his fear.

Someone pulled me back and threw up their shield. Something thunked against it, creating a dent, but the shield protected us.

"Stay close," a woman said. I recognized the Auripoan soldier as one of Dyana's companions, one of the future queen's closest confidants. There was a haggardness in her face — though I guessed she would be around Dyana's age if not younger. "There will be fewer spears in close combat."

The Auripoan soldiers formed a barrier between me and Petre and the Norte army. I doubted my troops knew who I was without my crown showing.

The Auripoans were like a spear, slicing through the bowels of the Norte army. With Asander at the point, the Norte Mirrors fell away. My heart raced, knowing we'd crash against the real soldiers of flesh and bone soon.

Seeing our movement, green cloaked Dacians converged on the fresh Norte troops as well. With the Auripoans gutting through the middle of the Norte battalion, the Reflections were out of the line of sight of the Mirrors controlling them. My Dacian soldiers cleared away the floundering Reflections. The Reflections were excellent fighters, so my soldiers had to pounce on the slightest advantage.

"D-don't let them touch you!" I shouted. The bald Norte Healer poisoned with merely a finger. And we suspected Clarifiers could cause nightmarish visions through contact with flesh.

Asander's momentum stalled as he battled two Norte. A woman crouched nearby, eyeing Asander's every movement. Unlike every other soldier, she had no weapon in hand. Next to me, Dyana's companion swung her sword but didn't parry away, clearly trying to protect me. She pressed forward, scattering the Norte converging on us. She'd get herself killed if she worried about exposing me. I bolted out from behind her, my sword wide, and sliced the outstretched hand of the crouched woman. She screamed and leapt toward me. I skipped back, unsure what her power was and not wanting to find out.

Asander rushed to my side. Around me, Norte lay bleeding. Real blood. Not Reflection mist. I spun, springing on the closest attacker. Then the next. I was vaguely aware of Petre behind me and Dyana's companion on my left. I focused on quickly calculating the danger each Norte warrior brought. Behind the front line, several Norte were not engaged in the battle. Some appeared to be fighting no one, obviously manipulating their army of Reflections as their bodies moved to fight invisible people. Others simply stood there, still as the dead.

Borsea was among them, staring ahead, watching. What was she waiting for? Seeming to sense my stare, her attention shifted. I stepped back, putting Asander between Borsea and me. Asander thrust forward. I looked over in horror at being exposed. But Borsea's gaze remained on the battle, not on me. Still, I struggled to breathe.

If she saw me, she'd blind us all and send the entire Norte army after me. Her victory would send all of Dacia spinning.

What was I doing in the middle of a battle? Putting myself at risk was putting the kingdom at risk. I should be up on the mountain top with the captain.

Asander cried out. One Norte was on the ground, bleeding, with Asander's blade through his chest. Another Norte was gripping Asander's extended hand. Asander's intense focus shifted into confusion, gazing wildly about him. He waved his sword, nearly hitting Petre.

A Clarifier.

Dyana's companion pulled a slender knife from her boot, flicking it straight into the soft area under the armpit and the boiled leather breastplate of Asander's attacker. The Clarifier's eyes grew wide. But with his free hand, he ripped out the blade and was about to stab Asander with it.

I leapt forward, slamming my shoulder into the Clarifier's stab wound. I spun into his chest and slashed down, cutting his upper arm. He stumbled. I dropped to my knees and rolled backward, not wanting to risk touching his flesh.

The Norte's grip had fallen away. Petre barreled into his brother, knocking him to the ground and out of the Clarifier's reach. The Norte had lost the Auripoan dagger and was pressing a hand to the wound under his arm as he retreated.

He had no idea the scratch on his arm would be his undoing.

Borsea's voice called out to the Norte. They lifted their cowls.

"Cover your eyes!" I dropped down on Asander, trying to cover his face while I ripped my cowl up over my face. Through the cloth, I couldn't see a thing. But I felt a faint pulse of magic. I dropped my cowl. The Norte were falling back. As they went, they took the lives of blinded Dacians within their reach. They could have slaughtered more, but they didn't linger.

Petre dropped the edge of his cloak from his face, blinking, as he straddled his brother who was still trying to buck him off.

"Get down," I hissed at Petre. "Cover yourself and Asander with his shield. When the field is safe, d-drag him to Pari."

Dacian soldiers were fumbling, their swords awkwardly outstretched into the air. I rushed after two Norte who fell behind, busy with killing as many of my blinded soldiers as they could. I screamed, chasing after them. With the rest of the Norte further ahead, I knew with my blade, I could defeat them. But the fact that I could clearly see was all it took for them to abandon their bloody task and scramble to catch up with their fellows.

Seeing them flee, I fell to my knees, heaving.

A voice boomed across the valley. "You have only tasted the power of the Norte. Surrender now. You are as helpless as newborn babes in the jaws of a snow leopard."

I scanned the area where the Norte had retreated. I couldn't see a particular Sonus speaker, but from this angle, the Norte's roughly constructed barrier was visible. From where my captains stood, we could only see a portion of the Norte's blockade tucked behind the mountainside at an angle. A cloud of dust indicated movement midway up the mountain above the Norte in the gray rocks and white snow. Concealed from the prying scopes of my captains was a creature unlike I'd ever seen. A massive leopard as white as the snow with speckled fur. Even from a distance, I was in awe of its enormous head and jaws, and powerful paws. A Norte rider sat astride the animal's back, scanning the valley. I crouched down, willing myself to look away. Had the rider noticed my deliberate movements? A cold chill burrowed deep inside my chest. I was an unintended witness to something the Norte had kept hidden. A weapon.

Snow leopards.

THE TORCHES barely cut through the darkness. The Luminaries did little better. The sun set early behind the mountains, true night setting before those on the ground could be searched. The injured were carried back down the canyon. The dead, to a pyre.

Dogs searched the area, sniffing for injured among the rocks. I looked alongside Midnight with my Luminary stone until the captain led me away. I couldn't understand his words; my mind buzzed.

The valley between the battle and the camp was a blur of shadowed movement. Asander had been taken to the infirmary. Someone else escorted me back; I don't remember who. In my tent, Rubia paced.

Rubia. I hadn't expected her. How long had it been since I'd seen her? Moons? I stared, vaguely aware of something in my heart. Relief? Gratitude? I couldn't tell.

"Nicoleta." Her voice was firm. I needed firm. "When I'd heard you were evaluating the burned village, I couldn't stay behind. I didn't when the fighting would start, but I knew it would be soon enough."

She sat me down, handed me a mug of tea, and started to unfasten my boots.

"Rufus?" I struggled to form words.

"He's Healed. You're too hard on yourself."

My Ghoster was a kind man, readily forgiving.

"Asander?"

"The hallucinations will be gone by tomorrow," Rubia assured me.

"Tulia?"

"Assisting Pari in the infirmary."

My gaze slid to Rubia's hands as they worked the knotted laces. I already suspected the medical tent would overflow with the wounded, but Tulia's absence and Rubia's silence confirmed it. I would never again leave my tent without my sword and an emergency packet of herbs that could save a life on the battlefield.

I tightened my hands into fists. More than my herbs, Luminary cream could have saved many. My soldiers had the concoction but didn't know how to use it.

No, they hadn't had *time* to use it. My strategies to protect them were woefully inadequate.

The flap swung open, and Jamil entered, his face dark. In his hand was a missive with an icy-blue wax seal. The Norte. I knew what it would say before I snapped the wax.

To the pretender who sits on the Dacian throne,

Deliver your head to us by dawn, and your soldiers will be spared.

Borsea Caracalla, Commander of the Norte Army

More than the threat, the name grabbed my attention. Borsea *Caracalla.* Seeing the name snapped me out of my daze. I shoved the letter back into Jamil's hands. He read, his face impassive. When he finished, he waited for me to dismiss Rubia. When I didn't, he handed her the letter.

"The threat and promise are a bluff," Jamil said. "Furthermore, Borsea wants you to know who she is. Another mind game."

Rubia crumpled the paper. "Caracalla, indeed. Do you think it's true?"

"It's p-possible she and Tatiana were related."

There was no similarity in their facial structure or magic. But sometimes siblings were as different as summer and winter. It would explain Borsea's jealousy of Tatiana; Borsea was not the chosen heir.

"I'm not giving up," I said. "They'd k-kill the entire Rose Court and essentially turn all Dacians into their Lilac-slaves. I will f-fight as long as there is air in my lungs."

Rubia gave me a proud nod.

"Though I made a mistake. I risked my life on the field. I wanted to warn the Auripoans, but my actions put our entire kingdom in danger." I glanced at the door flap to make sure it was closed.

"I don't approve of what you did. But from what I gather, you saved many lives." Jamil folded his arms. "Don't take that as my encouragement to do it again."

"I saw something I think the Norte meant to keep a secret.

They didn't anticipate anyone p-protecting their eyes so complete-ly." I tugged at my Luminary scarf. "I saw a snow leopard."

Rubia shot to her feet, one of my boots in her hand. "Did you hit your head? Snow leopards are nothing but a myth."

I gently took the boot from her, placing it on the ground. I was pushing her too far. "You're right. My imagination, perhaps," I soothed. "More importantly, I learned we are outmatched. The Norte could have killed us all on the field. Why didn't they?"

Why didn't they unleash the leopards on us? What other magic were they hiding? I rubbed the tight muscles in my neck as Rubia returned to unlacing my other boot, her brows furrowed.

"We need help from the Getaens," I said. "I'm going to send word to the Red Valley clan that I'm coming for a visit."

"That's a bad idea, Empress." Jamil frowned.

"It's a wonderful plan, Nikka." Rubia tugged off my other boot and moved to the straps on my boiled leather breastplate. "My clan was protected by the Red Valley. They could be your allies, too."

"You remember the clans how you want to," Jamil said to Rubia. "They aren't the benevolent protectors you imagine."

Rubia jerked the boiled leather from my body, revealing dark sweat underneath. Rubia signaled for Jamil to turn around while I changed. Even with his back to us, he continued arguing with Rubia. It was fascinating. Rubia's tongue was as sharp as ever, and Jamil rarely argued so harshly with me. I listened as they battled out the advantages and dangers of seeing the Getaens without me stuttering a word. Glorious.

When Rubia tapped his shoulder, Jamil spun and faced her. "Have you ever seen *the* Red Valley clan? Not scattered riverland clans or other allied clans, but where the Red Valley clan leader resides?"

Rubia's brow furrowed, pulling on the scar near her brow. "Yes. I remember a seaport."

Jamil raised an eyebrow. "Anything else?"

"Fine, I don't remember much. It's been over two decades, so I don't recall every detail," Rubia brushed off his criticizing stare.

Asander and Petre's voices carried from outside the tent.

"There's a reason you don't remember." Jamil pressed his lips together as the prince's arguing grew louder. Jamil avoided looking at Rubia or me, before inviting the princes into the tent.

Only Petre entered, his face red, and I suspected it wasn't from the cold.

"I'll fetch Ziba for your evening Protections," Rubia said, seeing Petre's sour mood. Jamil hurried to escort her, giving us some privacy.

"How is Asander?" I asked.

"He'll be fine, but he's too disoriented to discuss anything sensibly at the moment, so Dyana is taking him back to our tent. Pari said Asander was fortunate the Clarifier was pushed away before the full dose was inflicted. A bit of the Coatys' luck, I guess." Petre flashed me a sad smile. "Pari's medicine will speed his recovery."

"Thank you for letting me know."

Petre leaned against the table. "What are we going to do?"

He wasn't referring to just his brother.

"I have some ideas." I explained to him about Sonus magic and surprised myself by sharing what had happened with Rufus.

"Are you going to let that mistake, that failure, hold you back from trying again?" Petre asked.

I squeezed my eyes shut, seeing Rufus on the ground, feeling his ribs crack under my hands. "I don't want to. I'm afraid," I said ineloquently. "B-but after what I've seen, we have to risk it."

Petre's face skewed in pity. "War is —"

Shouting and scuffling sounded just outside my tent. Midnight sniffed the air but didn't growl, then Asander bounded inside.

The air crackled with palpable tension between the princes.

"Brother," Asander's thick, harsh accent was so heavy I could barely make out the word.

"I thought you were going to rest," Petre said.

I sensed that any wrong word could shatter the fragile peace between them, and I'd be walking on shards of glass.

"I would if I thought your brain wasn't full of dung." Asander took a menacing step forward.

Before they could begin a brawl that would bring my tent down, I blurted, "I'm going to train people to use Sonus magic."

They both looked annoyed at my interruption, not commenting on my declaration. I continued, ignoring their posturing. "Asander, you should be the first to know I'm going to the Red Valley Clan tomorrow."

Asander tensed. I could only imagine the concentration it was taking him in that moment to focus on the real world and push away the nightmare visions he still experienced.

"I'll remain here." Petre's voice was tight. "It's just as dangerous to try and travel to Auripo as it is to stay and fight."

Asander's nostrils flared, and he leaned forward, ready to argue. But then he paused and looked at me, his face growing a deeper shade of red. He was unable to command his brother to do much of anything — only Dyana or I could do that. Inside, I winced. Asander was no longer in control.

I looked from Asander to Petre. Two brothers who, despite their disagreement, were closer than two sides of a bronze bit. Asander's presence at my side had helped demonstrate Auripo's official support and confidence during my speeches, but I was ripping him apart. And me. I hated watching a friend suffer on my behalf. Besides, now that my recruitment speeches held sway, was his presence crucial?

"The Dacian captain is well trained, but he hasn't seen a real battle for over a d-decade," I said. The only time in the last forty years that the Dacian army had fought in a battle was during the brief Red Valley clan uprising fifteen years ago. "You're much younger yet already have many times the b-battlefield experience."

Asander's brow furrowed, his words slow. "Are you sure?"

"You're in no state to travel, but you'll be well enough to advise the captain in a few days."

"I assure you, I have managed fine without him for the last eighteen moons," Petre argued. "I've been fighting since before we ever came to Dacia, so don't leave him here on my account."

Asander clenched his jaw, his hands curling into fists at his sides.

I raised my hands to calm them both.

"Asander is critical to our success," I said. "He can help train our soldiers in using the Getaen tools like the eye cream and the Illuminator scarves that will be arriving. Dacians are wary of magic, but Asander can help change their hesitancy to urgency. Think about how many soldiers might have lived if they were confident in using the Luminary cream and quickly applied it?"

Asander fumbled for my Sonus stone until the magic pulsed. "There's something I want to say."

"Wait until you're feeling better. Tomorrow?" I asked, gripping the stone hard enough so that Asander wouldn't accidentally bat it away.

"You saved my life," Asander said.

"We all did."

"You got that Clarifier off of me. Others tried, but you succeeded. My mind, I can't... "

Who knows where the Clarifier would have thrown the dagger had I not stopped him, but none of us would have survived that battle without each other.

Asander took a breath. "I'm in your debt. I want to make you an offer."

"Asander, perhaps when you're feeling—"

"Let me finish. My offer." Asander shook his head hard. "I'll be loyal to you. If that's what you want. I'll have no other mistresses. If you'll be true to me, I'll be true to you. That's my promise."

Dyana barged into my tent, her ponytail even messier than usual. She had a barley roll in one hand and a piece of dried fruit in the other, which she jabbed in the air toward Asander. "Sorry, that one escaped from me."

I pulled the Sonus stone out of Asander's grip. I would've been shocked by his offer, but he was half-dazed and unlikely to even recall our conversation later.

"You thought you'd find him in the kitchens?" Petre said, mockingly.

"It's never good to scheme on an empty stomach. Besides, people learn when they listen. You might try it some time." Dyana turned serious as she faced me. "We need to send a letter to King Eusebes. The magic we witnessed on the field is new to us. Our people will be caught unaware. I'll take Petre with me."

"I was c-considering sending Petre to help train recruits in Moesia," I said. Petre had been fierce on the battlefield, but training in my hilltop childhood home would be far safer than the battlefront. With his brother safe, Asander could focus on my army again.

Asander's face softened. Petre frowned but was pulled into a debate with Dyana on the effects of magic, too fixated to notice that Asander brightened with a mischievous glint in his eye. "Nicoleta, if I may make a request."

Good, we're back to 'Nicoleta.' "Yes?"

"For the battlefront, I have a request." Asander's accent thickened as he sped through his clumsy words. "Something I trust only Petre to retrieve. He should travel home with Dyana."

A dawning realization came over Petre's face.

Dyana grinned.

"No. No." Petre took a step back. "I request to stay here. There's no *way* I'm fetching your blasted creature. I don't care what you say — it's part viper! And it hates me. Fetch your own horrid bird!"

Mama and Papa finally met with me. I'd known it was coming. They confirmed my worst nightmare.

I am a Seer.

Mama's voice trembled, explaining to me that she'd been Protecting my mind as well as she could. Though her veins are thick with magic, I am beyond her powers. But she promised not to give up. Papa cried, but if anyone can find a way to stop my Seer powers, Mama will find it. I know she will.

Mama left the Red Valley today, traveling to allied clans in search of a stronger Protector, or anything that can help me. I feel lighter, knowing she's going to fix me.

— ESME

THIRTEEN

RED VALLEY CLANHOLD

Leaving most of our things at the Curat camp, I took a small contingency to the Red Valley. Forgoing the carriage, six of us rode south on horseback: Ziba, Pari, Rubia, Jamil, Thadeus, and me. My concern for Ziba's stamina was unnecessary; she seemed impervious to the weather and the strain, as did both of my Own. But Rubia and Pari struggled as did I after five days of hard riding.

I hadn't wanted Rubia to join us, but she'd insisted. How could I deny her? Returning to the Red Valley was the closest thing to returning "home."

After seven days of riding, stopping only for recruitment speeches in villages, we crossed the Dacian River. According to the maps, we were in the Red Valley territory, but no record of the capitol's exact location existed. After three more days of staying at inns and talking to locals, we seemed no closer to finding the clan leader.

I sunk into a chair in the corner of a tavern that Jamil had selected. Though this far south was even warmer than Moesia, the tavern owner kept a low fire burning. Jamil saw me settled on cushions before leaving in search of another past Getaen connection. I grew too warm near the flames but was too tired to move my saddle-sore body. Muscles hurt that I hadn't even realized existed.

Over the past week, I'd begun processing my shock from the battlefield. I'd killed Reflections before. Both Tatiana and Yasmine had eventually died from injuries I'd inflicted. But I'd never seen so much immediate death. At least Mama's death had been due to natural causes, however grim. I struggled to comprehend the horrors of battle.

Jamil had advised that we keep my identity quiet. To any casual observer, it appeared as if I traveled with only Jamil. I missed Tulia's bright friendship even more sharply because neither my advisers nor my Own spoke with me in public.

Jamil had said we'd have more luck with a Getaen-only contingency. I had a sinking feeling that I was the reason that Jamil hadn't been successful in connecting with the elusive clan leader — I wasn't full Getaen.

Ziba, Pari, and Rubia huddled together in quiet conversation two tables away. My Own, Thadeus, stood by the fire, watching the few people coming and going, only an arm's length away from me at all times.

"Anything else, m'lady?" the barkeep asked, clearing my bowl. She'd seemed wary of me at first, but when I spoke Getaen, she seemed to let down her guard a bit. "Perhaps another barley roll?"

"Yes, please." They were exactly how Mama had made them.

Pari and Ziba laughed at something Rubia said, drawing the barkeeper's attention.

The barkeep smiled. "Nice to see sisters getting along so well."

"Sisters?"

Pari wasn't much older than me, but Rubia was older than my mother. Ziba was nearly old enough to be my grandmother. Though Rubia's petite size always made her appear younger at a glance, and the firelight's glow softened Ziba's features.

"I'll see about your barley roll, m'lady." She took my bowl and disappeared. I wondered what she would say about her visitors if she knew they served the empress. Perhaps Jamil's caution about my identity was for their safety as much as mine.

The front door swung open, banging on the wall as a Dacian entered. Even my advisers looked up from their conversation. He looked familiar, but from where, I couldn't remember. He inquired with the barkeep about something. If he requested a room, I knew none were available. He frowned, sparking my memory of him: the Weaver Emissary.

Ziba called out, getting his attention. He let out a sigh of relief and scurried to their table. The barkeep scowled at my advisers but continued with her work. After the barkeep brought me a roll, Ziba stood and moved to the fire, stopping near me.

"Some of the emissaries," Ziba whispered and held out her hands to the dying embers, "took the opportunity to come to the Red Valley and evaluate the Getaen resources, shore up contacts, and do some trading before the battles get worse."

Before Ziba could specify *which* emissaries, the front door eased open. I held my breath.

It was Jamil.

I should have been relieved it wasn't Marcus, but I could only muster a weak smile as he sat down in front of me. Ziba stood near Thadeus by the mantle, both pretending not to listen.

"I secured us an invitation to see the clan leader." The lines around Jamil's eyes were strained, though his news was what we'd been hoping for. "It will be me, you, Ziba, Pari, and Rubia. We leave tomorrow morning before dawn."

"Perfect." I eased back into my chair.

"What about the emissaries?" Ziba whispered, her back to the barkeep.

"The Weaver Emissary has been blundering around, asking for invitations." Jamil gave an almost imperceptible jerk toward where the weaver sat, mopping his brow. "He's been quite the spectacle. The Getaens are unlikely to help us as it is — bringing dead weight will only make it more difficult."

"I'll break it to him gently," Ziba said. "I hear he didn't come alone. Would you like me to inform both emissaries?"

Jamil paused, and his finger twitched. "The Agricultural Emissary has been much smarter about his inquiries. At least he attempts to comply with the Getaen ways of doing things."

I took a slow breath in, trying not to look, or worse *feel*, ruffled by the fact that Marcus was in the Red Valley territory.

"I hate for them to waste a trip, especially if we can assist them," I said.

Jamil's jaw clenched, and I could only guess at his thoughts.

"They're here to prepare for war," I reminded him. "That's a safe assumption. The weaver, as clumsy as he is, probably needs more wool for socks and undergarments. And the Agricultural Emissary is likely looking for additional food resources."

Jamil's nostrils flared. Whatever he thought of my plan, he did care about those in the military. He leaned forward, his voice a whisper so low I doubted even Ziba could hear.

"The Red Valley Clan is protected from outsiders. They'll never find it without the clan leader's permission."

"A city cannot hide. One of the emissaries will eventually find it."

Jamil's brows drew closer together. "Not even Cassus VI found it. He had skirmishes with the clan but never discovered the city center. Never even *saw* it."

"Can't I invite the emissaries to join us?" I asked.

"An empress does as she pleases. But consider how it will be received. This is already dangerous. Even more so for outsiders."

Jamil had not wanted us to come to the Red Valley, but he'd complied with my request. "What aren't you telling me?"

Jamil put his head in his hands, not responding. I'd about given up hope of him divulging anything when he finally signaled for Ziba and Thadeus to leave us alone. Jamil switched to speaking in Norte, a language we were more proficient with than most citizens.

"Are you positive you want to take this risk?" Jamil asked.

"You make it sound like we're going to meet Zalmoxis himself," I said.

"Chances are that not all of us will return."

"Then let everyone make their choice. For me, I'm going."

IN THE PRE-DAWN GLOOM, before the messenger from the Red Valley clan arrived at the tavern, Jamil requested a meeting with the emissaries to explain the dangers. I'd purposely not attended. Even so, Ziba rapped on my door soon after they started and handed me a glass. Then she watched down the hall to make sure I wasn't caught spying. With my ear to the glass, I could hear the three men.

"How dangerous?" an unfamiliar man's voice sounded. I guessed that was the weaver.

"Assume you're headed into hostile enemy territory." Jamil's voice was flat.

"All I want to do is help Dacians survive this coming crisis," Marcus said. "It's worth the risk for me if I can help feed even one more soldier and save a life. I'm in."

I pulled the glass away from the door. Even hearing Marcus' voice made me short of breath. I shook my head and marched back to my room, repeating to myself that I esteemed none of my emissaries over the others.

When the messenger arrived, Jamil was able to procure the permission for the two emissaries to join us. Any others who arrived after we left would be redirected back to Capidava by Thadeus, who would remain behind. As Jamil had predicted, no other guards, other than himself, would be allowed. Fortunately, he was the Thorn I trusted most.

With my black steel dagger hidden and my short sword sheathed where anyone could see, seven of us followed the Getaen messenger: Jamil, myself, Rubia, Ziba, and Pari, followed by Marcus and the weaver emissary.

We rode for over an hour, seeing nothing but the expanse of mustard-colored sand. I repeated Norte phrases under my breath to keep my mind from drifting to Marcus riding four horses back. Our tall, fair-haired messenger gave few instructions. His sharp jaw was pronounced as he ground his teeth. His discomfort only caused me to be more curious about where he lived. I'd assumed the clan leader lived in a city, but so far, every clan had been essentially a village — the inn and tavern being the largest structures.

We passed through the soft sand and dropped into a canyon of hard sandstone striated with bands of white, yellow, and rust-red. Past mid-morning, we rose out of the shaded canyon and returned to soft sand and the sun's pounding rays. Waves of heat shimmered in the distance. Sweat beaded down my back.

I squinted. Ahead was what appeared to be a smooth, shimmering spot, but it was too far away to know what it was. A strange oasis? Over the next hour, the area seemed to rise from the sand. Was it my over-heated imagination? Jamil didn't seem to notice anything amiss though his back and shoulders were tense. Behind me, Rubia was leaning forward in her saddle, her attention on the same area.

My horse started to sink in the sand. Jamil whistled, and I realized my Own was following exactly behind the messenger. I'd let my gelding veer to the right. We trudged through sand until she put down a hoof and *thunked* against solid ground. She stepped up and cautiously followed Jamil. I was again grateful that Jamil had matched me with a calm horse. As long as I followed directly behind Jamil, my gelding stood on solid ground. If she wandered a hoof to the right or the left, she sunk. Fortunately, she learned quickly. From Ziba's cursing behind us, I assumed her horse was a little more stubborn.

The unseen path curved as we grew closer, and we could gaze on the dome growing up out of the ground. No matter how far we traveled, the dome never seemed to get closer, yet it grew steadily larger. I swished the last of the liquid around in the bottom of my waterskin, determined to save the last swallow.

"Zalmoxis. That dome is large enough to cover the entire Moesian hill," Rubia said behind me.

I spoke to her over my shoulder, "You're surprised, too?"

"It's beyond anything I've ever heard of. Ever imagined."

As we descended an embankment toward the mountainous dome, I relented and drank the last of my water. Below, red earth broke into fissures, the land cleaved apart by unknown, ancient undulating rivers that likely once flowed from the Dacian River to the sea. The iridescent covering sat like a bubble of water in the midst of the crags though what was inside I couldn't see.

As we drew closer, a gate became visible. We stopped the horses though the messenger scowled at our delay. Ziba and Pari shook out the fine, summer cloak they'd brought me and secured the *crown of lore* on my head. I was not pinned, primped, and polished to Tulia's standards, but we had few options in the middle of the desert.

Next to the towering dome, I felt as small as an ant. Through the semi-transparent walls over the city, swaths of colors were visible: browns and grays, but also vibrant reds, oranges, and purples. The dome itself had a blue sheen that pulsed with magic so thick that it burned the back of my throat. I clutched my sword at my hip, reassured by its presence.

Although, if I used a weapon here for any reason, it would be the end of any Dacian-Getaen alliance — the sole purpose of my coming and the only hope of our winning the war.

The messenger quickly guided us through the gate. The spicy smells of home greeted me long before I saw the city proper. Jamil smoothly followed the messenger, but Rubia and I practically reared our horses, gasping. Pari's jaw dropped, her eyes wide, and Ziba looked delighted.

"Zalmoxis bury me alive," the weaver exclaimed behind us.

"Spectacular," Marcus said.

Jamil paused several paces ahead of us. "Empress, please ride at my side. The rest of you, stop gawking."

I forced what I hoped was a composed, regal air; I took my

place next to Jamil. But I couldn't help but stare at the strange sights. The houses were made of adobe, not so different from those in Moesia, but were stacked on top of each other and painted bright colors. I tried to count the dwellings. They varied from five to eight homes stacked vertically, but it was hard to tell with the irregular window placements. White dresses and camasas, vibrant aprons, and bedding dried on lines strung above us, casting purple, red, and orange shadows.

The baked, red-clay streets bustled with freckled, round-cheeked children with all shades of light ash blond to dark rust-colored hair. The men's clothing was similar to what I'd grown up seeing, including the wide belts. But the light, billowing materials were a looser cut. The women wore dresses that hit at the calf, showing their sandaled feet with half-fotas instead of double-aprons. Two women were laughing, their backs to us. As we passed, they stopped mid-discussion, choking on their words as they craned to see me on the other side of my Own. They pointed at my crown, but I couldn't hear what they said. Jamil's frown deepened.

"We must be quite a sight — I'm guessing not many Dacians are invited here," I observed.

"Forgive me, Empress, for not telling you more. I made an oath long before I met you." Jamil gave a baleful apology. "Perhaps I was wrong, but I felt it would be worse for both of us in the end if I broke it."

I pitied Jamil's conflicted feelings, but part of me was disquieted. If Jamil had kept the existence of this massive city and its strange magic a secret, what else was he not telling me?

The maze-like streets wound organically, passing brightly colored awnings that marked the entrances to a variety of shops. Children giggled and ran past us, flowers tucked into the girls' braided hair.

We arrived at a tall, cream-colored adobe structure. Jamil helped me dismount, and servants took our horses. The messenger led the way, but Jamil seemed comfortable as if he'd been here before, his dusty boots thumping against the terracotta tiles. At the top of an intricately-carved, winding stone staircase, we found ourselves in a room as large as the throne room. However, instead of a wall of glass, it was open to the outside, a wide balcony overlooking a green inner courtyard.

The messenger led us away from the balcony to the opposite wall with several high windows. Nearby, sage incense burned; I assumed it had a bit of Healer magic infused, to sharpen the mind. Several formidable pelts from wild animals covered the floor and soft, colorful cushions were arranged in a circle.

On the far side of the circle, an ample-sized man sat on a massive, bright red cushion. His belt disappeared under his round belly, and his neck was hidden beneath three chins. His blond hair was thinning, but his blue eyes were sharp, probing me for weakness.

I fought the urge to hide behind Jamil. Instead, I stared back at him, willing him to look away.

He didn't.

"Empress Nicoleta Aurelian, daughter of Leila of the Sea Mist clan, has requested an audience." The messenger turned from the man on the cushion to me. "Please be introduced to Cyrus Thushtra, leader of the Red Valley Clan. Ruler, protector, and speaker of the allied clans of the southern Getaen Sea."

The messenger stepped back, and Cyrus gestured for me to sit on one of the other large cushions furthest from the incense.

As Jamil introduced the rest of our party, the clan leader gave only Rubia a slight tip of his head in respect. The others he didn't acknowledge. When Ziba dared utter her gratitude for receiving an invitation and dipped in a gracious curtsy, Cyrus narrowed his eyes, scrutinizing her. Then, unlike Dacian conventions, Cyrus gestured for Jamil to sit across from me. Whether or not the clan leader was indicating my Own's comments were equal to mine, I could only guess.

"To what do I owe the pleasure of your visit?" the clan leader spoke to me, his lip curling.

Pushing aside his distaste, I sat up and spoke my prepared words. "As you have undoubtedly heard, the Norte have their sights on Dacia."

"What does it matter who holds my leash?" Cyrus said, almost lazily.

Jamil's face was as stone, his gaze on my forehead.

Thanks for the help, Jamil.

"The Norte and the Theracians will fight over Dacia like two d-dogs with one b-bone. Your lands are in the middle. What do you think will happen during the i-inevitable war?"

"Or perhaps you'll defeat the Norte. The Dacians have long been our protectors," Cyrus said in a mocking tone.

We would lose to the Norte without magic. "No one knows the future."

The wrinkles around Cyrus' eyes deepened as he seemed to probe my meaning, but the expression quickly washed away. "No future is certain, that is true. I had hoped for a happy future for my daughter, Essa."

I flinched. The emperors before me had treated Cyrus' daughter poorly.

Cyrus continued, "I already paid the price to stop one war. Would you have me sacrifice another child to stop this one?"

"Essa was fiercely loyal to the emperor. And she was g-good to her friends." I felt Pari and Ziba at my back. "The p-plague was too much for her."

"She was treated like a servant," he spat. "At best." Cassus VII had taken Essa as a mistress but never as a wife.

Pari's voice squeaked from behind me. "She was a lady of the court, buried as a proper consort to the emperor."

The clan leader turned to Jamil. "If you bring traitors into my home, please do me the courtesy of telling them not to speak. Every syllable defiles my ears."

Jamil swallowed. My fingernails dug into my palms. Without Cyrus' support, his people would never rally to our side. But how could I work with this man? And could he work with people he despised?

Before I could speak, a woman burst into the room. She wore a simple dress, and her unbound hair swept across her face. How could she even see? Her bare feet slapped across the floor. A sun-spotted woman rushed into the room after her. Jamil jumped to intercept the woman as she barreled toward us.

"She is her," she shouted, pointing at me over Jamil's shoulder. "The one who bites from the sky."

"Jamil, careful. Do not harm her," Cyrus warned, pushing himself to his feet with a grunt.

The woman's nails clawed at the air between us. I shrunk away from the wild creature just as Marcus moved to my side, his hand on his dagger.

"Count to ten, Essy." Cyrus held out his hand to the younger woman.

She gripped his forearm with one hand, her fingers digging into his flesh. Cyrus tenderly brushed the hair out of her eyes. The young woman's gaze darted around the room. She locked eyes with me — piercing blue eyes. She pushed away from Cyrus, lunging for me again. But before she could reach me, Jamil caught her up in his arms.

The older woman huffed, holding her side as she leaned against the clan leader. She shook her head, sadness and defeat in her reddening eyes.

The younger woman reached over Jamil's shoulder, swiping at the air, trying to reach me. I sat, dumbfounded.

Cyrus looked pained as he murmured to the older woman. "She's getting worse."

I was stabbed. Pain ripped through me like flames.

My sisters' screams woke me from my dream. The cool, stone walls surrounding me disappeared, and my warm, bright room appeared.

My clothing clung to me as if I'd jumped into the sea. I clutched my side, moaning. I lifted my hands away, expecting to see blood. But there was nothing. It was another dream.

My crying sisters' brought the scorpion caretaker. My three sisters were clinging to one another, and the scorpion gave them a sympathetic look. She glared at me and told me I was an abomination. She dragged me to our bathing pool in the center of our room. She didn't even wait for scented oils or salts to be brought. She just demanded I wash away my sweat and tears.

The scorpion caretaker moved me into my own room. I feel so alone.

— ESME

FOURTEEN

EAVESDROPPING

"What do you make of the clan leader," Ziba asked me as she tapped my arms, performing my evening Protections.

I peeked through slitted eyelids, surprised at the interruption of her meditative work. "He's plenty angry with the crown."

"What did you expect?" Ziba ran two fingers across my forehead.

"I don't know what I expected, but I'd hoped for an open conversation. The Getaens are in danger, too. But he's too prideful and upset to listen."

"As empress, it is *you* who needs to listen," Ziba said. "What does it hurt you to let him share his pain with you? The fact that he was honest is a good sign. He wants to trust you even if he doesn't realize it."

I recoiled at her words. She was right; I had come wanting the clan leader to understand our plight. But I hadn't been ready to listen. If I wanted him to see me as a partner — a partner he needed — I had to approach him differently.

Wearing my ornate crown would only serve to remind him of the Dacian throne that he deplored. I would need to leave it secured in my room in the future. Though the strange woman who'd interrupted our meeting frightened me somewhat, I was grateful to her. She'd given me a chance to come up with a new strategy before Cyrus considered the matter of war to be closed.

"Who do you think the two women were?" I asked. "The leader seemed very close to the older woman who came in. Is she Cyrus' wife? She didn't seem very... "

"Very what?" Ziba asked, a bite to her voice. "Courtly? Haughty? You of all people should know these characteristics do not make a good leader."

I took a slow breath in and then out. Ziba was right — I had assumed the older woman was too unrefined to be a clan leader's wife. But I didn't know the Red Valley nor the politics here, and I certainly didn't know Cyrus' family.

"If she was his wife," Ziba continued, "who was the girl?"

"His daughter," Jamil's voice sounded.

My eyes popped open. Jamil stood a few steps away near the open archway to my room.

"You should be more careful about your gossip," Jamil said. "The halls echo."

"I was finishing anyway." Ziba slid a pillow under my head. Often, I dozed off while she worked, but not tonight.

I grabbed Ziba's hand before she could leave. "Thank you. I appreciate your advice and the work you do. I know coming here couldn't have been easy."

Ziba put her other hand over mine, soft and warm. "I appreciate your saying so. But do not worry about me." Her voice deepened, and her hand squeezed mine a little too tight. "I have looked forward to a meeting like this since I was your age. The moment I saw you, I dared hope you could be the one to truly unite us. To heal the rifts that spider out from the crown. I will do anything within my power to see you succeed in that endeavor."

Ziba released me, promising to return at sunrise before she left. Seeing how she and Pari had been treated by every Getaen outside the castle, I had nothing but sympathy for her plight.

Jamil pulled my Sonus stone from my things and sat next to me. I pressed my fingers to the orb, feeling the magic pulse.

"The clan leader's wife is Yutab Behar," Jamil said, shifting the orb so the weight was balanced between us. "I doubt he intended to ever allow you to meet her. Cyrus is protective of his family. If bards include Yutab in their ballads, even if Cyrus *suspects* the subject is his wife, he never requests it played, and soon those songs lose favor."

I raised my brow at Cyrus' strange behavior.

"Don't be quick to judge people you do not know, even if it's not the kind of relationship you would choose," Jamil continued. "Cyrus and Yutab dote on each other. She appreciates their family privacy, especially when it comes to their daughter."

"Essa?"

"Yes, Essa, but primarily the daughter you saw today. Her story is Cyrus and Yutab's to share, but she's two years younger than Essa, and it appears her health has deteriorated," Jamil said. "As far as Essa, most people here don't care much for her or Dacian politics. Between the nearby bustling port and the city itself, the Red Valley people are occupied with their own lives. Why would they travel to Dacian cities where they'd be scorned? Few have given much thought for the daughter who joined the Rose Court."

"Do the citizens here know that Essa was essentially Cassus' mistress?"

"She was a lady of the royal court." Jamil frowned. "That's what the people know. Anything else would only be rumors that would quickly be replaced with other more interesting things like festivals, puppet shows, or candies."

My Own seemed to mock his people, but were Dacians so different? I chewed the inside of my cheek, still trying to understand this place.

"You were right," I admitted, griping the orb tighter. "The Red Valley isn't what I expected. Without the plague, could Moesia have remained this vibrant?"

"The plague struck Getaen cities and villages with equal force as it did Dacian ones. Instead of plundering like Cassus did, my people worked together."

"You knew this but did nothing to stop Cassus? You were an Emperor's *Own*. If anyone could do something, it would have been you." I tried not to be outraged with Jamil, but for a moment, the choking darkness of the hole under Papa's study floor came back to me. It wasn't Jamil's fault I had been forced to hide there, listening to soldiers ransack our home and beat my father, waiting and hoping they would leave without setting our home on fire. But the rage and terror bubbled up within, demanding an outlet. I clenched my fists and pushed those memories aside as I had learned to do with so many other hurts. An empress didn't have time for self-pity.

Jamil shook his head. "A Getaen Thorn, influencing a Cara-calla? Now who is being foolish." He gave a hint of a smile to take away the sting of his words. "Even when you and Irena convinced me that Cassus needed to be removed from the throne, I expected to die in the attempt."

"Then what were you doing there all that time, next to the emperor, if not to sway him to help Getaens?"

Jamil opened his mouth and then clamped it shut. He released the orb so quickly, I nearly dropped it.

"Get some rest, Empress." Jamil marched to the open doorway, slowing as he passed to inspect Rubia's small tray of herb teas. Next to the doorway, Jamil pointed to a brass-like button embedded into the wall.

"Press this when I leave. Only you will be able to come and go. No one else. Between this and the guards at the entrance to the sleeping quarters, you'll be safe."

He stepped into the hall and gestured to the doorway. "I'm waiting, Empress."

I was unnerved by his sudden departure but hurried and pressed the brass button. The space between us shimmered as if a wall of magical glass had just appeared, morphing Jamil into indistinct black shadows with a pale face, capped with a blur of strawberry blond.

There was another brass button below the first.

"If you need me, I'll be in the next r—" Jamil was cut off when I brushed the second brass button and I heard a slight click inside the adobe wall as if something had shifted.

I brushed the second brass knob again.

"—for Ziba in the morning," Jamil finished.

"So, the magic in the walls — it's Protection and Sonus?"

"I don't know the magic here as well as you might think," he said. "But, yes, that's likely."

He fell silent, and I wondered if he knew my mind was whirling. Magic was brilliantly woven into the walls of this home. Combinations of magic we hadn't even begun to explore seemed commonplace here. The Red Valley clan had kept magical capabilities to themselves. *Jamil* had kept them secret.

"Good night, Jamil," I said, not keeping the irritation from my voice.

Jamil pivoted and marched away. I curled my hand into a fist and punched the brass knob again, silencing my room. I skulked across the room to the balcony, overlooking the vast courtyard.

Jasmine and something more pungent I didn't recognize wafted up from the expansive gardens. I was on the third floor of the complex with two more levels above me. A barrier wall on either side blocked the view of the adjacent balconies. The household wrapped around the square, courtyard garden, and balconies on the right were visible. One of the balconies was much wider than the rest, and I guessed it was where we'd met with the clan leader earlier. The rooms on the left and across the courtyard were only two stories, lending to an awe-inspiring view of multi-level homes in the distance, blue Luminary lights in the windows.

Under different circumstances, I would have loved to explore every nook and cranny of this place. Papa would salivate when I told him about it. But between my frustration with Jamil and

Cyrus and the deaths I'd seen on the battlefield, it felt wrong to allow myself to feel joy or try to satisfy my personal curiosity.

Not wanting to even hear Jamil on the balcony next to me, I stomped into my room and pressed a brass piece near the balcony. Sure enough, another Protective wall shimmered into place. I tapped the brass button below it, guessing it silenced the room.

Wanting to fall asleep quickly, I grabbed a sleeping draught but found only a partial packet. Wanting to leave Pari and Rubia in peace, I dumped the remaining herbs into a mug of still-warm water left by the servants and made myself comfortable on the pallet of furs on the floor. Though I dreaded my frequent nightmares, sleep overtook me.

Some part of me knew I was dreaming, but still my heart thrummed. Mama fought in a battle but with only her bare hands. I could barely move. A snow leopard growled, but from where? I couldn't get to Mama. My sword was slippery in my hand. Desperate, I threw my blade, but I was shrinking. A snow leopard bound forward, striking me, sending a shock through me. The imagined blow knocked me awake.

I shot up in the dark, the back of my camisole wet against my skin. Panting, I rolled to my knees, fumbling for my short sword. My shallow breathing only caused me more dizziness, but my hand knocked against the pommel. I clutched the Canina Thorn to my chest and squeezed my eyes shut. Picturing endless desert, I calmed my breathing.

With my sword tight against my body, I moved to the side of the pallet, wanting fresh air. Without thinking, I walked right through the Protective barrier — the thrumming energy awakening my senses like I'd been slapped. The sky was lightening in the west, but the sun wouldn't rise for hours.

A blue glow spilled over Jamil's balcony, pulling my attention.

If he was already awake, we might as well get to work. Before I could return to my room, Jamil spoke.

"I wish I could explain it better." My Own's voice held depths of emotion, compassion. "Help you make sense of it."

I paused, wondering if he'd heard me and if this was an awkward apology over the wall.

"But Essa's arm was amputated. She was rid of the disease," Cyrus' voice rumbled. "I don't understand how the plague killed her."

I blinked, surprised the clan leader was awake and with Jamil at this hour.

"Her will to live died along with Cassus. Whether you believe it or not, she loved him."

I stepped back, not wanting to overhear their painful, private conversation.

"She sent word of your loyalty to her," Cyrus said. "Your father was proud of you until the day he died. We knew it must have been hard, torn between your loyalty to your clan and the throne, though Cassus was a witless and selfish man, so perhaps that made it easier."

Who did Cyrus think Jamil was devoted to? I swallowed, my mouth dry, wondering who would Jamil protect now if he had to choose: Cyrus or me?

"You and Essa were like an island to each other, the only ones that knew of this place. I always admired your wife's courage to agree to have her memory altered in order to stay with you." There was a pause before Cyrus continued. "I'm sorry she died in the plague. In the end, the curse took both your wife and my daughter."

I leaned against the far partial wall and forced a deep breath. *Altered memories?*

"Essa mentioned Irena ended up a Protector like her mama," Cyrus said.

"Yes."

"Why do I sense you're hiding something about your daughter from me?" Cyrus asked.

"Why do I suddenly regret giving you information on everyone who arrived with me?" Jamil asked.

"Except precious little about your empress."

"You would lose your faith in my loyalty otherwise."

"Jamil, don't try and distract me with a moral abyss. Tell me what you're hiding about your daughter. Quickly, now. I'm tired."

I clutched my sword tighter against my body. Essa was a Sensitive. It made sense her papa was as well. I'd have to be even more thoughtful with my words.

Jamil finally broke the silence. "Irena has a thriving business. I had hoped she would be content with her shop in Capidava. But she has something different in mind. She's asked for permission to serve Lady Katalin, a noble of the Rose Court." Jamil paused. "Lady Katalin is also serving in the empress' stead while Nicoleta is away."

"Of course, you will not allow it." Cyrus sounded agitated.

"On the contrary, I followed your example and allowed my daughter to make her own choice."

I winced at the rebuke. Surely the clan leader wouldn't appreciate harsh words from someone so far beneath him.

"I trusted Essa. Too much," Cyrus said, his voice hard. "She was wrong."

If Cyrus was a Sensitive like Essa, no wonder Jamil hadn't revealed any secrets to me. Cyrus would have quickly figured out that Jamil had betrayed his trust. And Jamil wouldn't be in a position to sway the clan leader in any direction, including joining us in the war.

At least I hoped that was Jamil's plan. Either way, I couldn't imagine my Own intentionally putting me in danger.

"Essa did find happiness," Jamil said. "And though she wanted and deserved more, the emperor didn't keep his relationship with Essa a secret. In his own way, I think he tried to express whatever love he was capable of to her."

Someone shifted, bits of sand crunching underfoot. Then Jamil continued, "Essa missed her home terribly, but she never regretted saving people's lives. Nicoleta is so much like Essa in that regard. They both care deeply about others. In fact, Essa helped Nicoleta in a way that only she could — by showing the Rose Court that a

Getaen could be one of them. It enabled Nicoleta to take a path that was already partially trodden.

"The Dacian empress isn't one of us."

"She was raised by two capable clanswomen. She is Getaen enough."

They fell quiet, and I realized I was trembling.

"I hope you're right," Cyrus said.

I tip-toed to the doorway, holding my breath.

"I kept my oath to you," Jamil said. "I revealed nothing of this place outside these walls. If I've earned your trust, tell me what else is bothering you. I don't have to be a Sensitive to know something is wrong."

Cyrus heaved a sigh. "I'm tired, Jamil."

"There will always be some excuse."

"All right, all right," Cyrus grumbled. "The dome is weakening."

I shook my head, sure I'd misheard.

"The Protections? They've stood for a thousand years," Jamil said.

"It's the truth, Jamil. They could last another fifty years, but I fear they won't last through the end of this war. Without them, we'll be visible. Vulnerable. We've kept ourselves hidden for so long. But without them, even the safe, narrow trail in the sand will vanish. More concerning than the travel from the west is the eastern side of the city. We'll be exposed. In generations past, no one predicted the Protections would be in danger, and the port has grown dangerously close to our walls. What once was a two-day ride is now mere hours. Travelers will undoubtedly discover it. We'll become a target."

"What can I do to help?"

"There's nothing you can do. Our best Protectors are working on it, but the artifact is disintegrating. It has been since I was a boy."

"My father mentioned the dome before, but I know little of it. A gift from the original Norte who settled here, yes? It's a wonder it's lasted this long."

"The timing of this war couldn't be worse. We could be caught on all sides. If we don't find another artifact to power it, we're doomed."

Movement on the lower level of the complex caught my attention. A servant was walking along the open hallway on the second floor, her back to me. The home was beginning to stir. I staggered back into my room, sweating.

The shield around the city was failing. And the clan leader was looking for another artifact to fix it. I clutched my sword in my trembling hands. The Canina Thorn was created by a warlock, with gifts of mythological proportion. But it was only two hundred years old. Surely, the Red Valley had something ancient and more powerful in this magical city.

But from the sound of the clan leader's voice, they didn't. And if I were in his place, I'd do whatever was necessary to restore the dome.

My dreams hold me for longer periods. I constantly fight them.

Papa is gone to meet with Cassus VI to try and negotiate peace. He took my older brothers and sister along with him. My eldest brother will likely become the clan leader, and Essa will be his adviser. Essa is said to be the strongest Sensitive in generations, and she is already included in many of Papa's meetings.

If I could control my Seer powers, I would be useful to the clan. I could advise my brother like Essa. Perhaps people will be less afraid of me if can show that I'm helpful.

—— ESME

FIFTEEN

WHAT THE SEER SEES

I quickly washed up and grabbed a comb, intending to find Rubia. If anyone could help me sort out what I'd just overheard from Jamil and Cyrus, it was her. Outside my room, the clan leader's wife waited.

"Good morning, we have not been officially introduced. I am Yutab Behar, Cyrus' wife." Her white hair was again pulled back in a tight, practical braid, and she wore a simple dress with a half-fota wrap apron. "I was hoping to speak with you. Alone."

Her gaze flicked to Jamil's door before she noticed the comb in my hand. "You must be looking for someone to braid your hair. Who? I'll take you."

"Rubia Bythesea, but it can wait."

"No, no. I will take you there." She smiled. "Rubia is the only Getaen guest here to *not* work at the castle."

I tensed at her implied insult toward Pari and Ziba, not to mention me. I spoke up as I accompanied her down the hallway. "Rubia always despised those who worked at the castle, too." Yutab nodded in approval, but I continued, "Until she got to know them."

Yutab's face hardened, and she stared straight ahead. We

walked through the halls in uncomfortable silence until she blurted. "Where is my grandson?"

I started at her words. "Excuse me?"

"Essa's son, Cas. What happened to him? Did he die with her?"

"I-I d-don't know."

She shook her head, her eyes widening. "He died? Or is he lost?"

"No, not —" I checked over my shoulder and pulled out the Sonus stone that I'd brought for my conversation with Rubia. I held it out to her. She touched the stone, pulling quickly back when it pulsed. Then, either her curiosity or desperation must have gotten the better of her because she pressed her fingers to the stone again.

"Essa's son was in danger." I gave her a hard look, willing her to understand so I wouldn't have go into horrifying details of his abduction. "I hid him away and had everyone's minds erased, including Jamil's. I only have a fragment of memory from that time. But he is protected."

"Don't tell me, then. I don't want to be a weak link in his safety." She clutched her free hand to her chest. "Knowing that he's cared for... it brings me such relief. Not knowing is the hardest." She took a moment, gathering her emotions. "You mustn't speak of the child here. No one knows of him, not even my husband. Essa wanted it that way, for Cas' sake."

I pitied the grandmama before me. "I considered bringing him to you —"

"No, you did the right thing. He would have had a very hard life here." Yutab paused, pressing her fingers harder against the Sonus stone as she stared straight ahead. "Cassus VII never claimed his child, not publicly. I know because I kept waiting for the announcement to arrive. It never did. But our people would have rejected him, too. The moment Cas appeared here, his Caracalla blood would have... "

Yutab's voice trailed off, but Jamil had already explained that

Essa's son would have been rejected at home. I kept that memory though Jamil hadn't.

Yutab continued, "Anyone with a grudge against the Caracallas might decide to take out their frustrations on the emperors' innocent, young descendant."

I had hidden Essa's son to avoid him becoming a piece in someone else's game. Still, I hadn't expected to get any reassurance that I'd done the right thing. Though I'd trusted Jamil, to hear his grandmama's viewpoint was still a relief.

"Do you think he is happy?" Yutab asked.

"I placed him in the very best place I could. I cared for him, too."

She blinked back tears and released her grip on the stone before checking over her shoulder again and continuing down the wide hall.

As soon as I was back in Capidava, I'd have Cas' name repurged from my memory, but that was a simple task. More heartbreaking was that Yutab did not petition to have her daughter's only child brought to the Red Valley; she *knew* a Caracalla would face incredible challenges in this clan.

Bringing the Getaens to the aid of the throne would be even harder than I thought. Perhaps Jamil was right all along — this was a futile trip.

Yutab stopped at a doorway. "This is Rubia's room." She glanced over her shoulder before quickly whispering, "I cannot tell you how grateful I am for your insights. I will sleep much better at night."

A servant approached and Yutab made small talk about the dinner menu until we were alone again.

"I will leave you now," Yutab said. "Any more time together could draw suspicion. No need for anyone to be curious about what we're discussing."

Especially not your husband, someone who will definitely *know if his wife is lying or hiding something.*

Yutab curtsied. I stared as she strode away, frozen with shock.

Her curtsy was the first deference I'd been paid by anyone since arriving.

I turned to face Rubia's semi-translucent wall. Curious, I pressed my hand against the Protective magic but was unable to penetrate the barrier. I took the dagger from my boot, intending to slam it into the wall like I would to a practice dummy. Fortunately, I decided to be less aggressive. The dagger ricocheted off the magic and clattered to the floor, leaving me with an aching wrist.

Rubia bounded to the door, and the magic fell away. I barely had time to retrieve my dagger before she pulled me into her room with a gleeful smile. She sat me down and began combing my hair as she gushed about everything on the estate. I rubbed my wrist, half-listening, no longer in the mood to discuss what I'd overheard between Jamil and Cyrus, nor could I say anything about the conversation I'd just had with his wife.

Besides, Rubia left her door open just like she often did back in Moesia. Soon, Pari wandered in with her comb. She plopped down in front of me, and I braided her hair though my wrist complained. Bantering back and forth, Pari giggled when Rubia pointed out she was using a Getaen word incorrectly.

When the breakfast bell rang, a servant guided us back to where we'd met the clan leader initially and seated us all on cushions around a low table. Before the meal began, Yutab introduced us to her three youngest daughters; the one who had tried to attack me was noticeably absent.

With Cyrus seated across from me, I was able to study him throughout the meal. He stifled several yawns as he pushed food around his plate. Did the clan leader have the same guile I'd seen in Essa when we first met? Or did his underlying anger indicate an erratic ball of hurt? With my options narrowing, I analyzed him with the little time we had.

Yutab sat next to her husband, but she was attentive, asking about my family, my interests, and Rupea castle. She spoke noticeably little about herself. Further down the table, one of her daughters sat next to Marcus, asking him one question after another.

Marcus' Getaen wasn't terrible, but she laughed and helped him with some of the pronunciation. Marcus caught my gaze, and I quickly jerked my attention back to my plate.

When Yutab slipped away to speak with a servant, Cyrus must have felt some pressure to attempt conversation.

"Jamil tells me your papa is a scholar," the clan leader said. "A student of Getaen culture. Would you be interested in visiting one of our Historians this afternoon?"

I tried not to smile, but I was sure my face brightened. "That would be lovely."

Papa had wanted to travel to the clans for this very purpose. He wouldn't want me to squander the opportunity. If any insights on the Norte magic were recorded in Getaen histories, this might be our best chance to find them.

The servant tapped Cyrus on the shoulder. Looking over at Yutab, Cyrus quickly joined his wife. The two of them looked calm as they turned their backs to us in a hushed conversation. Jamil's eyes darkened, but no one else seemed to pay Cyrus and Yutab any mind, still chatting over breakfast.

The Weaver Emissary, seated on the other side of Jamil, spoke up. "May the emissaries visit the port tomorrow?"

"Excellent idea," I said. It wouldn't hurt to have Marcus at a distance.

"They'll need special permission from the clan leader." Jamil was curt. "Otherwise there will be... complications."

"We don't need permission to explore *inside* the dome," Ziba said. "I plan to explore the city."

"That's not a good idea," Jamil warned.

"It's not like I have a traitor brand on my forehead," Ziba snapped. "For once I'd like to wander among my own people. To be a *normal* Getaen."

"You could never be normal." Pari grinned, her freckles crinkling.

"Pish." Ziba swatted at her. "I'll be back this afternoon. I need more supplies for the empress, anyway."

Yutab paced away from her husband as she bit her nail. Only her profile was visible, but her face was pale.

Something was wrong.

Cyrus gave Jamil a solemn nod from across the room, beckoning him.

Jamil stood and walked over, and I followed without invitation. The corner of Cyrus' lips frowned for a moment as I joined them.

"I've just received word of Theracians along our southern border. According to my spies, they are amassing an army."

AFTER THE NEWS of the gathering Theracians, Cyrus claimed he needed time to consider the situation. But from his red eyes, I suspected what he needed was a nap. Yutab kindly cleared the courtyard gardens, giving me a place to think.

I paced along the paths, thinking. The Theracians couldn't have physically mobilized so quickly. At most, the Illyrians could be gathering as they were on our southwest border, but they'd need an infrastructure to support the troops. They couldn't possibly be ready to fight. Still, I was anxious to discuss this scout's revelation further, and sway Cyrus to join us.

We returned for lunch but hours before Getaens typically ate. My guess was that Cyrus woke up hungry, and the household bent to his whims. Showing my annoyance with his lack of consideration for everyone else would only make negotiations more difficult; I stayed silent. Even so, with the news of the Theracians, the conversation was stilted and forced. At least Cyrus had made arrangements for us to see the Historian, as he'd promised.

With Ziba still exploring the city, only Pari, Marcus, Cyrus, and I followed Jamil through the courtyard to another part of the estate. Ornate murals covered the walls. Even the ceiling featured detailed scenes of Zalmoxis torturing the dead.

Pleasant.

This wasn't the ideal setting for negotiations, but neither of us had time to waste. My emissaries could stay for weeks if necessary, but I hoped Cyrus would send troops south. I needed to return to the war at the Curat in the north. For every quick, idyllic moment here, there could be long, drawn-out terror in the mountains.

Part of me wanted to demand the clan leader's fealty and bring his people to arms within the hour and be done with it. More and more after becoming empress, I felt myself slipping into stubborn impatience. But the Getaens were not fully under the thumb of the crown, and furthermore, brute insistence had never been my way. I had to be cautious or else I'd end up in a futile battle with my own people.

I signaled to Marcus and Pari to slow, and I kept pace next to the clan leader, Jamil two steps ahead of us. I could feel Marcus tracking my every movement, but I didn't look back. If I did, I'd lose my focus.

"I want the Red Valley clan to be safe," I said to Cyrus. "My mama's clan was once a sworn ally. To protect you is in my blood."

"You want to save your own skin," Cyrus said.

"If I wanted to save myself, I wouldn't have crawled into the jaws of the wolves in the Rose Court in a wild attempt to end the p-plague."

Cyrus shot me a look of near-respect.

I pressed forward, ignoring my discomfort at having Marcus and Pari witness my unpolished negotiations. "I could try to sway you by pointing out that your clan has clearly not been paying the agreed ten percent tax to the crown. And that your traders grow fat and wealthy off of a monopolized port, marking up prices for intermediary traders and buyers in Patridava."

"We defend our ports and land, not the crown. Therefore, we pay plenty in taxes."

"The Dacian crown p-pays to maintain the road. The P-patridavan governor employs Thorns to keep travelers safe. I'm not threatening to increase taxes but asking you to recognize that a significant p-portion of your p-people's wealth is possible thanks to your fellow Dacians."

"We earn our way by the sweat of our brow, no thanks to the throne." The clan leader quickened his pace. "Buy your soldiers and save your kingdom. I will not risk mine."

I stayed right next to him, defiantly. But my stubbornness wouldn't change his mind. I had to rip away both our bandages, exposing our wounds to stinging truth.

"Our t-treasury is as low as the magical P-Protections around this city."

Cyrus stopped short. "What? Where did you hear that falsehood?"

"You don't want to believe it, but we need each other." I spoke truthfully. If I lied, Cyrus would sense it.

"Who told you about our walls?" Cyrus grew more agitated and looked to Jamil. "You?"

"I did not speak a word of it to her," Jamil said, his face a mask.

"I'm able to sense magic," I said. "I feel it in the sword at my hip and in other objects, too. Anyone can learn to do it. But few do."

I hadn't sensed the Protections failing — in fact, I was in awe of the radiating power. I couldn't imagine the strength the dome originally emanated. Still, my statement was technically true.

I'd merely overheard everything I'd revealed. Confirmed truths. Cyrus was surprised, but his body language hadn't changed — he wasn't convinced he should join us. At this point, I had to scramble and hope my guesses about the magic were correct. Perhaps I could find a foothold, even impress Cyrus enough to convince him that I was a leader worth listening to.

"The ancient Protector who cast the original spell over this city was impressive," I spoke slowly, attempting to control my stutter. "I assume the Protection has layers of spells, including magic that enables travelers to traverse a narrow path on *top* of the sand. Plus," I paused for effect. "A d-deterrent spell?"

How else would travelers not regularly stumble upon this city?

Cyrus tilted his head as if re-evaluating me. Thank goodness I'd overheard Jamil's conversation or I'd never have known about the Protections failing.

I straightened — realizing Jamil had acted strangely. He wasn't careless, yet he'd held a private, important conversation where I could overhear every word. It took all my resolve not to look at my Own in that moment. Jamil knew I often awoke with nightmares. He had the opportunity to take half my sleeping draught, knowing I would likely wake. Had he been listening for me on my balcony, waiting? Did he *want* me to know the clan leader's secrets without actually telling me?

If I could have hugged Jamil, I would have, but I wouldn't break eye contact with Cyrus. Rubia had always hoped there was a negotiator deep inside me, a skill prized among Getaens — I was amidst one of the most important Getaen negotiations of my life.

"When your city is discovered, it'll be ravaged." I dug into the clan leader's worst fears. "You should hope for the Theracian hordes because the Norte magic is more powerful than you can imagine."

Cyrus brushed off my comment. "The Norte and Getaen magic are born from the same waters."

I waited for him to explain his naïve statement. He didn't.

"He hasn't heard," Jamil said.

A flash of confusion crossed the clan leader's face.

"The Norte Mirrors can split themselves so that one body can make two, three, or even a dozen. I call them 'Reflections.' Their army can go from ten people to fifty." I snapped my fingers. "And you won't even realize that there are fifty more b-behind you until there's a dagger in your back."

"Myths," Cyrus said, but lacked conviction.

"The empress speaks the truth. I've seen it for myself," Marcus moved to my side, speaking in Getaen. "The Norte can make the air brighter than the noonday sun, blinding your army."

"They can poison with a mere touch," Pari added.

"They can cause nightmarish visions, too." Jamil's tone soothed as if he were approaching a trapped animal.

Cyrus looked at each of us and then at Jamil. "May I? I have to be sure."

Jamil presented his wrist, and Cyrus pressed his fingers against my Own's skin.

"Everything we've said about the Norte is true," Jamil said, before going into great detail about what we'd personally seen and experienced. My Own paused at the end of his explanation, and his voice lowered. "Their magic is dangerous, and their greed includes your lands."

"Your stories are unbelievable." Cyrus dropped his hand and took a deep breath. "But I believe you."

"So, you'll join us?" I asked.

Cyrus fell quiet. He didn't pace. He didn't fidget. The lack of movement was more disconcerting than if he'd shouted. He glanced up at Jamil and then closed his eyes for another moment before speaking.

"I will defend two areas — the ports and the southern border."

"We will need an army in the south," I agreed. "However, Theracians don't have magic. We need Getaen magic at the Curat against the Norte."

"I hesitate to send magi so far from home. Without them, our army will be spread too thin."

"I will send a half battalion south to help defend the border with your non-magical portion of the army," I said. "Then you can divert those with magic to the north. You know that's where they're needed."

The clan leader folded his arms, taking a step away from me.

"What if Lazica sent aid?" Marcus interjected.

Cyrus laughed, dark and joyless. He responded in perfect Dacian. "Lazica is too busy making coin on everyone else's wars. Their little pocket of earth surrounded by jagged, ore-filled mountains affords them many luxuries, including a large mercenary army."

"What if some Lazicans worry that the Theracian Emperor has eyes for their luxuries?" Marcus asked.

"I'd say they'd finally come to their senses." Cyrus threw up his hands. "But they believe themselves untouchable. So any promise of aid from a lone Lazican or their judges is given by a fool. And only twice the fool would believe them."

"I agree, clan leader," I interjected. The Lazican council already conveyed their disinterest in joining us. "Lazica loves profit, only. And they're blind to the fact that their wealth makes them a target."

Marcus stared past me, his fingers on his chin, deep in thought.

"Unfortunately, by the time our far eastern neighbor recognizes their foolishness, it will be too late for us," I prepared to dig deeper into Cyrus' fears. "All clan leaders and their families are in grave danger. Our conquerors will devour you, your family, and your closest allies."

Just as the Blood Conqueror did when he originally conquered the Getae.

Cyrus was still, but I could see in his eyes: I'd struck a nerve.

"Fight for Dacia, because you rise or fall with us," I said. "Send your magi north, with me."

Cyrus furrowed his brow and tucked his thumb into his wide belt, wrapping his fingers along the side as he leaned back and appraised me.

"I will consider it." The clan leader spoke in a serious tone. He spared another glance at Jamil. "As a show of good faith, I offer you a trade."

Jamil shifted his weight, never a good sign.

"Jamil tells me you need an adviser?" Cyrus asked.

"Yes." I braced for his counter negotiation.

"I offer to send with you one of my own advisers. And in exchange, I request that you leave one of your people here with me."

A hostage exchange? I hadn't come all this way to gain a spy in my court and leave one of my advisers or emissaries behind.

"That is too generous of you," I said.

"It's an agreement I insist on. It's a traditional show of trust. I would appreciate it if Jamil returned home, to the Red Valley."

It was as if the earth opened and I was endlessly falling. My knees felt weak. A warm hand pressed against my back, steadying me. Marcus had slid closer, just behind me.

Cyrus continued, "His daughter, Irena, would be welcome to join him as well."

Jamil's hands formed fists at his side. That was all I needed — Jamil would not be staying.

I spoke slowly, fighting to keep calm. "Clan leader, while I appreciate —"

"I can stay behind," Pari stepped forward. "Essa was a good friend, and it would be my honor to reside in the city she loved so dearly. Besides, I'm a decade older than Essa was when she left home, so I'm that much more prepared. If you'll accept me, I would be pleased to stay."

My stomach churned. Getaens who had served the crown were an insult to Cyrus. Even if the clan leader accepted her, I wouldn't allow my tender-hearted Healer to be exposed to such derision.

"But surely Jamil of the Red Valley would be the more logical choice?" Cyrus spoke more to Jamil than anyone.

With Jamil's original promise to watch over Essa completed, of course the clan leader would want to provide a way for his citizen to return home. I respected that.

"I'll leave it up to Jamil." I trusted my Own to navigate this storm. He knew Cyrus and the Getaen traditions, and he knew Pari even better than I did.

"Clan leader," Jamil said, "I am honored, and I hope I am still welcome after I train a replacement as the head of the Empress' Own after the war. This is not the time for me to abandon the crown."

"I understand," Cyrus said though he looked disappointed. "After what you have quietly done for Essa, you and the empress are always welcome to return."

The clan leader looked down at Pari as if looking at a rodent.

"She is the finest Healer outside of the clans," Jamil said. "She is honorable. She was loyal to Essa to the end. And she will be a trustworthy addition to your household."

The clan leader gave me a curt nod. "She will suffice."

Zalmoxis, I can't leave Pari behind to suffer this treatment.

Cyrus spun on his heel and led us down the hall. "Now, let us visit the Historian of Norte migration. If anyone knows Norte magic, it's her."

THE HISTORIAN RECLINED on plump cushions, her back crooked and stooped. Thin strands of hair were pulled back into a braid under a gauzy veil. While Yutab and her daughters put nothing on their faces, the Historian's cheeks were dusted pink and her thin lips tinted. She kept her eyes closed as servants attended her, barely acknowledging us as Cyrus spoke.

"Our tradition is to select Historians at a young age, based on their memory and a knack for learning. We have few written records."

The Historian seemed unruffled when the clan leader requested her to recite the history of the ancient Protectors. She shared lore of how the dome connected to the earth's core. When the mages' secrets were still known, the city had expanded, twice the area beyond the original borders.

"Two hundred years after the creation of the dome, magi pushed the boundaries, perhaps beyond the artifact's capabilities," Cyrus muttered. "Perhaps the Protection would have lasted longer had they not." He tapped his fingers against the hilt of his dagger, but his gaze dropped to my short sword.

"So, a Protector and Bonder combined magic?" Pari tapped her chin. "Isn't that what the lore means when the shield around the city was *connected* to the earth? We've been experimenting with combining simple magic, and usually a Bonder is employed to, um, Bond the elements or magic together."

Cyrus and the Historian looked at each other. Then, the elder woman sent all but one servant away with a wave of her hand. "There are tales of long-ago events that might have resulted from *combinations* of magic."

"We have done layers of magic like what you've seen in the doors," Cyrus said. "But *combining* magic in the way you're describing is slightly different. You've employed Bonders in an interesting fashion; I'd like to hear more."

Pari animatedly shared insights from my adviser's recent experiments. The Historian interrupted my Healer several times with questions.

"Perhaps this trade will work to our advantage," Cyrus tucked his thumbs into his belt, again. "Zalmoxis must be distracted to allow such luck. We could learn from you... what was your name?

"Pari," she said.

"You believe the Bonders tapped the power from the earth's core, not the Protectors," Cyrus clarified. "And they bound it to the Protector's power."

"It's possible Protectors *and* Bonders created the dome," Pari said. "Yes."

"Pari, would you work with my magi? Share with them what you've learned?" Cyrus asked.

"I would be delighted." Pari beamed.

My heart pricked, seeing her genuine interest. She wanted to stay?

Pari was another friend slipping like water through my fingers. Though she had been divided between her loyalty to her Getaen friends and the crown, she'd never betrayed me. In fact, she'd saved my life after I'd been poisoned and again during the Battle of the Rose Court. Though she was always gracious, I knew she'd been sent to work at Rupea Castle as a child and was judged for a decision that wasn't hers. But she wasn't bitter.

"Why is the Norte magic so different from Getaen, then?" Jamil asked.

The Historian's hand shook as she unclipped a large key. "Norte myths and origins are recorded. We Historians don't hold them in our mouths because the information was written."

The servant left with the key, returning shortly with a bundle wrapped in threadbare, light blue silk. The servant placed the bundle on a low table. The Historian leaned forward and unwrapped three clay tablets. She invited Cyrus and me to sit down. Up closer, I noticed indentations on the tablets — Norte script. The language of magic.

The Historian adjusted the records so they were side by side — three of them. The servant held a magnifying glass in front of the text, moving it slowly as the elderly woman translated.

"Magic is born in the north. The cold protected the first Norte, granting them life by infusing their souls with magic. Magic is as much a part of them as the breath in their lungs. The cold kept its children close, to hone and harden them. Its children became like shards of ice. Over time, a new kind of magic emerged. A strange, unwelcome anomaly. After many generations, more children were born with this lesser magic." The Historian adjusted the large magnifier. "According to this lore, the cold rejected those children, resulting in the diseased magic. This magic was not held within but oozed out. Those unable to wield magic for themselves are weak."

Oozing? How does magic ooze? Flow?

"The bottom of this tablet is a record by those with the diseased magic." The Historian cleared her throat. "We don't hold magic inside like our brothers and sisters. We cowered in fear for generations, believing we were less than our brothers and sisters. Only when we realized that our strength was in the giving did we dare rise up and leave."

The Historian pushed aside the first tablet, and Cyrus spoke up. "This tells us very little about how their magic works."

"It does say Norte magic comes from within," I said. "The Illuminator, B-Borsea, she didn't p-project the light with her hands. She, *herself,* lit the air. The light emanated from her body."

Cyrus's brows scrunched together.

"It's hard to explain," I said.

"Per these records, Getaen magic was born from the same waters as the Norte but developed differently," Pari said.

"Like ice or steam. Different, but both are forms of water." Cyrus tapped two fingers against the palm of his other hand.

"We know what some forms of the Norte magic can do," I said. "But this helps us fill in the gaps. For example, based on this information, my guess is that Norte Protectors can strengthen themselves."

"But not others?" Cyrus mused. "What of Sensitives?"

"Lord Jovian spoke of the Norte grabbing his wrist while asking him questions," I said. "Just like you did with Jamil. The noble didn't speak, yet the Norte got their answers. I think they can read minds."

Cyrus shook his head. For the first time since we'd arrived, he looked worried. "What are the limits? Can they pull things from your mind that even you don't recall? Memories from your childhood? All of these magical abilities, they must have boundaries. If we know them, we can use that to our advantage."

"We have no idea what Bonders can do. Nor Seers." The latter magic could unravel our best plans.

"My wife has studied Seers in great depth. Any line of text or oral history, she knows it." Cyrus looked to the Historian. "You've recited to her everything on the Norte Seers, I imagine."

"Many times over the years," the elderly woman confirmed. "Based on what we know and what you've just told me, Norte magic is more potent. But, that could be of benefit in this instance."

"How so?" I asked. Having a *more* powerful Seer couldn't possibly be good.

Cyrus walked across the room, his back to us as he stared at a woven tapestry on the wall. The Historian ignored him and continued. "From the history, we interpret that the Norte Seers struggled with insanity, almost from birth. There's no record of a cure. If that's the case, even if their Seers do See visions of the future, they would be unable to communicate them."

The possibility flooded me with relief. I smiled at Jamil, but he was looking past me, to the pensive clan leader.

The Historian ran a bony finger down the second plate. "Most of this plate relates to their splitting into groups, hoping to find their own land or assimilate with other peoples. Here, in the Red Valley, they were welcomed into a vast population. They fought in skirmishes alongside them, intermarried, and created the dome long before the Blood Conqueror."

"That's unhelpful," Cyrus muttered. "What of the last plate?"

"This was written about sixty years later by a child who escaped with the original Norte." The Historian drew herself up before reciting the words. "Away from the source of the magic, I do not know if our magic will weaken. Even if it does, it will have been worth it. The stories of the bitter north are a nightmare compared to the warm, plentiful river lands. Plus, the newly-created Protection around this city will allow our children to grow fat on fish, melons, nuts, and olives instead of scraping meals from scraggly vegetation. However, I write this warning for my children: Care for the Protections in the way you've been taught. For the day that they fail, nothing will stand between you and the Norte. When they come, they will come with all the vengeance of their bitter forefathers who didn't obliterate us when they had the chance."

Even with the Historian's tremulous voice, the words condemned the clan's actions. Their ancestors had warned of the Norte, warned of securing the Protections. I sensed Cyrus' attention on me. With a hungry glint, he eyed the hilt of my sword.

The Red Valley needed an ancient artifact; Cyrus knew the lore surrounding the Canina Thorn. I set my hand on the pommel and leaned away.

Pounding feet sounded outside the door. Cyrus reached toward me. Before I could jump up, someone barreled through the entrance, a blur of white clothing and red hair.

"No, Papa! No! I've seen where that path leads!" It was the same woman again. This time, her hair was pulled into proper braids. Her shin connected with the low table, knocking it over and the tablets with it.

"My darling Essy, be calm." Cyrus caught her in his arms as the servant stood protectively in front of the Historian.

Jamil waved for me to get behind him. Marcus brushed my shoulder, his hand already on his dagger.

"Total destruction. *Death to all.*" The woman repeated the words over and over as Cyrus held her. "Don't touch the sword. No sword. Don't touch, Papa. Don't."

"Of course not, my darling." Cyrus stroked his daughter's hair. "I would never dream of such a thing."

He looked at me, our eyes locking for a moment before he jerked his gaze down, his hands trembling as he tried to calm his daughter. No matter what he said, for at least a heartbeat, Cyrus had considered taking my sword by force. Even if I hadn't seen the greediness in his eyes or the desperation in every line of his body, I would've suspected his intentions.

Because if I saw no other choice for saving my people, I would have done the same thing. But I wouldn't have hesitated.

Mama returned, thank the stars. She is prepared to try out new Protection techniques she'd learned in the river lands. I'm sure she knows from her servants that I'm 'awake' fewer and fewer hours of the day, but neither of us mentioned it.

I am excited to tell her about some of my dreams, knowing she'll be able to help me contain them. I'm especially interested in a warrior I keep Seeing. Papa has said that not many women serve in the Dacian military, so she must be Getaen. She wears a crown, a curved short sword at her side, and sometimes her eyes flash like gold in battle. She's called the Golden Protector, but I call her the Golden Warrior.

— ESME

SIXTEEN

STARLIT GARDEN

Gripping my upper arm, Jamil rushed me to my room, depositing me with instructions not to open my door for anyone until he returned. Part of me was unsettled that an older, far more experienced leader would panic and attempt to steal my sword right off my body. Would he try again? Should I attempt to escape the city? I had some compassion for his instinct, but I would not relinquish our greatest weapon so the clan leader could hide his city away, leaving the rest of the kingdom to rot.

Unexpected footsteps sounded from the balcony. I spun and pulled my sword from the sheath at the same time, facing the intruder.

"Nikka?" Rubia scowled, folding one of my maramas. "Put that thing away before you hurt someone."

I jogged to the balcony and ran my fingers over the brass knobs, protecting us both. Under my indignation, I was afraid. Outside this room, I was in danger. Unless Cyrus came to his senses, he could strip me of my sword. Would I bring my armies to force him to return it? I couldn't. Not with the Norte attacking. But without my sword *nor* the Getaens, all the strategy in Cornara wouldn't change the inevitable: death for me, my family, and all the nobles, and subjection for the commoners.

"Why are you on edge?" Rubia turned serious. "What happened in your meeting?"

"It was fine." An obvious lie. "Jamil just enjoys randomly dumping me in my room with instructions not to leave."

Rubia leveled her gaze at me and punched her hands against her hips, causing the scarf to slap against her thigh. I muttered an excuse about the heat making me short-tempered. For a moment I thought she'd pry, but Rubia let it go and told me about her exploration of the clan leader's home.

It was no surprise that she'd used her charms and made friends with several of the servants. Rubia plopped down on my bed next to a tray of food as she talked about the grand tour the servants had given her. Rubia picked through the nuts, picking out her favorites.

"There are seven — *seven* — intricate sculptures so beautiful that each would make you cry. They line the corridor to the private wing," Rubia gushed. "One for each of the clan leader's children. The detail is so fine; I'd swear unknown magic was employed, but the servant told me the Red Valley artisans are the best in Cornara."

"Of course you would wrangle a tour of the private wing."

"Only the main corridor. Not up the stairs. But that only made me more curious to see it."

Given time, I'm sure you'll figure out a way.

"Wait." I raised an eyebrow. "Was this servant who showed you around a hopeful, male admirer? Though Rubia was older than Papa, she always had more than a few men trying to garner her attention.

"Oh, a message arrived," Rubia picked up a blue disk from behind the fruit. "From your prince, I assume."

Don't think I didn't notice you changed the subject, I thought as Rubia handed over the disk.

I hadn't heard from Asander since I'd left the Curat camp. I settled myself next to parchment and pen, ready to take notes. Then I snapped the glass and heard Asander's voice.

Nicoleta,

It was eerily quiet for five days after you left. Our soldiers had just grown comfortable enough to dare to sleep when the Norte struck again. Our enemies are true experts in mental warfare. Our troops were valiant, and with help from the Luminary scarves you diverted to us, we were able to avoid the blinding light. I think our Norte Illuminator friend was frustrated. She quickly pulsed a darkness, and then a light. It was effective in blinding a portion of our army, but not all. Fortunately, her move caught some of her own people off guard, too. Our most recent adaption seemed to send them into a quicker retreat than usual.
But any joy we might have felt at beating back the Norte was cut short when we heard blood curdling cries from the mountains. They sounded like women screaming. But some of us know that sound: mountain cats. Only what we heard today was much, much louder. I will be honest; the cries shook me to my core. Dyana told me of the creature you saw. Still, we don't know exactly what the Norte have in store for us. No one is sleeping.
With any luck, Petre will return soon with my bird. Like your dire wolf, my wings bring me great comfort.

"Very romantic, that one," Rubia said. "Not even 'respectfully yours' at the end. Honestly, Nikka."

"He's tempered as he knows you or Jamil were likely to hear it," I said in his defense. I was even more certain Asander's offer of faithfulness was a rash response due to his Clarifier-induced mental-state. He'd been painfully honest about his expectations of our relationship. However, if Rubia knew the prince had injured my heart in the slightest, she might take it upon herself to slowly poison him.

"Oh, I should tell you what else I learned." Rubia quit picking through the food and sat up. "Did you know that our minds will be wiped when we leave this place? It's standard practice. No wonder no one remembers this domed city. The only exceptions are for people who were born here and are merely visiting the port city. Something in the doorways recognizes its people. Of course, I'm bitterly disappointed. I must find a way to secretly write about this city. I want to remember everything."

"I should have guessed at the layer of Clarifier magic." I bit the inside of my sore cheek. Cyrus could steal my sword and send me out the door, and all I'd know was that my sword went missing. I'd have no idea how or by whom.

"The rumor is that we'll remember some of the people, even some conversations, but the city itself will be a blur," Rubia said.

I flopped down on the furs and stared at the ceiling while Rubia ate the fruit. Marcus had followed Jamil and me to my rooms. I suspected he was still nearby, and I was tempted to look for him.

I could use his strategic mind right now. I'd done a decent job of keeping my emotions at bay around Marcus since we'd arrived in the Red Valley. It helped if I treated him like the sun and didn't look at him directly.

Rubia forced me to take a bite of melon, but it soured and made my already upset stomach twist. I'd felt on the verge of some small illness since Patridava, and all the worry was making it worse.

Finally, Jamil returned, and I lifted the Protection for him.

"The clan leader requests your audience," Jamil said.

Rubia frowned. "Do you think it's safe? The servants might help us escape."

"Escape to what?" I asked, though the thought of running had crossed my mind. "Without the Red Valley clan, we're doomed."

"Empress, I suggest you seal the room behind us," Jamil said. "The Protection will keep Rubia safe. Only the clan leader could walk through the closed doorway."

"That tells me a lot about your expectation of this meeting." Rubia folded her arms.

"It's just so Nicoleta doesn't worry about you. We need her focused."

Rubia scowled and turned her back on Jamil. I squeezed her arm before leaving her locked away.

Jamil guided me up two more flights of stairs, to the top of the structure. The clan leader was sitting on a cushion with Yutab next to him. She leaned forward, her body taut, as she seemed to counsel him. His face was pale, and he shifted on his cushion when he saw me, barely able to make eye contact.

My advisers, Pari and Ziba were already waiting, standing a few steps away from Cyrus. Yutab stood, giving me a sympathetic look.

It chilled me.

The clan leader cleared his throat and invited me to sit. I could either die today or die in moons when the Norte overran us. It didn't really matter which. I sat, staring straight into Cyrus' face.

"Empress, I am willing to do anything to save my people even if it means taking something important from you." Cyrus was blunt. "But it comes to my attention that your sword may be of better use to my people on the battlefield. That is what our Seer claims, anyway."

"Seer?" I choked on the word.

"Suffering teaches us who we are." The clan leader ignored my question. "I must heed the Seer. Pulling apart visions is difficult. So many possibilities. But occasionally, many roads lead to the same destination. Often that destination is generations in the future. Or the past. Rarely is it in our time. But it seems —" Cyrus ran his hand across his throat and visibly gulped. "Y-your decisions have thrust you into a prism point. You are the prism, the directional outcomes are all influenced through you. With you, we all live or die."

His words should have shocked me, but I was just relieved not to be robbed. If the clan leader was finally, completely convinced of his need to align with me, this was my chance to push forward, unveiling my next step.

"You must know that Dacia needs more than the Red Valley clan. I plan to go to the High Sands and the Roe Deer clan as well."

I knew if I had the Red Valley clan in the fight, the others were more likely to follow. Though they didn't get along well with each other, they would beat back anyone who threatened the other.

"The clans won't listen to you," Cyrus said without emotion.

"I will beg them to consider what happened last time they didn't work together and the Blood Conqueror brought them all under Dacian rule. History will repeat itself. This time the Norte and Theracians will fight over our lands like dogs over scraps from the high table."

"As we are going to war together, we can write a request together," Cyrus suggested.

I hid my smile. His offer was even better than I'd hoped for. But, then again, Cyrus had already vacillated from considering helping me, to requesting a hostage trade, to impulsively contemplating stealing from me. Though he hadn't gone through with any of those ideas, he'd been tempted. I needed to know his conviction was true.

"I didn't think Seers existed." Though I'd learned Norte Seers existed, I'd never met nor heard of a Getaen equivalent. Not even Marianna had turned out to be a true Seer.

"There are several Seers in the Red Valley alone. I'm sure there are more elsewhere." Cyrus' attention seemed to fade to someplace else. "At first, a parent might think it's merely a fanciful, childhood imagination. But then, one day, the child will dream of something real. Something they couldn't have known."

Pari and Ziba leaned forward, apparently as intrigued as I was.

"Then, they'll start daydreaming," Cyrus said. "Or that's what the parents assume is happening. But then one day, they cannot wake the child from the daydream. The child could be screaming, their limbs flailing, and all a parent can do is keep them from hurting themselves or others until it passes."

Cyrus' nose reddened, his voice cracking. "And that's when you can no longer deny it. That one day soon, your child will be lost to you forever, lost to dreams they can no longer decipher. A long stream of intense haunting visions forever."

"I-I am sorry," I said, sympathetic to Cyrus' family's struggles.

"That is why Yutab attends to her," Ziba asked softly. "As a Protector, she tries to shield your daughter's mind."

Cyrus nodded. "But our daughter's power is too strong. We're forced to resort to other measures. I hope that Yutab and Pari can come up with something between them, something with a Bonder that can come up with something to help her. Anything to keep her with us a bit longer."

"I offer my assistance as well." Ziba stepped forward.

Cyrus raised a brow. "Because you are a Protector?"

Ziba bit her lip, nodding. "I have been a Protector for longer than Pari has been alive."

Cyrus leaned back and flicked his fingers as if flinging dirty water away from him, and Ziba stepped back. He was about to say something that I assumed was a stinging retort to my Protector, but fortunately, he was interrupted by two servants. They were guiding Cyrus' daughter who shuffled across the room. Cyrus reached up, and she practically fell into his arms, resting her head against his shoulder.

"This is Esme, my daughter and Seer," Cyrus said. "Essy, do you know this young woman with the gold circlet on her head?" Cyrus asked her.

She stared at me, a bit of drool on her lips, and nodded.

"What do you See?" Yutab asked. She took her daughter's hand, and the young woman snapped her attention to her mama.

"Mama? I'm sorry," Esme said. "I keep drifting."

Yutab blinked back tears. "You are doing wonderfully, Essy. Just focus on Nicoleta's face."

She opened her mouth and a sickly gasp erupted from her lips. She jerked her head to look at me again. My insides folded in on each other in a squishy crunch as her words struck.

"A throne. A Dacian Emperor. He is slain and turns to ash.

"A throne. A golden woman. She is a warrior. She loves the people.

"A throne. An Empress with a black countenance. She smells of death and envy. She wields the day and the night. At her feet, bodies are heaped upon the earth. She rules all the kingdoms. She chews them in her mouth like glass.

"A throne. An Emperor rules. He holds many flags. He battles the cloud people all his days.

"A throne. An Empress rules. She has no magic, but she is clever. There is a time of peace. Our only chance."

I took a step back, not understanding.

"Papa, the clans fall." Tears well in the Seer's eyes. "The one who wields the day and night, she steps on every clan, crushing them with bloodstained boots." She jerked against her mother's embrace. "Screams rise from where she treads."

Esme's muscles relaxed and her head lolled back, but she snapped back to attention, her face contorted. I knew that feeling — straining to focus. To speak.

"You are the golden woman," Esme spoke to me, as if each word pained her. "Your destiny is set."

Cyrus' nostril's flared. He moved as if to whisk his daughter away, but Yutab shot him a warning look and he stilled.

The Seer licked her lips. "Golden one watches a slaughter. Cries over dead bones and lilacs laid at the feet of the throne. She tears a hole in the sky. Crashing of metal." The Seer touched her chest, her hand in the shape of a claw.

I mimic her action, one I recognize, clutching my orb in my palm.

"Your destiny always remains the same," the Seer said. "You die."

～

"WHAT HAPPENED?" Rubia asked when Jamil escorted me back to my room.

229

"Good news," I said, deciding to share only the best part and omit the worst. "The Red Valley clan will join us in battle."

Jamil rarely corrected me, but the way he looked from me to Rubia, I knew he was about to tell her what the Seer had predicted.

"Jamil, if you'll excuse us, I would like some time with my mother, alone."

I didn't want him upsetting Rubia over nothing. Even if Yutab's daughter was a Seer, from what I'd gathered, she'd only Seen verifiable visions of the past. In her relatively short lifetime, her family hadn't actually confirmed that any of her predictions of the future had ever come to fruition. Furthermore, to say that *all* paths led to my death was complete nonsense. I, of all people, knew magic was open to interpretation.

Jamil gave me a *look*, right before he left. One that said we would be discussing this further.

Rubia seemed to sense my unease and distracted me with stories of the bustling city. She called for dinner to be served in my room and then unbraided my hair while she hummed a Getaen lullaby.

For moons, she'd been surprised each time she saw my hair had been cut just past my shoulders. However, for the last several weeks, she'd consistently remembered the change. I celebrated each milestone, no matter how small. Between her humming, the incense she selected, and her gentle combing of my hair, she calmed my nerves enough that I could finally eat.

It was far too early for sleep, but my eyelids grew heavy. As I drifted, I was overcome with how much I still needed Rubia. I'd always need my mama.

When I awoke, the room was dark. Rubia was on a pallet of blankets on the far wall. I tried to go back to sleep but couldn't. I thrummed my fingers against my thin blanket and considered the most productive middle-of-the-night tasks I could accomplish.

I tip-toed across the room and picked up a Ghoster disk and dropped a strand of Asander's blond hair into the liquid. Not wanting to wake Rubia, I slipped out onto the starlit balcony to create a response to the prince.

Asander,

I received your message. I hope you are fully recovered and that your bird has arrived. Here, things are going as well. We hope to leave within the week.
I have a request I was not able to make in person before we left due to your ailment.

I considered saying, "due to your half-dazed stupor from the Clarifier magic," but I didn't.

I would like you to vet possible candidates for a special unit to work with me. I want people who have a natural ability and confidence in using the magic that you and I have experimented with. I will evaluate your suggested selections when I return.
Also, I have just the thing for the gifts from your father.

I set the disk down, not giving a salutation at the end. The prince would know my voice. Or I hoped he would, anyway. Even without specifics, Asander should know exactly what I needed: soldiers who were willing and able to use Sonus magic. I could practically envision my units' spears flying at deadly speeds, more potent with Auripoan black metal tips from King Coatys. I grinned at the thought.

Back in my room, I slipped the blue disk into a pouch. Out in the hall, there were no guards or servants. It was strange not to have my Own with me at every moment, protecting me.

The Seer's words whispered in my mind. I shook off the ill-fated warning and hurried toward the main courtyard, intending to cut across to the servant quarter's entrance. A house like this never fully slept. With any luck, someone could deliver this message to my Own in the nearby town.

As I neared the gardens, I heard footfalls coming up the hallway behind me. I told myself it was just an early riser, but I put my hand on my hilt as I turned, not wanting any surprises. It was Marcus, still too far away to speak to without shouting.

I slowed as I walked through the courtyard, wondering if he would hurry to catch up. Near the servant's quarters, I waited for Marcus to reappear. The sky was lightening, but the crescent moon still hung as if on a string of glittering stars, casting enough light to reveal anyone approaching on the main path. But through the lush garden, the only person who approached was a servant.

I handed off the message with my instructions and headed back to my room. Stomping across the pebbled path, I chastised myself for looking for my emissary like a forlorn schoolgirl.

I have a normal, professional relationship with the agricultural emissary. Completely normal. *Marcus is an old* friend.

On one of the side paths, I again spotted Marcus. He wasn't looking at anything in particular. It was as if he were waiting. I slowed, hesitating.

Marcus squared to face me, and I stopped short, rooted in place. He drew closer, and the smell of simple lye soap sent my treacherous heart fluttering.

"Want to talk about it?" Marcus asked.

About how seeing you makes me sweat and stutter?

"After the Seer's prediction, I came to see you last night," Marcus said, searching my face. "Jamil said Rubia was tending to you. You were in capable hands, but still, I couldn't sleep. And I couldn't wait for morning — I took a walk to clear my head. How are you feeling?"

"You're kind to worry, but I'm not bothered by her words."

"From what I've heard, Seer magic is notoriously unreliable. Still... " Marcus cupped my elbow in his palm and the feel of him, even through my sleeve, warmed me. "It was unnerving."

"I can't think about it," I said, trying not to remember how the Seer seemed to look *inside* my head. "Otherwise, I will be anxious. And I can't afford any d-distractions."

Including you. I pulled my arm away from Marcus but couldn't bring myself to walk away.

A blue Luminary light appeared on the second floor of the estate. The household was awakening. In the relative darkness of the garden, we wouldn't be immediately noticeable, but we didn't have long before the dawn would banish the shadows.

"I do have a question for you, though," I said. "B-back at the Curat, I went onto the field to warn the Auripoans about Borsea. I would have d-died that day, but someone threw an ivory hilted d-dagger into my would-be killer. Most nobles have ridiculously ornate, impractical weapons. There's only one d-dagger I've seen that is not only functional but boasts a carved, ivory handle."

I tore my gaze away from Marcus, looking at where his camasa hit the hollow of his neck. I could barely force my next word, both dreading and longing for an answer. "Why?"

Why do you keep risking your life for me?

"I will always be your steadfast support," Marcus said.

I bit my lip, not risking meeting Marcus' eyes, afraid of what I would do, of what I would invite. My stomach twisted. I couldn't care for Marcus in a romantic way. I shouldn't.

"When I saw you headed for the battle, how could I not follow?" Marcus took a small step closer. "You were incredible, like liquid lightning on the field."

With every word, the garden felt like it was tilting. I swallowed, desperate for even ground.

"And the Lazican wax for my tent? You must have thought to send that moons ago, well before even I knew I'd be at the b-battlefront."

"I'm loyal to you as the empress but also as a friend." Marcus grinned. "Anyone who knows you would know you'd be in the thick of things."

Another light appeared on the second floor. It wouldn't be long until most of the household was awake. Our chance to talk alone was slipping away much faster than I wanted.

"We haven't discussed what happened in Lazica." I'd received the letter from their council and heard about the merchant from Liviana but nothing directly from Marcus.

"That's another reason I couldn't sleep last night. The conversation about hostages is one I've had before. My family has long been considering an exchange with a merchant family in Lazica. I hesitated to agree because the arrangement would also entangle my family." Marcus paused as if he was struggling with something.

I reached out, but before I could touch him, Marcus sucked in a breath.

"It's critical that we gain Lazican support, isn't it." A flash of pain crossed Marcus' face.

"With their support, I think the other clans will be easier to sway."

Marcus gave me a slow nod. "I'll do what I must to bring them to your aid."

Something in his words pierced straight to my heart. The lightening sky revealed Marcus' messy hair, the circles under his eyes, the curve of his lips. And the emotion in his face made me struggle to breathe. We stared at each other, neither speaking — once we stepped out of the garden, the moment between us would be gone forever.

Several more lights appeared, but instead of going our separate ways, Marcus closed the distance between us. He tucked my hair behind my ears, the movement so tender it caused all sorts of emotions to explode from the carefully protected boxes inside me. His fingertips lingered on my neck, sending a thousand shocks down my spine. The moment made me braver. Or insane.

I leaned forward, drawn into him. He bent closer, kissing me lightly on the cheek. I closed my eyes, soaking in the feel of his lips as they brushed my skin. He ran his knuckles down my neck, hooking his finger around the leather string near my collar bone before he stood taller.

"You're a brilliant woman, Nicoleta. Wherever you lead, I will follow. Where ever you send me, I will go."

I couldn't speak. I could barely stand.

Noises sounded above, shattering the shared moment. Footsteps crunched on the main path. Though it wasn't improper for me to be with my emissary, Marcus was still standing close enough for me to feel the heat from his body.

I should have released Marcus with a flick of my wrist, but I found myself entranced. I'd been navigating our relationship well for days. But one small slip sent me tumbling into an abyss. I couldn't afford to fall any further.

I forced a deep breath and stepped back just before a servant strode past, busy with the waking dawn. Then, I spun around and followed behind her though every part of me screamed to stay.

Essa waited and waited to speak with me. I could feel her, even hear her.

But I couldn't reach her.

Thankfully, she was patient, and I was able to concentrate long enough to return. She told me the war with the Dacians was over, and she was going to live at Rupea Castle.

I cried, and she held me. I will miss my sister, but also my heart sunk when she told me I'd been Seeing for a week without waking.

Mama's Protections didn't work.

I might have visions of Essa or anyone in my family, but it isn't the same. Seeing isn't real. I'm watching events that might have happened, or could still happen... as a helpless bystander.

—— *ESME*

SEVENTEEN

THE GREAT SHIELD

When I returned to my room, a servant was waiting. Cyrus had invited us for a tour of 'the Protection points.' Rubia quickly prepared me though we weren't sure quite what to expect. Jamil escorted me to the front of the house where Pari and Ziba were already waiting. Though I told myself not to, I kept looking over my shoulder at the doors, expecting a glimpse of Marcus.

It had been an hour since I'd seen Marcus, but I could practically still feel his kiss on my cheek. Was he saying he still cared for me? His kiss wasn't a 'friend' kiss. It felt like a lot *more*. Or was that just what I'd wanted it to be?

"The emissaries already left for the port," Pari said. "You just missed them."

I felt my chest flush. My foolish heart was obvious. I steeled myself, staring at the side of the house where five polished palanquins with sheer curtains erected around them were being carried by four men each. Cyrus appeared behind us and waved them off.

"Bring the horses," Cyrus said. He turned to us, his lips slightly pursed. "Refined Getaens of status use palanquins, but Jamil said you prefer horses."

"Thank you," I forced a pleasant expression at his subtle insult.

"As we are allies, I will show you our sacred Protection," the clan leader said.

Allies, but not *equals* as far as Cyrus was concerned.

"Perhaps together, we can further your work in strengthening the dome." I assumed that was the real reason Cyrus was taking the time to reveal the details of the magic. The glint in his eye confirmed it.

"I have already begun to compose my letters to the Roe Deer and High Sands clans. With any luck, they'll join us —" Cyrus was briefly interrupted by whinnying horses as they appeared around the corner. "Ninety percent of my military magi will follow you north to the Curat. The rest will accompany the non-magical units in the south."

"Thank you. Sending soldiers into battle is not an easy decision."

Cyrus' grip on his reins tightened. "To that end, Yutab asked me to petition Healers and Protectors to join the battalions in the north and the south."

My jaw went slack. If Cyrus or Yutab requested magi assistance, far more Protectors and Healers would join than if I stood on a platform and begged for volunteers. "They could save many lives in both our armies."

With our growing knowledge, evolving tactics, and the magi's support, we had a chance of survival. Only a sliver, but it was preferable to inevitable defeat.

Cyrus puffed out his chest before approaching his horse and confidently mounted with ease. On my gelding, I rode next to Cyrus, Jamil leading the way. Ziba rode directly behind me, another reminder of her support to keep me safely on the throne.

As we rode, the people of the city gave both Cyrus and me differential nods. But irritation shown in their faces when they looked at me. I couldn't say that I'd have felt much differently if an empress had shown up unexpectedly in Moesia when I was growing up.

"The Historians met, which is unusual in and of itself. I'm

afraid that each of them has been told too many times of how special and essential they are. Though that is true, when working together, their combined knowledge can unlock many mysteries. They argued into the twilight hour and then sent for a little-known matriarch in the lower city. The matriarch confirmed the rumors that she is a descendant of a slave who escaped from the Norte. With the tales passed down over generations, plus the Historians teachings, they believe the Norte Bonders are affiliated with animals."

"But Bonders work with objects." I thought of the disk I'd just sent to Asander. "Amulets, usually."

Cyrus gave subdued, humble nods to a group of people clustering in a plaza. Once the street constricted again, the crowds left behind, Cyrus continued. "This slave ancestor served one particular couple and they cared for two wild animals. Then the parents gifted each of their newborn children an infant beast."

"Getaen Bonders have nothing to do with animals," I said and almost immediately recalled the Norte astride the snow leopard on the mountainside. Was it Bonder magic that enabled the rider to tame the beast?

"It gets stranger," Cyrus continued. "One night, the animal mauled one of the children. The family was heartbroken and mourned the loss. During that time of upheaval, an opportunity to escape materialized, and the slave took it."

"I think the wild animals are snow leopards."

Cyrus' shoulders fell. "Zalmoxis, *snow leopards.*"

"I can see how the Historians concluded they were Bonded — a magical connection. No other magic could keep an animal from eating such a convenient meal."

"You've seen them?"

"One. A white cat taller than a horse, and three times as wide."

Cyrus looked about as sick as I felt. My stomach hadn't stopped churning for days.

"Perhaps special training is required with the Magi and the animal?" Ziba suggested. "Or magic we haven't considered?

Cyrus narrowed his eyes. "What other magic could account for the snow leopard's strange behavior? A Ripper?" Cyrus looked over my shoulder at my advisers. "Rippers are welcomed by no one. The Norte people fear them even more than we do. When they are discovered, they are killed. The records are clear on that. Otherwise, Rippers become tyrants, too powerful to stop. It is best to always be wary in case one lurks, a wolf in sheep's clothing."

"Fortunately, we are not the Norte," I said, attempting to calm his sudden temper. "Besides, are not Getaens inherently more generous? Instead of keeping magic within themselves, they use their magic to serve others."

I turned to flash my advisers a pleasant look, conveying the importance of keeping Cyrus content. Pari was patting Ziba's arm, and my Protector looked as stiff as dried grass.

Behind them, a messenger was running to catch up with us, her face bright red.

"Cyrus," I said, halting my horse.

Cyrus dismounted and met the girl as she arrived. The people on the street scattered, giving the clan leader privacy as the runner conveyed her message. Cyrus looked back at me, his expression troubled.

Jamil and I dismounted and joined him, and Cyrus signaled for the messenger to repeat her words.

"Our ships intercepted, battled, and subdued three Theracian ships," the messenger said. "None escaped. The captains were questioned. They were headed for Auripo."

"Theracian ships?" I was surprised, but I realized I shouldn't have been. Emperor Saam was more comfortable on the water than anywhere else. "It makes sense. All the same, I can't believe they've already deployed."

"Three ships are likely a reconnaissance mission," Cyrus said. "Still, they are working quickly. I'd calculated that any movement before summer to be remote, but I underestimated the Theracians. My navy must be prepared for a southern offensive by spring."

"I'll send word to move the half battalion south as soon as we return to your home," I said.

"And I will deploy early scouts before they arrive." Cyrus' face paled as if memories of past battles weighed on his shoulders.

"Tomorrow, we finish our preparations together and then I must return to the Curat Pass."

"Things will change for my people sooner than I'd expected," Cyrus said, his face becoming determined. "Gems form under pressure. Salts are created by a suffocating heat. Seeds germinate in the dark. Some strength only emerges through trials. We will transform and be more powerful for it."

We remounted our horses, but for the rest of the journey to the outskirts of the city, we were silent.

As we traveled, the structures grew denser, and maneuvering horses through the crowds became increasingly difficult. Near the wall of the dome, servants took our horses. We approached a structure carved into a wall of red rock. Passing a set of columns carved into the face, we entered a windowless space. The far wall was lit by Luminary-infused crystals, spilling bright blue-white light. The room was narrow, only wide enough to fit three of us shoulder-to-shoulder, but the ceiling was several stories tall. We climbed the stone steps carved into the wall.

Jamil set a slow pace for Cyrus. My desire to hurry to the top grew with each step. I chanced a glance back at Ziba, expecting her to share a look of frustration. But she was staring past me, grinding her teeth.

At the top of the stairs, we emerged onto the rooftop. It was still early, but the sun beat down on the red stone. Papa would have loved this place, perched at the edge of the expansive city, feeling the crackling magic at his back.

Cyrus pointed at the sky, a smear of blue through the shimmer of magic. "The keystone hangs above, holding the dome in place."

Pari squinted. "I don't see anything."

Shading my eyes, I found the dark spot above what I estimated was the center of the city. I pointed it out to my companions as I asked Cyrus, "What is it?"

"No one knows. We'd have to build a scaffold to reach it." Cyrus had tempered his emotions well today, revealing little for me to study.

"The magic extends from the Protection points on the ground, up to the artifact in the sky?" Pari asked. "And the artifact essentially holds three walls of magic in place?"

"Correct, but there's more to understand." Cyrus turned to a young man approaching us. He had fine, ash blond hair, similar to Rubia's, just long enough to be secured in a thong at the nape of his neck. He matched Jamil's height but was about Marcus' age. "Ah, Jalab, I see you are on duty today."

The Getaen gave us all deferential bows. A linen marama draped across his shoulders similar to what Getaen miners used to shade their faces. But by the look of his burned cheeks and peeling nose, he rarely used it.

"I couldn't help but overhear you," Jalab said. "I can explain more about the artifact and the dome. Come this way."

We followed Jalab toward the edge. The dome's edge landed on the roof, a line of delineation across the center. Like a blanket, it "fell" off the sides of the structure and continued across the river-cut canyon, following every divot and rise of the ground.

"Amazing," Pari breathed. Ziba stood behind us all, her arms folded, her gaze on the blurry desert beyond. "The magic emanates from the artifact down to the Protection points and is Bonded deep in the earth."

The layers of magic were beyond my comprehension, but the essential magi for this dome seemed to be Protectors and Bonders.

"The magic is grounded in three points around the perimeter of the city. The dome curves to each point, creating a circle." Jalab led us to the other side of the structure. Where the dome met the red stone, the blue-tinted Protection turned white, veins of dull yellow-green pulsing down into the earth. "This is a Protection point."

"Protectors, like Jalab, monitor the points for weakening," Cyrus said. "These points were once veined with vibrant green. The change in color was our first indication of strain, though those attuned to magic noted a variance even earlier. When the magic is drained, the walls will fall."

Jalab shuddered.

I couldn't give the Getaens my sword, but another possibility came to my mind. One I would consider carefully. It might not even work. If it did or it didn't, either way, Katalin would be livid — and for good reason: the move would give a piece of my authority to the Red Valley clan.

I see a woman named Leila. She wears an orb that is smashed on one side as a pendant around her neck. My dreams are nearly constant, and they are confusing. This one, especially so.

Sometimes Leila looks Getaen, like she could have been from my clan. The orb is so powerful it almost hurts.

But sometimes Leila looks different. She has darker blond hair, and she wears the orb on a leather thong. And sometimes with her, the orb only has a drop of magic left.

The orb is always the key to the plague.

My Seeing gets mixed up sometimes. I struggle to understand the many different endings to the same story, not knowing which will be a reality, but knowing any of them could be.

— ESME

EIGHTEEN

THE RIPPER

After returning to the clan leader's home, I instructed Jamil to make preparations for us to leave at dawn. In my room, I picked up the box that held the *Crown of Lore*. I nearly dropped it when Pari burst into my room.

"Ziba is gone." Her eyes were wide with fear.

"What do you mean '*gone.*' Gone where? Into the city again?" I asked.

Rubia pushed past Pari in the doorway. "What's the fuss all about?"

Pari bit her lip and brought her hands up to her face. I barely made out mumbled syllables through her sudden burst of tears.

Rubia pulled Pari's hands away. "Speak up, child."

Pari yanked her hands from Rubia's grip. "You have no idea what just happened today. Everything Ziba has worked for, for *years* was just torn away. Her hopes, her dreams... everything. I have no idea what she'll do. But she left quietly, which worries me even more."

I jumped to the doorway and pressed the brass Sonus button. "B-but Cyrus agreed to join our army. Now, we have a chance!"

"We do." Pari gestured to the three of us, sniffling back tears as she spoke. "But not Ziba. Somehow, Cyrus figured out her secret —

much faster than either of us expected. And this morning, when we were riding, he issued her a threat."

Rubia grabbed Pari by the shoulders and gave her a firm shake. "Calm yourself, child. What secret? What threat?"'

I pried Rubia away before she upset Pari even more.

"Cyrus mentioned that Norte killed her kind. That they were dangerous and never would be accepted." Pari covered her mouth.

Rubia pressed her lips together in frustration at Pari's unhelpful explanation. But I'd recalled the clan leader's specific threat.

"Cyrus said that the Norte executed *Rippers,*" I whispered. And Ziba interpreted the words as a threat?

Oddities about Ziba started to make sense. Ziba was not a natural-born Protector. She was a Ripper. She'd lied to Cyrus — a powerful Sensitive — and he'd detected her subtle manipulation.

Pari raked her fingers through her braid, pulling out some of the strands. "I fear she's been repressing anger for a long time, and it's possible she'll lash out."

Ziba was on the run, hurt and angry somewhere in the Red Valley clan, possibly still in this very house.

RUBIA RUSHED to ask the servants whether they'd seen Ziba while Pari and I searched the guest rooms. If I couldn't find and calm my adviser soon, I'd have to alert the household for their own safety.

"Cyrus is a fool," I said to Pari. "He threatened Ziba without getting to know her. He judged her by her magic but then didn't have someone following her at all times?"

"He is used to being obeyed. In the Red Valley, he *is* the law," Pari said under her breath as we exited the room and strode down the hall. "He probably thought Ziba would consider his warning a kindness and slink away in the night."

"He doesn't know Ziba," I muttered. "Would she go to the

port?" Ziba had enough coin and skill to escape to anywhere in all of Cornara.

"No," Pari returned from a balcony. "She'd make a statement. She's not a gracious person by nature. After today... she's capable of doing anything."

"No wonder Ziba figured out Rippers were blocking the Norte magic."

We jogged passed the emissaries' rooms as their Protective doors were engaged and entered the next bedroom. "How long have you known?" I asked Pari.

"Essa told me about a year after I'd arrived at Rupea castle." Pari checked the balcony. "She said it was time I knew the truth about Ziba but not to be afraid. Essa reassured me that Ziba would never steal anything from either of us. Ever. Nor magic from anyone unwilling to give it. As I grew older, I began to figure out that Ziba took things from others quite regularly, making trades with the vulnerable."

"What can a Ripper take?" I asked as we darted to the next room.

"I'm not sure but definitely different forms of vitality. The luster of hair, the strength of bones." Pari paused, not looking at me. "Eyesight."

Pari started for the balcony, but I grabbed her.

"Surely, you don't mean Marianna," I said. The mystic was a child when an old witch in the castle offered her a trade: freedom in exchange for Marianna's remaining sight.

"Marianna was young but losing her eyesight, anyway," Pari whispered, still refusing to look at me.

I dropped my hand as if Pari's words burned me.

"Ziba's older than you realize," Pari whispered.

I groaned, bile rising in the back of my throat.

The faded round scars on Marianna's temples were the same size and location as the blisters I'd noticed on Essa after she'd died.

"Ziba lied to herself," I said. "She told herself she wouldn't steal from either of you. The ultimate deception — one even the teller believes. Otherwise, Essa would have stopped her. But Ziba did lie — she stole from Essa."

"No," Pari stepped away. "Essa was in constant misery — I'm sure she begged Ziba to end her pain."

Essa had been reduced to a sunken husk. How could Pari not have seen it, knowing the magic Ziba possessed?

"Don't fool yourself, too, Pari. Don't fall into the same trap that ensnared Ziba." I spun on my heel, staring down the corridor. If Ziba wanted to make a statement, where would it be? The city center?

No. It would be an attack on the heart of this place. What would devastate Cyrus — cause him the deepest wound? The clan leader was pompous, but he esteemed one thing, one person above all else.

"Pari," I shouted. "We must find Yutab!"

Our feet pounded against the terracotta stone as we raced to find Rubia. We didn't make it far before Rubia intercepted us in the courtyard.

I grabbed Rubia's shoulders. "Show us Cyrus' family quarters."

"They're upstairs, but they'd never grant us access," Rubia said.

"Show us the way," I demanded.

Rubia raised an eyebrow but hurried us down the main corridor. Then, we turned right down another hallway that led to a stairwell.

Rubia skidded to a stop. A Getaen guard lay on the ground. Rubia and Pari fell to their knees, checking his pulse and feeling for injuries.

"He'll survive, but he'll have a headache." Pari probed the back of his head with her fingertips.

"Hopefully, the second guard will be as lucky," Rubia said. "She must have taken him hostage."

"How would she have knocked one guard unconscious and captured another one?" Rubia shook her head. "They're both twice her size."

"She's actually quite good with a dagger." Pari sounded almost apologetic. "It was a hobby at one point."

You might have mentioned that sooner.

"Pari, run to the main entrance and alert the guards," I said.

Pari sprinted away. If she hoped to remain under this roof, she needed to show her loyalty to Cyrus, immediately. Trusting Pari's sense of self-preservation, I left Rubia to tend to the fallen guard and alert the steward.

As I rushed up the stairs, I was tempted to cry out for Ziba, but she was too stubborn for that. I'd have to find her. I tip-toed down the empty hall, wishing I hadn't left my boots with my concealed dagger. The Canina Thorn would kill her, but I wanted an explanation, not her death. I passed an opening to a massive bedroom. The three ornate beds were dwarfed by the large space. A reflection pool sat in the center, lotus flowers clinging to the sides.

A servant was leaning out a window, banging the dust from a pillow with her back to me. I hurried further down the hall.

I paused at the next door, slowly peering around the corner. It was a smaller room, far less luxurious. The floor was covered in soft furs, pillows placed along the back wall near a large bed. In the center of the bed, Esme sat, blinking at Ziba, who had her hands on the Seer's temples.

I slid the sword from my scabbard without thought.

"Step away from her, Ziba." I raised my sword, giving no other warning as I advanced on my former Protector.

Ziba slowly moved her hands away and faced me.

With a lunge, Ziba could touch my flesh. What would she take?

"Why didn't Marianna reveal you were the one who took her sight?" I asked.

"She probably didn't realize it was me. My voice has changed over the years." Ziba flashed a frightful grin. "Though I admit, I didn't realize at first that she was the same girl. She'd changed, too. I never intended for her to have the ability to see auras. But that is the beauty of being a Ripper; we can inadvertently create the most unique forms of magic. Sometimes, we have so much magic mixing in our veins that some slips out in interesting ways."

When you steal more magic, you mean.

"I'm better at controlling it now," Ziba continued, rising to her feet, a satchel resting at her hip. She seemed taller. Or maybe I was just seeing her for who she was. Far more mythical and powerful than I would ever be. "If only the clans could appreciate what I have to give. An Empress of our blood sits on the throne because of me. *I* am the reason that they have an opportunity to be truly free. *I* delivered you on a silver platter."

All this time, I thought Ziba wanted a Getaen on the throne to elevate all our people. But she wanted *herself* elevated in the eyes of the Getaens.

"Instead of thanks, all they see is a Ripper. They condemn me for magic I never asked for." Ziba shot out a finger, pointing at Esme. "You will see there is a balance in all things. Seers and Rippers are crucial to each other. I've given her a taste of what she *could* have had if her father could have looked past his prejudice."

"I would have given you a chance." I took a step closer.

"Truly?" Ziba scoffed. "You figured out what I was, and the first thing you did was hunt me down with your sword."

"I found you transferring magic from someone incapable of giving permission!"

Ziba's nostril's flared. "I thought you were more than what you are."

I slid my sword back into my scabbard. I had no magic for Ziba to steal, and in hand-to-hand combat, I could best her. I could at least keep her from Esme until guards arrived.

"If our positions were reversed, you'd have already killed me," I said.

"Perhaps." Ziba stepped toward me. We were toe to toe. "Or perhaps I'm feeling nostalgic about what could have been. Either way, it doesn't benefit me to have the Norte in power. They'll figure out what I am even quicker than Cyrus."

Ziba reached into her satchel, and I tensed, ready for a glint of metal. But instead, she pulled out a pebble. "You don't come after me, and I'll cause you no trouble. If you're tempted to find me, just remember that I know everything and everyone dear to you."

Ziba whispered something under her breath, the small stone held between her finger and thumb. Swiftly, she stepped back and pressed the pebble into Esme's palm. I jumped to snatch it, fearing Ziba's mischief. But Esme curled her hand around it.

"Ziba, what is this?" I snarled as I tried to pry the woman's fingers open. Glancing over my shoulder, I noticed another guard slumped against the ground.

And Ziba was gone.

"Who are you?" Esme said.

She stared up at me, and I stumbled back. Without the half-dazed look on her face, I realized her features were so much like Essa's that they could have been twins. The same intelligent eyes, freckles across their button noses, and high cheekbones.

"Do I know you?" She looked around, taking everything in. "And where am I?"

I stepped away from Esme, uneasy. What had Ziba done?

"Leila." She cocked her head, looking at the True Key around my neck. "A wild rose in your hair."

"I'm Nicoleta. My mama's name was Leila." My voice trembled. The idea of talking to a Seer, a *lucid* Seer, made my insides turn to water.

Her eyes widened. "You are the Golden Warrior. I've seen you many times."

Yutab pushed past me, practically knocking me over. "Essy! Essy, my dearest. Are you hurt?"

"Mama!" Esme gasped as they embraced. Esme opened her mouth, but then her attention turned back to me. She stilled.

As Esme took a step toward me, Yutab shifted enough to see the fallen guard. Yutab grabbed Esme's fisted hand, holding her daughter back as she cried out for a Healer.

"You are a vessel for magic," Esme said to me, her focus so invasive I wanted to hide. "Like a blue ghoster vial."

Every word she said filled me with dread. I didn't want to hear my future. Rubia said Seers weren't real. She was wrong. I wanted to press my hands to my ears, but at the same time, I soaked up Esme's words like dry clay.

"Unleash the plague." Esme tapped her sternum.

Someone brushed by me, running to the fallen guard.

"What is this, Essy?" Yutab had pried open her daughter's hand. "Where did you find a dirty pebble?"

"That's no mere pebble," I gasped. "It's Ripper magic."

Yutab frantically knocked the pebble from her daughter's hand, shouting.

Esme shook her head, her eyes going in and out of focus. Her face scrunched up again, straining as she pulled away from her mama, clawing at her chest. "The plague is not gone. I see it."

I clutched the hilt of my sword. The Canina Thorn still carried the plague. That was the truth. But the eerie intensity in which Esme said it rattled me. My back thumped against the far wall. My knees weakened, and I slid to the ground, clutching the True Key at my chest.

Servants rushed past me as Esme devolved into hysterics. "Release the plague."

The servants fought to restrain Esme. Ziba had cut exactly as she'd intended, a cruel wound as Yutab would soon discover. The pebble held enough magic to show Yutab and Cyrus what Esme *could* have been if they'd accepted Ziba.

"The pebble, it had Ripper magic." My words were a rasp, drown by Esme's cries.

But now, Cyrus could scour all Cornara and never find Ziba again. She would be sure not to leave a trace.

Mama's eyes were red when I awoke. She was very plain, not knowing how much time I had today. She confessed she'd gone to every allied clan and spoken with anyone who claimed to have information about Seers.

She hasn't figured out a way to save me.

But she swears she will never stop trying.

I'd already known, but hearing I only had a short time forced me to face the truth. I cried as Mama brushed my hair and braided it with a pile of flowers. It didn't take her long, and she wiped my eyes and took me for a walk in the gardens.

I wiped away my tears in the gardens. There is no relief from the curse that plagues me. There is no time to waste.

— ESME

NINETEEN

CROWN OF LORE

The Ghoster disk balled up in my hand as I explained to Cyrus how they worked. Pleased at the invention, Cyrus agreed to exchange locks of hair, knowing safe communication was vital. We avoided talking about his blunder in threatening Ziba. He'd detected her lies but hadn't bothered to find out more about her.

"Will I remember being here?" I asked.

Cyrus puffed out his chest. "Earlier, I said that you and Jamil were always welcome back. And I meant it. You are the only two who will retain your memories of this place, though. Including Ziba, if she somehow escapes the city."

You underestimate her yet again.

Yutab had secretly thanked me for telling her everything I'd witnessed between Ziba and Esme. I wouldn't be surprised if Yutab had already begun her search for a Ripper to help control her daughter's Seer abilities.

Jamil slipped into the room, a large satin box in his hands.

"Perhaps Ziba was right in one way," I said. "There is a push and a pull in all magic. Seers and Rippers balance each other."

"Never speak of that infernal, nefarious magic here," Cyrus said.

Instead of responding, I signaled for Jamil to come forward. My Own handed the clan leader the box. Opening the satin lid, Cyrus' eyes grew wider.

"Don't get any ideas about wearing it." I ran my finger across the detailed branches and leaves of the crown. The emeralds winked at me, making me wistful. It was a significant symbol, and it would have filled our treasury to the brim if I'd offered slivers of it to buyers. But it could never be sold, nor worn, by anyone other than me. "This crown killed the last emperor. Though not as old as your current artifact, it holds reserves of ancient magic summoned by the most powerful warlock of the Blood Conqueror's time."

"Why would you do this for us?" he asked.

"This is a gift to my friend and *our* people."

Cyrus closed the satin lid and reverently pressed a hand on top. "I shall save it for as long as I can. My son can use it as a positive symbol to rally around."

The city would need the crown in years, not decades. Was Cyrus planning on fighting and dying in the near future?

Seeing my expression, Cyrus excused everyone from the room, including Jamil.

"When the fighting is over," Cyrus sighed, "I will hand over my title."

"Isn't that when your people will need you most?"

"It's a tradition all clan leaders learn from their mentors. Something I will teach you, too." Cyrus caressed the box lid. "When you became empress, you did something fantastic; you stopped the plague and rallied the people to a new crown. The plague was your predecessor's fault, and they blamed him."

"Rightly so," I said. "Not just Cassus VII but his father and grandfather, too."

Cyrus continued, "But you destroyed the one thing that was keeping warring kingdoms at bay. That was your doing."

I pressed my lips together, unable to refute him.

"Still, we can blame all this on Cassus V's poor judgment."

Cyrus gave me a conspiratorial look. "Later, when trouble arose, you changed the structure of the Rose Court."

I raised my brow. "And I thought you didn't care about Dacian castle gossip."

"I have kept track of your rule, of course." Cyrus brushed off my remark, sliding the satin box onto a table. "Because you changed things, which not everyone loves, it saved your people again. However, when trouble rises a third time, the people will have grown wary of your ability to rule."

"But emperors stay in power until they die."

"But should they?" Cyrus steepled his fingers in front of him. "A seat of power eventually poisons the ruler. Wait and see. Especially in times of war, it will change you. Trust me on that. I've had my own troubles; every leader deals with complicated, flawed systems and cultures. What all clan leaders learn is: first, divert blame to your predecessor. The second time trouble appears, make changes — as you did to the Rose Court. The third time, pass on the mantle to the next in line.

"This war will be the third obstacle I see our clan through as even the most successful wars bring bitterness. When the war ends, I will hand over my title to my son. The people will blame me for the hardships of the past but will have hope in a fresh leader. And my son will still have my quiet guidance. How much better would it have been if the last emperor had been there to help you?"

I winced.

"Well, imagine if your papa had been the one teaching you," Cyrus said, escorting me from the room, securing the doorway with a Protection behind us. "Just because every Dacian before you has done things one way doesn't mean you can't insert some of our Getaen ways into future dealings."

Jamil, my emissaries, and Rubia waited outside near the main doors of the estate.

Cyrus continued, "Sometimes it takes a person from the fringe of society with a different perspective to step in and make imperfect improvements. You could be a great leader if you choose to be."

I pondered on Cyrus' unexpected parting words of advice. Had we become confidantes? Partners in the coming battles, our destinies tied together? It was more than I had hoped for.

In front of the estate, a crowd of people had gathered. Our horses were waiting, and Pari stood nearby. A servant held up a bag of Sonus powder, and Cyrus smeared some across his lips before raising both his hands.

"Getaens of the Red Valley," he bellowed. "It has been my profound honor to greet Empress Nicoleta Aurelian. She is both bright and compassionate with a great love of her Getaen blood."

The crowd was riveted as he spoke with passion about Mama's Sea Mist clan. He only hinted of the battles ahead, instead focusing on outside kingdoms hungry for our riches and of the attacks in the north. When he was finished, Cyrus turned to me, and in a grand gesture, he bowed.

My mouth went dry as I tried to feign calm. Several in the crowd gasped, and others looked at each other, unsure of what to do. Jamil dropped to a knee, followed by my emissaries and Rubia. Then, the messenger near the horse and the rest of the household. With a great whoosh of clothing, the crowd knelt displaying their loyalty.

After Jamil helped me mount my gelding, we rode through the streets. The news must have traveled quickly, as everyone we passed bowed or curtsied along the way to the city gate.

The people didn't yet know that my visit was a harbinger of war. The younger citizens wouldn't think much of the attacks near the Curat, other than it being exciting news. But the older generation would tremble, connecting my visit to the Theracian ships spotted on the sea, and know that war wasn't just in distant Auripo or in the far north of Dacia but would cut through their lives as well.

I move through a busy marketplace, colorful streamers overhead. Vendors bargain, the atmosphere light, and I bask in the activity around me. People gossip about the young empress' death. A strange anger, frustration, and sadness vie for my attention. I swallow and turn to the crowd around me, ready to begin my work.

Reaching out, my fingers grazing a portly man. I'm no longer hungry.

I brush my hand against a young woman, and the ache in my knee disappears. That was surprising. I'd had that pain for weeks.

I stand next to a woman squabbling over the price of apricots. She claims she cannot afford the whole bundle, but thanks to my Sensitive magic, I know it's a lie.

Something about my skill tugs at me.

Wait, I'm not a Sensitive.

I'm a Seer. In yet another dream.

My visions feel so real. My dreams usually leave me exhausted, but this one is worse. My stomach churns. Only one type of magic can draw another's essence. A Ripper.

— ESME

CHAPTER

TWENTY

RETURN TO CURAT CAMP

After seven days of riding through bouts of pelting, frigid rain, my cheeks were covered in little red welts. When snow began to fall, I counted it as a welcome reprieve. Finally, back at our Curat camp, we found beleaguered soldiers slumped around soggy fires, leaning against crude walking sticks, or lying on the frozen, muddy ground. Cold droplets dribbled between the evergreen needles, and the soldiers' soaked clothing stuck to their backs.

Midnight bolted to greet me, a squire running after her. The young man greeted me, quickly explaining they'd suffered heavy losses. I handed over my gelding and trudged to my tent, searching for Asander.

Empty.

I pulled one of the guards at my door into my tent.

"Where is Prince Asander?"

"Near the fighting." The guard was lean with a crooked front tooth.

"Is there active fighting right now?"

"No, no. But the prince eats and sleeps in a cave near the front. The Auripoans —"

Irena pushed her way past the guard, cutting him off. "I'm glad you're back."

"What are you doing here?" I asked. "I thought you were helping Lady Katalin at the castle."

"Lady Katalin sent me here to help the injured."

Irena snatched a carved wolf used to weigh down scrolls from the table. She slid out a Ghoster disk from the bottom of the weight. "Pretty clever place to keep it safe, don't you think?" She handed it to me. "I have to get back to the infirmary, but I'll let my papa know I'm here before nightfall."

"Before you go," I stopped her, "what happened while I was away?"

My guard and Irena exchanged glances, and she nodded for the guard to speak. "Our army was getting better at blocking the light from the Illuminators. Even when the Illuminators changed their call signals, many of our soldiers guessed at what was happening. We should have lost half our army in that battle as the Norte did not retreat quickly. They took their time, attempting to slaughter us at our most vulnerable. But those units who had weathered the magic and could still see well enough to fight, they pushed the Norte back, pushed them back through the mountain, closer to the river. But the soldiers ran into a heavier blockade. Still, we secured that pass and have held it."

"I arrived shortly after that battle," Irena said. "Our army was buoyed by the small victory. Plus, I traveled with supplies and more magical resources from Rupea castle."

"The Norte usually wait a few days between strikes." The guard turned to Irena. "From the survivors, you've probably heard more details than I have... "

Irena swallowed. "The Norte returned before the sun rose. Our soldiers heard the collective roar of the Norte, announcing their advance. Our army rushed to engage them in the far valley, but instead of facing blades, they were stoned."

"Our armies have shields, do they not?" I asked.

"They used their shields, of course," Irena said. "But the stones hit with incredible speed and accuracy, smashing mostly legs and ankles but also shoulders, ears, and anything that wasn't covered." She looked at me cautiously. "Sonus magic, perhaps."

"It makes sense," I said. I planned to use a similar technique with my unit.

"They made the ground rumble," Irena said, her voice flat. "They didn't quake the whole earth but enough to frighten half our army. It was a shock. Between the ground and the rocks and being unable to properly evaluate who was controlling the Mirrors… "

"It went badly." My guard shifted his weight to his heels. "The fighting finally let up just yesterday."

The flap to my tent flew open, and Jamil stomped in. Irena spun around and wrapped her papa in a tight hug, her eyes closed tight. "I'm so sorry. I know many were your friends."

Jamil hugged his daughter back, resting his cheek on her head. "I should have been here."

"I fear you may have your chance to die in battle." Irena released her father, promising to return later. She slipped away, back to help those she still could.

I waved off my guard, who returned to his outside post. Jamil ran a hand down his face, his shoulders slumped.

"Those soldiers were the most experienced in the kingdom. Asander requested them. They'd survived fighting in Cassus VI's campaigns." Jamil leaned against the table. "Now, they're gone. Our Dacian army has been dealt a bigger blow than I think the Norte even realize."

Tulia began to enter, a copper kettle in her arms, but Jamil sent her away. I wanted to console Jamil, my constant shield and protector. For me, this was a tactical tragedy, and the enormity of the human loss hadn't slammed against my heart. I couldn't allow it to if I wanted to stay focused. But for Jamil, he had just learned of these deep, personal losses. Before I could utter words of sympathy, he cleared his throat, his eyes narrowing. His usual mask of calm was gone, and every line on his face demanded a fierce response.

"I've already sent a message to Captain Lucius," I said. "I've requested five units of Imperial Guards to complete the promised half-battalion in the south. That half-battalion leaves the castle vulnerable and the Rodnic Valley virtually barren of soldiers. And here, we don't have enough soldiers to hold another battle. We must use the new recruits."

"They're not ready."

"Some have had two moons to train. Besides, we don't have a choice," Jamil said. "We must rely on the magi."

"The Red Valley army can't do it alone, and you know it. If the magi arrive and immediately see how... diminished we are, they could very well turn back."

"Cyrus' army will be two weeks behind us."

"Perfect," I said. Cyrus had advised restructuring when things got ugly; my army was about to see a flurry of changes. "That's about how long it will take for our recruits to arrive."

I sent a messenger to inform Asander, if the prince could be found, that I had returned. I didn't expect him to greet me, but it was polite to keep him informed of my whereabouts. Tulia finished preparing me a warm bath, and Midnight promptly sidled up next to the sealed wood slats. On Tulia's way out, she instructed the guards to protect my peace at all costs.

I nearly cried with joy when I slipped into the tub of not-freezing-water. As a bonus, it was clean. It was essentially a large bucket, but I was simply grateful to soothe my saddle-sore body. Between the tub, the copper kettle near my bed filled with boiling water, and the rocks fresh from the fire and buried in the sand under my pallet, the tent was luxuriously warm.

With my mind clear and sharp, I cracked the disk from Katalin.

Empress,

I trust that Irena and the supplies arrived safely. I employed the bandit, Garipy, and his associates to protect the caravan. They are useless when it comes to building or farming, but they have proved useful in this line of work. Plus, they seem to enjoy it. I also sent six Capidavan guards plus two more disguised as servants, in case the bandits got any foolish ideas as I'm sending valuable goods.

Katalin was to the point. I grinned, imagining her with her nose slightly in the air as she dictated this "letter."

The caravan is more than wagons of food and clothing. I secretly sent a friend — one who not even Irena knows of. They have something important to tell you, personally. Whatever it is, it wasn't even divulged to me.

On another note, you'll be pleased to know that the Roses are practicing with weapons. Somehow, the required training of our youth sucked the excitement out of daggers. But Lord Jovian has turned dagger throwing into a fashionable sport. There are targets, rules, points, and, most importantly, honor to be kept. I must say, avoid ever angering Lady Tyne. Her aim is dead on.

Katalin let out a haughty laugh. Between Katalin's humor and the news of the Roses, I chuckled in relief. Midnight lifted her head, confused. I didn't blame her.

Also, I have been working with the engineers at the university to create a system that diverts waste away from the water sources of the lower classes. The pieces of your coronation dress are bringing in a steady flow of coin from around the kingdom, and I find that if the Lilacs and Poppies are healthy, they are more likely to be able to help in the fields or volunteer as recruits.

I almost hope you disapprove of my idea and come running back to the castle directly and relieve me of my duties. The litany of annoying complaints is driving me mad. I hope this war ends quickly before I decide to run into the Dacian Mountains, never to be heard of again.

Least interestingly, Emperor Saam has sent a letter, requesting we speak with a diplomatic envoy.

I sat up, splashing water and practically dropping the crumbling disk into the tub. Saam wanted to talk?

Katalin's voice turned more disdainful.

I sent him a letter that you were traveling but that you *would contact* him. *If he's trying to assassinate you, he'll have a difficult time tracking you down. And in the meantime, it should keep his envoy from Rupea castle.*

Keep that blade of yours handy. I look forward to your return.

The last of the disk crumbled, and I brushed it off my hands, musing over Katalin's letter. Her plan for clean water was clever. I whole-heartedly approved of her helping the poor. It never would have occurred to me to engineer such a thing.

I leaned my head back, somewhat relieved at Katalin's frustration with running the kingdom. I wasn't the only one who found it to be no small task. I was glad to have her take some of the weight if only for a time.

More immediately urgent was the information about Saam. He was looking for me. And if so, it would only be a matter of time until his spies reported I'd returned to the Curat. Whether he hoped to negotiate, which I hoped, or kill me, which was likely, I didn't know. I'd have to plan for an attempt at either.

I was also curious as to who this mysterious friend was that Katalin had sent. They certainly couldn't approach me while I was sequestered in my tent.

I hopped out of the tub and dressed. Without complicated

aprons nor my armor, I easily dressed myself in a thick camasa and pants. I needed to make myself approachable without being vulnerable.

I pulled on my boots, strapping a layer of fur over the top for the brisk evening. My dagger secure at my ankle and the Canina Thorn at my side, I pulled out a bag of Sonus powder. Tulia had sewn a loop so I could fasten it to my belt as I'd told her I wanted to always have it within reach. I secured the powder, and my heavy cloak mostly hid it from view. Then, I stepped into the moonlight, Midnight at my side.

Ashy snow had begun to fall, blanketing the earth. Even Zalmoxis wanted to cover the ugliness of this muddy camp. The guards outside my tent fell into step behind me.

I held out my hand. "Please remain here."

My Own were never far, and I wanted the newcomer to feel comfortable approaching me. "Let Tulia know she can retire for the evening."

I strode toward the western edge of camp, encountering fresh snow and fewer people. Fires burned high, many of the soldiers already asleep. Though Katalin wasn't a spymaster, I couldn't help but think it would have been fine for her to tell me *who* was coming in a secret message shared in my secured tent. But, no one was an expert in *everything*, not even the illustrious Lady Katalin Vulpe.

I heard someone jogging through the crunchy snow to catch up with me. My heart leapt into my throat, and my hand moved to my hilt. Even so, I didn't cry out to the soldiers a stone's throw away. Some part of me knew it was Marcus even before he called out to me. If it was the way he charged the air around me or just his gait, I didn't know.

"What are you still doing up?" Our conversation in the Red Valley garden courtyard rushed back into my mind. But how much could Marcus remember?

"I was going to ask you the same thing. I had planned to talk to you in the morning, but I recognized you across the field.

"What did you need to talk to me about?" I asked as we

walked, Midnight striding between us. This might be even better for a friend to approach me. A casual conversation with my emissary could be the perfect cover.

"When will your new Protector be arriving?" Marcus asked.

In exchange for Pari's stay in the Red Valley, the clan leader offered to send a 'proper' Protector to replace Ziba. I'd explained the absence of Ziba, Pari, and the results of the negotiations to my companions once we'd left the Red Valley because their memories had quickly faded. Jamil pretended he was similarly affected, but his lack of questions confirmed he remembered everything just fine.

"Between the water for the glass houses and the wells in the Red Valley, I'm concerned about our own water supply."

"Whatever for? Water is literally falling from the sky right now."

Marcus held his hand up, catching flakes of snow. "This is not the river water we're drinking, nor using to water our crops. At least, not until spring."

A new potential problem. *Fantastic.*

"An army can survive for a week without food," Marcus said as we walked in step with each other. "They'll be weak, yes, but they can live. Without water? Only days. And what if our water were poisoned? What if our water *source* was poisoned — our drinking water tainted and crops ruined?"

I walked faster, wanting to escape Marcus' warning. His concern was remote, ridiculous even. I had plenty of more imminent worries. "You think they'll travel around Dacia, dipping their hands into every well?"

"I think far less will destroy us," Marcus said. "Imagine if ten farms are poisoned. Or ten fields used for grazing livestock. As the food is traded around the kingdom, no one will know if their next bite of food will be their last."

My irritation grew with Marcus' fantastical fears. I didn't have time for them.

I stopped short as large flakes of snow fell harder. Any relaxing lightness I'd felt was gone. Now I wanted to punch something. I headed back for my tent.

Marcus followed, keeping up with my furious pace. "What if the Norte poisoned the glaciers that fed the lakes high in the mountains? Just send spies to evaluate the area. What would it hurt?"

I spun and faced Marcus, my heart pounding. "We have too few spies and fewer soldiers. Sending even a single person on a fool's errand into the b-bitter cold northern mountains in the middle of the winter is r-risking their life for no reason. And I need every spy we have, watching the Theracian b-border in the south, the Curat Mountains, not to mention the entire Rodnic Valley. We don't even have enough spies for b-basic reconnaissance."

Marcus opened his mouth to argue, but I cut him off.

"D-do you know how much p-poison a Healer would have to put into the water to effect acres and acres of food? With a vain hope that some d-distant grasses will absorb their p-poison and kill our cattle?" I took a breath, my body shaking. I had just garnered an ally, we had a chance to win. Why bring me this distracting, remote worry? I fisted my hands behind my back and lowered my voice to a whisper so as not to stutter. "You are right. The Norte are extremely dangerous, but they're not foolish."

Marcus started, but I held up my hand to stop him from speaking.

"Don't talk to me tomorrow." I strode back to my tent, feeling Marcus behind me, but he was wise enough not to say a word.

Faces change in an instant, time moving forward at a great pace. One group converging on another, eating them until they are no more. And they are both gone, born anew as another personage entirely. Hundreds of years pass in a heartbeat, like a shooting star falling for eternity. Old civilizations are conquered and reborn anew, become old. The cycle continues.

—*ESME*

CHAPTER
TWENTY-ONE

I punched my pillow. Despite my exhaustion, I couldn't sleep. I tried to roll over, but Midnight had pinned my calves. With all my strength, I bucked her — but under her weight, it was merely a nudge. She shifted, huffing her displeasure.

I missed Pari. I missed Ziba. Dyana had returned to Auripo. I didn't know the location of Asander's cave. I was angry with Marcus and his demands. Though Tulia muttered in her sleep across the tent and soldiers stood watch nearby, I had no one I could talk to.

I couldn't shut off my thoughts. Irena and my chip-tooth guard's words came back to my mind. The Norte had employed a range of magic in their most recent battle, but not the snow leopards. So far, I'd been the only one to even see one. Perhaps the cats were not as fearsome as the myths implied.

One magic we knew existed, which had yet to be deployed, was the Healer's poison. It would have been easy for the Norte to lace their swords, arrows, or even their shields, efficiently, painfully ending us. Why hadn't they? The Norte had freely used all magic they'd already revealed... except for the Healers.

Or perhaps they *were* being utilized. Just not here.

I stared at the roof, which sagged under the weight of the snow. Marcus' words grated at the back of my mind. I frowned.

Impossible.

The Norte couldn't poison our food supply. But if they did, it would be disastrous — even if the Agricultural Guild were able to convince people to save the stores of food rather than eat them this winter. Our plan depended on *some* spring and summer crops. Or, as Marcus said, if the Norte only poisoned random farms, the people would be gambling their lives with every meal. Even for those who could scavenge in the wild, we might not know what portions of land had been poisoned until it was too late.

Mind games — exactly the kind the Norte played. The Healers might not be absent, just diverted elsewhere. But would they send their Healers to the glaciers that fed our water supply in the middle of winter?

Tatiana and Borsea were as tough as rawhide left to dry for ten seasons. They were capable of traversing the icy terrain. And, yes, from what I knew of the Council thus far, they would definitely risk their Healer's lives.

But who could I send to scout? Who was as tough as the Norte, but stealthier, able to hide?

Crawling out of bed, I wrapped myself in my blanket and called out a perimeter check to the outside guards. When they verified my tent was secure, I plucked one of Katalin's hairs from a fuchsia pouch.

If I were wrong, I'd be sending scouts north when I really needed them east, in the Curat Mountains. The question was, did I trust Marcus? Not Marcus, my friend, but Lord Constantin, the emissary — his knowledge and skill. Was I anticipating the Norte's next move, or was this yet another mind-game causing me to jump at ghosts?

I sucked in a breath and plucked up the liquid disk. When it balled-up in my hand, I spoke my instructions to Katalin, my heart pounding.

"Discretely, send spies into the northern mountains. Utilize those from the list Liviana sent, and inquire to see if any bandits are fit for the job." I whispered to the marble-size orb. "I need to know if there is any enemy movement in the glaciers that feed into our water supply. I'm sending my best scout to deliver this message. Assign him to assemble the team. Time is critical."

After commending her project that would improve the health of the poor, I updated her on the events of the Red Valley.

When finished, still wrapped in my heavy blanket, I leaned out of my tent and handed the glass disk to a guard. "An urgent message. Send this with Julius, back to Rupea Castle for Lady Katalin."

The guard slipped the fragile disk into a pouch and bolted away. I was betting on Marcus' intuition. Zalmoxis would be more than delighted to punish Dacia if I was wrong.

"Few are awake at the thieves' hour." The crooked-tooth guard was stationed at my door. "Is there anything I can get for you?"

The term "thieves' hour" was a common phrase where I grew up, but I'd never heard it elsewhere. "Are you from Moesia?"

It was too dark to scrutinize his expression.

"Never been there," he said. "Why?"

"No reason."

I shut the flap of my tent and crawled into bed. I didn't recall falling asleep, but it seemed like Tulia shook me awake moments later.

"Sorry to disturb you, Empress, but the sun is coming up."

While I was still half-asleep, Tulia helped me into clean, close-fitting trousers and a camasa. Then, without warning, she splashed frigid water on my face and scrubbed, rudely waking me enough to want to rip the scratchy cloth out of her hand.

"That's better." Tulia stepped back, hands on her hips.

"I can't feel my face."

"You should have scrubbed better when I'd poured you a proper bath. Next time, you won't waste the opportunity." Tulia stuck out her tongue and made a hideous face.

"I didn't get *that* dirty on the road," I defended myself.

Tulia snorted a laugh, tripped over Midnight, and collided with Irena, who had entered the tent at precisely that wrong moment.

"That was embarrassing." Tulia attempted to turn her clumsiness into a joke. She was generally obsessed with grace and presentation, and she rarely showed the silly side of herself to others.

Irena didn't smile. Instead, the Protector clutched a bowl to her chest, her eyes tight. Her solemnity was a stark reminder of her work, strengthening soldiers before they went into battle.

Tulia scooped up my dirty clothes, an excuse to leave.

"Empress, it would be my honor to Protect you if you'll allow it," Irena said.

Irena had helped save my life after I'd been poisoned — a shocking emergency. She was offering to serve me as Empress, a risky step toward being ostracized by her people. Jamil had already crossed that line but at the behest of the clan leader. This was different.

"Thank you." I lay down, humbled.

Irena's magic worked through me, strengthening me from the inside. With Ziba, I was used to a more powerful swell. I tensed, realizing that the entire time Ziba had been strengthening me, she'd been using magic she'd taken from someone else. Maybe many people. Ziba claimed to not steal magic, but I felt like a snake slithered through me, leaving me ill at ease.

Outside, the camp came alive. Pots banged, and wooden wheels squeaked. When Irena finished, I gripped her hand and sat up. What could I say?

Midnight whined, her nose at the door, ready to leave.

"It is my honor to serve the empress." Irena was resolute. She gathered her things, promising to return each morning.

A moment after Irena left, Tulia entered, brush in hand. While she tugged my hair into a practical braid, I secured my short sword and Sonus powder at my waist.

Outside, voices grew louder. Some men began laughing. It had been so long since I'd heard anything jovial; the happiness jolted me.

"Empress," the chipped-tooth guard called, his voice becoming familiar. "Prince Petre has returned."

"Thank you," Tulia called out as she finished securing a simple golden circlet on my head. She gave me a tight smile before leaving. I hesitated to follow; Petre would undoubtedly take me to see his brother, and I hadn't seen Asander in weeks. I fidgeted with my sword, readjusting it, before pulling myself taller. I stepped outside, and the morning chill slapped me.

Past the two black-clad Imperial Guards flanking my tent, the campsite was blanketed in a layer of white. I squinted, the morning light half-blinding me as it bounced off the glittering snow. Petre was steps away, joking with a unit of Dacian soldiers as they ate breakfast.

"Would you like an escort?" the crooked-tooth guard asked.

"No, thank you." I glanced at him then jerked my full body in his direction, staring. It was the guard from yesterday, but not quite. He had black hair and coloring of a Dacian but with Getaen features that looked eerily familiar.

"Rufus?" I whispered.

The lean guard flushed, subtly letting Midnight sniff him.

"Go check on Rubia." I quickly dismissed the other guard with barely a glance.

"I was wondering how long this effect would last." Rufus, in the guise of the chip-toothed, lean guard, looked down at his hands.

I checked over my shoulder just as Petre looked up at me. I grabbed Rufus' arm and yanked him into my tent before the prince could draw attention to me or Rufus. Midnight dragged her paws back inside, realizing she wasn't free yet.

He bowed. "It is I, Rufus Highsands."

I couldn't take my eyes off of him. I felt his hands, his arms, his face. Though he had been lean for a guard, he was actually broader than I remembered. When I touched his shoulders, they shrunk down. I jerked my hand back.

His body physically changed at my touch.

"I-I d-don't understand." My mouth moved, but the remaining words stuck in my throat. I had stopped his heart while experimenting with magic. And now, here he was, in my tent, a blend of two people: the guard and himself.

Rufus' soft expression seemed at odds with a Thorn's usual scowl.

"I recovered after the incident in Moesia," he reassured me.

He was too kind. My egregious misjudgment had nearly killed him. Rufus waited patiently, giving me time to process what I was seeing.

"Oh! You're the secret friend Lady Katalin sent." I clutched at my orb. "No wonder you could stay hidden during your travels. What magic is this?"

"While I was abed, I reflected on many things, but mostly on the magic you'd uncovered. I wondered if you'd discovered merely a branch when there was a whole tree. I theorized many possibilities. Most turned out to be nothing. But one... " Rufus lifted his arms and turned around... "became a brilliant disguise."

"Empress!" It was Petre, outside.

"Who else knows?" I asked Rufus.

"Empress Nicoleta," Petre sing-songed. "We have a surprise for you!"

"Only the two of us," Rufus said. "Once I teach you, erase my memory."

"If Tulia sees you, she'll figure it out. Or Jamil, or Rubia... "

"I'll hide in a wagon to sleep. No one will bother an Imperial Thorn."

"Stop interrogating your guard! I have something you *definitely* want to see." Petre drew out the last syllable.

"Find me tonight," I whispered.

Midnight whined at my side, reminding me of her immediate

need for relief. I hurried to the door, emerging back into the morning chill. Petre nearly knocked me over with a massive hug.

"It's g-good to see you, too!" I couldn't help but smile. "I'm relieved you've safely returned."

"I had to cross through treacherous Norte-controlled mountains, not to mention traversing the entire length of my kingdom. Yet, you only beat me by hours." Petre's mouth twisted into a teasing smile. He grabbed my shoulders. "I have some bad news for you as Asander's betrothed."

Despite Petre's light-heartedness, I was anxious to get away from my tent and allow Rufus a chance at escape before Tulia returned. "B-bad news?"

An earsplitting screech reverberated through the camp. Everyone crouched, covering their ears, looking wildly around. Midnight's hackles rose, a low growl rumbling from her chest.

"*That* bad news." Petre gave Midnight a playful scratch behind the ears. She deigned to let him touch her, but her ears stayed straight up, her nose pointed in the direction of the screech.

Jamil jogged over to us and gave Petre a nod. "Your Highness."

Petre straightened. "Good to see you again. I've only just returned with my brother's bird as he requested."

"Ah," Jamil said. "That explains the… "

"The ear-splitting cry of demon spawn? Yes, that's her."

"Shall we?" I urged them both away.

Petre led us north through the camp as he spoke. "Dyana stayed behind with her old battalion. They lost several members, including their captain. The king requested she lead them until spring." Petre's face faltered for a moment before returning to his jovial tone. "Asander will stay with his precious bird at the edge of the camp, keeping her calm. My brother thinks she's the most amazing creature that's ever winged through the air, but I'm warning you to keep your distance. She's a petulant thing that only obeys Asander — and only when she chooses."

Petre handed me a small bag. "There are folded, labeled parchments inside. Each holds a snippet of hair per your request. My father never liked the idea of magic, but when Dyana showed him how your blue-ghost-disc-things worked, he decided that magic had its uses."

I tied the bag next to my Sonus powder, not missing a step. Midnight padded next to me, her hackles raised and head down. I did my best to mimic her light tread through the crusted snow.

Through the trees, something moved. Midnight growled again. This time, her lips curled, revealing her canines. It was hard to comprehend what I was seeing up ahead, but as we grew closer, a massive beast with tawny feathers came into view.

"Zalmoxis," Jamil cursed under his breath. "That's Asander's bird?"

Petre whispered, "I refer to her as 'the castle pest,' but you can call her what you wish."

A twig crunched under Petre's foot, and he grimaced. The creature's gaze immediately swung to the prince. She rose up. Her claws flexed and dug into the snow and earth. I stopped short, trying to process the sheer width of the beast as her wings extended. Tip to tip, this bird could stand in the middle of the Dacian River and touch both sides.

I held my breath. Jamil's hand was already on the hilt of his sword. But how much could my Own do against that beast?

The creature jutted her beak forward, unfurling a deafening screech before it was cut off suddenly when something was thrown in the air. She caught the object with a snap of her sharp beak. Asander threw another morsel. A mouse? A vole? The bird could have easily snapped off Asander's entire hand. Or half his body.

Asander said something in a low, calm tone. The creature sunk a few inches, her wings tucking back. She turned around, walking on four legs like a dog. No, like a cat with a thick, long tail.

"That is no bird," I hissed at Petre, recognizing the creature from mythical drawings.

"Technically, she's a griffin," Petre said. "But according to our lore, griffins are brave and embody the grace of both the wind and clouds. But she's a raging storm."

"Empress, please stay here while I discuss the wisdom of this with Prince Asander," Jamil said.

"That won't be necessary." I jutted my chin in Asander's direction. The prince was striding toward us, yet I barely recognized him.

Asander had grown a short beard, and his eyes sparkled. "Nicoleta. You have safely returned."

Over his shoulder, Asander's griffin craned her neck, staring intently at me with a single golden eye.

"I'm so sorry about the battles while I was gone. I have heard the most terrible things." Saying it out loud seemed to drop a new weight on my shoulders, especially saying it to someone who fought in those battles.

"I fear the snow leopards you mentioned are real. We've heard their cries at dawn and dusk, nearly every day. Sometimes they're eerily close. I'm grateful Petre was able to fetch Baise, my griffin. We will need her."

"What else do you need?" I tried to avoid eye contact with the griffin. Midnight was tense, refusing to sit.

"The guilds are working to keep us supplied," Asander said. "And I received your message and formed a special unit. It is a good idea, but we desperately need more soldiers."

"I have some good news," I said. "The recruits should arrive in two weeks, along with all the magi from the Red Valley army."

Asander leaned back on his heels. "This is good news. How many?"

Jamil spoke up, "The clans only have a few hundred trained guards, and most don't have magic. Only magi will be sent here — around fifty soldiers."

"Only five units?" Asander's face fell.

"They're fifty skilled magi," I added. "They'll fight like an army of five hundred. They were enough to stop the entire Theracian army from attacking Auripo after your grandfather revolted."

"You've traded five hundred soldiers to observe a southern border not under attack, in exchange for fifty here?" Asander's face purpled. "We'll be defeated before spring at this rate. We need to make the army compulsory."

"Let's evaluate the Getaen army when they arrive." I couldn't explain my reasoning when he was this upset, so I redirected the prince. "Introduce me to Baise?"

He swallowed a retort and guided me forward. "Baise is a formidable ally. I think, in time, you may enjoy riding her yourself."

As if understanding Asander's words, the beast jumped to her feet, extending her wings, and let out a screech that rung in my ears. I fell to my knees, pressing my hands to my head.

I was horrified and excited at the same time. If this creature hated the snow leopards with even half the animosity she felt toward me, maybe we had a chance after all.

I Saw mermaids sitting on mountains of bright metal, laughing and throwing gold coins in the air. Their piles grew as they traded arrowheads to the north, spears to the east, daggers to the south, and swords to them all.

When I woke, I had my brother verify with the Historians that mermaids are the Lazican symbol. We'd been taught all the kingdom's symbols when we were younger, but I didn't care much about foreign kingdoms. Seeing them in my dreams is different — living their lives makes me far more interested in learning about them.

— ESME

TWENTY-TWO

ANOTHER'S LIKENESS

Jamil and I trudged through the snow, leaving Petre and Asander to another brotherly argument.

"Our spies in the Curat Mountains should return any day now," I said. Six had started the journey with Dyana and Petre but split up in the mountains. "I need to know the Norte movements."

"War is chaos," Jamil said.

"You must have been very young when you fought in the Red Valley army and against Cassus VI."

"I thought I'd put it behind me, but this brings it all back." Jamil ran a hand across his neatly trimmed beard. "What do you think about the Lazican shipping merchant?"

"Who? Marcus' contact?" I blinked, trying to follow his quick change in subject.

"At the Red Valley's port, Lord Constantin sent a message. I'm assuming he's made an agreement with his contacts in Lazica."

"He will inform us of his negotiation when it's settled," I reassured Jamil, pushing my own curiosity aside. If the offer was risky and involved the crown, Marcus would have requested approval first. "I just hope whatever he did actually works. We need Lazica."

I turned my thoughts to Rufus' Ghoster disguise. If I were to reveal this secret to anyone, it would be Jamil. But I preferred to keep my secret weapon's existence between Rufus and me, for now.

"Per the captain, our soldiers pushed the Norte army back through the pass," Jamil said. "Our soldiers occupy the Norte's abandoned campsite and are scouting the area. But our enemy destroyed evidence of their numbers or dwellings, taking the bulk of their supplies as they retreated."

A shrill cry echoed through the trees, and Jamil and I both looked back over our shoulders toward the griffin's location.

"I'll have the Auripoans moved to the northern side of that camp where the prince's beast will have more room," Jamil said.

"Do you think Asander can control her?" I asked.

"It would explain why he's survived so many battles."

Back in the camp, I busied myself with missives, trying not to think about Rufus sleeping off the last of the magical disguise. The captains and I gathered around the maps, evaluating the remaining army and the recruits, and making adjustments. My stomach was growling when Petre and Asander arrived at our war council.

"I have a message from Dyana," Petre said, handing me a blue disk. "I would have shared it first thing, but Asander's bird was so loud; I couldn't delay the introductions."

I dismissed the captains, clutching the message in my fist.

"Only you can break it, but she intended for Asander to hear the communique, too," Petre said.

I nodded at the brothers and snapped the disk. The edge began to crumble. Dyana's voice boomed inside the tent — she spoke in an irritated tone in her native Auripoan.

"The magic is capturing your words, so go right ahead." Petre's voice responded in Dacian, obviously knowing we'd hear his response. The real Petre in the room grinned, but it didn't reach his eyes.

"Empress Nicoleta Aurelian," Dyana's voice became more subdued as she spoke in Dacian. "Upon returning, I received more grave news. Not only were our battalions beaten back in the attack on the castle earlier this winter, but the Scythians have waged war as if in summer. The attacks are unprecedented. I suspect that our enemy is in league with the Norte. Or, at the very least, with someone who has promised to reinforce their troops. Without outside help, the Scythians will dwindle. And, so will we."

Dyana paused, thankfully, giving me a moment to absorb the gravity of her message.

"King Eusebes is true to his word in his alliance with Dacia," Dyana continued, "Though we are pressed on the east, we are sending a full battalion west. While the Norte are engaged with you, we hope to surprise them with a rear assault. However, with the Norte's short bursts of fighting, the timing will be critical.

"We believe the Scythians are a bloody distraction, and we are changing their game. We have already deployed our finest spies to the west."

I clutched at the True Key, overwhelmed. The Auripoans risked losing their own battles to aid us. I knew the Auripoans' bold move was in hopes of winning the greater war, but seeing their trust and dedication to Dacia took my breath away. Not only was Dacia's survival on my shoulders, but Auripo's as well.

"We are tired. We are hungry. We are worn thin. But we are not beaten." Pausing, Dyana took a breath. "We are coming, Nicoleta. Keep an eye on the Curat Mountains, for we will be there soon."

The disk crumbled to dust in my hand. I curled my fingers around the fragments, clutching them to my chest. We had to hold the Norte. Our enemies couldn't break us, nor could we allow them to retreat into their territory. If we were successful, the Norte would be flanked, pressed between two armies.

"Nicoleta," Petre said quietly. "Can you send food to our people? When the Norte withdrew, they burned every storehouse they could."

"Of course, she'll send supplies," Asander said.

I blinked. Asander didn't control the supplies. "We can't send food just to have our p-provisions fall into the hands of the Norte."

"We can't expect the battalion to survive the trip, let alone fight, if they're starving," Asander shot back. "Dacia has the food. Just send it!"

Petre took a half step away from us.

"I know you want to help your p-people, but we have to think this through. We don't know the location of the Norte. We must wait for my spies to return." I wanted to slam my hand against the table. If I hadn't sent my best spy to lead an expedition into the northern, Norte Mountains, I could have sent additional spies east, to scout for the safest routes to Auripo. I hated that we were spread so thin. What if I'd just sent my spies in the wrong direction?

Asander's face darkened. "This isn't hard. Take the food south. Cross the river. Meet the Auripoans. Save all our lives."

I curled my hands into fists. I wanted to point out that if Auripo had built a proper port, we could easily ship them the supplies. I bit my tongue. Auripo had been engaged in war for decades, not to mention sharp cliffs lined their shore, leaving few safe access points.

"This war cannot only serve Dacia." Asander leaned forward. "We can't give everything and Dacia give nothing."

My jaw dropped, and my words caught.

Midnight growled. Asander shot her a glare, but I didn't shush her or send her away. I stood frozen, torn between what I wanted and trying to see things from Asander's perspective.

"I'll leave you to tend to Dacia's needs." Asander's nostrils flared. "It's what you do best."

He stormed away, and I didn't stop him.

∽

I FUMED as I paced inside my tent. I knew Asander had agreed to marry me for Dacia's resources, his plain inference of such was like a punch to the stomach.

Of course, I wanted to help Auripo. But we had limited resources, and to rush blindly through hostile mountains was foolishness. I wished Asander would use his head rather than his heart to guide his decision-making as I had when I agreed to a marriage in name only.

The tent door rustled as Tulia shuffled in, carrying the large, steaming copper kettle. I jumped over to grab one side of the handle, settling the container near the table to stave off the cold night air.

Tulia wiped her brow. "There's a page here for you with a message from Lady Katalin."

"Send them in." My stomach rumbled.

"I will, and then I'll grab both your dinners." Tulia rolled her eyes at Midnight already leaning against the copper kettle.

A tall page entered, letting in another gust of cold air, as Tulia slipped out. The page pulled back his cowl and gave me a bow.

"Good evening, Empress." It was Rufus' voice.

I jumped and grabbed my Sonus stone, pressing it into his hand. My guards regularly checked the security of my tent, but this conversation was highly sensitive. I had to be careful.

"Rufus? How many disguises do you have?"

"Only these two," Rufus said. "The disguises are of real people, and I obviously couldn't get their consent to steal a lock of hair and impersonate them. I don't like to do it, but the secrecy is necessary."

"How does this work?" I used my free hand to scrunch up the material of his cloak and then prod his elbow. "You feel real. But you somehow look younger, Dacian, and... are you taller?"

"With a well-matched disguise, the magic can last a full day. As you saw, it fades rather than just disappearing all at once." Rufus flashed a modest smile. "Relatively small adjustments stretch the magic to its maximum duration. But say I was dressed in these clothes and I wanted to pretend to be a large woman wearing a full dress and curly long hair, then the spell would unravel in a few hours."

This discovery could shift the balance of the war. I dropped the

Sonus stone into Rufus' hand, then requested the guards do a perimeter check, and then I triple-checked the secured door flap.

I marched back to Rufus and pressed my fingers to the Sonus stone. Even feeling the pulse of magic, I dropped my voice.

"I want to try it."

Rufus squirmed. "Perhaps someone less visible? Like Tulia or even Jamil. I'm sure either would agree."

"No, I don't want anyone else to know yet."

"You are the empress, and I'll do as you command. But I fear letting you jump off an unknown cliff."

"You've already tested yourself multiple times, so it isn't much of a leap. What *you* did was brave."

Rufus shrugged. "As a Getaen in a small village, existing was a risk."

"After you left your village, you could have lived comfortably in a city like Moesia. Why did you come to Rupea when you knew it would put you back in a hated position just like when you were a child?"

"I figured that Zalmoxis couldn't take me any lower than I'd already been. And I survived." Rufus flashed a hint of a rueful smile. "I learned to gamble everything as I knew I could survive with nothing."

Under Rufus' quiet and reflective demeanor was a bold risk-taker. "I trust your work."

Rufus sighed. "Who do you want to pretend to be?"

I glanced at the fuchsia-colored pouch. "Lady Katalin."

"You could, but it's harder to hold a smaller form. If someone goes to put a hand on her *disguised* shoulder, they could hit your *real* shoulder; the invisible barrier will reveal the magical illusion."

"So, I should pick someone larger than me?"

"Yes, but not excessively so. The closer the match, the longer the spell."

"I have one of Gul's hairs."

"She's a stronger match. When the spell begins to wear off, if someone brushes against you, they'll go right through your illusion, similar to putting one's hand through a blue vision ghost.

"Is it possible to break the spell early? Can I end the magic when I don't want to be Gul any longer?"

"Probably, but I haven't figured out how, yet. For now, the spell must wane on its own."

I pulled one of Gul's hairs from the pouch and handed it to Rufus.

Rufus shrunk away. "I think if we had Gul's clothes, it would—"

"Just do it. You already said a hair was all that was needed."

Rufus bit his lip but nodded. From his pocket, he pulled a vial similar to what held Mama's blue vision. He uncorked the top and dropped in Gul's hair, "Almai eodi."

I expected him to tell me to drink the mixture, but he reached the vial up to the top of my head. The rim of the glass lightly touched my scalp. I squeezed my eyes shut. But I didn't feel any liquid, or burning, or... anything.

"Empress," Rufus whispered. "Look."

Smoke billowed down my shoulders, rolling in a thousand swirling clouds down my arms. The mist fell over my face, my torso, even covering my trousers and boots. The smoke thickened, clouding my vision. I was like a sheep wearing a woolly coat.

"I brought two more prepared vials, and I can make more when I track down the ingredients," Rufus said.

"It's possible Rubia or —" I stopped short of saying 'Ziba.' "Rubia has fine taste in ingredients. Check with her." The smoke started to dissipate. "I visited the Red Valley Clan; Ziba and Pari opted not to return."

"I imagine that was difficult." Rufus' left it at that, not prying.

"It still is. They kept a lot of secrets." My voice sounded strange. Deeper. "Part of me is confused, and... I don't know. Mostly, I just miss them."

Everyone had their secrets. Did loyalty equate to total honesty?

"Sometimes, focusing on the best parts of people is the wisest thing to do." Rufus brushed away the last tendrils of the fog. My royal clothing had changed to rougher, looser fitting trousers and a belted, long camasa. Rufus continued, straightening my collar. "I've lived long enough to recognize a genuine person. There are too few of them, Nicoleta. You are to be cherished."

His simple and genuine admiration caused a lump in my throat. Perhaps it was caused by the strangeness of the spell or the happiness at seeing him healthy, but his words resonated inside me.

Rufus pressed the Sonus stone to my palm again. "It's odd to see your facial expressions on Gul's face. I've never seen her even close to emotional."

I sniffed back my tears before playfully smacking Rufus' shoulder. "What happened to cherishing me?"

Rufus pressed two fingers above my heart, his face somber. "Emotions make us human." He stepped back, tilting his head to the side in wonderment. His lip trembled. "It worked. My masterpiece."

I inspected my larger, stronger hands, ran my fingers through my thick, straight hair. I was a stranger in my body. But it wasn't mine — it was a borrowed illusion, yet it felt as real to me as Rufus' disguise had. I tentatively walked around. The way my feet rolled against the ground was different. I jumped up and down, testing my balance. I felt like a child exploring the world for the first time. I patted my torso, my hips, and lifted my leg before stomping my foot against the dirt. Midnight whined but licked my hand.

Rufus handed me the stone again. "Your voice might sound deeper in your head, but the tone hasn't changed much. The Norte may be able to alter their physical body, I assume every organ. My illusion is like a costume draped over you. You'll need practice mimicking Gul's voice. But if the bards can do it, you can, too."

"Your masterpiece is going to get us into the middle of the Norte camp without them ever knowing." It was time I struck directly at the heart of the Norte. "And I know exactly how we'll do it."

I have Seen the same woman several times. Does she impact many people? My people?

Leila reads different languages. She calls herself a linguist. She wears wild roses in her hair like Getaens do. She travels with a man — her husband, I believe. They travel the kingdom, and they have a daughter they dote on.

In some of my dreams, Leila has a son. Sometimes, the husband is a noble. I can tell because he wears a dagger, which is a Dacian tradition. Sometimes, he's a warrior prince with a crown.

I can't help but wonder how many different versions of the same life I've seen. Or if it's different lives altogether. A father and daughter, or a mother and son — their lives connected and crashing together in my visions.

— ESME

TWENTY-THREE

SAAM'S OFFER

Fortunately, the guards took me seriously, and no one was admitted near my tent, not even Tulia. Unfortunately, the next morning, I still looked like Gul.

I'd already told my guards I was sick, but hoping to burn through the disguise faster, I did my exercises until I was dripping with sweat. I let myself be distracted by the maps, calculating the length of time it would take the spies to begin their search of the northern mountains. Another five days, at most? Then I studied probable routes the Auripoan battalion would take as they traveled west toward Dacia to flank the Norte army.

By the late afternoon, my arms and body seemed back to normal, so I sent for Jamil. When he arrived, I assured him I was 'feeling better' and got right to work.

"Has Ivan spoken with the Agricultural Emissary about options for sending food to the Auripoans?" I asked. I'd tasked the captain adjutant to research the options and bring them to me.

"I believe they're in discussion right now," Jamil said.

"I'd like to be there." I'd successfully worn out my Gul-Ghoster disguise a few hours earlier than Rufus had predicted because of all my exercising; I could participate in the conversation.

"Would you like lunch before we go? You haven't eaten all day."

"I'll eat when we get back."

I grabbed my cloak. I stunk from my exercises, and my hair was a mess, but I wasn't trying to impress anyone. Outside, the dusky light kissed me with a bitter chill.

"Please inform Tulia she can return, and give her my deepest apologies for making her find a different place to sleep last night," I said to the guards at the door.

Past Jamil's tent, I was somewhat surprised to see the Auripoans around a fire with some of my soldiers. The Dacians were huddled forward as Petre regaled them with a battle story. I caught a glimpse of Asander through the crowd. He sat with rounded shoulders, his knitting needles flying. The light from the fire danced across his face, but didn't reveal his hidden thoughts.

Jamil led me past other groups of soldiers who were knocking snow off their tents and warming themselves around the fires. When we arrived at the wagon depot, Marcus was deep in conversation with Ivan. Even from a distance, Marcus noticed us arriving and straightened as we approached.

He bowed, but I could tell he was guarded. And why wouldn't he be — I'd commanded him not to speak with me after our argument.

"Ivan's explained the Auripoan situation," Marcus said. "We've been discussing possible delivery routes."

"We don't know the thickness of the ice in the north," Ivan said. "We could build a bridge upriver, but there might be a more efficient way."

"By ship is the most efficient," Marcus said. "The Roe Valley clan has the closest port to the Auripoan border," he added. "We could skirt the coast, anchor, then take rowboats to the shore. Auripo's shoreline is primarily cliffs, but someone in their party must know a usable path. The problem is in directing an Auripoan supply line or contingency to meet us. They don't even know we're coming."

"Prepare a caravan of goods," I said. "If we don't hear back from the scouts in two days with knowledge of a safe route, we'll go to the Roe Deer clan. Asander will have to get word to his people to meet us."

"I'll begin immediately," Marcus said.

"Ivan, please apprise Prince Asander." I dismissed him and turned to Marcus.

"Do you think your Lazican shipping merchant will come to our aid?"

Jamil took a step back, usually indicating he felt it was not his place to comment. But he kept walking, stopping five paces away, his gaze sweeping the area.

"Let me explain," Marcus said. "My papa and this Lazican merchant have known each other all their lives."

At his serious tone, I clutched my gloved hands behind me, bracing myself.

"Our apples are an exotic luxury in Lazica. Over the generations, our families have grown close." Marcus glanced up and held up a hand for a wagon driver to wait. "The merchant honored our family with an offer of exchange. With royals, there's a threatening undertone when it comes to hostages. But wealthy families of Lazica do this to build strong relations with other influential families of neighboring kingdoms."

"And you agreed? Who are you sending?"

"My little sister. She's always begged to travel, and she's the right age. My parents delayed making the arrangements, cautious of any reason that might have denied me the emissary position. Because we didn't readily accept the offer, I spent much of my time in Lazica smoothing ruffled feathers. In the end, part of the reason I found new favor was *because* of my emissary status; the more influential the family, the better the exchange."

"Who are they sending to Dacia?"

"The Lazican merchant has two sons and two daughters. I told them I'd be happy to host any of them."

Some of the tension uncoiled from my shoulders. I'd expected some horrible concession in securing the Lazican ally. "They may trust you to host each other's families, but what makes you think they'll help us in war?"

Marcus stepped closer, his voice almost a whisper. "They're trusting me with their child. Money and resources mean far less to this family than their own flesh and blood. An agreed exchange insinuates they'll leverage their influence to protect their child, including any *kingdom* in which their child resides. Though, if Lazica is attacked, the merchant will expect the Dacian crown to assist in kind."

I rolled my lips together. "Thank you for b-being straightforward with the expectations."

Unless Lazica would commit fully and openly to being an ally, I couldn't make any promises of aid on Dacia's behalf. It was all I could do to protect my own kingdom, let alone the very kingdom creating weapons for our enemies.

Marcus stepped back, and I realized how close we'd been standing. Marcus glanced at the waiting wagon driver, and I studied his profile before he turned back to me.

"Clarifier magic dulled my memories of the Red Valley," Marcus paused. "But I remember feelings. Snippets of where you were standing or things you said. We talked, didn't we? In a garden?"

Heat rose inside me. Marcus hadn't mentioned our conversation since, and I'd assumed he'd forgotten. I resisted the urge to touch my cheek where he'd kissed me.

"I actually hadn't agreed to host anyone, not until after you and I spoke in the Red Valley," Marcus confessed. He paused, and I couldn't help but get swept up in his stormy gray eyes. "I'd not committed while I was in Lazica because I wasn't ready to move forward with anything that affected my personal life — traces of you were in all my thoughts, in everything I did."

His admission tore through me. I wanted to blurt out that I still cared for him, that Asander would never love me, and that I didn't love him either. But what would that accomplish? It might feel good for a moment but would ultimately only cause us both further heartbreak.

"But I understand, as I have for a long time, that the crown must do what is right for the kingdom. So, I am tempering my emotions. Our conversation in the Red Valley garden pushed me to remember my promise to you. I'm forever your devoted servant, and I committed to help preserve Dacia. So, I resolved to let go and move forward."

"I'm glad." The words tasted like acid, but I offered a stiff smile. "No matter what, I will always cherish your friendship."

There could never be anything more. My insides twisted into a hundred knots. I don't know why we kept allowing ourselves to be drawn to each other, a vicious cycle that only burned us both. But what could be done? We'd be working together. And he was a trusted ally when I had too few.

Even when we'd argued, he'd respected my boundaries. I hadn't even told him I'd done as he'd advised. He didn't sulk or push but supported my decisions anyway.

"Lord Constantin." I hugged my arms around myself. "Thank you for telling me your concerns about the water. Please don't ever quit sharing your expertise just because I don't want to hear it."

"I would never dream of it." Marcus gave me his half-grin, but it felt broken.

I hoped the intensity I felt every time I saw him would fade sooner rather than later. It was torture. I signaled to Jamil and gripped his arm as we returned to the camp. Jamil must have noticed my measured breaths because he directed me straight back to my quarters.

My fiance waited outside my tent.

"Asander," I said a bit sharply. I felt raw and rung out after seeing Marcus, and I didn't have the energy to deal with the prince's moods. "Ivan informed you of our caravan of supplies to Auripo?"

"With Baise, I can make the arrangements to coordinate the transport. I can fly there and back in a matter of days."

The sun had dropped below the trees, but I could see well enough to notice Asander's tentative expression as he held out something he'd knitted.

"A gift. It just never seemed the right time to give them to you." Asander licked his lip. "I realize that was my fault."

I unfolded the gift: long, woolen socks. Expertly knotted, they were beyond my skill. "These are exquisite."

"They're dark green, for Dacia. I wove in a thread of red, representing me, and a thread of yellow, representing you." Asander put his hands over mine, holding the socks between us. The gesture was wooden, but it was kind.

"I don't know what to say." I was surprised at his peace offering. "Thank you d-doesn't seem like enough."

"If you'll forgive me and consider my earlier offer of singular fidelity, that's enough," Asander said.

Asander opened my tent's flap and bade me goodnight. I stood inside, basking in the smells of barley stew, my fingers running along the nubby socks, and listening to the prince and Jamil's muted discussion on shield styles. I'd assumed Asander either didn't remember or regretted the offer he'd extended while still under the Clarifier's influence. Was I wrong? And if I was, what did that change?

Away from the other soldiers, my own special unit used white Sonus powder on their fingers in an attempt to push rocks off a log. After two days of practice, they'd only wriggled the stones that lay *just* beyond their fingertips.

Fortunately, I had help in training them: Rufus. He had pretended to arrive by horse, and only Jamil seemed to question our story. Asander and I stood on the edge of the field, evaluating my unit's progress.

"Your Sonus wielders will never be as potent as a single

Auripoan with a disk bow, but it will catch the Norte off guard, which is excellent," Asander said.

"They might surprise you," I responded coolly. "Liviana is doing well."

Along with the others, Marcus' sister had been invited to join the unit without knowing I'd be the captain, nor knowing the full extent of the training.

While I had been away in the Red Valley, Asander had done as I'd asked and appraised soldiers based on their natural spear and javelin abilities and their magical aptitude. All of my Sonus recruits were sworn to secrecy. I'd have to eliminate another two if they couldn't master the needed skills soon, and a Clarifier would blur their minds as to the magic we were manipulating. I intended to keep my unit secret until they stepped foot on the battlefield.

Asander looked over at Liviana as she sent her rock tumbling off the log with a pathetic *plop*. "She's the best of them?"

Not wanting to dwell on my unit's tepid performance, I changed the subject. "I have news you'll like to hear, my prince. I've put out a call to the Healers and Protectors. The first twenty to volunteer to serve the Auripoan army and have their supplies in order will be paid an additional gold piece for six moons of service."

Asander lifted a hand to his mouth, but he quickly fisted it and tapped his chin, trying to hide his emotion.

"I promised to help your people," I said, "but I'm not one to rush headlong into action. I won't be that kind of ruler, and I hope you can respect that."

Asander nodded but didn't meet my eyes.

"We haven't heard back from our scouts in the Curat Mountains." We'd been rotating groups of scouts east, through the mountainous terrain, for over two moons. Some didn't return. And with our strongest scout redirected to the north, acquiring timely information was a struggle. "I fear the current teams have been captured or killed. Our best option is to send the caravan of goods, Healers, and Protectors by sea."

Asander straightened. "I'm ready to leave at your command to coordinate the supply line and guide the Dacian ships to safe anchor locations. And as the scouts have not returned, I'll gather information on Dyana's battalion myself; I'll bring back the information we need."

"Please be careful. The Norte… I'm nervous." Could they mount an attack against an air-born griffin? If they'd spotted Petre earlier, they might have prepared an attack option. "They've been quiet."

"The Norte have fought using this strategy from the beginning. Days of nothing, then rapid attacks," Asander said. "They're dictating the pace of the war. But when the might of the Auripoan army comes down on them… we'll end them in one day."

Asander's firm belief in a decisive victory was inspiring. I wanted to tell him of my brilliant plan to spy on the Norte — thanks to Rufus' Ghoster illusion. But I pressed my lips together. I was going to great lengths to hide my Sonus unit; I wouldn't risk even whispering of the Ghoster magic's newfound ability until absolutely necessary.

I hadn't decided who I would send to infiltrate our enemy. The candidate would have to be both a confident liar and wise enough to know when to keep their mouth shut. Someone with survival instincts. If Valentin were alive, I would've sent him. Asander was an option, but was he the best one? He could fight his way out if discovered, but I wanted someone unlikely to be revealed in the first place. Asander's volatile emotions served him well on the battlefield, but a cooler head and craftier heart were needed for any chance of success. Plus, knowledge of the Norte language would be essential. Who knew how many chances we'd get to spy on the Norte before they caught on? I had to choose my spy carefully.

"Before you leave, did you gather the black arrows your father sent?"

"They're in a bag inside your tent. What's your plan?"

"I'm going to ask the most skilled Getaen blacksmith to make a set of weapons for my Sonus unit — javelins and spears. My Sonus unit will be able to throw their javelins harder and faster than anyone else."

"If only they could properly channel the magic."

"You were just as terrible in the beginning." I lightly elbowed him in the ribs. "The javelin tips will be iron. We'll use the black Auripoan metal for the spear tips."

"But we were gifted arrowheads."

"A blacksmith will have to melt, re-size and shape them. I know that only the finest craftsmen of Auripo are allowed to touch black metal, but we must make do."

Asander frowned. "Let me take the arrowheads to Auripo for reshaping."

I had prepared for his inevitable concern. "I need you to focus on a route for a ship full of goods and people. It won't be an easy task."

"I must prepare for my flight," the prince bid me a brisk goodbye.

"Asander." I stopped him, not wanting to part on a sour note. I lowered my voice. "I need you. Return as soon as possible."

Asander softened and took my hand, guiding me across the field just far enough to garner my unit's attention. Angling himself so that we were on full display, he gave me a farewell kiss on the knuckles. Then he jogged away down the path that led to the northern camps where his griffin waited.

I blushed, feeling my unit's attention. Thankfully, Rufus cleared his throat and restarted the training. One of my Own rushed down the path and spoke with Jamil. Nodding furiously, the two of them grew animated. I joined them, and Jamil gave me the update.

"The Red Valley army is only a day out. They've sent an advance party to apprise us and to start laying out their camp."

"They're only seven days behind us?" I expected them to take two weeks to arrive.

"Six and a half," Jamil said. "And we need to prepare for a full century of soldiers."

They already sent a hundred soldiers. Did I hear that correctly?

Jamil continued, "Plus another hundred support individuals: Healers, Protectors, farriers, blacksmiths, carpenters — everyone Cyrus thought we would need."

I opened my mouth but was too stunned to speak.

"There's more. The Roe Valley clan has sent a representative as well, letting us know they await your command. I wouldn't be surprised to hear from the High Sands clan, too."

I grabbed Jamil's arms. Making sure he was real. His words were real.

"You were right. I was wrong," Jamil said. "Going to the clan was the best decision you could've made."

I let out a yelp and jumped up and down, my heart soaring. I didn't care that I was right, only that... I was *right*. So many things could have gone horribly amiss, but in the end, I convinced all the Getaen clans to join us. I hugged Jamil, cried, and hugged him again. He stood like a fence post, but I didn't care.

"You know what this means?" I shook my Own.

"You'll easily have your Healers and Protectors to send in the caravan to Auripo, for one," Jamil said.

I could hardly contain my excitement. When Asander returned with information on the *flanking* Auripoan army, we could send in a spy to infiltrate the Norte camp. Between the Auripoans, the Norte spy's reconnaissance, the Getaen clans, and my Sonus unit, we could possibly have all the pieces we needed to strike — to pierce a hole straight through the heart of the enemy's offensive, turning this war upside down.

Nine days after Asander left, battle raged. I was too far from the fighting to hear the fray, but not knowing what was happening set my teeth on edge. The latest report was favorable — our forces, combined with the Red Valley army, had pushed the Norte back, but not into full retreat.

I focused on my Sonus unit, training in a secluded area, guarded by a wide perimeter of my Own. They'd made steady progress since we'd begun. Not surprisingly, the Getaen Sonus of the group had surpassed the others and had taken over for Rufus in the training exercises. While he was an excellent teacher, Liviana was the more compelling leader and was my second in command.

"Your practice with the Norte language is paying off. The vibration is much stronger," I said to one of the recruits. He gave me a quick nod, extending his white-tipped fingers toward a stone two paces away.

With any luck, Asander would return today. With the Red Valley army and the new recruits, both the main camp and the one deeper in the mountains were full. I was depending on Asander for information on the Auripoan army before I sent a spy into the Norte camp. If I deployed the spy too early, the Norte plans could change by the time the Auripoans arrived.

Seeing Jamil approaching, I signaled to the Sonus in my unit to take over the training. I jogged to meet my Own, Midnight trotting at my side.

"This was delivered half an hour ago." Jamil handed me a letter with a purple wax seal.

I raised my eyebrow and tried not to snatch it from his hand. Emperor Saam's messenger had found me at last. I waited until I was at the edge of the camp before I snapped the seal.

Most Esteemed Golden Empress,

Thank you for hosting us in Dacia. I apologize for departing before we could finish our discussions. I am pleased to see that you have retained the crown, and I would like to resume our negotiations.
I look forward to seeing you in person again soon.

Emperor Saam Oeagrus

I thrust the letter back to Jamil. "Who does he think he is? He acts as if his closest adviser hadn't tried to kill me."

Yasmine had succeeded in murdering Marianna. My throat closed, my body shaking. I stormed away from the training area. Jamil hurried after me as I ranted.

"How d-dare he request anything. He didn't think his ships getting caught crossing the sea, nor his troops gathering on our border was worth mentioning. He was only at Rupea, in the first place, to decide if he should d-double cross me or not. And I'll bet he suspected Yasmine's nefarious intentions but didn't stop her."

The more I thought about Saam, the angrier I grew.

"Empress," Jamil said softly, stopping me in my tracks.

I spun, ready to argue, but realized why he'd interrupted me. We were in an area of the woods I didn't recognize. Pine trees huddled all around, covered in fresh snow.

"It was wise to get your frustration out without an audience. But there's a risk in wandering further. The clouds are thickening and moving fast."

Midnight searched the immediate area as I paced back and forth, not admitting that I'd impulsively stormed in a random direction. That wasn't like me. I shook out my hands, remembering what Tulia had told me: think like Katalin and tamp down blinding emotions.

I muttered to myself, "Katalin would think ten steps ahead. She'd see the different angles."

Jamil scanned the area and back toward camp, not commenting.

As I paced, the snow compressed down revealing patches of mud. I wrapped my cloak tighter against the wind's bite. "Theracia is coming to war whether we want them to or not. But they *shouldn't* be able to march for a year, perhaps two."

"Yet, we've caught their ships and seen their gathering troops." Jamil scratched his beard.

I had held tight to a thin strand of hope that we could win the war before Theracia joined. Even after we'd been alerted of the ships, I'd had hope. Yet, I had to prepare as if Theracia was further along in mobilizing than we'd believed possible. But *how* far along were their preparations?

After we'd questioned the Theracians we'd detained after the Battle of the Rose Court, we quickly discovered they were in lesser positions of trust and were not even aware that the emperor was fleeing. They had little information to share beyond their businesses, estates, and Theracian life.

Several had asked not to be returned home. Apparently, Saam had a habit of publicly stoning those who had been captured in the past. The stories of the emperor were the most useful insights into my enemy.

"Saam's vanity has no end," I said. "He believes the God of the Sea has destined him to rule all of Cornara. He has his own, malformed ethical code."

Theracia wanted colony states. Though Saam might do a few paltry things for us, in the end, he'll crush Dacia with his demands of heavy taxes and our citizens in other wars.

Jamil cursed under his breath. It took me a moment to realize it was a Norte word. I blinked and looked up at him. I'd been trying to figure out who to send as a spy when the answer was right next to me the whole time. I'd been considering younger options, but Jamil was a cool-headed, stealthy, experienced soldier. And he knew the Norte language. He was well into his fourth decade but was twice as fit as people half his age.

He tilted his head, considering me, but I didn't offer up my plans, and he didn't ask. Even in this remote location, it wasn't secure enough for me to explain.

"If I can speak to Saam, perhaps I can uncover some of his plans," I said, redirecting my thoughts back to the issue at hand. "Moreover, I'm willing to talk to him again even if there's only the slightest chance we can avoid bloodshed."

We trudged back to camp, the only sound the hushing of our cloak hems over the snow and the crunch of our boots. Smoke billowed from fires above the trees, the heat carrying ash and embers into the sky.

As we neared the camp, an Imperial guard approached us. I picked up my pace, hoping for news of Asander's return.

"A Theracian representative is here to see you," the guard reported.

"Now? Already?" I asked. "Is Emperor Saam with them?"

"Just the representative, along with another representative from Illyria."

I splayed my fingers at my sides. I had not been given time to mentally prepare to meet with representatives. I was half-tempted to send them away. But the one thing I could not afford was to ignore a threat as great as Saam. At the same time, I had no idea what I *should* do to avoid becoming Theracia's next vassal state.

However, I was out of time to figure it out.

I rapped the Canina Thorn at my hip. "Send for Tulia and Irena. I have a negotiation to prepare for."

Inside my tent, Irena performed her Protections, and Tulia dressed me in an intimidating soldier's uniform, but without my leathers. Jamil entered as she selected my crown: a thick circlet with a massive emerald in the center.

"The representatives sent the emperor's letter just ahead of their arrival," Jamil said.

"Interesting." I held still as Tulia secured the crown. Saam wasn't the type to make a request and offer to see me if he didn't intend to keep that promise. So why send his representatives instead of coming as he'd said. What kind of game was this? Perhaps the representatives were in preparation for a future meeting. "I can understand why Saam would send a Theracian representative, but why the Illyrian?"

I knew little of the Illyrians except that they had been conquered long before I was born. They were seafarers, like the Theracians, but worshiped many gods. Zalmoxis was more than enough god for me to avoid, let alone dozens of deities.

"We will soon find out," Jamil said. "As soon as you're ready, I'll send for them."

Without Pari or Ziba, or any of my advisers, I felt like a bug about to be swallowed. Ziba had lied and manipulated many people, but she'd constantly reminded me of my capabilities, instilling me with confidence. I felt her absence keenly.

Jamil was my most trusted guard, but he wasn't in the habit of advising me outside of the protection I needed. He was a vigilant Thorn, but he'd been trained too long to be subservient to the crown.

A guard announced, "Theracian delegates to see her majesty, Empress Nicoleta Aurelian."

Tulia cursed and shrunk against the side of the tent, out of the way. My mouth dried, and my knees turned soft.

The guards opened the door and led in two men, both blindfolded. The first was a slender Theracian with a trimmed mustache and perfectly combed hair. He removed the blindfold, revealing cruel cunning in his deep-set brown eyes. Another man followed, unfastening his blindfold. He had the same black hair as the Theracian, but the Illyrian had a lighter complexion. Like Jamil, he had a military precision to his step but appeared to be a decade older with deep wrinkles around his mouth and eyes, undoubtedly from years of scowling.

The Illyrian bumped Tulia as she made her way out, clearly on purpose, and spat something in another language under his breath. The Theracian smirked but otherwise ignored the interaction. I narrowed my eyes at the newcomers.

The Theracian stepped forward. "I am Romnic Ghorba, official representative to Emperor Saam Oeagrus, and this is Captain Kekad Dardan. Emperor Saam sent us to discuss the terms of your surrender."

I gripped my hands together behind my back. It didn't matter that I had no response to such a demand because the Theracian delegate continued with the lengthy terms. Ridiculous terms I'd already rejected when Saam had visited Rupea Castle.

My fingers tingled in my grip. I wanted to tell them to get out of my tent, but I had to salvage something from this meeting.

"Are you not going to inquire as to the health of your people?" I asked. "They're all healthy and have been well attended." I could have dumped them into the city prison or even the dungeon. Either would have been warranted considering their kingdom's involvement in the plot against the crown.

"If you're expecting a ransom, you're sadly mistaken," Romnic droned. "They are responsible for their own payment."

Inwardly, I wanted to scream. Instead, I changed tactics.

"No other kingdom has magic like the Norte. They've been stalking Dacia for decades like wild beasts — now they're pouncing. If you think they'll bring you to the feast, you're wrong. They won't even leave you to your own meal. To the Norte, you're nothing but delicious oysters to crack. Dessert. They will eat you up and spit out your bones."

"You do not know Theracian might," Kekad spoke in heavily-accented Dacian as he stared at me, not hiding his disgust. "Attempting to fight brings destruction. Illyrians mightier than you. We destroyed. You destroyed, too."

Ah, the reason for bringing the Illyrian became clear. He was my warning. The proof of the futility of fighting. I was unnerved by Kekad, but not in the way that Saam had intended. This Illyrian was a doll to Saam — a puppet to control. The colony state, like the man, had lost its agency. I refused to let ours go without a fight.

"I offer Theracia a chance to join us," I tried not to sound like I was begging. "No matter how strong you think you are, the Norte are stronger."

"Disappointing. If that is your only argument, we have nothing more to say here," Romnic said.

Romnic and Kekad both turned to my soldiers for their masks. My guards looked to me. I shook my head and waited for what seemed like an eternity before the delegates reluctantly returned their attention to me.

"Tell Emperor Saam *my* warning," I said.

Romnic tapped his toe with impatience. However, the Illyrian captain gave me a curious look. Pity perhaps?

"The emperor thinks he'll marry the future Norte crown," I enunciated each word. "Or he thinks he will take the crown for himself. B-both will be wrong. The opportunity to join with us is now." I nodded to my guards, who handed over the blindfolds.

I stared at the door after the two men had left, my chest heaving.

"That wasn't a negotiation," Jamil glowered. "That wasn't even a discussion."

"What did you make of them?" I asked.

"Captain Dardan must have been a child during the Illyrian wars," Jamil said. "Conquerors often put responsibility for quailing local unrest with native rulers — ones deemed easy to control. The Blood Conqueror did the same within the Getaen clans. That tells me a lot about the captain."

"They came to deliver an ultimatum. And we learned nothing." I was more determined than ever to get a spy into the Norte camp.

Jamil folded his arms. "At least, the delegates had little opportunity to glean information with the blindfolds. We could detain them, but Emperor Saam would never attempt to communicate with us again."

Tulia rushed back into the tent, the hem of her dress wet. She pressed a folded piece of parchment into my hand. "That Illyrian, I think he put this in my pocket. I noticed it right before I started washing the clothes.

I unfolded the note, deciphering the scrawl: "conch shell."

"The Illyrians gave me a conch shell after I ended the plague." A strange gift, still back at the castle.

"What are you going to do?" Tulia asked.

"Send for the shell." I hoped Katalin had done as I'd asked and not sold it. "There's something about it we missed."

When I awoke, my skin was raw with scratch marks all up and down my arms, legs, face, and even my torso.

I'd had the Lilac Plague. No, I'd only Seen it, but the pain felt real.

The scorpion-caretaker was gone. Mama said she sent her most trusted adviser away after she returned home to find me scratching, bleeding, and crying. Mama apologized for not noticing my ill-treatment sooner.

I could barely form words, I was so relieved. I hated the scorpion and hadn't realized it was possible to live without *her cruel shadow over me.*

— ESME

TWENTY-FOUR

GRAVE NEWS

The bitter winter cold had set into my bones. No matter how much I tried to warm myself, I never seemed to be able to shed the chill. Even in my tent with the hot coals buried plus the steaming, copper, pumpkin-shaped kettle, I couldn't stop shivering.

The bonfires got larger, woodcutters bringing in a stream of split logs. The Red Valley clan had pitched fine tents, and the Auripoans taught them how to modify the structures, allowing for fires inside. Most of the smoke rose up and out through carefully engineered holes. The remaining debris was a small price to pay for heat.

But most of my troops didn't have fine tents. They placed their lean-to structures around fires, the fronts open, the backs pinned down to reflect the heat.

Before the soldier's evening routines, I met with Rufus in my tent for an update.

"Between Rubia and I, we have all the supplies to prepare another Ghoster disguise," Rufus said. "We had to find someone with nutmeg, which took a while to track down."

"And no one knows what it's for?" I asked.

"Rubia knows it's a secret and didn't ask questions," Rufus

said. "Thankfully, she lied to Lord Constantin, so hopefully, he won't be suspicious."

"You got nutmeg from the Agricultural Emissary?"

"He was one of the few people who thought to bring dried spices. And I'm glad he did. Can you imagine how much worse the dinners would be without them?"

I grimaced. "They can't get much worse."

"That's your royal taste buds. Trust me, these meals are palatable, especially for… " Rufus trailed off. From the snippets he'd shared of his past, he'd been an unwelcome Getaen, essentially a Lilac as he drifted from town to town. My heart broke for him.

Rufus cleared his throat. "I think that poor lad is freezing. Lord Constantin's tent is away from the main bonfires, near the depot. It's strange because the folks in the Rodnic Valley generally favor a particular container that they fill with boiling water—"

Rufus pointed to the copper, pumpkin-shaped heater between mine and Tulia's pallets. Midnight had dragged a blanket over and was curled up next to it.

"—like that one," Rufus said. "The emissary forgot to pack his. He won't make that mistake again."

I cursed under my breath. Tulia obviously knew that it was Marcus' but had decided my comfort was more important. Or hers. It was hard to say for certain.

Rufus held up a Ghoster bottle. "I only have one for a trial practice. The new one that Rubia helped with will be done soon — we'll use it for the real *event*."

My guard announced Jamil just before my Own entered.

"The fighting has stopped," Jamil announced. "Half the Auripoans are coming back from the caves to camp here for a few days."

"Good, I need to talk to Petre." I hadn't approached Petre to discuss it, but Asander had been gone for over two weeks. We'd expected him back days ago. I needed to infiltrate the Norte, and I couldn't wait for Asander any longer. I needed to update him on some of my plan.

"I can fetch the prince for you," Rufus offered, moving to the door.

"No, I need to speak with both of you," I said, holding out my Sonus stone. I waited for them to press their fingers to the surface. "Rufus, I spoke with Jamil last night about the Ghoster disguise, and he's agreed to be the spy."

"Would it be prudent to perhaps send someone who knows the Norte language better?" Rufus said, timidly. "Possibly someone from the Red Valley clan."

I knew he meant: *Someone with magic will know the Norte language.*

"Another person might know the language better, but I trust no one more. We will test it on Jamil tomorrow."

"Of course, Empress," Rufus said.

I dismissed the Ghoster so he could return to his work. I placed the Sonus on the table and tugged on my gloves as I looked over the map. "I get tired of all the waiting, Jamil."

"War is chaos."

"So you've said."

Of the few scouts I had to send through the Curat, the only ones to return had investigated the southern end of the mountains, near the mouth to the sea. So as of a few days ago, the Norte hadn't completely blocked access to Auripo. Yet.

"The battalions are ready to attack?" I asked.

"They'll be ready," Jamil confirmed.

"I'd planned to send you into enemy territory shortly before the Auripoans arrive. But, without Asander, we'll have to estimate Dyana's timeline." We planned to press the Norte, hoping the distraction would protect the Auripoans as they flanked our enemy. "In the meantime, if the Norte attack someplace other than the Curat, we're vulnerable."

Jamil nodded. "Let's hope Julius and the spies that Lady Katalin sent him with into the Norte mountains return with good news."

"If they find nothing amiss, that means I diverted spies for no reason." I tapped my finger on the map.

"We've been strategic with the battalions, spies, and all the resources we have," Jamil assured me.

But would it be enough? Without Asander or the information from scouts, I would be sending Jamil in blind and hoping the Auripoans appeared shortly after he returned.

"I need some air." I pushed out of the tent into the biting wind that kicked loose snow through the air. Around the fires, soldiers shoveled soup into their mouths. The sky was still hidden under thick clouds, making the days feel like endless night.

Jamil and I trekked through the snow to find Petre. Near the Auripoan camp, the only sign of life was the slow curl of smoke coming out of the top of the tent. An Auripoan sentry seemed to appear out of thin air.

"Empress, we weren't expecting you." The Auripoan stilled as Midnight approached. "Would you like me to clear out the tent for you to speak with the prince?"

"No, I hate to disturb everyone after returning from battle," I said as Midnight returned to my side. "But I do need to speak with the prince."

The sentry ducked into the tent, and Jamil's gaze darted from Midnight as she trotted around the trodden area to the nearest trees.

Petre emerged, tugging his fur-lined cloak on over the top of his undergarments. "Nicoleta, is everything all right?"

"Yes, yes, were you asleep? I apologize. Had I known, I wouldn't have disturbed you."

"I should have come to see you when we returned," Petre said as the wind began to pick up. I pulled out my orb for more light, and the three of us huddled closer. I noticed a bit of crusted yellow powder around Petre's eye: remnants of Luminary cream. "I just collapsed with exhaustion. The fighting was brutal. The Norte employed new tactics. The Illuminators switched their calls. Instead of warning their soldiers of light, they actually warned of darkness. So most of our soldiers used the wrong side of their scarves."

My heart wrenched. The Illuminator-caused blindness was terrifying.

"Some of the newer scarves are layered inside with both kinds of material — for light and dark. It wasn't as effective but better than nothing. Many of us were able to use our Illuminator cream in time." Petre pointed to the eye with the crusty material around it. "Your Illuminator is a genius. Without him, we would have all been killed."

My teeth chattered with the cold wind stinging my cheeks, and Midnight pressed up against my legs.

"What about the orange-sting?" I asked. The Getaen magi had used it effectively in the last battle.

"The Norte used their scarves more efficiently this time," Petre said. "They couldn't see, but they figured out that by backing away the moment the orange-sting was released and covering their eyes until out of the radius of the poison, they could continue fighting."

Another reminder that the first time I used my Sonus unit, we had to hit hard.

"There's more," Petre raised his voice over the growing wind. "Usually when we attack, we have to go through a horde of Mirrors' Reflections. But this time, they hid Clarifiers amongst the Reflections in the front lines. Their Reflections were able to slay nearly every soldier who had been touched by a Clarifier. By the time we realized what was happening, the damage had been done. They used their switched-Illuminator-calls and retreated."

"How did the Red Valley soldiers fare?" Jamil asked.

"Better, now that they're getting past the shock of experiencing the true power of the Norte. They're better trained than the Dacian soldiers, thank the stars. The Red Valley soldiers dipped every arrow and sword in poison. Even a graze burns like a hot poker. They also brought a few weapons and amulets created by Bonders through the years. None as powerful as your sword but definitely worthwhile; one slices through metal."

The wind whipped, kicking up drifts of snow as the sky darkened.

"Do you think Baise could fly in a storm like this?" I asked.

"Asander is brave, but he's not a fool. If a storm is bearing down or in severe weather, he hunkers down and waits it out." Petre shivered. "All the same, I expected him back already. All he had to do was fly to the castle, make arrangements for our people to meet the Roe Deer's ship, and signal to the ship's captain where to anchor."

"Asander may have decided to oversee the transfer of the goods," Jamil offered. "Maybe accompanied them back to the castle."

"You don't know my brother," Petre shouted over the wind. "He's quite adept at delegating what he considers the 'non-dangerous' tasks. I'm normally not concerned, but my gut tells me something is wrong."

"If... *when* Asander returns, please send someone to inform me immediately," I said. "Go rest, Petre, and come see me in the morning. There's something I need to tell you, but it can wait until then."

Jamil and I hurried back to my tent. The wind cut through my cloak and threatened to push me off my feet. Jamil grabbed my arm, helping me stay on the worn path.

Outside my tent, a lone figure and two Imperial Guards looked like they were about to be blown away. We grew closer, and I realized it was Marcus. I shoved him into my tent, stomping the snow off my boots.

"Careful, you'll get me wet!" Tulia shrunk away from us as she finished making my pallet for the night. She looked at Marcus. "What are you doing out in this storm?"

"A messenger came," Marcus said, handing me a letter with Katalin's fox stamp. The bottom corner was marked with an X. Something urgent. "The young messenger was exhausted. I told him to rest and I'd bring you the letter myself."

I broke the seal before Marcus finished speaking and found a blue Ghoster disk secured inside along with a map. I snapped the disk, and Katalin's voice filled the tent.

I have grave news. I received your request to send scouts north. Several bandits have requested work, and I selected the three fittest who had experience with similar terrain. A total of six spies entered the mountains, including the scout you sent and the bandits. They returned today, only an hour ago.

The good news is that all returned. The bad news is that they discovered several Norte camps. They have marked them as accurately as they could on the enclosed map.

Empress, I do not think the Norte would have allowed our scouts to return had they seen them, but I cannot be sure. Either way, the scouts reported that while some camps are small, some are significant and had more soldiers arriving daily.

I cannot help but be concerned. I fear we are poised to fight the wrong battle. Please advise.

The four of us fell silent as the wind pounded against the tent. I looked to Marcus, stunned. Even if I knew what to do, no one could travel safely until the storm passed — it was crucial that my response didn't get lost en route, regardless of what it was. I slammed the map onto the table, pressing my fingers against the edge so as to not smear the snow-damped ink.

Had every battle up until now been merely distractions from the Norte's real ploy? What were our enemies up to?

I SLEPT RESTLESSLY, staring at the now-cold kettle as the tent began to lighten. Before Marcus left last night, I'd congratulated him on the agricultural guild's approval and recent completion of the first glass house. And though I knew the kettle was his to begin with, I asked him to take it as a reward. He thanked me but declined.

I pushed away any wistful feelings that threatened and sat up. My stomach had been unsettled all night. Ignoring it, I racked my fingers like a comb, ripping apart my tangled braid.

Irena slipped in for my Protections before the sun rose. She was finishing when Rubia arrived.

"Tulia mentioned you haven't been eating well since Patrida-va." Rubia set my breakfast at my side.

Irena's brow furrowed. "This could explain why you've been weaker than I expected."

I pressed my hands to my gurgling stomach. "I haven't had an appetite. I supposed I had a minor illness that would go away."

Rubia paled and looked to Irena. "Could someone have tainted her food?"

Practically flinging me to the ground, they began poking and prodding as they urgently discussed my symptoms.

Panic rose in Irena's voice. "I can't believe I could miss something as obvious as poison."

"In Patridava, you partook from a communal tray," Rubia spoke quickly, trying to decipher what could have gone wrong. "We haven't heard word that the governor or his family is ill."

Irena tapped freshly oiled fingers against my temples. "It's not poison."

Rubia let out a sigh of relief before spitting more questions. "Is she overwrought? What brought this on? What happened in Patridava?"

"Running a kingdom might be considered a minor strain." My sarcasm was more to calm myself than anyone else.

Irena continued to mutter magical Norte words under her breath as she tested my body. She kept nodding, progressing through an array of movements, tapping and running wet fingers across my wrists, ankles, and hovering her palms above my stomach.

Irena froze. "Does the pain come and go?"

I pressed my fist into my belly. "Yes, but it grew more intense in the Red Valley."

Irena looked up at Rubia, fidgeting. "I hate to be presumptuous, but I think I have a diagnosis."

"Speak it, girl." Rubia leaned forward, eyes narrowing. I grimaced, doubting that Irena had seen this protective, impatient mothering-side of Rubia.

Irena folded her arms. "If the empress represses... emotion. That might drive her to sickness. Something changed in Patridava and grew more difficult to ignore in the Red Valley."

I had put so much sadness, pain, and regret into the boxes in my mind, shoving them away. It made sense they were making me physically ill. "Since becoming the empress, there's been much to process and little time to do so."

"But something changed in Patridava?" Irena prodded.

"I don't know. I just need to be healthy."

Irena softened, her arms relaxing into her lap. "I'm sorry, Empress. There's no shortcut for falling out of love. People who think they can just turn off their feelings are lying to themselves."

I wanted to sink into the floor. I could not still be in love with Marcus. My emotions were not making me *sick*. Nonsense. Yet the pain in my stomach was real — an echo of poison, not a figment of my imagination.

Admittedly, when I saw Marcus in Patridava, past feelings resurfaced. But I had moved on — I'd dug a hole and buried what I felt for him. Yes, sometimes those emotions bubbled to the surface, but I just buried them again, and I would keep doing that because that's what was required of an empress.

I pushed to my feet, stumbling to the table.

"I was afraid of this," Rubia said in a low voice behind me. "I knew Marcus was trouble from the first moment I saw him."

I huffed and dug through one of the trunks, pulling out several more maps. "We don't have time for this. We're at *war*."

Zalmoxis, I couldn't have feelings for Marcus. I wouldn't.

"Fine." Rubia turned to leave just as Jamil and Tulia entered.

"I-I didn't expect to see you this morning," Jamil stuttered, fidgeting with the rolled-up map in his hands.

"I don't know why not. I'm here almost every morning," Rubia said.

Behind Jamil's back, Tulia looked from Rubia to Jamil and dramatically feigned gagging before she grabbed a brush.

"Were you able to get all your supplies for Rufus?" Jamil asked.

"I don't see how that's your concern," Rubia flicked her braid over her shoulder and pushed past Jamil, leaving.

Tulia groaned.

Jamil's nostrils flared. "The Empress and I have things to discuss."

Irena shot her papa a sympathetic look and left, but Tulia took her time finishing my hair and picking up my clothing before she sauntered out.

"Why is Rubia so annoyed with you?" I asked.

"I wasn't pleased that Rubia and Irena came to the battle-front," Jamil said, his tone overly casual.

I could understand Jamil's concern for his daughter, but not why he would be upset about anything Rubia did. I considered defending her, but experience had taught me that Rubia could speak for herself.

I turned back to the map of the northern mountains on the table.

"You brought the mountain riverways map?" I asked.

Jamil set it down on the table. "About eighty percent of all the Rodnic Valley is fed by streams and rivers that branch off one substantial river fed by the Norte Mountains."

"And that river comes from a glacier. What do you want to bet the Norte are sitting on that very ice cap at this very moment?"

I added the rivers to Katalin's map, tracing them back to their source, which led me right to the glacier where the majority of the Norte camps were clustered.

Jamil ran a hand down his face. "This changes everything."

A broken family.

A griffin king. He betroths his little sister to someone. She's angry and destroys something valuable.

Who are they?

When are they? *They don't look Dacian or Getaen. The Auripoan symbol is the griffin, so perhaps this is their royal family? They have not been an independent kingdom for long, so I think this is the future.*

Though I can't convince myself it matters. I keep drifting, Seeing their lives rapidly unfold before me.

—— ESME

CHAPTER
TWENTY-FIVE
A PRINCE RETURNS

"We need to send troops to the Rodnic Valley." I pressed my fingers against the map. "I'm inclined to believe Emissary Constantin — the Norte are planning to poison the water."

"If they haven't already," Jamil said.

"Would they poison the river and then attack the valley?"

"Poison and attack the same locale?" Jamil nodded. "Yes. That's the point. They'll eliminate the local population, allowing for easy occupation."

"Not to send more troops is foolishness."

"It's a risk," Jamil said. "Unless we know how to prevent the poisoning, our soldiers could die without a single blade."

"It's a bigger risk not to. I'll send five units. I'll also send word to Lady Katalin, offering to pay recently freed slaves to become our eyes and ears in outlying areas."

"A sound maneuver," Jamil said. "That will require little skill and will enable the trained spies to do more complex work."

"Nikka, we got your message. What do you need?" Rubia spoke as she entered my tent, Irena right behind her. I explained the poisoning and asked what our options were.

"It *might be* possible to pull the poison out," Rubia said, exchanging a look with Irena. "With the help of the Red Valley magi, we could try. They've already done things we thought were impossible."

Possibilities might be endless. I thought about Rufus' Ghoster spell.

"Protectors will want to get to the water *before* it's poisoned," Irena continued. "To try and fortify the land, blocking any damaging magic."

"Whether or not we can remove the poison, we need to know if it's already begun," I said. "I'll dispatch a Healer and Protector to the Rodnic Valley as soon as this storm passes. Any suggestions on who?"

"We'll find a suitable pair to travel to the Rodnic Valley to evaluate the land," Irena said.

I dismissed Irena and Rubia to their work. As much as I wanted to fret and discuss the poisoned water, I was anxious for Jamil to test the Ghoster disguise.

I tapped my dagger, sword, Sonus powder, and emergency packet of medicine. I never left my tent without my supplies. Outside, the clouds were a gray blur beyond the massive falling snowflakes, but the wind had died down.

I followed Jamil through the woods. Midnight trotted through the trees, snowdrifts grazing her chest. Despite everything, the blanket of snow made the morning beautifully peaceful.

"I can't help but think these battles have a purpose beyond mere distraction," I said. "Why else send Borsea here to fight? She's no empty-headed tool, merely a commander for show. As Tatiana's personal guard, she proved more than capable. If they planned the main assault for the Rodnic Valley, why risk her life in a distraction?"

"Perhaps the Norte anticipate overcoming our armies here," Jamil said. "They might consider poisoning Rodnic Valley a last resort, preferring not to damage lands they intend to claim."

"Or crush our army here and then subdue the people through

terror? While Dacians feared poison, the Norte would know which water and food to avoid."

"They'd have all the knowledge, all the power," Jamil said. "But why not send Healers to fight here? Even one could have tipped the scales in their favor."

"Maybe they didn't think they'd need them." I hoped the Norte's sense of superiority was a weakness we could exploit as we did in the Battle of the Rose Court.

We fell silent as we passed a group of soldiers finishing breakfast. Jamil gave them a nod before continuing, "We could move west to the Rodnic and surprise the Norte in the mountains. If we disrupt their plan, we might send them crawling back home, at least for a season."

"But the Norte will return another day. We have to come up with strategies that will stop this war for generations, not moons."

I sensed Jamil had an argument, but he kept it to himself as Rufus came into view, a satchel slung across his chest. After the last skirmish, one of my Own had retrieved a hair off a dead Norte soldier about Jamil's height, which Rufus used. For a quarter hour, we followed Rufus northwest before dropping into a gully. With Midnight stationed at one end, Rufus spilled the potion onto Jamil's head. A thousand swirling clouds enveloped him.

When the clouds rolled away, I gasped. I knew it was Jamil, but seeing a Norte looming right before me sent an instinctual chill of fear down my spine.

Jamil looked at his hands with awe. "No wonder you kept this magic a secret." His voice was only slightly deeper than usual.

"You'll need to practice manipulating your voice," I said. The plan was to capture an injured Norte and question him with a Clarifier. Then, the next time the Norte fought, we would make sure they discovered Jamil, disguised as that captured soldier. "You must convince them you're gravely injured. Just in case you're touched by a Sensitive, a potent medicine will blur your memories for about an hour. The Norte should send you straight to their Healers, assuming they have them. From there, your real work begins. We need to know how many battalions they have. The number of troops. Other tricks and schemes they have planned."

Jamil moved around like he was a toddler at first. But eventually, he started running, jumping over fallen logs. He practiced with his sword and then a dagger, his movements jerking a bit but quickly improving.

"Your disguise will fail within a day," I said. "The easiest way to return to us is if you're sent back into battle, but you can't depend on it. You'll need to study routes through the Curat Mountains to sneak back. It doesn't matter what you learn if you're caught."

"The information in your head could be our downfall." Rufus gave us pitying looks. He had advised me to equip Jamil with poison in case he was caught. But I refused to consider such a dark option.

"Just make sure you get out of there," I reiterated.

Jamil pulled Dacian clothing from Rufus' satchel, putting them over his Norte uniform. With gloves and the cowl pulled low, Jamil was completely covered. If anyone saw his alabaster skin, our greatest secret would be exposed.

"We need to test something," Rufus said to Jamil. "I should have experimented on myself when disguised. I apologize. I don't know why I didn't think of it sooner."

"It's done." Jamil extended his arm and pushed up the sleeve. His forearm was wrapped with a bandage. "I cut myself right before I put on the Dacian clothing over the Norte uniform. I came prepared, mentally and physically, to fully test the magic."

I grabbed his hand, inspecting the bandage — splotches of bright red dots formed a line up his arm. "Why?"

"To see if the disguise will bleed. To test the level of pain," Rufus said.

I squeezed my eyes shut, my experiment and plan becoming more real. "I can stitch your arm if needed."

"I was careful not to cut too deep," Jamil said.

"When I stubbed my toe or knocked into something, it was painful." Rufus cringed. "Slightly dulled, perhaps."

Jamil slid his sleeve back over the bandage. "I didn't want to make a fuss about it."

"I want to inspect the cut," Rufus said. "Now and also when the disguise fails. I want to compare the wound between the Ghoster image and your real flesh."

"Of course." Jamil led us back to the camp along a different route from earlier. Though with Midnight and my fine clothing, it was obvious who I was. We drew too many stares.

"See you soon." Rufus winked before jogging away. We'd already planned to split up and meet at Rufus' wagon, which was out of the way.

Moments later, a page approached, and Jamil stiffened at my side. I considered sending the page away and seeking her out later, but Midnight was already moving to intervene, sniffing the girl. When my dire wolf let her pass, the page gave me a low curtsy.

"Prince Petre has sent word that Prince Asander has returned."

"Thank you," I dismissed her, hoping she wouldn't look too closely at the man next to me. Her gaze flicked to Jamil just before she turned on her heel, but my Own had pivoted away.

Instead of going to Rufus' wagon, we circled toward the Auripoan camp. Shouts resounded all around as soldiers rushed toward the pass. Every camp was vacant, or soon would be, by the way the soldiers were tightening their boots and securing their cloaks.

"Either the captains are switching all the battalions at once," Jamil whispered. "Or the Norte have struck harder than usual today."

The timing couldn't have been worse. Jamil was wearing a disguise which wouldn't dissipate for a day. And another Ghoster vial wasn't ready yet. We could have saved the one we just used and attempted to send Jamil over as a spy during this very battle if only Asander had arrived a day earlier. Even an hour with the information of when Auripoan reinforcements would arrive.

If travel-weary Asander jumped into the fray, we might *never* get the information we needed.

I spun to Jamil. "Go to the wagons. I'll find you and Rufus later."

Jamil grabbed my shoulder. His pale eyes were icy cold. I shivered and reminded myself that the unrecognizable man before me was Jamil. He was the one I trusted most with my life.

"I need to stop Asander. You know he'll be first into battle, and... " *If he dies, so will any information on the flanking Auripoan army.* If I didn't find out approximately when Dyana would arrive, I was flying blind. It was crucial that I sent my spy north at just the right time.

Jamil's grip tightened. For a moment, I didn't think he would let me go. But he pinched his eyes shut and withdrew his hand. "Be quick, and stop him. He's too valuable. Don't let him die."

～

As I passed my tent, two of my Own emerged from the nearby trees. With a flick of my wrist, they knew to follow me.

We raced through the camps while thick snow continued falling, passing others trudging toward the mountain pass. On the north side, the Auripoan camp was abandoned. I clutched the orb at my neck, calling out for Asander.

He was gone. They all were. I kicked the snow, cursing Asander's need to be in every fight.

"Find Prince Asander. He has crucial information," I said to my Own. I recognized Thadeus, the Patridavan. The other guard was older and had been promoted after the Battle of the Rose Court. His close-cropped hair revealed faded scars on his cheeks and nose. He led the way, and Thadeus followed behind us, Midnight at my side.

We melded in with the throng of troops. Before, I had ridden a horse along this near-empty road. Now I felt suffocated, unable to see past my Own in front of me. A screech echoed through the steep valley. Everyone covered their ears and bent low, faces furtively looking skyward. There she was, a gray-gold griffin streaking across the sky toward the battlefield.

Everyone gawked, breaking into excited chatter about the creature above. I bit my cheek, fuming — I'd be lucky to get to the battlefield by sundown at this rate. Thadeus tapped my shoulder, and I spun to see him holding the reins of a magnificent grey and white horse. He helped me into the saddle while the scarred guard mounted his own steed.

"Stay, girl," I commanded my dire wolf.

She whined, her ears down. But I wouldn't bring her. She would protect me but also signal my identity on the battlefield.

"I've got her," Thadeus assured me, holding Midnight's scruff.

Even with the horses, we couldn't progress through the pass clogged with soldiers.

"Your crown," the scarred Own suggested.

I tugged my hood back, missing the warmth, but my crown shone in the sunlight like a beacon, commanding my soldiers to make way. Midnight howled. Between the cry of my dire wolf and my glinting crown, soon the road was cleared, and we raced forward. Strands of my hair pulled free of my crude braid. My cheeks burned with cold, and my eyes watered, but I didn't slow. I imagined Asander exhausted, fighting. Every moment stretched like an hour. I tried to shake off my concern that Asander would be hurt as he seemed impervious to injury. But his bird would attract attention, and she'd never experienced Norte magic. I checked the skies, hoping for even a distant wing, but found none.

The pass widened, and we rode through the old battlefield where the air still stunk of burnt flesh. Galloping across the field, we started up the next canyon path. Soon, we passed the old Norte camp where now our Dacian flags snapped in the wind. My muscles tensed. I hadn't been to a battlefield in weeks and never this deep into the mountains.

I heard the battle long before I saw the rough fortifications and the defending soldiers. The crude structure delineated our land and the fight beyond. I pointed to the line ahead.

We slowed our horses as we wove through the soldiers guarding the entrance through these mountains that led to our camp.

"Make way! Make way for the Empress!" My Own shouted, prompting my soldiers to shift their bodies and shields, allowing us to move forward.

As we grew closer to the conflict, the cries and clanging grew louder. I gripped the Canina Thorn's hilt, my fingers growing slick, memories of my last fight flooding my mind. I wiped the flakes of snow from my lashes, and I tucked my cowl over my crown, hiding it as we squeezed through the last of the make-shift wall before we entered the battlefield.

"Look for the griffin!" I cried.

The fighting was beginning to split — one portion pressing deeper, closer to the Norte, the other attempting to keep the Norte from flanking them, pushing themselves further to the right. Guessing the position of the Auripoans, I pulled my reigns to ride to the right, to the southeast side of the field. My Own held up a hand, signaling we should stop.

"We're away from the fight here. It's best not to make you an easy target, Empress," he said.

"I need to get to Asander." The information was too nuanced to quickly explain and send another soldier into the fray to retrieve it.

"If he's there," my Own pointed east, "he's in the thick of things. How important is it that you get to him?"

I drew my sword. "If he dies, it puts our entire strategy, all our soldiers at risk."

My Own gave me a quick nod. I dug my heels into my horse's flank and jolted forward, quickly coming to the outskirts of the fighting. My Own maneuvered his mount to flank me, slowing just enough to grab a shield from a Norte Reflection that was fighting no one. He bashed the metal against the Reflection's twin who was fighting a Dacian soldier.

My horse reared. A javelin extended from the horse's front shoulder. Someone yanked me from the saddle. As I toppled, I slashed my sword to defend myself but pulled my strike as I caught a glimpse of Dacian green.

Something clanged against my Own's shield. He jumped from his horse, which reared and fled back toward relative safety.

We need to requisition proper war horses. I shook my head at the thought. I had greater worries at the moment.

Between my Own and a Dacian soldier, we pressed through the Norte. For every Dacian and Auripoan, there seemed to be three Norte. The close proximity made it nearly impossible to determine a Reflection from who was real. I spotted a Norte disjointedly fighting, a clear indication of a Reflection, and I darted to cut them down before hurrying back to my Own.

"Stay at my back, Empress. Let others cut down the Refl —" My Own cried out, falling to his knees. A Norte stood over him, bringing down her sword. I didn't think, I just thrust, burying my sword in the space between her breastplate and armpit.

She screamed and stepped toward me, but she couldn't raise her sword arm. She would have rammed into me, but the Dacian Thorn slammed a foot into the side of her knee, sending her into the mud.

I leapt over her, inspecting my Own. He clutched his wrist, blood pulsing between his fingers. His hand had been severed. I didn't recoil, my Healer training taking over.

While I ripped the bottom portion of my camasa, my soldiers fought off more Norte attackers. I wrapped the strip of cloth around his forearm, above the wound. I looked for a stick, finding an arrow instead. Snapping it in half, I wrapped the cloth around the arrow and then used it to cinch the wrap tight. With each turn of the arrow, I checked for spurting blood. When the bleeding was a trickle, I knew the tourniquet was tight enough and tied it off.

"Lie on your back and apply pressure until someone can haul you back to the Healer's tent to properly staunch the bleeding."

He winced and shook his head, staggering to his feet. "I'm near useless without my sword arm, but I can put my body between you and the enemy, and that's what I'm sworn to do, Empress."

I pulled him back down and ordered two Thorns to get him to safety. The battle was so loud that I could only see their lips move as they grabbed my Own, pushing through the chaos as other soldiers cut a path, enabling them to escape the fray.

Still crouched, I scanned the area. Rising up over the heads and shoulders of the fight was Baise, her talons slashing before launching into the sky. Near where she'd attacked, I noticed a group of Auripoans.

"Asander!" I screamed, but my voice was lost in the deafening noise.

With a swipe of Sonus powder to my lip, I cried out, "To me!"

All Dacians close enough to hear moved to my side, following my command as we drove deeper into the heart of the fighting. As we closed the gap between the Auripoans and us, the griffin dropped down again. The Norte drew back, but as they did, I noticed something crouched. It would have blended in with the snow-covered ground further away, but here, in the churned mud, the snow leopard was no longer camouflaged.

I cried a warning, but it was too late. The snow leopard launched into the air, its claws raking the griffin. Baise screamed, flapping her wings but only getting a few feet off the ground. Still, she slashed a front claw into the leopard, leaving red stripes.

Sensing weakness, the Norte rushed forward. They all lifted their cowls — but there was no signal. I cried out a warning, my magically enhanced voice carrying to the soldiers near me even over the screams and metal clashing. I covered my eyes. A pulse of magic, stronger this time. I waited a heartbeat, no more. Then pushed my scarf down with one hand and lifted my sword into my basic stance, ready for the onslaught.

Cries grew louder. In the distance, my soldiers fumbled, fighting to recover from the Illuminator's assault. The Norte didn't quickly retreat. They attacked. I couldn't, wouldn't stand by. I stumbled forward, putting myself between the enemy and my soldiers, my Canina Thorn already raised.

I lost count of the number of times I met Norte, blade to blade. Mirrors, Illuminators, Sonus — I didn't know one from the other. For once, I was grateful for the cold. If any of the Norte were Clarifiers, they'd have a hard time finding any of my skin to touch.

"Empress!" Petre shouted. Around his eyes, Illuminator cream glistened. He pressed against me, shoulder to shoulder, as we made our way to the Auripoan position. Just ahead, Asander and several Auripoans were pushing back the Norte. Baise was on her feet, but her wing hung at an odd angle.

Together, Petre and I moved to fight alongside Asander. The prince's face was dirty with circles under his eyes, unwashed hair tied back. How long had he been traveling? I silently cursed him for not remaining back at the camp.

Screams sounded, and a snow leopard bounded through the soldiers. On its back was a Norte rider, one hand gripping the base of the leopard's neck, the other brandishing a sword.

"They're coming for you, Empress," Asander said, looking at his brother. "We won't let them take you." Petre nodded and moved to join his brother in making a human shield for me.

The leopard closed the gap, and I readied my blade. I didn't know how high the creature could leap, but it might leap over my would-be protectors.

Instead of attacking me, the snow leopard pounced on Asander, sinking its fangs into his arm before turning back for the Norte line, my fiancé dragged like a rag doll.

"Asander!" I screamed. Petre seemed frozen in disbelief and horror. I spun away from him and leapt onto the griffin's back. She couldn't fly, but she could run.

"Go!" I screamed. Baise charged, nearly throwing me off. Where her feathers met fur, I dug my fingers, grasping the leather harness.

With my complexion and fighting alongside Petre and Asander, the Norte must have assumed I was an Auripoan. But riding on the back of the griffin, I made myself a target — and we were headed right for the heart of the Norte stronghold.

Around me, Norte had their cowls lifted again. I jerked my scarf up just in time for a faint pulse of magic. I realized the griffin must have been blinded from the first burst of Illuminator magic. She was tracking Asander on scent.

I shoved the scarf away to see Norte retreating back to their line of safety. The griffin crushed several as she raced unseeing toward her master. The leopard carrying Asander was more cautious, not wanting to maim the Norte soldiers scattered across the field. Baise closed the distance between us and the leopard. With a pained screech, the griffin lifted up off the ground and angled down toward the Bonder. I couldn't reach the leopard with my sword, not even close. I ripped the dagger from my boot and flung it at the leopard, sinking the blade into her hindquarter. The leopard dropped, screeching in pain, sending the Norte around her scattering. The Norte fled, not engaging with Baise, only intent on returning to the Norte line and securing it.

All the better for me.

The leopard slowed, limping. Baise rammed into the leopard's side. The snow cat clawed at the griffin. Baise screeched and scored her talons across the leopard's side. I jumped from the griffin onto the back of the leopard, surprising the Norte rider. He lashed at my legs, a dagger in hand.

I flinched but managed to riposte with my short sword, nicking the Norte's back. With any other blade, it would've been a flesh wound.

The leopard swayed, and I let go, sliding to the ground. The leopard tumbled. I rushed to the mouth of the beast. Asander lay in the leopard's slackened jaws, but he wasn't moving. My breath caught. I wedged my boot against the cat's upper jaw and used my sword as a lever, prying Asander out.

I began dragging him away through the muck when the Norte rider stumbled around the leopard's head. Crying to his beast with unfocused eyes, he didn't seem to notice the painful blisters that I knew were forming across his back.

The griffin was bleeding, Asander wasn't responsive, and my remaining army was on the far side of the field.

As the Norte streamed back to the mouth of their section of the canyon, a few of them broke off, running toward us. I stood up, ready to engage them. Asander stirred; I needed to get him away from here.

"Nicoleta?" he groaned. Blood was pooling in several places on his chest and arm. Puncture wounds from the leopard's teeth.

The ferocity of the icy men and women baring down on us shocked me, even after moons of battle. I couldn't fight their army alone. We had to run.

I sheathed my sword and pulled Asander into a standing position. Cursing his size, I pushed him, shouting at him to grab Baise's stirrup. The griffin screeched at the Norte, flapping her good wing, which seemed to keep the advancing soldiers at bay.

Baise squatted down. Asander tried to hoist himself up. With a burst of frantic energy, I shoved him up and over the griffin's shoulder. I grabbed the strap, pulling myself up, and wrapped an arm and leg across the prince.

"Go!" I yelled, and the griffin bounded back toward the Auripoans. Asander hung limp in front of me. His back was soaked. I gripped him tighter, desperate to keep us both from sliding off.

We passed Dacian soldiers, exhausted on the field. I couldn't tell if Asander was breathing. The Healers at camp were too far away. If I didn't treat the prince on the field, he'd bleed to death long before we reached magical Healers.

I pulled Baise to a halt. Soldiers helped me lower the prince to the ground. Pulling out my emergency pack of herbs, I yanked off Asander's damaged armor. And I got to work, uttering words of magic.

∼

"Nicoleta?" Asander groaned. He lay on my bed pallet in my tent, a much quieter location than the sometimes raucous Auripoan camp.

"Good morning, princess." Petre grinned at his brother. "You've been out for two days."

"Leave him be," I scolded Petre though there was no malice in either of our words. "Your brother is lucky to be alive."

"He's lucky you were there." Petre's voice lost its sarcastic edge, and he moved closer to Asander. "Nikka saved your life. Probably three times. She did lose the dagger, but not to worry; I went back for it."

"You're a dolt," Asander whispered. "What happened? The last thing I remember is fighting and... Mother Earth, is Baise all right? Is she alive?" Asander tried to sit up, but Petre and I pushed him back down.

"Your vile bird is fine. Or will be, anyway," Petre said.

"She's the reason you're alive," I confessed.

"Oh, don't give that stubborn creature all the credit," Petre said. "You dressed Asander's wounds right on the field. It's a rare talent to stay calm with all that blood. Trust me."

"After you've treated people with the plague, nothing much is a shock." The plague was blisters and rotting flesh. Puncture wounds were not nearly as disgusting.

Fortunately, the snow leopard hadn't clamped down, destroying Asander's organs. Clearly, the Norte desired a live, royal hostage.

Even with my skills and Rubia's Healing, Asander would need a full moon of strict rest. Possibly longer.

Petre gave his brother a strained grin. I'd already warned the younger prince that Asander was still in danger of internal bleeding if he didn't rest, not to mention infection. Though, as long as Asander continued Rubia and Irena's ministrations, we expected him to survive.

"Asander, this is very important," I said softly, taking his hand in mine. "Did the Roe Valley clan deliver the goods along with safe passage for the Healers and Protectors from the Red Valley?"

Asander was quiet, his eyes searching the roof of the tent. "Yes, but I had to lead a caravan to the location. After what I saw in Auripo, I feared a spy was amongst them." He gripped my hand tighter. "The Scythians have been brutal. The Healers and Protectors could save us from extinction."

My stomach dropped. This was the army I was depending on to save us?

"Did your father send a battalion west as promised? An army to flank the Norte from behind?" I wasn't sure if it was my hand or his that shook.

Asander's eyes darted across the roof again. "Yes, Dyana is with them. Ten days. I calculated ten days after I returned here."

Meaning, if Asander was correct, we had eight days to prepare. Jamil didn't have much time.

We'd snipped a locket of hair from a captured Norte Mirror who'd bled to death shortly after the battle. We'd tried to save him but to no avail. Still, we'd heard his voice, and a Clarifier extracted a bit of information before he died. And he was Jamil's best match. As soon as the Norte struck again, Jamil would place himself amongst them as the near-dead soldier they'd left behind.

Asander pressed my knuckles to his lips, pulling me out of my thoughts. "I owe you my life, blood sister."

"Then I command you to drink this." I held out a mug of warm tea in my hand. The sharply-sweet scent of fennel nearly covered the more delicate notes of nettle and dandelion. The herbs would help Asander rebuild his strength. I'd added a splash of lemon and squandered some of our precious honey to sweeten the concoction.

Asander drank it obediently before lying back and falling into a fitful sleep.

Petre tapped his fist to his chest. "To my blood sister."

I made a face but then sobered at Petre's frown.

"What does that mean? Blood sister?" I'd heard Asander

mention the term in the past but hadn't paid much attention to his military talk.

"Exactly what he said. He has pledged his life to you. A rarity, but not unknown. Those who live to see the other side of battle are offered a residence with the king, exactly like a sibling. It's an Auripoan code, you might say. My father has blood siblings from battle as well."

"But Asander has saved my life many times in battle."

"But he didn't put his own life in unnecessary peril to do so, did he?" Petre raised his brow. "We all fight alongside each other. What you did was different. Even without the wedding, you're officially family. If you accept the title, any one of us would give our life for you, and we'd expect the same from you."

"It doesn't sound safe to be a blood sibling." I frowned.

Petre chuckled and shrugged. "I guess you could think of it that way. But Asander is a good person to have in your debt. He won't deny you anything you ask."

Assuming we had a child, I wondered if Asander would agree to stay away from fighting for a few years to raise our heir. But I would never ask him a personal favor he didn't *want* to give.

Leaving Asander to rest, I walked Petre back to his camp, Midnight at my side.

"Petre, are you taking command of Asander's battalion until he's healed?"

"It should have been Asander's second in command, but... " Petre swallowed.

"I'm very sorry for your losses." I hoped Petre would see he needed to officially take command of the Auripoans, and soon. "Well, I have information, but it's only for the captain of the Auripoan army."

"Forcing my hand, Empress?" Petre sighed. "Well done. Played like a true leader. Tell me your news."

With my Sonus stone, I silenced our conversation. I updated him on the encampments our scouts had detected in the Norte

Mountains, the possibility for poisoning, and of relocating a portion of our troops to the Rodnic Valley.

Petre's eyes widened before he composed himself. "That explains the quiet this morning. I thought perhaps you'd moved troops to the mountain camp."

"Our troops will relocate to the mountain camp," I said. "Once we flush the Norte off the glacier, they'll likely congregate at the Curat. The time has come to make our stand."

"We've lost many of our best soldiers; we can't take much more." Petre's cheek twitched.

"We'll have to use what and *who* we have to turn the tide. But I have a few more tricks up my sleeve."

"They better be explosive, or our families won't live to see the summer."

I cuddled a kitten. She was white with a few black flecks in her fur. I could sense the kitten's contentment — I know we will be a good pair. She purred so loudly that it woke me. I wouldn't mind Seeing that vision again.

— ESME

TWENTY-SIX

A BLOOD SISTER

I shouted to my unit. "Now!"

Twelve javelins flew at their targets, some even hitting them. My unit was making great gains, but a test on a windless afternoon was nothing like a snow-blown battle when emotions were high.

It'd been four days since Asander had been injured. Three days since I'd sent a half-battalion to the Rodnic Valley along with a Protector and Healer. But they wouldn't arrive at their destination for another half week.

Jamil arrived on the edge of the practice area, snow hitting his shins. Further up the canyon, the snow was deeper. My second in command took control, and I jogged to Jamil's side.

"Have the Norte struck?" I dreaded the attack, but the sooner Jamil could infiltrate, the better.

In the last battle, we'd lost over eight hundred soldiers. Every death sickened me. I might have worried that the Red Valley soldiers would abandon us to seek refuge in their protected dome, but they stayed fast. Even with them, how long could we last?

"No sign of the Norte," Jamil said. "One of the scouts returned today."

"Only one? What did he say?"

"Two days ago, along the southern route, they encountered the advanced party of Auripoan soldiers. Dyana was with them." Jamil handed me a shiny blue disk.

"What happened to the other scout?"

"Our scouts were intercepted crossing the Curat. One escaped, but the other didn't." Jamil paused. "This means two things: First, the message the other scout carried was captured, the one from Dyana to her brothers. The Norte won't get anything from it, but neither will the princes. Second, the Auripoans are close. I hope that Dyana's private message to you will indicate when they can flank the Norte."

"We need to get you into the Norte camp, and quickly, before the Auripoans arrive. I don't want you accidentally killed by our allies."

Jamil nodded and flexed his wrist. The scabs on his forearm were nearly all gone. Once we realized that his real flesh could be damaged underneath the Ghoster disguise, it became even more important to sneak him in and out of the Norte camp with care.

"An injured soldier surviving longer than a couple of days on the battlefield is implausible, so we'll need to snatch a freshly-injured soldier from the field, question him, then use the Ghoster disguise. I've already made preparations so we can secretly make the switch."

"Well done."

I snapped the disk. Dyana spoke in an overly formal tone.

Empress Nicoleta Aurelian of Dacia,

We have suffered mightily, but the king has dispatched us to assist you. My unit leads with a century of soldiers to follow two days behind. Your scouts met us at a fortuitous time as I just received an urgent message from the castle. Firstly, they are grateful for the supplies you have sent. Secondly, King Eusebes Coatys succumbed to the injuries he received when the castle was attacked. My husband has returned to the castle to assert control over the kingdom.

I gasped. Dyana was no longer the future queen of Auripo; she was queen.

When Dyana continued her message, her tone deepened. She sounded more like the confidant woman I knew, but her voice resonated with emotional turmoil.

With the losses, the mourning, and fear, Dacia's comfort in the form of medicine, Healers, Protectors, and food saved us from drowning in our despair. I am honored to fight at Dacia's side.

With those words, the rest of the disk crumbled. I stared at the dust, my heart pounding. Though we were giving all we could to each other, both our kingdoms were unraveling.

"Nicoleta," Jamil said softly. "Do you want me to tell the princes?"

I blinked, realization dawning on me. "No, I should be the one to tell Petre and Asander that their father has... died."

Later in my tent, Tulia prepared me as I took deep, calming breaths, steeling myself. When Tulia deemed me ready, one of my Own escorted me to the new Auripoan camp. Jamil had sent word ahead, so only Asander and Petre awaited me inside their spacious tent.

I brushed my hand down my camasa, resisting the urge to fiddle with my orb. Instead, I sprinkled a Sonus circle around us, wide enough to include Asander's entire pile of fur pelts. I told them about the two spies and that one had been killed.

"The d-disk meant for you was intercepted. Mine arrived intact." I licked my dry lips. "Dyana gave me grave news. Your f-father succumbed to his injuries."

Petre paled. "I must return home at once."

I grabbed him before he could step out of the circle. "I am sure Dyana would advise against that. It's not safe to c-cross the river even for trained spies. If you're caught, you know too much. The Norte can p-pull your memories with a single touch. Not to mention a p-prince would make a valuable hostage."

Petre scowled and shrugged me off. For the first time, I saw what anger looked like etched across Petre's usually mischievous face. He pushed past me and stormed out of the tent and into the woods without his cloak. I turned to go after him.

"Nicoleta," Asander whispered. He struggled to sit up. I spun and knelt next to him, cursing these two stubborn brothers. Asander winced, pressing his hand to a wound. "Leave Petre be." Though, he stared at the door through which his brother had escaped.

I took Asander's hand, stroking his fingers. At my calming gesture, Asander relaxed back onto his pillows.

I ran my hand across his forehead. "No fever."

He gave me a weak smile. "Will you change my bandages? I don't want to see anyone else today."

I nodded and pulled the Healer's tray inside the Sonus circle.

"Asander, I feel like I've been keeping a secret from you," I spoke as I carefully unwrapped the cloth across his chest. "With your father... gone, what you're losing... I have to be honest."

Asander seemed to shrink away from my touch, but if I didn't tell him the truth now, I never would.

"I don't think Dyana intends to p-produce an heir," I blurted. "And if your b-brother doesn't name another, you are next in line for the crown."

My hands trembled, hovering over his chest, a portion of the bloody bandages in my hand.

Asander let out a long breath, which seemed to drag on for an hour. Finally, he whispered. "I know."

I wanted to smack him. "So, you knew you were g-giving up the throne when you agreed to marry me?"

"I suspected that if Dyana meant to have a child, she would already have one. They've been married for nearly a decade." Asander lifted himself up on his elbow, grimacing but bracing himself so I could unwrap the cloth around him more easily.

Asander's resentment at being stuck in Dacia made more sense, knowing he was aware of the full extent of his sacrifice.

I unwrapped the rest of the cloth, revealing puncture wounds in his chest, stuffed with special Healers linens that wouldn't be removed for another day. I balled up the soiled cloth and slid the clean one off the Healer's tray. As I wrapped, a heaviness threatened to suffocate us both.

"It must be nice to have only good memories to mourn," Asander said, breaking the silence.

I stared at him, not sure I understood his meaning.

"I can't help but think about all the things my father *should* have done. The man he *could* have been. I've been so angry with him most of my life. Angry with myself for trying to impress him, to garner his approval."

I finished wrapping the cloth around Asander's chest and arranged his pillows before settling down next to him.

"You are a b-better man than your father because you *choose* to be." I could see two paths laid out before me. I wanted to be a part of the Coatys family: to have Petre as a brother and Dyana as my sister. Tears started to burn my eyes, a lump in my throat. They were the best part of the alliance, but I had to let them go. "You and I both know that wise alliances are the d-difference between p-prosperity and extinction for a kingdom. So, I can't give that up. But I also won't take you away from a kingdom that needs you."

I swallowed, my throat growing thick, but I pushed forward. This was best for everyone. "Prince Asander Coatys, I release you from your engagement. You d-deserve to be the future king of Auripo."

"What?"

"We're a transaction between our kingdoms. Willing transactions but b-bought and sold all the same: the price of allied loyalty. Yet, I already have your word, your oath to always p-protect me."

Asander took my hand. "True, you are my blood sister, Nicoleta. I will always, *always* be loyal to you. But I can't promise that my older brother will align with Dacia."

"I trust that between you and Dyana, the new King Coatys will hold true to our alliance." Dyana would be forever loyal to Dacia after we'd sent supplies.

Asander nodded, his face twisting in pain. I poured hot water from the kettle into a mug and looked over the Healer packets. "Would you like something for the pain or something for you to sleep?"

"Sleep, please," Asander said.

I poured in Rubia's draught and helped him drink.

"Will you stay with me until I'm asleep? I would do it for my sister in this situation." Asander forced a grin though I knew the draught did nothing for pain.

"I'll even hum a Getaen ballad, but be warned, I'm tone deaf."

Asander started to laugh, but he gripped his ribs, wincing. I placed a hand on his arm; he relaxed as I began to hum, pretending that ending my engagement wasn't breaking what was left of my heart.

There had never been more than friendship between us, but some deep and secret part of me wished that Asander had cared to fight, to keep me even a little. Perhaps it was my vanity, or perhaps it was simple loneliness. More than losing him as a partner, even if never as a lover, I was losing a sense of belonging to a family I was just getting to know.

Yet, at the same time, another part of me felt lighter. I was free of the burden of keeping Asander from his throne. Though he would've tried to be a better husband than his father had been, I wanted more. I wanted love.

~

I HAD BROKEN MY ENGAGEMENT, and though upset, I was determined to return to my unit and finish the morning training. Thadeus escorted Midnight and me through the trees, skirting the camps to my units' secluded training.

Jamil intercepted us before we arrived, quickly dismissing Thadeus.

"You have a visitor from the castle." Jamil led me to a copse of trees where another person waited.

Hadrian pushed back his hood and gave me a solemn nod with a mischievous grin. Upon seeing his familiar face, I ran through the snow to greet him.

"What are you doing here?" I asked my illusive Illuminator. He carried a box and wore a massive pack strapped to his back.

"I was itching to get out of Capidava, and a delivery needed to be made." Hadrian held out the box. I took off the lid and peered inside. The Illyrian conch shell rested in folds of fabric. I picked it up, inspecting the plain shell once again.

"None of us could find any special markings, carvings, or anything of that nature, nor can we sense anything magical. It's robust, having survived a long time in the ocean. That's the only notable thing about it."

Hadrian set the box in the snow and pulled off his pack. "These are from Seneca though I helped with the design. A Protector and Healer contributed as well though Gul erased their memory afterward. We decided it's best to keep our inventions secret. Lady Katalin isn't even privy. It's something we created just for you."

I peeked inside the pack, unsure of what I was seeing.

"Well, try them on," Hadrian said, reaching inside and pulling out a strange boiled leather item.

"It's a gorget." He spoke quickly, his feet practically dancing. "We're almost certain that Norte Clarifiers and Healers must touch their victims to directly transfer their vile magic. This will protect you."

Hadrian placed the leather against my neck with one hand, trying to clasp it in the back with another but mostly fumbling. Jamil stepped in and secured it.

Hadrian clapped his hands. "This collar is Bonded to you and has Protector magic, extending your healthy mind and body."

If I concentrated, I could sense the slightest buzz of magic, which filled me with gratitude and wonder. "Why didn't Seneca come?"

"When the spies returned to the castle, we knew something was wrong. Lady Katalin didn't say, but we suspect fighting is coming to the Rodnic Valley. Seneca has ties to the area and wanted to be there just in case, so we left the same day but went different directions."

Hadrian pulled another item from his bag. As he held it in front of me, I jumped back, the sight of the article making my stomach drop. The piece of stiff, dark fabric was meant to cover most of one's face.

"An assassin's m-mask," I choked on the words.

Hadrian tucked it next to his chest, covering it with his hand, his face hurt. "It's a mask born out of respect for *you*. Created not just to keep your identity hidden, but the less skin you have exposed, the safer you'll be."

I struggled to push away my feelings of dread and held out my hands to Hadrian. "Thank you for the mask. I will wear it, knowing it was lovingly invented just for me."

Hadrian's thumb stroked the mask, and then he placed it gently in my hands. "The mask is the work of a Healer. Right now, the sage lining will sharpen your mind. A Healer can imbue it with whatever herbs needed to procure the effect you want in a fight."

I swallowed and pressed the stiff material to my skin. In a breath, everything came into sharper focus. The wind rustling my cloak was from the northeast; I smelled another storm coming. Midnight's panting was harsher. The spears knocking against each other grew louder, more defined. The magical effect wasn't as strong as the chewing sage Pari supplied before I'd met the bandits moons ago but more subtle and hopefully longer lasting.

I secured the mask behind my braid then turned to face Jamil.

"Your weapons match the ferocity of your heart," he said, gravely.

"Thank you." My words were muffled by the material. Not wanting to waste the magic, I removed it.

A page tore out of the woods, running toward my unit's field.

Jamil whistled. The page jumped, seeing us, then rushed to me, stopping with a curtsy.

"The Norte." She gasped for breath. "They've attacked!"

❧

JAMIL and I rushed back to camp where Rufus was waiting near my Own's tent, nervously pulling at his hair.

"You have the elixir?" Rufus asked Jamil.

"For the third time today, yes," Jamil shot back, tapping the pouch at his side. "You have the Norte Mirror's hair as backup?"

"Of course."

When they ducked into Jamil's tent, I rushed into my own, determined to accompany them. I grabbed pins, jabbing them through the loops Tulia had sewn into the hood of my cloak, and secured them to my simple circlet. I shoved my new mask into a satchel, leaving the multi-clasped gorget in place.

Nervous energy thrummed through my veins, but I took a calming breath; I had to save my strength. I'd need it for the battle ahead. I tapped the hilts of my short sword and black dagger, reassuring myself, then grabbed a packet of emergency herbs and a bag of white Sonus powder, and I bolted from my tent. Midnight nipped at my fingers, sensing the tension of the emptying camp. I ran my fingers through her fur, whispering soft words until Jamil and Rufus reappeared.

Jamil held out a long, light shield, and I thrust my arm into the strap and gripped the handle. I suppressed a grin. He wasn't going to argue, knowing he couldn't stop me anyway. He led Rufus and me into the throng of soldiers headed for the battlefield, many of them looking surprisingly refreshed.

"A new century arrived today," Jamil explained. "All one hundred are new recruits, so they'll stay back near the line for this one. They're coming primarily to observe."

I couldn't help but look for the designs indicating their city of origin. I caught a yellow geometric pattern on a sleeve.

"I thought the Moesian recruits had already arrived," I said.

"After your impassioned speech in Moesia, word spread, and more people joined the Thorns in every city."

My jaw dropped, and my heart soared. The people had heard my pleas. I gripped Jamil's arm but couldn't speak.

"It's a miracle," Rufus whispered.

"The earlier recruits only have weeks more training. Too soon, they'll be in battle," Jamil said.

His words were a slap of truth, deflating my excitement. We'd lost many soldiers with *years* of experience. I had to figure out how to fight smarter, or even with the added soldiers, this war would be lost.

Imperial Guards waited with our horses near the mouth of the canyon. As we traversed deeper and higher into the mountain, I feared we'd miss our chance to infiltrate the Norte. As each moment passed, everything that could go wrong tumbled through my mind. The Norte could retreat too soon. The spell might not fool them. Jamil could speak with the wrong voice, using wrong mannerisms... so many variables.

When we arrived at the battle-line, we made our last preparations near the protective barrier and thick lines of soldiers. With my new pieces of armor, gloves, mask, and my trousers tucked into my fur boots, the only exposed skin on my entire body was from just below my eyes to my forehead.

I was also nearly unrecognizable.

"Nicoleta." Jamil grabbed my hand and pressed something in my palm. "For Irena, if I don't return."

I glanced at the small blue vial. A Ghoster blue vision. I started to shake my head and insist that he wouldn't need it. But I couldn't lie to him or myself, so I clutched the vial tight and nodded before tucking it into my satchel.

I peered past Jamil and Rufus, watching the new Moesian recruits as the protection line shifted to create a gap allowing them onto the battlefield. Even on the outskirts, they'd be in danger.

Some recruits wore metal breastplates, but most wore boiled

leather like mine. They carried weapons my army had gathered from the dead, and I hoped they wouldn't join them today. Observing the first wave of the battle would give them a chance to recover from the initial shock as their innocence was torn away. I clutched at my orb against my chest, wondering how many swords, spears, and shields would be left without breathing owners.

If Jamil returned with excellent intelligence, we might stand a chance. Otherwise, we were as blind as if an Illuminator lit up right in front of our noses.

A familiar profile caught my attention. I leaned forward as the figure paused at the line. Marcus?

He gave a soldier a quick embrace: Liviana. I had requested my unit come to watch all the battles as well, to study our enemy. I hadn't expected Marcus to walk his sister all the way to the line. When she left to rejoin her unit, Marcus stared after her for a moment before turning to return to the camp.

"I need to stretch my legs," I said to Jamil though I was sure he knew exactly where I was going. I darted through the procession, weaving through bodies like a fish swimming upstream.

I tried calling his name, but my voice was muffled by the mask. Reaching him, I grabbed his shoulder. Marcus turned, and his brow furrowed. I am sure I was a bit terrifying dressed like a Scythian assassin.

"Nicoleta?" he whispered. "What are you doing here?"

I took his wrist, spinning him so he faced the mountain. I stood next to him, our shoulders touching, improvising a private conversation.

I removed my mask and whispered. "I should ask you the same thing. But, I saw your sister."

"A benefit of being here is I can support my sister," Marcus said.

"I haven't seen you since we received the message from Katalin," I whispered, remembering the red dots on the map she'd sent.

I had to pick my words carefully without a Sonus stone. "You were right about the Norte movements."

"I wish I hadn't been right," Marcus sighed. "But gaining this information is your victory, Nicoleta. You had your doubts. It was a risk to trust me, but you did. You weighed the information available and made the best decision you could. You're a good leader."

I allowed myself to bask in the comfort of Marcus' closeness, the chaos around us falling away. We naturally fell in-step with each other, especially in times of trouble. I realized I was still gripping his wrist. Marcus flashed me a half-grin, and my gaze dropped to his lips.

My stomach tightened, and Irena's words rang in my mind.

Though I was no longer tied to Asander, I still had to be careful around Marcus. He wasn't a necessary strategic ally to wed on behalf of the kingdom. I loosened my grip and stepped back.

My throat tightened as I tried to speak, but it sounded more like a squeak.

"Marcus..."

If someone else had stopped the plague, someone else wore the crown, things could be different. If when Marcus had met me in Moesia, if I had been a healer, or scholar, or anything else, I would have chosen him. I would have chosen Marcus a thousand times over.

"It's all right," Marcus whispered, giving me a pained smile. "Trust me, I understand."

His every syllable burrowed deep inside, connecting us in a way that I could not deny. I was tempted to step closer, my resolve failing, but Midnight nudged my hand, grounding me.

I had an enormous task to focus on. Marcus gave me a discrete bow. I turned and followed Jamil, Marcus' presence behind me like the sun, warming me.

If my feelings continued to rebel and refused to stay buried, I was determined to funnel the thrumming, frustrated energy and focus it, using it to propel me into battle. If my plan worked, Dacia would have our first advantage of this entire war.

Jamil pushed through the gap in the line, and I secured my mask. The clanging rang in my ears, rattling my teeth. Jamil surveyed the battlefield. We needed somewhere away from prying eyes to perform the magic.

Today, the fighting was more evenly distributed; without Asander and his griffin, we hadn't pushed nearly as deep into the Norte's side. Skirting the mountain, we worked our way south, keeping a distance from the heat of battle.

"There," Jamil pointed at a depression in the snow, the remains of a makeshift defensive trough from a previous battle. "I was hoping we could use a trench deeper on the field, but it's far too visible today — a Norte might discover the ruse."

"But that trough is too far from the fighting," My words were muffled through my mask. "It will be obvious when a Norte soldier pops out over that ridge."

Jamil glanced at Midnight. "It's too risky to take you any closer."

"Do what you must." I'd insisted on coming to help, but I was a liability. "I'll return to the line."

I hurried back toward the two dozen Imperial Guards who were dressed as common soldiers, ready and watching my every move. Their orders were to protect Rufus and me. They'd been told that our goal was to return a Norte prisoner to the fight with a message to deliver to the Council.

Jamil didn't invite my most loyal Own but, instead, asked the most obedient guards. I had always thought those were one-and-the-same soldiers, but as empress, I was learning that they were not. Near the line, at Jamil's signal, the Imperial Guards swarmed past me, cutting a path to the mound in the distance, pushing back the Norte.

One of the soldiers handed me a full-bodied shield with a small, narrow slit in the top, center. "Jamil requested we give this to you."

I frowned. Jamil had planned on leaving me behind from the beginning. Otherwise, he wouldn't have given me a slit-shield for observation. I grumbled under my breath, and Midnight perked her ears. I slammed it into the snow and got onto one knee, looking through the slit of the shield, my entire body protected.

Pinpointing Reflections was becoming easier, and my guards cut through them as they made their way to the mound on the southern end of the intense battle. While Rufus had a snippet of the Norte hair from the last attack as a reserve, grabbing someone on the field today would be far better.

Jamil and Rufus slid into the trench, disappearing from sight. My heart pulsed in my ears as I scanned the area, trying to guess who would be the best soldier for Jamil to imitate.

Midnight's hackles raised, a growl in her chest. Across the battlefield, two snow leopards had entered the fray. One bounded north, the other charging toward Jamil's and Rufus' position. I called out as I grabbed for my Sonus powder, my voice drowning in the clanging metal and soldiers' cries. But the leopard changed direction away from the trench and straight for the new recruits near our lines.

I shot to my feet, running to intercept the leopard though I knew I'd never make it in time.

"Bonder! Get back!" I screamed, swiping my powdered finger across my lips. "Back behind the line!"

Seeing the leopard coming straight for them, some of the recruits began to run for the protective barrier while others pulled out their swords to fight, but too many stood frozen in place. They had never seen a Bonder on a snow leopard before, let alone tried to fight one.

"Fall back!" I pumped my arms harder, my sword in hand, willing myself to go faster. The more-experienced soldiers holding the line shifted, allowing the heavy infantry to move to the front. They fanned their large shields across the line and readied for impact. Arrows flew down from higher on the mountain. A few shafts stuck in the hindquarters of the massive cat but acted as mere irritating splinters rather than mortal wounds.

Behind the heavy infantry, a line of lighter, foot soldiers braced their spears, creating a bristling wall of metal above the shields to welcome the Bonder. My seasoned troops were performing their maneuvers admirably, but the panicked recruits were now stranded between the spears and the leopard. The line split, but only a few would be able to retreat in time. Desperate, I dug my hands into the Sonus bag at my hip, coating all my sweaty fingers.

The snow leopard landed in the throng of recruits, knocking several to the ground, pulverizing others. Liviana had her feet planted, a single javelin in hand. What was she doing? Foolish woman.

This must be how Jamil felt every time I put myself in danger, idiotically thinking I could help.

I stabbed my sword into the snow and pulled my dagger from my boot, words of magic on my tongue as I aimed for the beast's neck and threw. My dagger sliced through the air, striking just below the leopard's ear. I cursed — I'd missed the mark.

The Norte Bonder on the leopard's back clutched at her own neck and screamed in unison with her mount. They turned, identifying me. The leopard let out a low growl and crouched, ready to pounce. I sucked in a breath, reaching for my sword. The leopard loomed, its gaze full of revulsion and hate. Midnight raced forward to intercept the beast.

As the cat leapt, so did my dire wolf, her teeth sinking into the leopard's front leg. Several of my soldiers chased after the beast, but their battle cries faded in the back of my mind. I dove into a rolling dodge that Dyana's training had drilled into me. My blood pounded in my ears. I got my feet under me and ran, wasting no time looking back. I rolled again, this time over my shoulder, tucking around my shield. I came up into a low fighting stance, the Canina Thorn extended, shield up, arm braced against my body, ready for impact. But no attack came.

Midnight was harrying the leopard while the recruits fought. A javelin protruded from the snow beast's ribs.

I charged back into the fight as the beast's eyes rolled up into the back of its head. The Norte Bonder let out a guttural screech that pierced the air as the leopard fell.

The leopard's tail jerked and then fell limp. I drew closer. Though the leopard had fallen at an angle, the Norte woman was still in her mount, too dazed or unwilling to retreat. When she noticed the Dacians closing in, she screamed a litany of curses that probably few, other than myself, could understand. Reaching the beast, I jumped and grabbed the fur near the neck, finding the hidden harness, pulling myself up.

"How dare you touch her," The Bonder screamed in the Norte tongue, pushing to her feet. "She is a sacred creature of magic."

"You never should have come." My voice was low and slow, and I spoke in her native language. "This is only the beginning." I wasn't sure she could hear me with my mask on, but her attention jerked to my face as I crouched on the leopard's front shoulder.

She laughed, so manically it sent a chill down my spine. Below us, Midnight howled. The Norte woman shrieked as she lifted herself to her full height and switched to heavily accented Dacian. "You are the empress Borsea cautions us about?"

"You should have listened," Liviana said from behind the Bonder, now on the leopard's back. The Norte woman spun, and her body jerked. The Bonder stumbled back, a spear lodged in her chest. Liviana leapt forward and jerked the spear free. The Bonder reeled back and slammed into me.

I lost my footing and began to slide off the leopard, arms flailing. I dropped my sword and caught hold of the Norte soldier, but momentum carried us. I groped for a handhold but raked the Bonder's arm instead. I grabbed a fist-full of fur, which slowed my fall. I landed on the Bonder with a thud.

Warm liquid ran down my arm. I scrambled back, wiping the blood away, trying to assess the damage. It wasn't my blood. The Bonder lay on the ground, an arm outstretched, reaching for her leopard. She shuddered, and her arm dropped. Her bright red blood steamed, seeping into the snow. I turned away from the sight. Liviana gripped the fur of the leopard and swung down in a surprisingly agile move.

"Empress." Liviana looked me over. "Are you all right? I didn't expect to see you here."

Midnight limped to my side. I scanned the field, searching for Rufus or Jamil. Rufus was half crouched outside the trench, and he was focused on me. The moment I looked his way, he waved both hands in the air. Even from a distance, I saw the sheer panic in his face. Rufus was rarely fearful of anything, even when I'd nearly killed him.

"Midnight, stay." I gave her the hand-signal. "Liviana, please see that Midnight gets returned safely," I adjusted my mask, hoping Liviana was the only person to recognize me — she'd need to keep my secret, for now. "The empress is back at camp and must be worried about her."

Liviana pointed to where I'd dropped my famous blade. "Whatever you demand, I will obey."

I picked up the Canina Thorn, wiped it across the snow and then on my cloak. 'No good ever came of a dirty blade,' Jamil's words rang in my head. Would I see him alive again?

I rushed toward Rufus without another word. Something must have gone terribly wrong.

I slipped on an icy ridge. My heart stopped as I fell, fell, fell. I slammed into a crevasse, my leg broken, my body aching. But I wasn't dead. I looked up, seeing walls of ice that extended a hundred men tall. I cried with self-pity.

Then, I was another person on the same mountain, slip-sliding my way forward along with many others. This time, I saw the swords and shields. Quivers of arrows. At my own hips were twin daggers, but I could barely feel them. Frigid cold made my fingers numb. I heard a voice, directing us. A Sonus, no doubt, but I didn't see a single Getaen around me or up higher on the mountain.

Up ahead is a cloud-person with white hair and marble skin. She's the one giving commands.

Then I slipped again. I fell, fell, fell.

— ESME

TWENTY-SEVEN

THE LATE BONDER

Canina Thorn in hand, I battled my way toward Rufus, half-tripping over strewn bodies, the smoke of dissipating Reflections obscuring much of the valley. An unnatural fog had risen around us as if from the bowels of the earth. As I grew closer, Rufus shouted for the two Imperial Guards near him to make way. They pivoted to let me pass as I slid down next to my Ghoster.

Jamil was lying unconscious. Unmoving. Blood at his temple.

"Zalmoxis! No!" I grabbed Jamil's wrist. My own blood thrummed — I couldn't feel a pulse beyond my own.

"He's alive." Rufus pressed a red-stained cloth to Jamil's temple. "But he's badly injured."

"The Norte are retreating!" one of the guards shouted.

The other guard added, "Odd. They usual—"

"Cover your eyes!" I screamed. I hadn't heard a signal from the Norte, but I was paranoid.

Soldiers on the field started crying out, including the one nearest to me. "I'm blind! Everything is pitch black!"

"Your Luminary cream!" Rufus shifted next to me.

I opened my eyes to chaos. One Imperial Guard was fumbling

around, the other chasing down retreating Norte. I pulled out my herbs, not seeing any that would wake Jamil. I jumped up and grabbed Rufus by the shoulders.

"Where's the Mirror Disguise? Did you use it? Is it broken?" I snatched the pocket hanging from Jamil's belt and dumped out the contents. The only thing inside was a round, black seed.

"How dare you?" I glared at Rufus and threw the deadly poison as far as I could.

"It was his choice!" Rufus pulled out a blue vial from a pouch at his side. "Jamil barely arrived before a Sonus hit him in the head with a stone. He was lucky it wasn't a spear." He looked at my arm. "You're lucky to be alive, too."

I glanced at the blood on my arm, the *Bonder's blood*. Then back at the vial in Rufus' hand.

"Rufus... send *me*." Across the field, the Norte were holding off my Thorns as they retreated. My heart surged in my throat. My opportunity was shrinking with each passing moment. I grabbed the vial and flicked off the cork lid. I wiped the Bonder's blood from my arm across the top. "This is a Norte woman's blood. Do you think that's enough?"

"Empress, no!" Rufus' eyes widened.

"I know the language. I know more of the magic than Jamil. Send me." I shoved the bottle back in his hands and crouched down out of sight in the trench. "I command you to disguise me."

"Your sword," Rufus said. "It doesn't align against your leg. Someone could feel it under the disguise."

I grunted and put the Canina Thorn in Jamil's empty sheath and dropped my cloak as well. The simpler my clothing, the better.

Rufus put the bottle on my head, his hands shaking. He whispered strengthening words and released the spell. Smoke circled down my arms. I peeked over the ridge. The Norte were disappearing into the unnatural fog, headed back for their side of the battle lines.

"How do I look?" I asked.

"The spell isn't complete. Most of your body is still covered."

I glanced down. Bits of bright white Norte soldier's clothing shown between the magic swirls. Rufus scrunched his nose. "Your eyes are frightening. I think it worked."

I stood up, staring down at Rufus. "If I don't return, tell Rubia and Papa that my last thoughts were of them."

I wanted to say something about Marcus, but Rufus smacked my forehead with something sharp.

"You can't show up without any wounds," he said. "You just lost your snow leopard in a vicious battle."

I hissed, gingerly feeling the welt and broken skin, blood already pooling.

"Jamil's escape plan was to get to the Curat River and move south," Rufus spoke quickly. "A scout and guard will head there tonight under the cover of darkness. They'll meet you down river in one day's time. Now, go!"

I ran for the Norte line, the cut bleeding like a mountain spring. Warm blood trickled across my brow and down the side of my face. I pressed my forearm against it, both trying to keep the blood out of my eye but also staining my white uniform. Rufus was right, I needed to look like I'd been through a battle.

Instinctively, I grabbed for the Canina Thorn at my hip, but it was gone, replaced by a sleek but unfamiliar sword with a straight blade. The fog dissipated away from the center of the fighting. The Norte line came into view, not a friendly face among them. I swallowed. In theory, this was a simple task.

As I drew closer, the line parted, letting me through with the last of the Norte soldiers. Enemy territory. The miasma of sweat and blood, heavy Norte slang, and air thrumming with magic hit me almost like a physical wall.

"Galtis, you look lost," a Norte woman said, her tone mocking and hostile.

I ignored her as I tried to get used to the heavy accents.

A man with a round face gave a sharp retort to the woman,

though it took me a moment to interpret his words. "Even without her Bonded companion, Galtis is your superior, you low-lit vulture."

The woman glared at me, saying something in slang about "meeting the vultures" as she plucked one of my disguise's braids, rolling it in her hand. Primal revulsion screamed in the back of my mind.

"Hands off." The man's lip curled as he jerked my arm, pulling me away and through the throng of Norte soldiers.

I'd forgotten to bring the medicine that would fuzz my mind for the first half hour. If this man was a Sensitive, I wouldn't last long.

My throat tightened, my pulse racing. I was exposed. The sooner I got to the Healers' tent, the better. The mass of soldiers thinned as we arrived at the camp. I swallowed a gasp. Cave-dwellings vertically layered up the mountainside. At the base of the mountain, the caves were marked with blocks of snow extending from the entrances, expanding the spaces.

"You must keep your wits about you, Gal. You know what happens to Bonders who lose their companions." He pushed me down onto a stump, speaking too quickly for me to follow, and I only caught "proving your mind."

I stared up at him. If this was a gentle warning, I hated to see a gruff scolding. At least, he confirmed our suspicion that Bonders were the leopard riders. What else could Bonders do? What would I be expected to perform?

The man snapped his fingers in front of my face and then lifted my chin toward the setting sun, seeming to check my pupils. I focused on the accent, pulling out his words.

"You need rest is all," he said.

Why wasn't he taking me to the infirmary? I touched my forehead, trying to match what I'd heard of Gal's voice before she was killed. "I need a Healer."

He furrowed his brow, looking me over. A familiar voice

sounded, snarling about losing a leopard, and footsteps stomped closer.

It was Borsea. Her skin was tight over her already pronounced cheekbones, her long, white braids swinging as she stormed toward us. I struggled to breathe. She was the last person I wanted to see.

The Norte man hoisted me to my feet. When he gave her a bow, I quickly followed with a curtsy. She looked at me expectantly. I clamped my mouth shut. If I stuttered, Borsea might begin to suspect.

Borsea dug her finger just below the base of my neck. "Why did you attack the north side?"

I hoped she would interpret the concern on my face as more pained than worried. My gorget was directly where she was pressing, hidden under my magical disguise. Borsea turned her attention to the man next to me.

"Bonders are full of their own self-importance." Borsea's tone was low-boiling fury. "But the Council gave me full command of our army here. Let *this* be a reminder as to the importance of obeying my command." Her finger dug harder into my chest.

The man's nostril's flared. "Yes, commander."

"Unfortunately, Galtis is not a *true* Bonder anymore. If you had done exactly as I commanded, she'd still be whole, and you'd still have a sister."

I stiffened. Was this man Galtis' actual brother? If so, he probably knew her better than anyone. How could I fool him?

"Galtis could be eligible for a new cub in the spring," the man said.

"Really?" Borsea said with a mocking laugh. "The Council rarely approves a second Bond, especially when the rider is past her prime." Borsea looked me up and down, her upper lip curling in distaste. "Why bother sharpening a blunted blade?"

Gal's brother curled his hands into fists. Borsea didn't flinch, staring him down. The man stepped back.

"I'll take her." The finality of his tone sent a shiver of dread down my spine.

"Good choice." Borsea lifted her chin and marched away. The man glared at Borsea's back.

Her dwelling wasn't far. Though all the entrances at the base were constructed from blocks of snow, the doors were cloth. When she threw open the door, I thought I saw large pillows and rugs. I'd imagined her the type to sleep on a slab of wood or jagged rocks.

Gal's brother motioned me forward. I had little hope he was escorting me to my dwelling to sleep off my supposed injuries. After Borsea's words, I knew I was in danger. We passed through camps with shelters dug into the snow, not all of them around a fire. Around our camps, soldiers on break were often crowded together, telling stories or drinking. But, the Norte soldiers were far enough apart that they could outstretch their hands and not even graze another's fingers. I thought Borsea and Tatiana had stood apart from each other out of mutual dislike, but perhaps it was a cultural precaution against each other's magic touch.

The sun sank, the shadows growing longer. A half-hour after we passed the last camp, the man slowed. Ahead, snow-covered mounds were alive with black feathered carrion birds.

"Where are you t-taking me?" I asked.

"Your mind is addled. Borsea is right. At least, I know for certain, so I can sleep well tonight."

I wasn't sure if I was interpreting his words correctly — they didn't make sense.

The black birds cawed and flapped their wings but were reluctant to fly away. I shuffled forward. Feathers ruffled in the wind, lying on lumps of alabaster.

My blood ran cold. The injured Norte were left here to die. I spun and grabbed the man's arm, my voice barely a whisper. "My injuries are not so severe."

He pressed a hand to his heart. "Losing a Bond beast causes madness. Bonders have the superior magic and the greater risk. You'd remember this clearly if your mind wasn't already slipping."

Warning bells rang in the back of my skull. I risked speaking further. "I'm sure Healers can extend my life a day or two. It isn't much for them. My mind will hold that long."

He slowed down like he was talking to a child, which I found actually helpful. "Gal, our only Healers are so drained of magic that they are barely able to raise from their beds. These battles have not been as simple as we'd supposed."

"But… " I scrambled for a new plan.

"Know that I will always honor you even if my own death follows on your heels." He stepped back, his hand on his hip. "We have already dealt the deadly blow to the Dacians. When you close your eyes, know that you played your part well."

Hearing the sound of metal sliding from a scabbard, I jumped back, pulling out my sword.

"What I do is a kindness, sister. Die quickly at my hands rather than be left to the ice gods."

"Let me make my b-bid to the gods." I would not die here. Not after all I'd done. My "brother" eyed my sword. I tossed it down and lifted my hands. The imbalanced weapon was useless to me anyway. "Do for me what you want another B-Bonder to do for you, when you are in my p-position."

Not taking his gaze off me, he picked up my sword from the snow. I held my breath, not blinking, not backing down. With a sword in each of his hands, I half expected him to cut me down.

"You always were the bravest of us." He spoke quickly about me taking my chances with the gods and staying away from the camp. He nodded his head as if willing a child to understand. "Remember, the sentinels."

As he trudged away, I was tempted to throw something at him, if only a snowball. He'd left his sister with no sword and no extra clothing, knowing no kingdom would take her in. The callousness of the Norte knew no bounds.

Once the temperature dropped, I would freeze, even in Norte clothing. Jamil would tell me to keep moving. To loop around the camp and make my way back to Dacian territory. Southeast from where I stood, I eyed a mass of trees, likely marking the location of the Curat River. I could give up my mission and follow the river south to safety. But I'd return with little more than the knowledge I'd come with.

I waited for night to fall, and then I crouched in the snow and crawled back to the Norte camp.

I cry out to Medauros, desperate for his fierce protection. We need the God of War to rise and help us defeat the Theracians, the kraken.

I whisper to Zlatna. I must keep my wits about me in the forest of the fairy queen. We need her blessing, not her curses. If she rises to help us, we will be victorious.

I hear the conch shell, and my heart soars. Our Illyrian gods will hear us. Our ships sail for battle on the Imens Ocean.

I watch in horror as a kraken curled her tentacles around our ships, sinking them into the water's depths. The city burns behind me. Our castle crumbles to rubble under the boot of the Theracian Empire.

I awoke, tears streaming down my face at the senseless violence.

—— ESME

CHAPTER
TWENTY-EIGHT
WHILE ZALMOXIS SLEPT

I crawled forward, my body aching from the bitter night and the strain of my protracted movements. Gal's brother had warned of sentinels, or sentries, depending on the translation. Their perimeter guards were likely Sonuses if I hazarded a guess. That's what I would have done.

The edge of camp was delineated by clusters of trees. A strip of barren snow lay in my path. I pressed my body to the ground, cursing the full moon, before crossing, watching, forming a strategy.

I had to avoid Borsea, of course. And the Bonders. The latter would be more difficult as I didn't know how to distinguish leopard riders. And Sensitives... I mentally added them to my list of people to avoid.

I shuddered at the thought of a Sensitive reading my mind. I'd reacted out of emotion when I'd discovered the black seed in Jamil's pouch — I was foolish to discard it.

Every gust of wind scraping across the barren branches stole my breath. But I couldn't delay. Between the twilight and my white clothing, I should be hidden from all except the sharpest eyes. I crawled forward. Every crunch sounded like a roar to me. A twig snapped ahead. I froze. Wind screeched through the swaying trees, and shadows danced. I took my chance and darted forward, moving my body with the shadows. As the wind died, I crouched next to the nearest tree.

Approaching footsteps sounded. I pressed against a trunk, unable to stop myself from loudly gulping breaths of air. A bright light shown on the surrounding trees, but fortunately, I was on the opposite side, hidden in shadow. The footsteps drew closer, the light brightening. I held my breath.

A howl sounded from near the bodies where I'd been.

"Blasted wolves," a woman said.

"They always come after a battle, thick through the forests. Clever little beasts," a man replied.

"Soon, all these forests and the wolves in them will belong to us," the woman said with no emotion in her voice. Only hard truth. She was talking about the Dacians — our symbol was the wolf. The Norte were confident of their victory.

They trudged on. I forced my shivering body to slide around the tree, keeping out of sight. Their steps had long faded before I could breathe easily again.

What am I thinking? I'll never gather information and return in one piece.

I pressed my forehead against the trunk of the tree. I'd come too far to quit. If I were caught, they'd dump my body with the others, never realizing Galtis was only a shell. Besides, the reward of success was too great to ignore.

I marched forward as if I owned the land. Which technically, on this side of the river, Dacia *did*. The first encampment was soon in sight. I felt Norte eyes on me, but no one tried to stop me.

Ten. There were ten soldiers in that camp.

I began my tally.

For an hour, I circled a section of the perimeter of the camps. Each group ranged from ten to nineteen soldiers. Many of them had dug holes into the snow for shelter. As their fires died down and they finished eating their dinner, a ground-up grain with an unappetizing consistency, many started to disappear into their snow caves. It was almost eerie how the camp seemed to curl in on itself. No music. No stories. Definitely, no laughter.

"Bonder," a man growled. "Get back to your camp, or I shall report you."

My heart jumped, but I did my best to act annoyed. "I'm on an errand for Commander Caracalla."

His face pinched, but he didn't argue as I continued. In the shadowed trees between camps, I paused. I'd assumed I could move around more easily at night as the Norte settled in. I was wrong. I sucked in a breath, debating. If I could hide, I could wait and lurk from the thieves' hour until dawn. It would be difficult to get an accurate count, but some information was better than none.

Then, I'd run for the river. The risk of someone recognizing Galtis in the daylight was too great. She wouldn't be given a second reprieve from death.

I hid behind a large tree trunk, out of immediate view of either camp. The encampments grew quiet, the dying fire crackling. After less than a quarter-hour of not moving, my muscles stiffened. The wind bit into my skin. I bent and straightened my knees and tucked my gloved hands under my armpits. Even with the layers of clothing, my toes and nose were going numb.

I couldn't stay here; I'd freeze. I moved through the shadows past the next camp, and then another, adding to my tally. In the following camp, one side of the area had a high snowdrift with six sheltered entrances, mostly re-blocked with snow to keep out the wind. The fire was closer to the other side of the ring, where soldiers simply had pallets of blankets. The four soldiers near the fire were asleep — the nearest drooling.

Unable to feel my toes, I shuffled near the fire, alert for hints of stirring. Putting my hands practically on the coals undulating with heat, I began estimating how much of the camp I'd seen. I had probably only walked a quarter of the total perimeter. Nothing deeper.

I needed to examine the section of mountain dotted with caves. The baskets and other accouterments indicated people lived inside. Based on the location and relative luxury, I anticipated unearthing the most valuable information there.

"What are you doing here?" a young man whispered.

I jumped to my feet. Past the snoring woman, a young man peered up from his blankets. His gaze fell to my empty scabbard. In his sleepy state, his words were slightly slurred but slow enough for me to interpret. "I heard the Bonders lost a leopard and rider today. You can't stay here. I don't want any trouble."

What would a Norte Bonder do in this situation? They probably wouldn't *run*. I slowly crouched back down by the fire. The young man took my action as an invitation to continue.

"Don't know why they have to kill you. Bonders are partly mad already. You'd have to be to ride those beasts."

I was too nervous to laugh, but perhaps that was for the better.

The Norte rolled on his back. "I met them once, you know. When I was a boy."

"Who?"

"The Dacians. In their northern valley. I went with my mother to do some trading one summer." He had an undertone of anger. Frustration perhaps.

"What did you think?"

"They seemed oblivious to what they had. Green fields. You can't imagine the number of cows. Horses. Houses made from *wood*. Luxuries their land affords them."

"They sound terrible," I agreed, not wanting to raise further suspicion.

"Spoiled and soft. But that softness made them... " his voice trailed off.

Kind? Creative?

"Naïve." His voice hardened. "Snuffing Dacians is an empty victory. They're like children. We should fight the Gets — the ones who betrayed our ancestors. They're the ones I want."

I ground my teeth and stared at the fire. This boy had no real reason to hate me. He inherited his prejudice. Yet, could I blame him when he'd been fed ugly stories and saw riches beyond his reach? This wasn't something one conversation could fix. If anything, talking would get me caught.

Footsteps sounded, but the young man didn't react. A servant walked up, wearing dirty clothing and a too-thin cloak. As he drew closer, my heart twisted so tight I couldn't breathe. The glassy-eyed servant looked Dacian with his tanned complexion and raven hair.

He dumped two split logs onto the fire. He seemed not to see me — like I wasn't even there. When he straightened, I covered my mouth, hiding my reaction. He *was* a Dacian — his worn-out Capidavan Guard uniform marked him as such. He'd somehow been captured and enslaved. His mind had been altered by a Norte Clarifier, I was sure of it.

Bile burned up my throat, and I dropped my gaze to the snow. I barely registered the Dacian slave leaving.

"You'd best get back to your camp." The young man pointed through the trees.

It took me several breaths to compose myself enough to speak. "I won't tell anyone that you saw me."

He visibly relaxed and closed his eyes.

"Since I'm not really here, what can you tell me about that servant? I've never seen him before."

"He's assigned to us Illuminators. Rumor is he worked at the Dacian castle before he betrayed the impostor empress." The young man chuckled. "He was wise enough to realize he was on the losing side of this war when Tatiana Caracalla arrived in the capital. He just didn't realize his role in the new kingdom would be serving us low-class folks."

I sucked in a breath, hoping the dancing flames hid my horror. The dazed soldier was one of the guards who'd turned against me in the Battle of the Rose Court. And this was his reward. My insides churned, vomit threatening. I stood to leave, but the boy interrupted me.

"I answered your question, answer one of mine."

I gave him a nod, swallowing the acid in my throat.

He yawned. "Why do we retreat in each battle when we could obliterate the Dacians?"

The Bonders must have been privy to more information than the Illuminators, or he wouldn't have asked. "I can't answer that."

His eyes closed, and he rolled over. "Then, you don't know either."

I backed away from the fire and then bolted toward the center of the camp, the only place I knew the Bonders were *not* sleeping. But I didn't make it ten steps before I fell to my knees and retched into the snow. The Dacian soldier had made his choice to betray me, but I would always be haunted by his face.

I wiped my lips and kept moving, forcing myself to count. Though my distress was burning my disguise much faster than Rufus had hoped, just a few more hours. From my calculations, we outnumbered the Norte soldiers. Of course, their magic gave them a distinct advantage, but at least I detected no secret battalion held in reserve.

As I snuck forward, the trees grew sparser again nearer the canyon wall. I caught glimpses of the moon through thickening clouds.

In the Norte camp we'd taken, I hadn't seen any caves like these. Had the Norte been camped here the entire time? Had they allowed us to press forward, letting us feel like we were winning? Either way, this was their stronghold. I doubted they would concede it. Yielding this site would oblige them to cross the river and make new camps on the Auripoan side, costing them valuable time and energy. They were literally dug in here.

I waited near the stump where Galtis' brother had spoken with me — where Borsea had sentenced me to death. I bounced on my heels to keep my muscles warm, only pausing once when two people strode by, whispering.

From my vantage point, I observed Borsea's dwelling. The snow walls glowed with a soft orange light, indicating a fire deeper inside her cave. Along the base of the mountain, torches marked the space between each dwelling — fifteen torches. No magical

Luminaries in sight. How odd that, with all her magic, Borsea couldn't put light into an orb or any object. *She* was light, but with no way to share it.

I strained to see where the horizon met the mountain above me. Once the sky was light enough, I'd count the cave dwellings and then disappear before the camp awoke. Though I wouldn't be able to see the caves higher on the hill for a few more hours.

A shadow crossed Borsea's tent doors. I stilled, bracing myself against the trunk of the tree in front of me. The figure grabbed a nearby torch; it was Borsea, her white hair pulled back away from her taut face. She strode past a few entrances before barging through someone's curtained entrance.

It dawned on me: there were no guards outside the doors. Borsea was like Jamil, a soldier. She wasn't a queen, constantly protected. She was her own protection. And she'd never suspect any spy would be able to get this close to her secrets.

I shook my head. I should count the caves and go. Just standing here was a risk. If I was caught, I had no way to protect myself from a Norte Sensitive probing my mind. Even if I could kill myself first, the best-case scenario would be that they would toss my body away before the disguise began to dissipate, giving Rufus another chance to send in a different spy.

Then again, the Norte were not going to retreat. If we posed any threat, they'd release another unknown terror on my army. We might not get another chance to spy. And Borsea wasn't in her room; an opportunity I could grab while Zalmoxis slept.

I crept forward, pausing to listen outside the door. Nothing. I pressed my ear against the canvas, hearing only the crackling of a fire. I pulled back the curtain and peered inside. No one.

Two steps past the entrance, which was made of snow blocks, the walls turned to rough stone. The floors were strewn with layers of rugs and furs. Massive pillows decorated the room, shades of violet or pale blue, several glinted with golden thread. This close, I recognized the patterns — Theracian. Emperor Saam was attempting to get into Borsea's good graces.

The cave ended ten steps further, the space naturally widening, making room for a fire pit, small desk, and a bed. The smoke rose through a hole cut into the stone. A draft swept most of the smoke away. Someone had engineered this space long ago. Perhaps years. The remaining haze itched my throat, and I stifled a cough, moving faster. Without my Canina Thorn, I was no match for Borsea should she return.

I darted to the low table and shuffled through the maps. The first was a detailed drawing of the mountains north of the Rodnic Valley. My hands trembled, flipping to the next map, and the next. Maps of the rivers. Maps of the *Dacian* fields.

In the corner of the desk was a dagger next to a small box. I jerked open the lid. Glass vials rested on a velvet cloth. Uncorking one, I took a small whiff. Healer medicine. Of course, Borsea would keep her enemy's magic hidden. Peeking from under the box was a letter. I shoved the box away, scanning the message. It was signed by the Council. Their scrawled Norte script was difficult to read. I narrowed my eyes, picking out a few words: water, poison. No surprises yet. I slowed, reading again. My breath hitched.

Poisoning commenced. Hold the Dacians until the first shoots of green.

My mouth dried. We were too late. The poisoning had already begun.

I staggered toward the door, the weight of the revelation too heavy to carry. I had to get this information to the Rodnic Valley. Or was I too late already?

Snow crunched outside. I'd lowered my guard for mere moments to focus on the letter, but that was my undoing. A shadow entered Borsea's dwelling. I lunged for the knife on the desk.

"Well, well." The man's voice was familiar. He stepped into the firelight — the Illyrian representative who'd demanded Dacia's surrender.

I had to silence Kekad before he alerted the camp to my presence.

The captain looked at me with disgust, sliding a long dagger from behind him. "You'd already be dead, but the Emperor would be disappointed to find blood on his finery."

The bright orange light of a torch passed by the snow-wall.

"Drop your knife. On your knees."

He had a longer reach. More experience.

I couldn't be caught. Not letting myself think, I sucked in a breath and plunged the small blade between my ribs. I partially retracted the dagger and cut across the muscle tissue, purposefully missing my vital organs. I stifled a cry, the pain registering through my initial shock. I stumbled, my shoulder striking the stone wall, warmth running down my side. I hoped the wound would convince them to throw me out with the rest of the dead and dying. Just another crazed Bonder, nothing more.

"Captain Kekad! What is going on here?" Borsea shouted.

"I followed this woman in here," Kekad growled. His Norte tongue was rough, but it was better than his Dacian. "I was about to arrest her—"

I threw the dagger at the Illyrian, just missing his eye, the blade clattering into the stone behind him.

Borsea reached for me, but Kekad grabbed me first. Pulling my arms behind me and upward, I was forced to my knees with a yelp.

"What do you expect after discarding me like refuse after I lost my Bond companion," I spat, determined to keep up my pretense.

A bead of sweat rolled down my back, and I willed my trembling body to look weak enough to discard. Borsea slid her sword from its scabbard. With a downward motion, pain exploded against my temple, bright lights flashed behind my eyes, and then I was swallowed by darkness.

SHARP PAIN in my torso ripped me from unconsciousness. I cried out, but it was barely a whimper. My head ached, and the stab wound throbbed deep inside. At the edges, the injury felt as if I were getting jabbed with a hundred needles. My face was planted on the ground. I tried to roll over, but I couldn't. My arms were tied behind me and tethered to a bolt secured into the wall of Borsea's cave.

So much for getting thrown out with the dead. I groaned. Tied up and alive was *not* an option. My breathing quickened, and sweat broke out along my upper lip. Light diffused through the snow walls, indicating the sun was up. But how high, I couldn't be sure.

Every breath sent daggers of pain through my lungs. Even with the Healing herbs in the mask and the gorget's Protection, the blade had done too much damage to overcome. My body undoubtedly spent a lot of energy, trying to save my life. I tilted my chin down, my cheeks scraping against the stone. My blood-stained, white soldier's uniform was still intact. None of my Dacian-self showed. But for how long? Could I convince them to cast me aside before Rufus' magic wore off?

I couldn't chance it. I twisted my wrists, and rope dug into my flesh. I pressed my feet against the cave to try and pry the bolt out of the rocks. My ribs screamed in protest. Still, I pulled and struggled until I feared my shoulders would be jerked from their sockets.

Footsteps drew closer to Borsea's cave. I dropped, slumping as if I were still unconscious. The tent flap swished.

Captain Kekad snarled about just killing me and something else I couldn't catch.

"You are in no position to question me." Borsea's voice was flat.

"Not questioning, only suggesting," Kekad said. "Theracia and her vassals only wish to win this war. Has the emperor not proven himself by distracting the Auripoan forces?"

Borsea let out a mocking laugh. "That is no favor to the Norte. Emperor Saam wants Auripo for himself. Why else would he work with those who rule over wind-ravaged shrubs?"

I kept my body still though pain screamed for my attention. Had the Theracians aligned with the Scythians? It would explain why the Scythians had inexplicably attacked during the winter.

"We want to keep as many Dacian soldiers alive as possible," Borsea said. "We'll deploy them to finish off the Auripoan army."

The footsteps drew closer, and then a boot connected with my injured ribs. Pain shot through me. I cried out, rolling with the blow.

Captain Kekad growled his accented Norte words, "Let's get this over with."

I winced as Kekad yanked me into a seated position, tears stinging my eyes.

Borsea stood over me, shouting too quickly for me to interpret through the ringing in my ears.

"Captain Borsea, may I?" The Illyrian's voice had an edge of irritation as he squatted down next to me. "Losing your Bonded companion must have been difficult."

Borsea's nostrils flared, and she turned away in disgust.

I shrugged, my head pounding.

Kekad's accent was unique, but because he spoke slowly, I could fill in enough gaps to understand. "It's understandable that you would want to hurt the commander."

He seemed genuinely concerned. He was an excellent liar.

The only reason I could parse his intention was due to the sage magic in the mask sharpening my mind. He seemed to be trying to cajole me into confessing my intentions.

I had to get under Borsea's skin. If I could make her lose her temper, she might follow her instinct and toss me in the pile before they figured out my identity. I cocked my head, realizing her weakness went beyond her temper. Jealousy. Mariana had warned me that Borsea was envious of Tatiana. It stemmed from the Norte culture. *Low-lit.* Galtis' brother used the term as an insult. The Illuminators were considered a "lower class" of magic. Even the Norte had their prejudices and class system. Borsea's weakness was her desire for respect, to rise above her Illuminator status.

I stared straight into Borsea's face. With any luck, I could goad her into killing me. "Everyone knows Borsea secretly uses lowly Getaen Healer magic on herself. I came here to find the proof."

Borsea's nostrils flared. She dug her thumb into the tendons of my shoulder and hissed. "Filthy beast kin. I will have you fed to the leo—"

She stopped mid-sentence, her grip loosening. What little I could see through my blurry eyes made me dizzy.

"God of the Seas!" Kekad gasped.

I wiped away my tears the best I could with my shoulder, just in time for Borsea to jab a finger at my chest. At my *Dacian* boiled breastplate.

A Norte man entered Borsea's dwelling. Every Norte I'd ever seen were tall and thin, but this man reminded me of a shriveled raisin, hunched over. His beady eyes moved from Borsea to me.

"Perfect timing," Borsea said before pulling at the smoking edges of my disguise.

No, no, no!

In a few heartbeats, she'd know *who* I was. I slowed my breathing, trying to prolong the inevitable. Bits of my arm began to dissipate. My face next, the smoke obscuring my vision.

Captain Kekad's knee pressed down on my thigh, holding me in place. I tried to wriggle away, but there was nowhere for me to go. Borsea reached for my hip. My mouth dried. Everything seemed to slow as she slid my sword from the scabbard.

"Impossible," Borsea stared at my breastplate, the embossed canina flower on the edge of the leather, a sister image from my Canina Thorn. Her eyes narrowed, looking from the canina to my face. Suddenly, she lunged, her fingers scratching through the disguise, vicious nails digging into my flesh. I screamed, trying to wrench away. Portions of the disguise were still firmly Bonded. But Borsea pinned me down, ripping Galtis' skin from my own. Waves of pain shot through my cheek crashing into my already pounding headache.

"It's me. It's *me!*" I cried through my tears, counting on Borsea to recognize my voice. I needed my wits about me as long as possible, not to be slowly bleeding to death, unable to shield my thoughts.

Something like glee flashed in Borsea's eyes. My chest tightened; she would delight in torturing me. My breathing quickened. Why had I thrown away Jamil's poison-seed?

Borsea leaned forward and unclasped my mask, dropping it away. Unfortunately, she switched to speaking impeccable Dacian. "Well, well, know-nothing child of a scholar. Let's see how you match up against a true Caracalla."

My cousins and I sleep in the mountains bordering the Ice Lands. Another chance to prove ourselves.

I share a cave with my brother. He did not pack well enough. He's shivering. Even though our skin is always white as the snow, he has a sickly pallor. There's nothing to burn this high on the mountain. If I lay next to him, he will survive. It could be a trick, however. He claims to be a Protector, but I suspect he's a Ripper like our grandfather.

I'm tempted to leave him to die. One less person to compete with to become The Chosen One of the Council. Only one Caracalla descendant can be selected. It should be me. Cassus V sits on the throne. Once he dies, the curse will unleash. When his son, Cassus VI, realizes he needs a descendant of Odon to stop the plague, he will have to relinquish the throne.

And I intend to take it.

— ESME

TWENTY-NINE

"Question her. Start from the day she took the crown and sort through every memory from that moment forward. She can piss where she sits. No breaks." Borsea spoke with perfect Norte diction, clearly wanting me to know my dreadful fate. The elderly Norte man who had just arrived stared at me with all the warmth and kindness of crow getting ready to peck out a corpse's eye.

"Borsea," Captain Kekad interrupted with a cool voice. "I will fetch a Council member to witness the interrogation."

Borsea and the elderly man both shot the Illyrian a disdainful look.

Kekad dropped his chin. "Remember the law, commander."

The Norte man, who I assumed was a Sensitive, spoke in a casual tone. "Questioning a foreign leader needs approval from a Council member."

Borsea pounded her chest. "I am the commander of this army."

The elderly Sensitive seemed impassive to Borsea's temper. "True, but your bid for the Council seat was denied. Targen's dwelling is not far."

Kekad kept his chin dropped as he spoke. "I can take news of the impostor empress' capture to the council on your behalf."

Fantastic. How kind of him. My eye throbbed, already swelling shut even as warm blood ran down the side of my face.

Borsea spun to face the Illyrian, my blood on her fingers, a smear of crimson on her leather pants. "No," she snapped. "I'll speak with him directly."

Borsea pushed past the men and disappeared through the door. With her gone, the tension in the cave only thickened. Kekad tapped his fingers as if counting as he shot furtive glances at my sword on Borsea's table.

"Where is Emperor Saam?" I demanded. "Too good to get his hands dirty, so he sends a colony state on his errands?" I hated the idea of my people becoming tools of Saam or the Norte Council.

"Can we verify her identity?" The Illyrian paced the room.

The Norte man didn't respond.

"It is wise to verify her identity before the Council arrives, yes?" Kekad asked.

The Sensitive gave a slow nod. He leaned forward. I pressed back against the stone, trying to avoid his touch, but the elderly man gripped my temples, pressing, restricting. My headache felt like it would split my skull. Memories rose unbidden. I had to keep Dacia's political secrets, so I focused on my childhood, on the plague. I would keep them guessing as long as I could.

"She is the daughter of a scholar." The Sensitive's voice quivered. "Ahh. A woman calls her 'Nikka.'" He released my head, leaving me feeling empty.

I'd failed my first attempt at deceit. But Lord Jovian had figured out the trick — so could I.

The Illyrian frowned, coming to a stop next to the Sensitive. Kekad clenched his jaw and bent his knees as if poised to attack. He drew his dagger and stabbed the Sensitive in the back. The Norte man gasped, his scream a gurgle. Horror snaked through me.

The Illyrian was out of his mind.

Kekad spun toward me, the fire behind him casting his long shadow over me. I gulped a breath, preparing for death. Kekad grabbed my arm and shoved me down onto my face.

"Be still," he commanded in his stilted Dacian, pressing a knee to my back. Then the pressure lifted and he jerked me to my feet, scraping my shoulder on the stone. "Hurry. We go before Borsea returns."

My wrists were sore but free. I pressed my hand to my stab wound as Kekad wiped his dagger on a velvet pillow.

"Why?" I gasped.

"You forced changes." Kekad tossed me my mask, and I tucked it into my belt. It would mark me, immediately.

"Conch shell?" he asked.

I nodded, fumbling through Borsea's things, finding my packet of herbs. I grabbed the ones I needed and shoved them against the wound between my ribs.

"So close. All plans... " He shook his head. "Ruined."

I had too many questions — my mind reeled and my tongue refused to cooperate.

Kekad ripped a pillow and wrapped a strip of material around my torso as a make-shift bandage. He tossed me one of Borsea's cloaks. Luxurious white fur lined with satin in a Theracian design. Saam was working hard to win Borsea's attention. Perhaps the commander was the choice for the Dacian throne as she'd hoped.

Kekad peeked through the curtained doorway. I didn't trust him, but for now, I didn't have any better options. Unlike Borsea, he wanted me alive.

The Illyrian muttered to himself in Illyrian then spoke in his accented Dacian. "I buy you time. Help get you to the battlefield. Escape."

"They'll expect me to attempt to run straight back through the battlefield. That's the first place they'll send their leopards. Take me to the river."

"Insane. You will travel a day. Two days. Instead of an hour." He paused. "Clever. That could work."

We burst out of the confines of Borsea's quarters into the cloudy afternoon. I pulled the hood lower as we crossed the open expanse, feeling nearby soldiers watching me.

The Illyrian spoke under his breath. "They think you a visitor maybe — spy or foreign contact. Visitors must have Norte escort. We not get far before stopped." As we crossed into the trees, the Illyrian continued. "The gods smile on us. You survive your dagger."

It was no accident.

"I was trained as a healer. I gave myself a wound that would take days to kill me." A *mostly* shallow wound; I never stopped hoping they'd toss me with the others to die, giving me a small chance to still escape.

"Your lungs. You rasped before."

I shrugged. Kekad seemed to be helping me, but I still didn't trust him enough to explain how the gorget's and mask's magic worked.

Targen's Sonus-amplified voice echoed across the camp. "A Dacian prisoner has escaped. Find her!"

Kekad put his hand to my back, pushing me faster. I'd been stripped of my Sonus powder, and my dagger was long gone, embedded in Galtis' leopard. All I had were my herbs and Borsea's cloak.

"I am loyal to my people. I pretend — I disguise like you — to Emperor Saam." Kekad struggled with the Dacian, but I nodded quickly, encouraging him to continue. "The Norte stronger than emperor will believe."

Shouts sounded behind us. We would be discovered long before we escaped the camp.

"Dacia's magic only hope to stop Norte." He hurried toward a denser group of fir trees, his stronger, longer legs breaking a trail through the snow for me.

"Dacia falls. Auripo next. Illyria next. Our ocean access valuable." He frantically scanned the trees. I took advantage of the pause to try and catch my breath. "Illyria is weak because Theracia takes so much from us. Our ways fading like the sunset; I help you to help my people."

The shouts grew closer, but Kekad raced onward. I struggled to keep up.

"When you took throne, I have idea. A coup — our people together: Dacians and Illyrians. But gods take away path." His voice was determined. He stopped and held out his hand. "Give me white cloak."

I unclasped Borsea's cloak and thrust it at him.

Voices sounded like they would bear down on us at any moment.

"Climb tree." He pointed at the nearby pine. "Wait. Then run."

Distant movement flashed between the trees. I stepped into Kekad's waiting, interlocked fingers and with a burst of euphoria, I jumped. Kekad pushed my boot, thrusting me upward. I grabbed the lowest branch, hooked a leg around it, and pulled myself up.

Below, Kekad had pulled up his heavy sleeve. He held up his forearm for me to see: a golden yellow strip of material wrapped high above his wrist. "For Illyria, crush the Norte and Theracians."

I blinked. I'd seen similar symbols of support before from my people. Never from anyone in another kingdom.

Kekad crouched in the snow. I didn't have time to urge him to run before soldiers burst through the trees. I froze, holding my breath, digging my fingernails into the bark. If the soldiers looked up, they'd spot me as trapped as any alley cat.

The Illyrian shot to his feet, throwing off Borsea's cloak, his sword flashing. He cut down a soldier and bolted away through the trees. I marveled that he still had the energy to sprint after our flight from Borsea's room. I was already exhausted.

The Norte soldiers pursued him, disappearing through the trees. Alone, my body trembled. Inside my clothes, warmth tickled down my side. I pressed my hand to my wound. I'd reopened it. I sucked in a breath, checking around me one more time. No sign of pursuit. I lowered myself, gritting my teeth. I landed with a thud, planted two feet in the snow, and then stumbled back, gasping in pain as the muscles in my side clenched.

I focused on Kekad's words, not his cruel fate as I grabbed Borsea's discarded cloak and staggered toward the river. Every sound I made seemed as loud as a thunderclap. A Sonus might be able to hear me a mile away, but there was nothing I could do. I pushed myself into a limping run. As I moved past deserted camps, I dug my hands into my pouch. I yanked out the herbs, gripping two that would slow the bleeding while the others tumbled to the ground. As I hobbled forward, I packed them into my wound, keeping the pressure with my fingertips as I told my legs to move faster. I didn't sense any more magic from my mask or gorget. I must have exhausted them both. What I needed was a place to rest before I risked moving further.

I pressed forward, focused on a line of thick trees next to the river. Though my footsteps blended in with the trampled ground, the drops of blood would give me away. No, the leopards would pick up my fear sweat even without my bloody trail.

Were the shouts growing louder?

My heart soared at the sound of gurgling water. I hurried toward the glorious scent-scattering river. A screech behind me stopped me in my tracks; my blood ran cold. A snow leopard. I curled my hand into a fist and pumped my arm, propelling myself faster to the thickening trees.

I skidded to a stop — the land dropped away just beyond my toes. Below, the Curat River raged through the crevice it had mercilessly dug for thousands of years. I dropped down the steep, muddy embankment, using my free hand to slow my descent. There was nothing to grab. I slid through the scree to the water's edge. Jumping to my feet, I moved south along the bank of the river, following the current. I slipped on the green-slimed rocks, nearly toppling to my knees. I had to avoid the more slick surfaces. I wiped blood and tears from around my eyes and took a deep breath, trying to slow my heart. Any trick I could think of to escape.

Another leopard screamed, much closer. The beasts would have no difficulty jumping down to the water and bounding across the rocks. I crouched down with a wince, tightening the straps on one boot, but removing the other.

Multiple leopards cried out. I practically felt their hot breath on my neck. I looked up in time to see one muscled leopard leap down next to the river. Crouched as I was, they hadn't sighted me yet. Clutching the boot in my hand, I sucked in a deep breath and leapt into the water.

THE SHOCK of cold instantly froze my limbs and lungs. I struggled for a breath when my face surfaced from the swirling blackness — no other thought was able to compete with the instinctual need for air. The Curat took me where it wanted. As the river churned me in its froth, I lost track of sky and river bottom, the water covering me completely. Abruptly, the water smoothed — I coughed and gagged, spitting.

A tree had fallen across the river. Rubia's old warning rung somewhere in the recesses of my mind — branches snagged swimmers like a net, trapping them below. I flailed my heavy arms, shifting my angle in time to be pulled into the safer current. As I passed around the tree, I grabbed the jagged, broken top. I could only grip the slimy section for a moment with my stiff fingers, but that's all I needed. I slammed my boot onto the trunk, leaving my scent, before the water sucked me further downstream. Anything I could do to confuse the snow leopards' hunt, the better chance I had of surviving.

I'd never been a strong swimmer, and the Curat was nothing like the meandering rivers Rubia had taken me to explore. I floundered, attempting to stay in the darker water, away from unforgiving boulders or debris. The river widened and slowed. This was my chance. I thrashed toward the edge, my body protesting. I seemed to weigh more than an armored warhorse. Putting every ounce of energy into my arms and legs, I paddled until my feet took purchase on rocks below. From there, I pushed myself from stone to stone until the water hit my waist. As the water grew shallower, so did the weight of my clothing. I felt like I was *wearing* a snow leopard. Swaying, I stripped my cloak. My grip failed, and I watched confused as the river stole it away.

I trudged toward the riverbank, my breath forming clouds. I could barely command my body enough to navigate the mossy rocks. Shivering, I wrapped my arms around myself, tripping along the river. My lips and ears tingled, my fingers and toes numb.

One more step; I didn't have the energy to look behind me. I might have delayed the Bonders by crossing the river and leaving my boot. But they'd eventually catch me. My only hope was to find my Thorns.

The sun set beyond the treetops on the opposite side of the river. Was I in Dacia or Auripo? I was hot and wanted to strip off my other boot. But I also didn't want to reveal my dagger. My lucky black metal blade had slain two leopards. I laughed, and the maniacal nature sobered me enough to remember I'd lost my dagger in battle.

I was freezing to death. My guards were likely hours away. I shuffled forward, noticing my bare foot was bleeding. I couldn't feel the cut.

One more step; my body was burning up. I pulled at my gloves, but they were already gone.

The bank flattened. I climbed the crest into the snowy embankment. Where were my soldiers? I'd been walking for what seemed like days. But someone had died so I could escape. What was his name?

One more step; my legs buckled. The Illyrian was dead. I'd failed him. I dragged myself to the nearest tree, half-fallen, leaving a hollow partially covered by its own roots. I dropped inside. If there were raccoons or other creatures taking refuge with me, I didn't care. I couldn't even cry.

Curling into a ball, I longed for Mama to appear. Even if only in a hallucination. Or a dream. Or in death. I closed my eyes and waited.

Theracians gather together. There are too many soldiers to count in the hot desert. But I See others, those the Kraken controls. He sends soldiers from the south up through lands of wild horses and sagebrush up to jagged, icy mountains.

— ESME

CHAPTER

THIRTY

A DESPERATE OFFER

Pungent herbs stirred me to consciousnesses, sharp and acrid, burning the back of my throat. I forced my eyes open, just a slit, blinking to clear the blurriness. The dim blue hue of a Luminary stone cut through the darkness — *Getaen* magic.

"Nicoleta?" Marcus whispered as he sat next to me.

Our eyes met, and relief flooded me. I didn't know how he'd found me, but he had.

"Thank the stars," Marcus said.

With his words, I burst into tears, releasing the terror of being captured, the horrors of stabbing myself, witnessing Kekad murder the Sensitive, his subsequent suicide escape, and the panic of running for my life — all the trauma I finally felt safe enough to *feel*.

Marcus gathered me into his arms, cradling me to his chest as I sobbed. As soon as his scent of mint registered, I wrapped my arms around his waist, burying myself against him. I should've been surprised he was here, but somehow he always found me when I needed him most.

His shoulders shook, and it took me one heartbeat to realize he was crying, too, which only made me cry harder.

394

"Nicoleta," Marcus whispered, his voice breaking. "I thought... when Midnight found you... you were so cold."

With my eyes adjusted, I took note of our surroundings. The two of us were in a crudely-constructed tent, two thick sticks holding up a woolen blanket with furs thrown over the snow.

Midnight lay stretched out between Marcus and the flap serving as the door, her body heat filling the enclosure.

I shook my head in disbelief. This could have been a dream. It *should* have been a dream. How was I alive?

Marcus leaned back, and his gaze roamed over me, taking note of every injury, every hurt. I swallowed hard and dropped my hand to my torso, brushing against a bandage under my camasa. But that wasn't the only dressed wound. I lifted my fingers, inspecting the linen wrap covering my hand.

"Rubia tended to you. She said your deep puncture wound will heal in a few weeks. The frostbite might take longer."

I inspected Marcus in the dim Luminary light. His reddened cheeks, bitten from frigid temperatures, dark circles under his eyes, and messy hair spoke of his sacrifice — his constancy. I drank in all of this and more. Every detail, from the shadow of dark whiskers on his face to the mud-splattered attire hugging his broad shoulders — he was still the most beautiful person I'd ever known.

Marcus brushed my tear-streaked face, his touch feather-soft. His fingertips lingered just under my eye. I frowned, realizing my cheek had been bandaged, too.

"I wanted to ask how you're doing," he said, his voice rough with emotion. "But I can see..."

I shivered as he caressed along my jaw. Then, his hand dropped, and he traced over my neck, sliding along my arms.

He glanced down at my lips, and everything inside me stilled. Heat rolled off his body, wrapping me in an embrace, and I swayed like a flower basking in the sun. Marcus was my light, my everything.

His hand gripped my hip, and my heart thundered, sending fire through my veins. More than anything, I wanted him. He should be the one at my side.

My breaths grew shallow, and drawing closer, I slid my arms around his neck.

Tilting my head, I closed my eyes, and his lips brushed mine. His kiss shattered me. Breaking me into a thousand pieces and then, as he deepened the kiss, I was whole. All that mattered was right here. Now. This.

All of the moons of waiting — of wanting — fell away. I couldn't think. Wouldn't. He tasted of salt and mint and... freedom.

Marcus pulled away first and rested his forehead on mine. Between his ragged breaths, he said, "I love you, Nicoleta."

I smiled at his admission. "And I love you."

He pressed his lips to mine, a brief kiss to seal our declaration before adding. "I know the crown must wed for the kingdom, but I don't care."

"What —"

"You're forced to carry the weight of our kingdom on your shoulders, and I see it's breaking you apart. Nicoleta, please, let me be your corner of safety. No matter what happens, I'll be there for you. Always."

Marcus held me securely, ever aware of my wounds, but I tilted my head and frowned. Surely he wasn't saying—

"Whatever time you can spare. Whatever piece of your heart that is free. If you'll have me, I'll take anything you give."

I clung to him, searching his face for the truth behind his words. He grinned, but instead of joy or triumph, my stomach twisted with sickening realization.

"What did I say that upset you?" Marcus asked, his breath tickling my neck. "Surely, you knew how I felt."

I blinked and then swallowed back the sour disappointment burning my throat. I'd been so selfish — greedy — especially when it came to him. Biting my lower lip, I blinked away fresh tears. Life wasn't fair. Not for me. Not for Asander. And most certainly, not for Marcus. Which made it that much harder to do what needed to be done.

I smiled — a sad, watery smile and then gently pushed him back.

"Marcus, I love you." The words rolled off my tongue, natural and easy because they were true. Every part of me cared for Marcus, and I longed for a life with him. "But what you're suggesting?" I shook my head. "I can't."

His eyes widened, and he blanched, so I rushed to explain.

"I love you too much to let you settle for scraps." My grip loosened around his neck as I stumbled and started through the words I hated to say. "You d-deserve more; far more than stolen moments and b-broken p-promises. You, more than anyone I know, d-deserve happiness. And I want that for you. A family. Children, perhaps. And a wife who can give you her *whole* heart, mind, body, and soul."

He blinked, all the warmth in his expression evaporated. I felt Marcus withdraw. His arms were still wrapped around me, but his heart no longer beat in tandem with mine. Even so, this was right.

"Marcus," I whispered, pleading with him to understand. I wanted, no, I needed him to be happy. "Jealousy will tear us apart. If you gave and gave and gave like that, you would grow to resent me. I can't cheat you from the future you d-deserve."

I love you too much to give you that life.

"You're mad now." I could see the pinched furrow between his brows. I could feel the stiffness of his arms. Even so, I forced the words out even though they were ashes on my tongue. "One d-day, when you meet someone else, you'll understand. And then you'll be g-grateful."

At least I hoped so.

My insides twisted, and my core fissured into shards of cold lead, tearing through my veins and eviscerating me from the inside out.

Marcus' expression sobered, pain ravaging his face. Pain I'd caused.

I wanted to tell Marcus I was lying. That I'd keep him for myself. I *wanted* to be selfish, so much, but instead, I chose *him*. I tucked my hands into my lap, my fingers still itching to touch him.

Marcus carefully laid me back down, anguish coming off him in waves.

"How will we bear being around each other?" he whispered, a hint of bitterness lacing his voice. "How can we —"

"We can't be alone together. Ever," I said. This decision was too hard to make again. "I forbid it."

He drew back as if I'd slapped him. Inclining his head, he said, "I'll do as you command. When we get back to safe Dacian territory, I'll safeguard we never meet alone."

"Wait... *When*?" I pushed myself up onto my elbows, raising my voice. "We're *not* in Dacian secured territory?"

There was a rustling behind Marcus, and the tent flap rose.

"Nikka?" Rubia crouched in the doorway.

Marcus moved back, giving Rubia room to fall next to me. She put a hand to my forehead. "Your fever is lower. My child, you scared me. I brought a tea so you can rest."

"How long ago d-did you find me?" I needed to report my findings, not sleep. "How long have I been unconscious?"

"Nearly twelve hours. We found you just after dusk. The sun will be up in about an hour. But we won't move for another day. Not until you're well enough to travel."

"We d-don't have time. Snow leopards are tracking me. My d-disguise failed. I escaped. I have information that is *c-critical* to get b-back to our army."

Rubia spat a Getaen curse that would make a bandit blush. "You're in no condition to talk, let alone travel. But I believe you. I know how ruthless soldiers can be when they want someone dead."

With a swish of canvas, Rubia was gone.

Marcus moved to leave, and I tried to grab his arm with my linen-wrapped hand. Marcus stiffened at my touch but waited.

"Where are we?" I asked Marcus.

"We're back on the Dacian side of the river."

"Back?"

"We wouldn't have thought to look for you on the Auripoan side of the Curat, but Midnight discovered a white cloak on their banks."

Outside, urgent whispers sounded. Then canvas dropped and tools banged against each other as people began packing. We had mere moments, but I was desperate to salvage any thread of friendship between us.

"When will I be able to hold my sword?" I asked about my frostbite, feigning like I hadn't just gutted us both.

"Rubia thinks she can save all your fingers, but only time will tell."

"Who is here?" I asked.

"A Scout, one of your Own, Rubia, and I. We could only take one of your Own without raising further suspicion that you were not at the camp."

"How is Jamil?" I asked.

"A serious concussion, but he'll recover in a few moons. He's in the infirmary with Irena. If he knew you were missing, I don't think even Rubia could have stopped him from coming."

I laid back, allowing Marcus to finally leave to pack. But he stayed.

I hated war. People were ugly. There was a greed but also a desperation. The way the young Norte soldier spoke, I knew he had been taught to hate without reason. Just as the Getaens hated Rippers. From what I'd seen, the Norte were frustrated and angry after generations of squeezing their existence from the sparse, snowy landscape.

When Borsea first arrived in Dacia, seeing the relative ease in which we lived inflamed her hatred in ways I hadn't understood at the time. Whatever the reason, The Norte felt entitled to Dacian soil. They had lured our army to the Curat and managed to keep us distracted while they put their greater plan into motion.

One of my Own, Thadeus, entered the tent, crouching next to Marcus.

"Empress, we're ready to leave," my Own reported. "We couldn't bring horses here due to the need for stealth. The terrain is rough, but as you're being hunted, we can use the supply sled to move you to safety."

Marcus and Thadeus shifted me onto the narrow sled, securing the blankets around me. I refused my mask, wanting to explain as we traveled. The moon and stars were smothered under the clouds although the far rim of the sky was a lighter blue. The breeze bit into any exposed flesh. As my Own strapped me in, I began relaying all I could to the four people around me. If the Bonders caught up to us, one person would need to survive to share what I'd learned. As helpless as I was, it wouldn't be me.

The sled was agony, and my body yearned for rest. When my voice grew too hoarse to speak, Rubia gave me a sleeping draught and pressed my mask to my face, the newly infused magic tingling my skin. When Rubia kissed my forehead, I *knew* she was worried.

I awoke to shooting pains in my abdomen and the blinding light bouncing off the glittering snow. Judging by the angle of the sun, it was late afternoon. I moaned, unable to move my arms.

"Stop," Marcus said. "The empress is awake."

The sled halted, and Rubia pulled the hood and mask away.

"P-pain," I tried to say, but the wind snatched my words.

My Own dropped the sled's rope, and Marcus tossed him a backpack. The two of them bustled, setting up a make-shift camp while the scout kept watch. Rubia popped a pungent sprig of rosemary into my mouth before she pulled out a small mortar to prepare a poultice. The magic took effect, dulling the sharpest edges of the pain.

"The tent is ready." Thaddeus' brows and lashes had tiny ice crystals clinging to them. He pulled the sled a few more steps, right into the tent. It wasn't a perfect fit, but it kept the biting wind at bay. "We can't build a fire. It could draw unwanted attention. I do apologize, your majesty."

I whispered a thank you as Midnight snuggled next to me.

Rubia entered with a small stone bowl in hand. She gave me a tight smile. There was no use pretending that what she was about to do wouldn't hurt. I arched my back, trying to make it easier for her to tug away the linens. Dried blood had melded raw flesh and the linen together. Without a fire, there wasn't enough melted snow to properly soak the bandages. I hissed as she peeled off the last layer of material, partially reopening the wound in my side.

"It's inflamed, Nikka. I won't lie, not that you wouldn't guess in a day or two, anyway. I'll do what I can with what medicine I have, but I need a good honey poultice to draw out the rot. We'll be back in the camp tomorrow. I have everything I need there."

"Tomorrow?" I knew the estimated travel time for Jamil. Even in foul weather, the spy should have returned before dusk the night after they departed. I was slowing down the movement of the group even more than I realized. Something tugged at the back of my mind. With my wrapped hand, I pawed at Rubia's shoulder. "When will the first shoots of spring arrive?"

"Here? Not for many moons. Why?" Rubia asked.

"What about at the b-base of the Curat Mountains. How soon?"

My Own spoke up. "Crocus can appear through the snow. That could happen any day."

"I need to speak with the scout," I said.

Rubia called him to my side, and moments later, he appeared.

"The letter I found. I just remembered something about the first shoots of green." I pressed my eyes closed, trying to recall the wording. "It said to hold until then. I don't know if they're going to attack, retreat, or change tactics, but it will happen the day after the first signs of spring. Or even that night." Perhaps Borsea, a low-lit, was made commander for a reason beyond her being a Cara-calla. "The Illuminators may have skills we haven't witnessed yet that could be used to their advantage in a night raid."

The scout nodded in understanding. "I'll convey this informa-tion to the captains."

"If you leave now, could you arrive by dusk?"

The scout nodded. "Sooner, even."

"Then go," I said. "The captains need my information as quickly as possible."

"Empress, I fear leaving you behind."

"Even if your footprints are lost in the weather, I can find the way." Rubia pointed west. "As long as we don't run into any Norte soldiers, we'll be fine."

"I'm not debating the merits of my plan. This is a command," I said.

We all knew that the Norte would keep hunting for me. Though I should have died on the river, Borsea would not be satisfied until they found my body.

"Go," I said to the scout. "I didn't expose our greatest Ghoster's magic for nothing."

The soldier gave me a nod. Through a slit in the door, I watched him pack as Rubia dressed my wounds. After he strapped on a massive pack, he disappeared. I couldn't even hear his footsteps retreating.

I AWOKE when the sled stopped.

"We're taking a short rest," Rubia said. She lifted my hood, holding a Luminary orb in her other hand, the light bouncing off the overhead ledge pushing away the night. "We're slightly protected from the elements here. If we hurry, we might be able to beat the storm. We're all exhausted. I don't think any of us have slept for three nights since we understood where you'd gone."

Thadeus disappeared over the snowy embankment, Midnight right behind him, a tiny blue Luminary light at her neck.

"Pretty clever, isn't it?" Rubia asked as she removed my mask. "The Luminary light is secured to a collar. I was surprised she tolerated it, but following her in the darkness is easier with the glow."

Marcus knelt next to me as Rubia went through her pack. He pulled a barley roll from his cloak with a forced grin. "A feast fit to tempt an empress' appetite."

He was right; the smell was amazing. His little kindnesses pricked at my heart. When we returned to our camp, I was torn between dreading and hoping for the day he'd stop putting me first. Marcus slipped away, leaving Rubia to tend to me.

"Why is Emissary Constantin here?" I asked Rubia.

"You're wondering why I didn't bring a Thorn, instead." Rubia gave me a knowing look. She clutched my mask and muttered an incantation. After a few moments, she continued. "Rufus came to me right after you'd disappeared into Norte territory. He told me what had happened on the field. Thadeus, the scout, and I were all supposed to meet Jamil though we hadn't known anything about the Ghoster magic. Before we left for the rendezvous point, Marcus figured out you were missing. He kept asking questions and, well, I invited him to join us."

I raised my brow. Rubia had never purposefully put Marcus and me in the same place at the same time.

"I was worried." Rubia brushed off my unsaid words. "I wanted someone who I could trust to put *you* before anything else." Rubia returned her attention to my mask.

I had more questions, but no answer would satisfy, so I let them go. I chewed the roll, the muscles in my face protesting where Borsea had clawed at me. I gingerly prodded my swollen flesh under the square patch of linen that ran from below my eye to my cheek.

"How bad is it?" I asked Rubia.

"No matter what happens with your face, or your fingers, or your toes, or anything else, you will be honored as the bravest leader to *ever* wear the crown."

Her words of praise stung. Guilt descended upon me. "I left a man to d-die in the Norte camp, let him create a d-diversion so I could escape. I have k-killed soldiers and animals in battle. I haven't freed all the Lilac slaves. I didn't stop the p-poisoning of the Rodnic Valley. Marcus even warned me, and I was too late. I've changed."

I stopped short of saying I'd become a monster. I swallowed the words, shocking even to me. Had I become something unrecognizable to myself? The Red Valley clan leader's words came back to me in a rush: *A seat of power eventually poisons the ruler. Especially in time of war. Pass on the mantle to the next in line.*

The advice hadn't made much sense at the time, but it did now. I felt like I was at a tipping point, my excuses for brutality becoming more elaborate and easier at the same time — a dangerous combination.

Rubia didn't correct me. Didn't scold. But she had a look of pity as she handed me a tea to help dull the pain. Before I could take a sip, Midnight leapt over the embankment, her ears perked.

Staring out at darkness, she growled.

My Own reappeared. "They're coming. The leopards. They've caught your trail."

Panic rose inside me as Rubia shoved things back in her bag.

"Impossible. I didn't hear the leopards screeching," I said, but no one seemed to hear.

Marcus roughly resecured my straps on the stretcher, pulling them tight.

"I have Sonus powder on my ears," my Own replied, grabbing his pack. "From that ridge, I heard them in the distance. We can beat them to the horses if we hurry."

Midnight bounded ahead with Marcus, sniffing out the scout's trail. Thadeus strapped my sled's rope to his waist as Rubia shoved the mask back across my face. The magic in the mask tingled against my skin, more like pinpricks near my injured eye. The sled jerked forward. Rubia hurried ahead. Marcus brought up the rear, alert for my pursuers.

Outside of the protection of the ridge, the wind immediately cut through my cowl. But I wasn't cold — my pulse thrummed. In the night, we'd crossed the peak and were coming down the other side. I kept my focus on the ridge above, waiting for a leopard silhouette to appear. My Own pulled me behind as he trudged across the face of the mountain.

A thud in the snow behind us nearly stopped my heart.

"It's just me," Marcus called out of the darkness. There was a crunch, and he slid down, coming into the glow of Rubia's bright Luminary. He'd slid down the front of the steep mountain, skipping the safer switchbacks.

"What did you see?" Rubia asked, her voice raised over the wind.

"Above this trail is a steep ridge that I noticed on the way up. I climbed up to try and locate the leopards. I couldn't see a thing, but I put Sonus powder on my ears, too, and I could hear them."

"They know Nikka's alive," Rubia said. "They probably sent at least one Bonder back to warn Borsea that she'd escaped."

"They might change their plans," I said. Rubia tipped my mask so I could be more easily heard. "Attack even sooner. Borsea probably thinks I know more than I do, but I didn't have much time to search her cave. Nor did the Illyrian tell me about the Norte plans."

A screech sounded in the distance. Rubia snapped my mask back in place as Thadeus strained forward. Marcus rushed to join him. They ignored rocks and divots. My muscles tightened, bracing for the jarring impacts. They cut the corner of the next switchback. I had the unsettling feeling of riding on one skid before it fell back to earth. Rubia kept a hand out, ready to steady the sled.

The clouds on the eastern horizon, were they lightening?

"I'll ready the horses!" Marcus shouted. I heard a crunch and then him sliding down the mountain.

"Daft man. He won't see a rock until he's maimed by it." Rubia cursed.

A leopard cry sent a chill through my bones.

"Rubia, when we get to the horses, take the Empress' gelding and go," my Own instructed. "Her horse is the slowest. I'll get the Empress situated on my horse, but you need a head start. Can you find your way?"

"The leopards aren't tracking me, even if I do get lost," Rubia said. "Even so, the path is easy enough to follow, especially with the lightening sky. I'll see you back at camp."

I scanned the top of the ridge for a blurring shadow. A leopard's cry sounded a mile away. But they could move quickly — a leopard could race straight down the side of a mountain.

"Over here," Marcus' voice carried up the mountain from below. "Give me your pack, Rubia. I'll strap it to Velos."

Marcus must have flown to the horses. Thadeus kept an even pace, his breathing heavy. I cursed my frozen, immobile toes. Rubia shouted, and hooves pounded in the dirt, fading quickly.

I kept my eye on the slight line above where the shadowed mountain met the pre-dawn sky.

My Own slid to a stop next to a massive stallion, and then he lunged to jerk my bindings free. "Emissary, get on my stallion. No questions."

The back of my neck pricked. "What are you planning?" I asked Thadeus.

Thadeus looked at the three horses, their bodies twitching, sensing danger. "I'm staying behind to slow the Norte."

"No!"

"They're on the ridge," Marcus shouted.

Thadeus yanked my legs free, not bothering to unstrap them. With a swift motion, he hefted me from the sled and shoved me on the stallion. Ripping a fur from my stretcher, he threw it at Marcus.

"Get her back to camp," Thadeus said just as a leopard cried.

I pointed to Velos, Rubia's pack strapped near the saddlebag. "My wound b-bindings are in there. Use them to create another scent trail. B-but then circle back to me. I command you not to d-die trying to slow them."

Marcus swung into the saddle behind me and dug his heels into the stallion, yanking the reins. The horse plunged into the forest, Midnight loping at her side.

I screamed over Marcus' shoulder to my Own. "D-diversion, only!"

Marcus wrapped his arms around me, keeping me in the saddle

as he held the reins. I wanted to demand he stop until I had made my point clear to Thadeus. But, I knew my Own would make his choice. I only hoped that I'd given him an option he might not have considered.

The stallion's hooves pounded through the snow, and the forest trees flew by. Midnight began to fall behind. As the sky lightened, the trees grew more distinct. Behind us, another leopard cried, closer this time. Marcus' grip around my waist tightened, and the stallion put on another burst of speed. Midnight cut into the forest, and I heaved a sigh of relief. Like Rubia said, the leopards weren't tracking her or my dire wolf. They wanted me.

From behind us, rhythmic galloping sounded. I glanced back to see Velos with Rubia's pack still strapped to the saddle. Once Velos closed the gap between us, she stayed right next to us. My Own was nowhere in sight.

I tugged the blanket tighter to my chest, numb and angry at myself, at my inability to keep even a guard, let alone Marcus, safe. Guilt pierced me. I wanted to scream; to let Zalmoxis know that he had won. That I gave up. I didn't have it in me to try anymore. I was, like the horses, running half-blind with fear.

The firm strength of Marcus' arm around me calmed me enough to stay focused. If I did nothing else, I would try to save him. I lowered one of my hands to the pommel, bracing myself so Marcus didn't have to hold so much of my weight.

Just as I did, a snarling cry and a crash came through the forest close behind us. Without thinking, I went for the dagger in my boot. It was gone. I remembered Marcus'. I shoved aside the edge of his cloak, finding his bandolier across his chest. But with my linen-wrapped hands, I fumbled with the handle. Marcus grabbed the knife before it slipped from my fingers.

The leopard cried again, and Velos pulled ahead, her flank wet with sweat. I glanced back, expecting to see the leopard ready to pounce. My heart thundered. I could see flashes of fur between the trees behind us. Even if Marcus hit the leopard, the beast wouldn't immediately fall. But it might slow enough to give us a chance to escape. I braced myself as the leopard and rider came into view. I threw off my blanket and took the reins from Marcus.

"You throw. I'll guide," I shouted.

Keeping a hand firmly on my waist, he twisted his body, flexing with the throw. The leopard screamed followed by the rider. Marcus' body jerked again and again, throwing knives. The leopard let out a high-pitched cry.

Ahead, something moved along the sides of the trail. Imperial Guards appeared, swords in hand. I recognized Liviana and other members of my Sonus unit. They carried spears, their hands white with Sonus powder.

I wanted to sob with relief. The wails of the leopard fell further behind as we arrived at the southern edge of our camp. Soldiers scrambled past us to intercept our pursuers. I didn't know how many were chasing us.

I suspected that once the Bonders realized that I'd slipped from their grasp, they would turn tail and run. They'd return to the Norte to lick their wounds and rise to strike again.

Our next battle would change everything in the war. We were done dancing — the Norte would not hold back.

But neither would we. By the time the Bonder's returned, the Auripoans might be ready to flank our common enemy. The Norte's prideful blindness hid the seed to their demise.

I am drawn closer to a cave surrounded by rows of teeth made out of ice. I sense my magic is born here. In the distance, further than human eyes can see, I can See several stone sanctuaries cut into mountains, glaciers at the peak.

I hear a growl, and snow leopards prowl in front of the entrance to the cave. I cannot draw closer. Not because of the leopard but because the magic forbids me.

I feel someone wrap a blanket around me, the real me. But I am trapped in this place, goosebumps crawling up my arms.

I've never been so frightened. And so in awe.

Until the magic released me, I could not go. I've never felt anything that powerful. If the Norte are connected to this magic, we should fear them.

— ESME

CHAPTER
THIRTY-ONE

WORDS IN THE WIND

I barked orders from my bed, refusing to sleep. The wind screamed outside, buffeting against the walls of my tent, leaning the entire structure. Tulia was off fetching hot water and coals per Rubia's demands. My earlier wave of energy waned. Rubia exchanged the spent mask for a sprig of sage to keep me from collapsing. I was halfway through explaining what had happened to my captains when Petre burst into my tent, his face pale.

He stood near the doorway as I wrapped up my final assessments to the five captains. "The Norte have systematically reduced our army. But we must be patient and wait for the Auripoans. This is our chance to strike a crippling blow."

Now that I'd confirmed the Norte plans for the Rodnic Valley, I re-assigned one battalion to the Rodnic Valley.

"Send this via messenger to Lady Katalin right away," I handed the blue disk to the captain. "She needs to be aware that the northern waters could be poisoned and create possible evacuation plans."

I'd also requested her to meet me in Findava. Katalin had over-seen the castle's needs for far longer than either of us had originally anticipated, and we had matters to discuss that were best done in person.

I dismissed the captains, weighted with the burdens of their charges. Rubia tried to send Petre away with them so she could inspect my wounds, but I called him back; the Auripoans needed to know the situation.

"There are so many rumors about the Golden Empress right now," Petre began, dropping down to one knee next to my bed pallet. "I don't even know where to start. You killed a snow leopard with your bare hands, stole a Norte's clothing and hid among them, wielded your Sword of Lore, and took down a hundred Norte, coming away with only a scratch. All this before out-pacing the leopards while riding bareback on a wild horse."

"Pah!" Rubia rolled her eyes as she gathered herbs to imbue into my mask.

"That's exactly what happened." I couldn't help but give Petre a grin. "Especially the killing of the leopard with my bare hands."

Petre's body relaxed a bit. "Then, I guess this had nothing to do with it." Petre held up the black dagger I'd lost. "I found it embedded in a snow leopard. Very odd adornment if you ask me."

I tried to snatch it from him, but he pulled it out of my reach. He gave me a teasing smile, but then he turned serious, cradling the dagger.

"My father commissioned this weapon with a mind that it would stay in our family." Petre paused. I held my breath. "His wish will be fulfilled; nothing has changed between us, Nikka. I'm too stubborn to think of you as a snobby Golden Empress. You are as dear to my heart as Dyana, and you will remain my sister forever."

Petre pressed the blade into my hands. I rolled my lips, a lump in my throat.

"I hope to visit the Rose Court, and I expect a dance at every one of your fine dinners," Petre added.

I tucked the blade into my lap and pulled Petre into a hug. My throat constricted, and all I could utter was a small, "Thank you."

"Stop sniffling in my ear. That's not very empress-like," Petre teased, handing me a kerchief with an exaggerated look of disgust.

"It's your fault for barging in after I've had a *horrible* day... and then treating me so kindly." I changed the subject. "How is Baise?"

"Unfortunately, Rubia tended that wretched bird. Her witch powers are downright frightening." He mockingly wiggled his fingers.

"Magi," Rubia muttered under her breath.

"I think the horrid beast could fly if she tried," Petre continued. "A Healer removed the wrapping that was keeping her wing pinned to her body, but Baise just moans and squawks like there's an arrow through her heart, not leaving the tent where Asander's recuperating."

"Some animals are more loyal than any human," Rubia said.

I glanced at the foot of my bed, worried about Midnight, who had yet to return. I hoped the dogs had picked up her scent.

Petre sat straighter, his voice serious again. "Asander and I kept the dissolution of your engagement quiet — maintain the appearance of unity. Unless you'd prefer to announce it?"

The princes' consideration went unnoticed by Rubia, who elbowed Petre away and handed me a tea. Between sips, I told Petre everything, even details I hadn't told the captains — the fear I'd felt. Desperation. Horrified at finding out my people were already being poisoned.

I cringed, the memories of my own poisoning too fresh in my mind.

"What can we do to help?" Petre put a hand on my shoulder. "Asander is past the danger of infection, but he's in no condition to ride. I know you won't make the same mistake my brother does in thinking the Auripoan army revolves around him."

"I fear the Norte will retreat before Dyana gets here. If the Norte escape back into the mountains... " I couldn't finish the thought.

"If they retreat and you think they're about to enact the next part of their campaign plan, we can give pursuit. Change the game."

"They lulled us into false confidence by allowing us to gain ground." I adjusted how I lay, trying to alleviate the pain in my side as I explained the layout of their camp. "They could attack from their caves up on the mountainside with little danger of us overtaking them. And, if they cut off the escape back through the canyon, we'd be trapped against the frigid Curat River on the east, and the ice mountains to the north. We can't take the bait."

"What if *we* cut them off before they can retreat? We can defeat the ones they send to the battlefield, especially when Dyana comes over the hills." Petre scratched at the stubble on his neck. "A cornered animal will lash out. We'll have to expect the worst."

"That could work, assuming the Auripoans arrive in time. Dyana is supposed to send a scout in advance with her plan."

I was missing something, but even with the sage, I hadn't figured it out. "Why try to distract us here at the Curat while they weaken the northern valleys? What's the point?"

We fell quiet. My mind refused to work the problem any further.

Petre dropped to both his knees, and he grabbed mine and Rubia's shoulders. "Don't you see? They're repeating a tactic that's already worked in Auripo."

Rubia and I stared at him, not following his thoughts.

Petre spoke slowly as if trying to explain it to himself at the same time. "We assumed the Norte wanted to occupy the Rodnic Valley. To control that vast land and town there and then work their way south, through Findava and every other major city until they reach Rupea Castle. But what if they don't plan to stay in the Rodnic Valley at all? What if they march around every city and cut straight south and launch an assault directly on Rupea Castle."

~

A SHOOTING PAIN through my abdomen jerked me awake. My memories of the last two days flooded back. I pressed my wound and breathed a sigh of relief. I was safe in my Dacian tent near the battlefront. Across from me, Tulia stirred, but her breathing settled back into its sleeping rhythm. Judging by the dim light through the now-still walls, it would be another hour until sunrise.

I'd calculated I'd slept for about twenty hours with the help of Rubia's medicine. Even with the cobwebs lingering in my head, I noticed Midnight had still not returned. I never thought I'd miss her bed hogging.

I held out hope that she survived the leopards and the storm, but Thadeus had little chance escaping either danger. Though it was possible, by some miracle, that he'd returned while I'd slept.

I stood slowly, avoiding dizziness, and stretched. I opened my mouth, and the scabbed tissue on my cheek tightened. The burrowing, deep ache reminded me of Borsea's fingers digging into my flesh. Her maniacal, blind fury had driven her, seemingly detached from her heinous actions.

After a measured breath, I took a few steps, willing myself to ignore the radiating pain through my body. My fingers and toes felt fat and strange. Now was my chance to inspect them without onlookers.

I shuffled to the Luminary at the doorway and stared at my bundled feet, not sure what to hope for. I unrolled my left foot; the swollen flesh was mottled violet and blue, especially on the tips of my toes. I unrolled the other foot — it was the same. There were several gashes, but they'd looked like they'd be completely healed in a day or two. But the frostbite concerned me. The body could only do so much healing at once. I pulled away the linen on my hands, inspecting similar discoloration and swelling. I tried to curl my hands into fists, but they only partly cooperated. It would be impossible to properly grip my sword. I gritted my teeth, determined to become Rubia's best patient. I had to be able to fight with my sword again.

On top of the table, missives waited along with two blue

Ghoster disks. Unable to sleep and wanting a distraction from my injuries, I huddled under my blankets and cracked the first disk. The Red Valley clan leader's deep voice sounded:

Empress Nicoleta Aurelian of Dacia,

I have news of a surprising nature. Three Lazican families have quietly sent aid. One is a ship builder and has gifted three warships to the Red Valley clan. They are very fine vessels, built in the Getaen design so as not to draw the ire of the Theracians. In the time after you departed, we have intercepted several Theracian vessels on the sea. All the goods were commandeered, of course, and we distributed the supplies to the soldiers at the southern border.

Your Agricultural Emissary is more resourceful than I gave him credit.

The disk crumbled in my hand. Lazica had joined the fight. Marcus had been successful after all, just not in the way I'd expected. Not in a way *anyone* expected. I would need to thank Marcus though I suspected he'd prefer not to see me for a few days. Or perhaps I was the one who needed time to gather my wits.

I snapped the second disk, and Katalin's voice sounded:

Empress,

I've made progress on your idea of buying the slaves and freeing them, but there are challenges.

I've sold several more pieces of Caracalla jewelry. However, the more jewels I sell, the more it drives down the value of each piece. I cannot squander our best resource for coin — as you hesitate to raise taxes. So, I'm left to balance ensuring we have enough funds to sustain the army and continuing to buy slaves' freedom.

Some freed slaves chose to join the army recruits, but many left for Patri-

dava where more opportunities are available. But now Poppies in Patri-
dava complain that their wages are being driven down.

All the reasons I'd disliked Katalin and kept her at a distance now seemed trivial. Considering how many people were actively trying to murder me and subjugate all our people, her missteps were infinitesimal in comparison. She'd become an ally, one who was doing the thorny tasks of unraveling the mess Dacia had created over generations.

I sent bards to the wealthiest Lazican houses with fantastic tales that
included the jewelry I plan to sell next.

Of course, Katalin was still a fox. I was lucky to have her working on the side of Dacia and not against us.

Also, the people around Dacia are rationing food, wanting to store for
the future and divert goods to the soldiers. They can sense the danger
and are doing what they can to help.

It warmed me more than I'd expected to think of the kingdom's people working together in every small way imaginable, creating a massive impact for good. We were not a large army, but we had clothing, supplies, and food.

This castle business is every bit as disagreeable as I'd imagined. Don't do
anything rash as I don't want to be in your shoes for a moment longer
than necessary.

I grinned as the disk turned to dust in my swollen hand. Katalin would definitely not approve of me risking my life to spy on the Norte. But it would make for an exciting tale, assuming I lived long enough to tell her myself.

Tulia stirred and sat up, shrugging off my blankets. I dusted the blue powder onto the ground, cringing at how my palm felt under my fleshy fingers.

"You're awake early," Tulia said, padding over to check on me. Her nose crinkled at seeing my hands, probably for the first time.

"Rubia left this paste for you to put under your tongue if you woke." She grabbed a stone bowl off Rubia's Healer table and handed it to me with a spoon. "I hate to see you like this, but... you were so brave."

"How angry is Jamil?" I put the paste under my tongue, the bitterness making my mouth water.

Tulia placed the bowl and spoon back on the small table. "He doesn't know. Rubia talked Jamil into allowing himself to be put into a deep sleep. She claimed it would help him heal faster, but I think she mostly wanted him unaware of the situation."

Rubia rarely used medicine that pushed one deeper into unconsciousness than her sleeping draughts. She must have been desperate.

Tulia sat next to me on my pallet, her voice soft. "When Emissary Constantin returned you to the tent, his face... I could tell that part of him still pines over the mysterious scholar's daughter. But, as you're the empress, I'm glad he's moving on with his life."

"Oh?" I asked, the paste stuck to my tongue.

"He has invited a Lazican family to send a hostage to his house."

"I hearm," I slurred my words, the paste felt like it was taking up too much space in my mouth. "His sis'er is going to Laz-ca."

Tulia patted my hand. The gesture was far from her usual sarcasm, which got my attention. "Sometimes I forget that you don't know the customs of the Rose Court. Hostages are Lazica's way of forming alliances. But it's also not uncommon for the child who visits to stay many years, and to marry someone in the host country."

I nodded. That made sense.

"The child often marries someone in the host family."

I accidentally swallowed the paste.

"Their families are already friends, after all," Tulia continued. "If the Emissary ever had a dalliance with one of the merchant's daughters, or if any was interested in him romantically, that daughter is likely the one to readily volunteer to move here."

"I'm happy for him." I tried to force a pleasant expression.

Tulia smiled and grabbed my hand. "Oh, I'm so relieved. Rumor has it that the young woman arriving is just a year older than you, and she is sure to be the *most* fashionable thing in the Rose Court. I am hoping to garner an invitation to the Constantin household to meet her servants as soon as she arrives."

I snorted, grateful for Tulia's lightheartedness. Of course, she would be thinking of fashion in the middle of a war.

"If you want me to oversee the arrangement, I will do so when we return. I promise."

I put my hand out to run my fingers through Midnight's fur — she was gone, of course. I rubbed my swollen fingers against the knot forming in my chest. Tulia left to do her morning chores, whisking away Marcus' kettle from our tent.

Marcus' arrangement would make it easier for me, in the end. I'd probably have to marry some noteworthy Scythian in order to stop the attacks on Auripo, or a Theracian prince to soothe the wounds of war. The crown represented Dacia; the kingdom came first and last. There was nothing else.

Dogs barked in the distance, startling me. I clumsily pulled on my boots and cloak. I opened the door flap to the pre-dawn. Only one Imperial Guard was stationed outside my tent.

"We heard the dogs," he said. A bitter chill whistled through the camp. "We're investigating the noise. We will report the findings immediately."

Had the dogs found Midnight's remains? Or my Own's? Irena appeared for her morning Protections, and I beckoned her inside my tent.

"What's going on?" Irena said. "You only have one guard, and he seems tense."

"Did you hear the dogs barking at the edge of camp?" I whispered.

"That's what woke me," Irena said. "But if the dogs are searching in the woods, why are they barking *in* the camp?"

I jerked my attention to the door. "You're right."

Shouts sounded. I tried to grab the Canina Thorn from under my blankets, but my fingers weren't strong enough to keep it steady.

I realized I'd been so used to Midnight subtly checking identities, I had forgotten to question Irena. And Tulia, for that matter. Though if either of them were Mirrors, they'd have tried to kill me already.

"A message, empress, from one of the cooks," said my guard from outside.

Irena raised her brow.

I grabbed Sonus powder and dipped my fingers in it. I held my hand behind my back and invited my guard to enter.

"What is the news?" What had my dogs discovered?

"The Imperial dogs are still searching in the woods. The disruption this morning came from a cook's dogs, in the 'camp deer' location on the south side."

"And?" Irena pressed him to hurry.

"Your Own survived the leopards and the storm."

"I'm sorry," Rubia said to my unconscious Own before waving a vial under his nose. "Thadeus, it's me, Rubia. Wake up, dear boy."

The trained dogs had already cleared him as my Own, not a Mirror impostor. After all our losses, I had tried to not get my hopes up that he would survive. Even now, his recovery was not assured.

More Luminaries had been arranged, lighting my tent in a magical glow. Thadeus started to sit up on his elbows, but Rubia forced him back down.

"I'm so sorry to wake you."

My Own's eyes wildly searched the tent. Seeing me, he looked relieved. "Empress, is it you?"

I placed a swollen hand on his chest. "Thanks to you, I'm alive."

Thadeus' breathing became shallow and fast. "I took your bloodied linens as you suggested. It was a good idea. I rode south through the forest." He lost his voice, and Rubia helped him take a sip of water. "Those leopards are fast even in the forest. Nimble. I tucked the linens into the horse's saddle and then bailed into a ravine after taking a sharp turn. The leopards either didn't notice me or didn't care. I suffered a few bumps and bruises. Instead of returning to our camp, I circled back to the base of the mountain. I lay in wait to see if the Norte had captured you. I planned to free you if they had. But by the time I was able to trek there, they'd already passed through. I saw smoke from a fire up high on the ridge."

Rubia gave him another sip of tea, and I caught a whiff of the calming herb blend. "I scaled the mountain. If the wind had switched... blown west, I would have been discovered. I climbed to the outcropping that Emissary Constantin had mentioned. The Bonder's voices carried well enough even from that distance. I couldn't understand their argument, but I had a Ghoster disk."

"Well done." Rubia unhooked his pouch, fishing for the disk inside.

Thadeus blinked, and his breathing slowed. When Rubia handed me the disk, my Own's eyes were closed, his body relaxed. With Rubia and Irena, I cracked the disk.

The Norte's voices shouted, but the wind made interpretation difficult. Irena and Rubia leaned forward. Though Mama had taught me much about the language of magic, they could likely pick up a few magic-based words as well. It took me a moment to distinguish the words in their rapid conversation.

A man was speaking, his voice angry. "It was a mistake to drag out these battles."

A woman shouted, her voice sounded nearer the disk. "Borsea lied. The false empress is strong."

The man spoke again as the wind picked up, but I caught the end. "— already killed two of us."

A familiar voice spoke. I leaned closer as I could have sworn it was Galtis' brother. "Borsea knows the greater plan."

"The greater plan, my chapped rear end!" the woman spat. "The Council diverts us to guide weak Scythians, Illyrians, and Theracians across our sacred mountains?"

Irena grabbed Rubia's wrist, the two of them sharing an incredulous look.

The woman continued, sounding almost delighted. "Such a pity, watching those Theracians fall into crevasses."

Galtis' brother spoke up. "The outsiders are not worthy of our mountains."

My mind reeled. The Theracians were amassing at our southern border. How many could possibly be in the *Norte's* mountains?

The woman's voice dropped below the shriek of the wind. All I could catch were more complaints about the Council.

Galtis' brother spoke again. "Enough! Our success is assured. Once we rule Dacia and Auripo, there will be no need to tolerate the weak kingdoms anymore."

The group fell silent, the disk only picking up the crackling of the fire and the wind. The Norte's argument seemed to have passed, and they spoke too quietly for me to confidently decipher them. There was a long period of wind before the blue disk crumbled.

I immediately sent for my captains and Petre. New strategies were imperative — I just hoped we weren't too late. When my captains arrived, Tulia and Rubia attended Thadeus while I relayed to my captains what we'd heard. While I spoke, I captured my words for Katalin using a disk, also including Petre's concern about the danger to the castle.

"So, the Norte are not the only ones who will greet us in the Rodnic Valley," Petre clarified.

"While the Theracians sent supplies over the sea, many troops traveled through Scythia," I said. "Their partnership with the tribes was more than just a ploy to destroy Auripo. The good news is, the Theracians are struggling with the harsh terrain. However, we can't underestimate them. What they lack in knowledge of the Norte they make up for in sheer numbers." I slid the disk for Katalin onto my table next to the box that stored my conch shell.

Captain Kekad had once hoped for an alliance, but that plan had crumbled when I was caught, and Kekad revealed himself the moment he helped me escape. If another Illyrian came forward with an offer to align, I intended to have the shell close. But until they approached me, I had to treat all of Theracia's colony states as enemies.

I handed the newly-created disk to my Imperial Guard, trying to ignore the way he looked at my hands and instructed it be sent to Katalin. I turned back to the captains in my tent with my chin lifted. "Every day the Norte wait to fight is another day the Auripoans have to get into flanking position. We must hold the Norte until they do."

"Have we heard from their scouts?" one of my captains asked.

"Not yet, but with yesterday's storm, that's no surprise. I expect it will be another two or three days. So, we will engage the Norte, keeping them in place until the scout arrives. Then, we'll strike with everything we have."

"If the Theracians are in the Norte mountains, they could intercept the Auripoans," Petre said.

"It's a possibility, but everything we've discovered indicates the Theracians are headed further west and will spearhead the movement to Rupea castle. I'm tempted to send yet another battalion back to the Rodnic Valley, but every soldier we divert puts a higher risk of failure here. So, I'm only going to send six soldiers: my second in command will take five soldiers from our unit to the Rodnic Valley. It's wise to have trained Sonus soldiers in both locations."

My captains didn't argue, but two of them shifted nervously.

"Every strategy is a calculated risk," I said. "If we send away our armies too early to intercept the enemy in the Rodnic, we'll be defeated here, allowing the Norte easy access to both Dacia and Auripo. If we don't get to the Rodnic Valley before our enemy's coordinated attack, they'll march down the highway, straight for Rupea Castle, leaving a path of destruction in their wake."

With the slightest miscalculation, we could lose everything.

I forced myself to wake, the warnings too dire to ignore. I fight to stay and tell Mama everything I've Seen.

The Historians must record our lifestyle, beliefs, traditions, and family genealogy. We must hide the records away as they will be more precious than any of the Blood Conqueror's treasure. And like his warlock of old, we must protect these records. Guardians must return.

In a hundred years after the death of The Golden Warrior, there will be a great war with the southern kingdoms.

Our Norte oppressors will be distracted. Most of our magi will die by the blade, but even if not a drop of magic remains, Getaens will long to be who they once were. They can practice our ways in secret.

Many paths lead to the Norte discovering that our descendants have rekindled Getaen ways, and they could eradicate them. But there is a chance it will not end in tragedy.

My clan must act, or face destruction... again.

— ESME

THIRTY-TWO

BATTLE OF THE CURAT

Two days after Thadeus had reappeared, I oversaw my Sonus unit with their white-powdered hands, throwing spears with improved accuracy. Two of them were Lilies, so Asander fashioned harnesses at their hips for daggers rather than javelins.

Even with the progress of my unit, the tension was driving me mad.

"You could probably join your unit tomorrow," Irena said. She, Rufus, and Hadrian watched the progress of my experimental magic-wielders. Irena inspected my fingers, pressing on each nail. "The coloring is improved. Rubia thinks your fingers and toes will be fine. And don't worry about the scaring below your eye. It's tight and uncomfortable, but Rubia said she can massage it so there will be less of a... lump."

If I didn't look at my reflection, touch my face, smile, or eat, I hardly remembered my injury. After what I'd seen, a scar on my face was a small price to pay. Esme, the Seer, had predicted much worse: death. Though her mama asserted that Seer's only saw possibilities, Esme's words were hard to ignore. Would this next battle with the Norte be my last?

Six days of eerie silence on the battlefield had passed. If I hadn't seen the caves in the mountain, I might have led my armies on an offensive strike, thinking we could push the Norte back into the river.

Because of the need to heed the Council, Borsea lacked the ability to quickly alter battle plans. I would gladly take every hour of the Council's dithering to enable the Auripoans another hour to arrive. I'd sent the only scout who had successfully trekked back and forth across the Curat River to watch for the Auripoan army. And this time, I didn't argue when my Own provided him a black seed.

After I dismissed my unit, I whispered to Rufus, "I need your help with something."

"I've been expecting your request." His eyes were sad when he lifted a blue Ghoster vial from his pocket.

We walked further from the camp. My Own sprinkled black Sonus powder around Rufus and me before withdrawing to keep watch for intruders.

First, Rufus was my witness as I spoke into two blue disks for High Judge Isidro.

Then I took a deep breath. I'd never seen the creation of a sacred blue vision. How was the magic done? Rufus poured a bottle of elixir on my head. I didn't even feel a drop, but my body became iridescent.

At my feet, he placed the same vial and nodded for me to begin. I stared past Rufus at the empty woods as I spoke. I tried to stay distant from my words, knowing if I began to cry, my throat would close, and I'd be a stuttering mess.

"If you followed Getaen tradition, it's been three years since my d-death. As you grew up in the Rose Court, this might be the only blue vision you've ever had the privilege of seeing. I hope that Rubia gave you more information on what to expect than she gave me." I grinned. "When we met on the dusty roadside, I never would have guessed at the wisdom you'd learned from hard experience, nor your capacity for compassion and humility. It is that way in life, isn't it? We don't know anyone unless we make the effort, nor do we know their potential until we give them the space and the tools to reach it. You are more than prepared to be the empress though you never aspired to it. I have instructed the High Judge to give you your choice in the matter, and you will have chosen your path by the time you see this. Whichever path you chose, know that I support it.

"I never had many friends... which may not surprise you," I suppressed a chuckle then sobered. "I wish I would have recognized sooner that you were not just an ally but a friend."

Before my emotions could rise, I picked up the vial at my feet. A pulse of magic took my breath away. Rufus was suddenly at my side, bracing me until I could breathe.

"Deliver this to Lady Katalin upon my death." I tugged on my gloves. Rufus had somehow gotten the vial stoppered after I'd finished. "And here are Ghoster disks for the High Judge Isidro. He *must* be the one to open them. I created two, just in case one were destroyed."

"It was an honor to witness your blue vision." Rufus gave me an almost forlorn look. "I will keep these safe."

He didn't try to convince me to wait until my wounds were healed before joining the fight. He didn't pretend I wouldn't end up in the fray. As the leader of our kingdom, I wouldn't be foolish with my life, but at the same time, we didn't know what the Norte had planned. Every time we thought we did, they changed their tactics.

As we got closer to the camp, my stomach growled, as I smelled stew. Before we could get dinner, my captain's Sonus-amplified voice carried across the entire camp.

"The Norte are attacking! To arms!"

"Now?" Rufus asked, confused. "A strike right before nightfall?"

He was right. The Norte usually struck at dawn. I could understand why they'd try to catch us unawares at night, but at dusk?

"Another one of their games," I said.

Tulia burst out of the tent, frantic. Seeing me, she pulled me inside.

"You can't grip your sword properly, but we can still protect you," Tulia said as she strapped on my leather breastplate.

I had a pouch of Sonus powder and the Canina Thorn at my hip, Dacian armor, and an Auripoan black dagger. I felt the spirits of the dead, their expectations and support around me. Kekad had sacrificed his life to help me, in a faint hope that we could stop the Norte. To honor him, I put a string through the hole in the conch shell and secured it next to the Sonus powder on my belt.

I secured my gorget and mask, and Tulia held up a small shield. I thrust my arm through, but the handle was difficult to grip. Thankfully, Tulia had compensated for my weakness by sewing me thinner gloves.

"Your unit is coming," a guard called from outside. "And your Own."

Outside, the camp was a swarming hive but subdued, without bawdy jokes or shouting. The knowledge was like a sober blanket over us — this was the final battle on the Curat. We had to hold the Norte until the Auripoans arrived, and we had no idea what our enemies had in store.

But we'd surprised the Norte with our clever resourcefulness. And we still had a few tricks up our sleeve.

My GELDING WAS SADDLED and waiting with Jamil at her side. Despite his black eyes, he helped me mount with ease as my remaining Own moved their horses into position around me.

"I should be going with you," Jamil said, gripping the reins. "My mind is fine."

"Half an hour ago, you asked me to pass you the dog instead of a spoon," one of my Own jested, trying to lighten the situation. "We'll make sure the empress is safe."

"We'll keep her well away from trouble," another one added.

"Then, you don't know her." Jamil turned to me. "I should come. I am tired of your dire wolf's whining."

One of my Own cocked his head, confused, and Jamil reddened. "Oh, Rubia said I was to keep that a secret."

I grabbed Jamil's camasa. "Rubia has Midnight?"

"A dog found him last night. Rubia threatened the man to be quiet about it for two days. Your dire wolf, Nikka, she's in bad shape."

Five of my Own stationed themselves in front, the tails of their horses twitching as soldiers rushed around us, the air thick with rising tension. I knew I needed to be at the front, but it didn't stop me from longing to see Midnight. She needed me.

"Rubia is tending to Midnight herself," Jamil assured me. "You'll be reunited with her soon."

I signaled to my Own to ride and followed them. If I returned, I would check on Midnight. No, *when* I returned. The remaining four of my Own rode at my side and behind me as we headed to the battle.

We converged with the crowd of soldiers squeezing into the pass. Every century, every unit was called to the battle. Only the wounded were left behind. The finality of the impact of this battle hung over us all.

My Own shouted for people to make way, and our horses' hooves dug into the trodden snow, propelling us toward the battlefront. My blood thrummed through my veins, every part of my skin buzzing. Near the line marking the end of our territory, the soldiers waited for instructions. My Own broke away from the mass, leading me up the side of the mountain to join the captains. The sun was setting behind us, and a shock of vibrant colors stained the sky. Without a word, the captain handed me the spyglass.

Across the field, the Norte soldiers waited. No shouts. No running.

Waiting.

"What's going on?" I asked.

"The Norte rushed onto the field and then suddenly stopped."

"What are they waiting for?"

"For us to advance?" the captain suggested.

I lowered the spyglass, looking at the field as a whole. The long shadows were fading as the valley descended into night. From the north, dark clouds rolled in. If it covered up the moon, we'd have a short battle. Or had the Norte selected tonight because of the clouds?

"They're waiting for darkness." I spun to my Own on the horse next to me. "Call for all the Illuminators to alight every loose rock they can find. Make the rocks as bright as they can. Give several to each soldier. Not for them to hold - that would make them easy targets — but to throw on the field around them."

I turned to the next Own. "Send my unit along the front edge of the mountain with a pile of Luminary stones hidden in their cloaks. When the fighting begins, have them throw the stones deep onto the field. Otherwise, we'll be fighting blind."

I'd wanted to be with my unit on the mountainside, but without my grip-strength, it was wiser to oversee the entire battle. Half my unit was marching to the Rodnic Valley with Liviana, and the other half was below. The Getaen Sonus had become my second-in-command, and this would be the first time my unit would be used in battle; and the last time it would surprise the Norte.

My Own disappeared down the mountain, and my captain turned to me. "Can the Norte Luminaries see in the dark? If not, I don't understand this tactic."

"That gives me an idea." I looked through the spyglass at the faces of the soldiers, looking for the young man I'd spoken to at the Norte campsite — the Illuminator. "It's possible that Illuminators, like Borsea, can see in the dark. If I can identify their location, we might be able to figure out their plan."

The front two rows all have their cowls pulled low, so I couldn't see their faces, so I started scanning the back rows, first.

I scanned the faces, only seeing two I recognized. One was the young man I'd spoken to, and the other was the woman who'd snored as she slept between us. "There. Two Illuminators in the second to back row of their century. I still don't see Borsea."

"The Norte often change their tactics." The captain's voice sounded like he was almost trying to reassure himself.

Something was wrong. The captain felt it, too. I squirmed. I hadn't heard any leopard cries. I handed back the spyglass and scanned the entire length of the field.

As the last color faded from the sky, one of the Norte called out a single note. The rest responded in perfect unison with a stomp of a foot. From their side of the pass, their line opened and a stream of single-file soldiers entered the field, each with a tall, narrow shield that had a concave, curved edge along the top. They poured in front of their battalions, creating a new front line.

At my captain's command, Luminary stones were thrown onto the field. The stones barely glowed in the fading light. The gibbous moon above would soon be shrouded by clouds. My heart squeezed. I needed to be closer to the field.

I wrapped my still-clumsy fingers around my sword, testing my grip.

The Norte advanced. With a cry, my army surged to meet them. We sent a volley of arrows, but many of the Norte responded, deflecting the shafts with their shields. The Norte closed ranks, tightening shoulder-to-shoulder, overlapping the shields, creating an impenetrable wall. Where the shields curved, spears thrust forward to impale any soldier who stood in their path.

Arrows soared toward my army, dark lines against the snow. The captain next to me cried out a warning, Sonus powder on his lips, carrying his voice. Our army lifted their shields, most able to repel the attack. With the growing darkness, the captain wouldn't be able to warn them again.

Our soldiers were forced to get creative, striking under the shields at ankles. When our soldiers tried to flank the Norte battalions, their lines curved back. The Norte quickly pressed forward. Some of my soldiers managed to rip away an occasional Norte shield, creating temporary holes in the lines with barely enough time to take down a Mirror.

Using their new strategy, the Norte pushed us back. Still, our army was not badly beaten. I leaned forward, straining to watch the shadows below. The dim blue lights helped, but not enough.

"Give *the* signal," I said to the captain. He cried out, and our entire army dropped to the ground. From the base of the mountain, javelins from my Sonus unit whistled through the air. Many were strong enough to penetrate the shields, sinking into their Norte targets. My soldiers waited for the cries and then jumped to their feet, pressing the Norte back.

Norte Illuminators began to glow. Not a blinding light like we had seen before — just enough to dispel the darkness for their fellow soldiers.

"The most valuable Norte soldiers are nearest to the Luminaries. Our soldiers need to focus there."

"The Illuminators just made themselves targets," the captain said.

Sure enough, a massive Auripoan soldier cut her way through the Reflections, approaching an Illuminator. As the Auripoan lifted her sword to cut down the Illuminator, another Norte darted next to the Auripoan and then away in a heartbeat. I couldn't see what the Norte soldier had done, but the Auripoan clutched at her neck. I recognized the brief gesture soon ended by the Illuminator's blade.

"The Healers are on the field today!" I shouted, my heart thumping.

The captain couldn't answer with the powder on his lips, but one of my Own whispered. "Zalmoxis, this really is the last battle of the Curat. It ends here."

My captain gave another cry. The clanging stopped. Then, the sound of javelins whistled through the air. Before I could speak, the crashing of swords sounded again.

This didn't make sense. "The Norte only had a few Healers in the entire camp. They would never risk Healers or others they absolutely needed." I paused, thinking through what that could mean. "Borsea doesn't expect the Healers to live. Which means they won't be able to heal any wounded."

Why would the Norte not leave a way to help any wounded? Were all these soldiers expendable in the eyes of the Council? It made sense. The low-lits, the Illuminators on the edge of the camp, were likely perceived as less important, the same way many Dacians thought of Poppies or Lilacs. No wonder Borsea wasn't among them. But where was she?

The Norte army was too small to sacrifice the twenty centuries on the field. Unless there were more Mirrors than I'd estimated. Warnings screamed in the back of my mind. Something was very wrong about this entire battle.

"I need to get down to the field. In this darkness, we can't see well enough to guide our soldiers."

Across the valley, on the far mountain, there was a distant roar. A thunderous pounding sounded, descending onto the field. My heart raced. We were unable to see the aggressors. But it could be Borsea with another battalion. The Norte were coming to slay us in the dark.

I started down the hill, my Own right behind me. As we drew closer to the line, a sense of dread weighed down on the last group of waiting soldiers. These were the most experienced, those waiting to be sent in when the Norte had tired. But I sensed their tension at the growing tumult of an unknown enemy across the field, rushing toward the battle.

One of the captains on the field shouted back to our secured line, Sonus powder carrying his voice. "The Auripoans are coming!"

"Where's Queen Dyana?" I shouted, guiding my horse among the soldiers so we could enter the field. Dyana had to be warned — something was amiss.

A soldier rushed toward me as we entered the battlefield, a Luminary in hand.

"Empress," he gasped. "Half the Auripoans have engaged. But

the captain believes the other half have attacked the enemy from the rear, nearer the entrance to the Norte camp."

"They could be falling into a trap. Warn your captain. I'm traveling to the Norte camp. Hurry!" A vision of Dyana charging forward came to my mind. She'd be expecting to combat the soldiers on the ground, only to be met with an arrow in her back, shot from the caves above. Even if she survived the first volley, she'd have to climb a vertical mountain face to reach the Norte archers. And that's if the Norte weren't prepared with some noxious liquid fire to pour down on her or anyone else that tried to prod them from their nests.

As our horses skirted the battle through the darkness, I unhooked the shield strapped to the hindquarter of my horse. Though we were attempting to stay out of the fight, we couldn't be sure we wouldn't be attacked by either army. The clouds had grown thick overhead. Few spots of light shone on the ground this far from the fight. The white of the Norte clothing blended with the night, but they still cast silhouettes when they fought near the Luminaries.

Several of my soldiers had swords that glowed. The Getaen Illuminators were quick thinkers, ingeniously using their magic. The light drew Norte attackers to the sword wielders, but at least they could see who they were fighting. One of the Norte hoods fell back. The glowing blade revealed his face. I gasped.

He wasn't a Norte Mirror, nor even a Reflection. He was a Dacian Thorn, one of those who had betrayed the crown at the Battle of the Rose Court. Had the Clarifiers twisted his mind, sending him to fight the Norte's battle for them? Or was he here of his own will, having already turned against his kingdom once?

I suspected it was the former, after having seen one unfortunate Dacian Thorn in the Norte camp. As I searched the Norte ranks, I realized this man wasn't the only Dacian fighting his own people. Even though they'd betrayed me, knowing Clarifiers had probably unraveled their minds made my stomach turn.

I dug my fingertips into the powder at my hip and wiped it across my lip.

"Dyana, stop!" I screamed. "Hold your position. Do not advance on the Norte camp. Return to me." But we were still a distance from the pass that led to the Norte camp. Could she hear me over the fight?

Racing to the Norte line, we nearly rode over Norte Mirrors who were strewn in the snow, their bodies dissipating and sending fog into the night sky. Another strange move by the Norte — assigning Mirrors to guard the last defense with mindless Reflections — it was as if they *wanted* us to invade their camp.

I slowed my horse and cried another warning. We were greeted by an eerie silence. My heart thumped, imagining Norte soldiers in every shadow. With my teeth, I ripped off my glove and coated my fingers in Sonus powder, waiting for the inevitable attack.

None came.

I called out again as we proceeded slowly.

A clanking of armor sounded ahead.

"Who goes there?" A man called in heavily accented Dacian.

I responded. "Those loyal to Dacia."

There was more rustling, and a woman shouted. "Why do I feel like someone has played a joke but I have no idea what it is?"

"Dyana!" I cried, riding forward.

"Empress, please, wait." My Own hissed.

I drew back my reigns, holding my horse back. I tossed my Sonus stone, the light arching over the head of my Own who had moved his horse to partially block my path. My stone landed and rolled before coming to a sudden stop under someone's boot. Dyana lifted it to her face.

"Empress, where's your pup? It's unwise to be approaching anyone without her," Dyana said with her typical dry humor.

"Zalmoxis." I slid off my horse, furiously rubbing the Sonus powder from my lips. I grabbed a bit of snow to wipe away the last grains. "You frightened the wits out of me."

"We can worry about that later. We're missing the fight. No one's here. This camp has been vacated."

"Are you sure?"

"Can't you feel it? They're gone. The question is, are they moving to flank your army while we dither here? What are they doing?" Dyana turned and whistled to her horse.

"No. No, no, *no!*" I groaned, suddenly understanding their move — their game. "The Norte must have fled after I infiltrated their camp."

"Wait," Dyana laughed. "I thought you just said you *infiltrated their camp.*"

"We have a lot of catching up to do, but right now, we have to end this battle." I grabbed my Luminary from Dyana and mounted my gelding. "The Norte probably thought they could stall us until morning if not longer. They took advantage of the darkness to fight, but they probably left days ago."

We raced back to the battlefield.

"Where would they go?" Dyana called out.

"To the Rodnic Valley. They had to move up their plans. They're hoping to cripple the food production and the people of the north, and then they'll lay siege to Rupea Castle."

"Bold," Dyana shouted over the wind in our ears.

"They originally planned to hold us here and then shatter our army in one debilitating swoop. Afterward, bearing down on the castle, surprising the Rose Court. Even if the people of Capidava managed to secure the wall in time, the people on the outside would be eating tainted food, dying from a strange, Norte illness. They'd bow down to the north. The Norte poisoned the food, so they not only know which fields are ruined, but likely their Healers can reverse the magic.

"That's a good plan. Simple, but deadly. But you disrupted it."

"There were two things Borsea didn't count on. She didn't expect the reinforcements from the Red Valley." I squinted across the field, seeking my Sonus unit. "And she didn't expect *me.*"

WITH THE AURIPOANS and my Own attacking the Norte from behind, now armed with the knowledge of the Norte strategy, we focused our attack. Those closest to the Illuminators were the most powerful, the Healers and Clarifiers; a single touch to flesh could bring death. Since we were unable to call out to my troops without alerting the Norte, Dyana deployed her spear-warriors, bringing the Norte rear guard to their knees.

As we stepped over the bodies of the dying, I noticed a gaunt man with the fair complexion of the Auripoans who was missing a hand. I grabbed Dyana's shoulder. "Is he one of yours?"

"No!" Dyana dropped to her knees, heedless of the fighting continuing around her. Dyana's head snapped up, and she scrambled to look at the next person. And the next. She wailed, loud enough to make my ears ring. I rushed to her side, my Luminary held aloft, passing the body of a soldier with dirty blond hair, and then a Dacian Thorn, still in his soiled Capidavan uniform. Dyana held down an Auripoan who had roused enough to attack her. He had an ornate griffin stitched into his camasa, but his armor was gone.

Unbridled anger unfurled from my stomach at the Norte manipulations. The Norte had purposefully left our own people at the periphery of the fight, knowing they'd die at the hands of their friends. I had my sisters' and brothers' blood on my hands, always.

Without thought, without a plan, I lifted my hand, my fingertips still white with Sonus powder. I cried out in the language of magic, not caring what I said.

"Palai!" A pulse of magic threw me back but knocked over a dozen Norte as if the hand of Zalmoxis had fallen upon them. Stepping forward, I repeated my actions, again and again. As I did, Reflections collapsed to the ground as their Mirrors were rendered unconscious or worse. I moved forward again, changing direction so I wouldn't come close to hitting my own soldiers. I kept a sharp eye for anyone without the icy locks and snow-white skin of the Norte.

I caught a glimpse of Dyana, fighting like a woman gone mad, alongside her own unit.

Someone crashed into me, knocking me to the ground. I shoved my hand against their shoulder. "Skenai!"

As the man flew back, I recognized him though the unreasoning rage in his eyes made him nearly unrecognizable.

"Kekad!" I ran to him as he pushed himself to his feet, ready to attack again. I applied Sonus powder across my lips, amplifying my voice. "I need a Clarifier!"

I struggled to rein in my anger. I whispered, letting the Sonus magic pulse from my fingertips just enough to keep Kekad from tackling me again. He hadn't been given a sword, no weapon that I could see. The Norte had put him in the line as a death sentence. He was drenched in blood, and from the pallor of his skin, much of it was likely his.

"Clarifier!" I screamed again.

"Empress?" A Red Valley soldier bounded to my side.

"Can you clear his mind?"

"Even if we have a Healer on the battlefield, I don't think we can save him."

"I know."

Kekad could barely stand, his face pale. I'd seen these symptoms before — he'd lost too much blood. No magic or herbs could regenerate it fast enough for him to survive. "Just do what you can."

While I distracted Kekad, the Clarifier approached from behind. She restrained his hands though he tried to buck her off. The Clarifier's hand slapped against the side of Kekad's face, her lips whispering words of magic.

Kekad's eyes rolled into the back of his head, his face crumpling in pain as he opened his mouth in an agonized scream. I rushed to his side as the Clarifier sat Kekad in the torn-up snow. I brushed off what little Sonus powder remained on my lips.

"Captain Kekad, I thought you'd been killed. I'm so sorry."

The Illyrian didn't seem to hear me, his body shaking. He didn't have long to live. I pulled herbs from my pocket and stuffed them in the wounds that likely caused the most pain. Kekad relaxed, perhaps from the herbs or perhaps because he was drifting into unconsciousness.

"Very cold," he whispered in Dacian. Around us, the sounds of the battle began to fade. I kept my focus on him. I didn't want him to die alone.

"I'll stay with you," I said.

"Empress?"

"Yes, Kekad, it's me."

"The water god welcomes me home. Send me properly."

I looked at the Red Valley soldier in confusion, but she just shrugged.

"Conch shell." He reached for the shell tied at my waist, but his hand fell short. "Play it."

I flung back my cloak and unhooked the shell, looking it over but at a loss as to what to do.

At my silence, Kekad blinked his eyes open. "Blow into it. No. Other end."

My lips buzzed as I blew into the shell, the pressure pounding against my injured cheek. I ignored the pain. The sound was an ugly squeak to my ears, but Kekad rested a fist against his chest. I blew again, the sound clearer, louder.

All around, the fighting paused. Then, continued just as quickly, the last of the Norte refusing to surrender. I glanced down. Kekad's hand lay against his chest, his eyes half-open, staring unseeing at the clouds.

"May you rest well with your gods," I whispered.

I turned to face the dark battlefield. I could hear a few skirmishes, though they'd be over soon. I never rejoiced in the death of others but knowing we'd cut down our own people left a bitter taste in my mouth and renewed the anger boiling in my chest.

The battle ended before midnight. We'd captured a few Norte, and our Sensitives and Clarifiers set to work questioning them without delay. From the early reports, they'd only discovered information that confirmed our suspicions.

The Norte had a three-day head start to the Rodnic Valley.

We had to alert the valley to the impending Norte's rampage. We struck our camp by the light of torches and Luminaries. We packed tents and supplies through the night, the wagons soon bursting. The Norte had to traverse over or around treacherous mountains. We had an easier, more direct route — we could possibly beat them to the valley.

As the gray skies lightened, I checked on Midnight in the infirmary. My dire wolf was thin, her paws injured. Rubia had kept her unconscious as she healed, much like Jamil. I was angry with Rubia for not telling me about Midnight right away. Rubia rushed around the infirmary, tending the wounded while she packed supplies. She was even less patient with me than usual.

"Spare me your griping. I spent long nights with an animal who's always hated me." She waived a roll of ripped up camasas that were now bandages.

"Midnight hates most everyone," I said. I ran my hand over my dire wolf's side, feeling the deep heave and slack of her breathing. I'd missed her so.

"She's on the mend," Rubia said. "She'll wake soon. Don't ask for more blessings. Zalmoxis will notice if you're greedy. Now, off with you." She shooed me out of the large tent.

Dyana waited outside. She offered me a cold slice of meat in a roll with a pickle and what looked like dried fruit.

"Even the mythical Golden Protector needs to eat," Dyana said. I ate gratefully as we walked to the Auripoan camp.

"Petre told me about your exciting trip to the Norte camp," Dyana interrupted my thoughts as she looked at the lumpy, scabbed sore below my eye. "Want to talk about it? What happened?"

"Borsea went to battle with my Ghoster disguise, and I was caught in the middle."

"I'm impressed. You survived to tell the tale. And you have a chance to save your kingdom." The lines of Dyana's face tightened. "I fear what has happened to mine. I was heartsick at leaving the armies behind as we had been brought so low. But I took what was left of my century and marched here; our only hope is in Dacia's survival. If we strike a decisive blow here, Dacia can reinforce Auripo to push back the Scythians."

"If it's any consolation, I think the Scythians are exhausted. I have reason to believe they've been aligned with the Theracians, possibly for some time. At this very moment, they're traversing the northern mountains."

"Better them than me," Dyana said.

"My point being that the Scythians, who are a people of horses and wide expanses, may be shivering, possibly *dying* on the mountain... they may be reevaluating their alliance right now." Though, it would likely take more than a few cold nights to get them to abandon their allies. "It's possible that Saam wants the Scythians weak. If so, and the Scythians find out, they could be a fractious ally."

"If Saam thinks the Scythians are brutish fools, he's sorely mistaken. The Scythians won't be easy prey for the victor of these battles."

A squawk up ahead caught our attention. Dyana scowled. "I love griffins in theory only. Their image may be on our flag, but that doesn't mean I see their finer qualities all the time."

I grinned. "Did Petre mention that I rode her?"

Dyana nearly choked on her food. "He left that out. How did you manage that? I swear, I leave for a few weeks, and I miss everything."

"It wasn't elegant, I promise. There was no flying. More like blindly racing around."

"Then I'm doubly disappointed to have missed it."

I was tempted to bid Dyana good-bye and avoid seeing the Auripoan army. I wasn't sure if things would be mildly awkward around Asander or horribly uncomfortable, especially with all the

Auripoans watching. Besides, I had a good excuse — I was accompanying the second battalion out of the camp shortly.

Even so, the idea of facing Asander was far from the hardest thing I'd had to do in the last few days, and I wanted to get this initial meeting behind us. We were still aligned, and I'd be fighting alongside the Auripoans again soon enough. So I held my head high, bracing myself.

The griffin skulked near where the tent had stood as the last pieces were hastily rolled into a tarp. Asander was on a pallet, propped up against a log. Upon seeing Dyana and me, Asander's face broke into a smile. Dyana rubbed her knuckles in his hair, creating a knotted mess.

"Stop! Have you no respect?" Asander tried to bat her away but winced and pressed a hand to his chest. "Didn't anyone tell you that a leopard tried to *eat* me?" He turned to me. "At least someone thought fast enough to bring my sweet Baise and come to my aid."

Heat crawled up my chest, feeling everyone's eyes on me. Something bumped me from behind. I turned to see the griffin. She rubbed her feathered head against mine, nearly knocking me over.

"Careful," Asander said to the creature. "Nicoleta has wounds of her own."

"Flesh wounds now," I whispered, still in awe of the towering animal.

"Petre," Dyana said, as the younger prince arrived. "Am I dreaming? Or is this beasty not trying to peck out Nicoleta's eyes."

"I guess — as the empress saved that nasty creature's favorite human, she has gained a bit of favor." Petre wrapped his arm around my neck and tousled my tresses.

The griffin lifted her wings in warning, and Petre jumped back, putting me between the bird and him. "Wings all healed," Petre muttered before turning to Dyana. "Nikka has made a devoted, new friend."

"My sympathies," Dyana said, and some of the Auripoans chuckled.

"It's an honor," I said more to the griffin than anyone else.

I cleared my throat and spoke to the Auripoan soldiers. "Put anything you won't need in the next week in the wagons. You are welcome to leave with my unit shortly. We will be riding hard for the Rodnic Valley, which from what I've seen of Auripoans, is what you p-prefer."

With a few grunts of approval, Petre and the soldiers hurried to stow their supplies and to ready their horses. Dyana helped Asander to his feet and then inspected the heavy wrap around his torso. Despite his injuries, he seemed more relaxed. I'd seen glimpses of *this* Asander before we were engaged, but never afterward.

Mystic Marianna had predicted that Asander and I could be happy together. She was a wise woman in many respects, but not in this. She had made her best guess based on our temperaments, but she wasn't a Seer. Part of me was embarrassed at how unhappy Asander had been. Another part was relieved. Another part didn't know *what* I felt, but I'd have to work through it later. One thing I did know — it wasn't my responsibility to make anyone fall in love with me.

Asander caught me staring and pulled something out of his bag, which he tossed to me. I caught the soft wool items as he sauntered over. Unrolling them, I discovered another pair of socks.

"I had some time to knit while you were gone," he said.

I ran my fingers over the yellow wool. I had never imagined how much I'd value a pair of thick, warm, hideous stockings until I'd spent a winter in the mountains. Asander's simple gift was worth more to me than any sparkling bobble he might have offered. "Thank you."

"If we both survive, I'll knit some out of that nubby silk that everyone seems to prefer in Moesia."

I grinned. Without the pressure of an engagement, perhaps we could be friends — a relationship that didn't feel stretched thin with frustrated efforts.

Dyana put her arm around Asander's shoulder, this time much more gently. "I'm sorry about your father. He fought to the end."

Asander blinked, his nose reddening. I squeezed Asander's forearm before Dyana took him aside for a whispered conversation.

"Empress?" One of my Own approached. "A captain is waiting to speak with you."

Although there were few people nearby, the captain and I held my Sonus stone to keep our conversation private.

"Our soldiers searched the Norte camp at first light. It was as you'd described," he said. "We focused on the dwellings at the base. Most of the snow-like walls had been demolished, creating a blockade to the caves where Borsea and the Council were housed. Between the lack of traps and the fact that bulky items had been left behind, they withdrew in a hurry."

"Any clues as to their plans?" I asked.

"On the far end of the leadership's dwellings, in the last cave, the furnishings were Theracian design. It was almost eerie how they left everything as if they only planned to be gone for a short while. I think the Theracian emperor or his representative resided there."

My heartbeat quickened. I hadn't considered that Saam himself might have been in the campground. "It could have been the Illyrian's room. Perhaps he'd taken a liking to Theracian items after living under their rule for decades."

The captain shook his head. "Besides the intricately carved wooden box and the expensive incense still lingering in the air, we found something strange."

The captain handed over a cylindrical case. It reminded me of the cases Papa carried maps in, only this one was small enough to fit in a pouch. "It was the only item inside the box." The captain leveled a gaze at me. "In the center of the table, next to a *Luminary.*"

Despised Getaen magic right under the Council's noses. Bold.

I examined the cylinder. A kraken, Theracia's symbol, had been embossed on the smooth leather. A Luminary indicated it wasn't meant for the Norte to find. Saam had taken a risk to make sure this cylinder grabbed my attention. I glanced back at the Auripoans. Only a few lingered, packing the last load of their supplies. Dyana was with Asander, her arm wrapped comfortingly around him.

I excused the captain, turned my back to the group, and focused on the cylinder. One end had been dipped in wax. I dug the wax away with my thumbnail. I tilted the cylinder and a letter slid out. Unfolding it, my heart sank. It was in Theracian.

I turned back to the Auripoan camp, weighing my options. The royal family likely knew the language because their kingdom had been controlled by the Theracians not long ago — and they studied their enemies well. Asander limped over to his griffin, who waited near the trees. The prince gave me a nod before slowly leading Baise toward the caravan. Dyana returned for her pack, and I made my choice.

I thrust the letter into her hand. "Can you read this?"

"What is it?" Dyana asked.

I pressed my lips together, not wanting to answer her.

"I know there are things you don't tell me because you fear what the Norte Sensitives will drag from my mind. But at some point, you have to trust that I'm skilled enough to not get caught."

I pressed my lips together before finally relenting. "I believe this is a message from Emperor Saam meant for me."

Dyana scowled and took the letter. Scanning it, her brows furrowed. "More games. This is written in Theracian but isn't worth the ink he used to write it. It's a trick he'd hoped would divide us."

"What do you mean?"

"Does the emperor know you don't read Theracian?"

"I never pretended otherwise."

"So, he knew you'd show this letter to someone who could speak Theracian, someone you trusted, probably me." Dyana tapped the letter against her palm. "Saam's acting as if this is a response to your offer of alignment. It's meant to look as if you are double-crossing Auripo."

"Do you doubt my loyalty?" I glanced at Asander, my no-longer-betrothed, disappearing in the distance with Baise.

"I think a petty man is doing what he can to sow doubt."

I scanned the strange, inked characters, wondering if Saam would dare risk the Norte finding him with Luminary magic. Perhaps the Council had sanctioned this act? I crinkled the note, shoving it back into the cylinder.

"There is another matter. I had hoped to meet with Lady Katalin in Findava. There are urgent matters of the crown that need to be discussed in person. But with the Norte already three days ahead, I'll have to send a Ghoster message instead. Would you like to be there for the creation? I can update you both at the same time. Then we'll ride for the Rodnic Valley."

Dyana tapped her chin. "How important is it that you meet with your steward? I have an idea, but it's dangerous... possibly insane. Did I mention dangerous?"

I checked over my shoulder, making sure we were alone. "It's critical that I speak with her. Petre thinks the Norte plan to march on Rupea Castle."

Dyana nodded. "Makes sense." She grabbed my arm and we hurried after Asander. "The dangerous path, then."

The clan leaders are hunted. Their entire families, starting with my brothers Cy and Bijan. Even the small clans scattered across the river lands. The cloud-people hunt them all.

Two of my cousins escape during the chaos. They're older now. But I recognize them. They carry the keys. They become the Guardians of our history. Our lives in their hands.

—— ESME

THIRTY-THREE

THE COST OF FREEDOM

The gray skies broke, patches of glorious blue peeking through. The wind whistled in my ears, making it almost impossible to hear anything except for Petre, who screamed behind me.

"I hate you, Nicoleta! I don't know why I ever thought of you as a sister!"

I laughed, the sound muffled by my mask. Gliding through the air on the back of a griffin was a glorious thrill. My heart soared even higher than we did. With a powerful flap of her wings, Baise caught a current, hurling us through the air. I laughed again, letting my hood fall back.

I don't know why I thought about Valentin in that moment, but I did. My Own would have *loved* this. I could hear his laughter on the wind, his encouragement to drink in the experience for the both of us. I let out a whoop, stretching one hand overhead.

"Nikka! Hold on with *both* hands and fly this blasted thing straight!" Petre yelled. "Why did I agree to this? Why! My balance is horrible. Ask anyone!"

Baise banked, circling in the air over the ant-sized caravan below. I put a gloved hand out, my palm covering the century soldiers I'd sent to the Rodnic days ago along with my Sonus unit.

Yet, seeing them only made *me* feel small; a speck of dust flitting on the air above the forest.

The biting wind stung my ears as we flew for Rupea Castle. Instead of traveling for a week to Findava, we'd catch Katalin before she ever left. We took several breaks in the first half of the day. Petre's legs wobbled although he insisted he was fine. When we took to the air, he let out a string of curses.

I had never felt so free.

As the day waned, Capidava came into view; gray granite in a sea of evergreen and black-limbed trees. A quarter hour later, we landed in the courtyard.

"Thank mother earth, the stars, the rock spirits, the river god…" Petre uttered behind me, seemingly oblivious to the dozen Imperial Guards rushing toward us, swords in hand.

I pulled away my mask and threw back my hood, grateful Tulia had insisted I wear a substantial crown.

The guards dropped to a knee. With some effort, Petre released his grip at my waist so I could jump down from Baise's back. I discretely helped Petre take the first steps in a semi-graceful manner.

Imperial Guards escorted us into the castle and past a guard with a trained dog at the doorway. The dog sniffed at our hands and barked at Petre, not allowing him entrance. I quickly clarified his identity with the guard, and we strode forward. Just inside, Katalin rushed toward us.

"Empress, what a lovely surprise." Lines of concern were etched across her forehead.

I dismissed the guards, and the three of us continued down the corridor.

"I apologize for the guards," Katalin said. "They're on edge, ever since we caught a Mirror as he tried to enter Rupea Castle."

"What? When?" I asked.

"That's not why you've come? My messenger must have just missed you." Katalin tapped her lip. "We've closed the upper gates.

Many of the nobles have left to fight alongside the farmers and villagers under their estate's protection."

"As they rightly should," Petre interjected.

"Prince Petre, please excuse us," Katalin said.

"I would if I was able, but Jamil told me that if I allow anyone to even *breathe* on the empress, he would tear out my toenails and then feed the rest of me to Baise," Petre said. "You don't want that horrid fate for me, do you?"

"At least take your annoying, princely self a step away."

Petre held up his hands in submission and wandered a few steps away, muttering loudly, "At least, we can be completely sure we're talking to *the* Lady Katalin."

Katalin linked her arm through mine, pulling me close. "Why is Petre here? Why are *you* here?"

"Asander was wounded," I said. "He'll mend, but it will be some time before he can fully command his troops."

"And they're no longer engaged to wed," Petre added.

Katalin stopped short, pulling me to a halt with her.

"The empress also has a stab wound, so don't yank her arm," Petre said.

Katalin's jaw dropped.

"This information is coming in the Ghoster disks I sent earlier, but I happened to get here first —" I started to explain, but Katalin gripped my arm again and rushed us to my chambers.

Inside my rooms, servants were frantically dusting and starting a fire. Katalin ignored them and led Petre and me into my bedchamber where not even my Own could eavesdrop.

I told Katalin about Rufus' Mirror disguise, of my spying inside the Norte camp, and of how we'd discovered the Norte had tricked us into staying at the Curat while they rushed to the mountains above the Rodnic Valley. Katalin's face paled, but she leaned forward, listening to every word.

"Petre has a theory and I fear he's correct… " I looked at Petre, giving him a chance to speak.

"The Norte are bold," Petre said. "Instead of attacking border towns like the Scythians, the Norte came straight for the heart of Auripo: our castle and the king. I think they'll ignore the Rodnic Valley, Findava, and the other northern cities, and march directly on the castle."

"Rupea Castle has never been taken." But even as Katalin said the words, she didn't look convinced.

"They likely already know the easiest route to the capital," Petre said.

I nodded. "Norte army is relatively small but powerful. If they move quickly enough, they could use little-traveled roads and flood through the gates before you could close them."

Katalin glanced from Petre to me then pinched her fingers along the bridge of her nose.

I took a breath, trying to stay calm though my own heart pounded at the mere idea of the Norte invading my home. "You need to prepare the city for siege."

"While not causing a panic. With all the changes... " Katalin dropped her hand away from her nose, her gaze falling to her feet. "I didn't want to upset you as you were in the middle of a battle-field, but some of the slave owners are refusing to sell. I've even offered coin from my own estate. They refuse."

"The slaves will rise up," Petre said flatly. "My ancestors did. Your nobles will wind up dead."

Katalin brushed him off. "Let's try to avoid all the melodramatic talk of murder and uprising, shall we?"

Petre's nostrils flared, and I put a hand on the prince's arm. "Where do most Lilacs prefer to go once they're freed?"

"Many are moving south, desiring work at the new glass houses the Agricultural Emissary designed," Katalin said. "The first structure was a success, and two more are nearly completed. But there isn't enough work available. And if we have to evacuate the entire Rodnic Valley as you've suggested, where will everyone live?" Katalin's voice tightened as she spoke. "How will we feed an army and the people?"

"One problem at a time," I said. Marcus and Sorin could probably come up with some solutions. "First, we need to free *all* the slaves."

"End it all at once. Make the law clear," Petre added.

"Thank you, *Auripoan* prince." Katalin brushed off her dress and turned to me. "I will send a final offer to the families."

"If they didn't listen to you before, why would they listen now?" I paced as Jamil had often done in this very spot. I was tired of dealing with obstinate nobles. But on the other hand, the kingdom needed them, too. "I have an idea. It's not perfect, but if I'm going to be pelted by a sandstorm, I'd rather get it over with at once. Slavery is done. For those who won't comply — a trial and a fine for every slave retained. If they don't sell in the next moon — they face prison and forfeit their lands and titles."

Petre stood taller and grinned.

"The nobles will have a difficult time with more changes," Katalin warned. "Traditions are being upended that have existed for centuries. Are you sure?"

"Nobles are like the scum on the top of a kettle of stew," Petre said. "Sometimes they need to be stirred up."

"These analogies of yours... " Katalin's voice was filled with sarcasm. "Brilliant."

I continued to pace the floor, ignoring them. I'd already dealt with the ire of the Rose Court and of the people in general. I didn't like it, but I was strong enough to bear it.

"Not to worry, my dear Lady Katalin, the scum always seems to rise to the top," Petre added.

"Well said, *prince!*" Katalin shot back.

I clutched the edge of the mantle, letting their bickering swirl around me. The Red Valley clan leader's advice came to my mind. He'd suggested making changes. I'd gotten rid of taxes on magic, given women opportunity to be Thorns, and shaken up the Rose Court. But I hadn't finished my changes to the slave trade.

I'd already put an end to new enslavement and to the buying and selling of slaves, a heavy blow to the treasury. There were a limited number of Caracalla jewels, and the war was costly. Even if we pushed the Norte back, there was still the poisoning of the Rodnic Valley.

I didn't have a solution. All I could do was take the next step, survive the moment, and fix things later. I had to trust that, together, my advisers could come up with possible solutions.

I turned and raised a hand. Katalin and Petre froze mid-argument. "Send for a Ghoster. I'll compose messages myself to the resistant families. A message from the empress in the form of Getaen magic should get their attention."

"You really are the Golden Protector," Katalin said, a hand on her hip. "I never realized how much we needed you. It's as if you kicked a few stones down a hill and started a landslide. Our entire landscape will be different."

Petre gave me a firm nod. "Kingdoms either have rockslides or earthquakes. One way or another, nothing stays the same forever."

My dreams are mixed-up. With great care, I can still pick them apart. But only just.

— ESME

CHAPTER

THIRTY-FOUR

EMPEROR OF SHADOWS

The stars were fading in the pre-dawn sky as Petre, Katalin, and I were escorted to the griffin. The courtyard had been cleared except for a few Imperial Guards and dogs on the perimeter.

I said nothing of who would sit on the throne in case I should die in battle, but Rufus had the blue disks for the High Judge with my last request: for Katalin to be the next in line for the crown.

"Nikka!" Papa called from behind me.

"I'll be quick," I assured Petre. Even when we arrived in the Rodnic Valley today, we would only have a small head start on the Norte army.

Papa fidgeted with the cylinder from Saam. "Your instincts are proving to be impeccable. This is, indeed, a coded message from the emperor."

The letter had been crumpled when I'd given it to Papa, but now it was smoothed back out, charcoal rubbed along the side, revealing characters I hadn't seen earlier.

"What does it say?" I asked.

"There were indentions along the side of this letter — writings." Papa rose up on his toes, excitement in his voice. "I worked with one of the scholars familiar with Theracian, but he said the words didn't make sense. I'm not even sure who had the idea first, but we cut the leather cylinder open. Inside was a cypher!"

"Hush, Papa." Over his shoulder, I watched Petre secure our packs to Baise's harness. No need to ruffle her feathers.

Papa opened the leather cylinder. Sure enough, a faded cypher was inked inside. It had clearly been created well in advance — years, or even decades.

"We used this old cypher to interpret the emperor's message." Papa's face fell. "He... he wants you to meet him. The night before the battle, he wants you to meet him."

"Where?"

"He doesn't say."

"Why bother leaving this note at all?"

Papa shrugged. "So you'll be expecting him?

"Saam might not know the date or location himself," I said. If and when he contacted me, I'd likely need to act quickly.

I pulled Papa into a hug. We'd spoken at length the night before and said our good-byes. I didn't want to dissolve into tears again, and Papa seemed to understand that. He held my still-bandaged hands for a moment before letting me slip away.

I mounted in front of Petre. Beneath me, Baise fidgeted, eager to be back in the air.

"Thank you for all you've done to keep Rupea running smoothly," I said, sincerely. "You have been invaluable."

"I wish you good health and luck on the battlefield," Katalin said. "I'm sorry you won't have your Midnight with you on the battlefield."

"I hope she improves enough to ride to the Rodnic Valley," I said, my heart tight.

Katalin gave me a firm nod. "I shall hope for that as well, then. Truth be told, I like Midnight more than most people."

"Except for present company, I'm sure." Petre waved to Katalin with a flourish. "I bid you a fond farewell, Lady Katalin."

"Try not to fall off the beast, prince. It would be such a

tragedy," Katalin said, but her words had no bite. She stepped back and curtsied deeply.

The griffin crouched, her muscles flexing, and then launched into the air. The ground fell away below us. Papa's hand rested over his heart. Katalin's fuchsia dress stood out against the cobblestones. The moment we were out of sight, she'd begin frantic preparations for a siege. Though, as Katalin and I had soberly discussed, Capidava's stores of food were depleted this time of year. And, unfortunately, due to the recent emperors' apathy and the plague, there weren't years of food stored like the people had set aside in generations past. Essentially, a siege would mean death for Dacia. But Katalin and I agreed that after all we'd done to save our kingdom, we wouldn't go down without a fight.

Petre had decided to follow my lead and wear a mask, so the ride was relatively quiet. In the sky, my mind was clear and sharp. I put myself in the Norte's shoes. Invading Dacia would make sense if they felt disadvantaged and bitter, especially if they also felt superior to everyone else. I mulled over how to use that to our advantage until the forest ended and the rolling hills of the Rodnic Valley came into view.

It was well past midday when I circled above the same field we'd used moons earlier to train new recruits. Soldiers scattered as we descended. The captains were shocked but grateful to see me. I quickly updated them on the Norte marching to the glacial mountains overlooking the Rodnic Valley.

A captain escorted Petre and me to the largest stable in Arcidava to inquire after a place for the griffin to eat and rest.

"Something Petre said keeps coming to my mind," I said to the captain.

"I often have interesting things to say," Petre said with exaggerated false modesty.

I punched him lightly on the arm. "When you said kingdoms either suffered from rockslides or earthquakes, I wondered if we could create a *real* earth-shaking movement of our own.

"Emotionally moving?" Petre asked. "Or using some psycho-logical tricks of our own?"

"I mean, a physical rockslide." Glancing around me, I grabbed a few rocks and piled them together on the ground. I tugged back the linen on my fingers and dipped them in Sonus powder. I knelt, the pile of rocks at my knees. I pressed my Sonus-covered finger on the top rock. It began to shake, small jerks of motion between my finger and the rocks below, causing the pile underneath to tremble. I pressed harder, focused on the task, and the rocks ricocheted off each other, causing the pile to collapse.

I held up my powdered hand with a grin. "Rockslide."

The captain's eyebrow rose. "Impressive."

Petre's grin widened. "That's a neat magical trick. But you only displaced a dozen small, *loose* stones. How are you going to bring down the mountain?"

The captain's face fell a fraction, but he turned to me, waiting for my plan.

"Half my unit left five days ago. I expect them to be here in three or four more days." It was a risk at the time, but now I was glad I'd done it. "Once we knew about the poisoning, I suspected the Norte planned to attack the weakened Rodnic Valley. I think they were expecting an easy, quick fight."

"We got the warning about not drinking the water until a Healer tests it," the captain said. "We collected fresh snow and rainwater while waiting for a Healer. Unfortunately, few magical Getaens are this far north."

"We have a Healer and Protector coming with the caravan. At the longest, it will be another four days. However, you make a good point. The Norte have been planning this invasion for decades. Why didn't they wait until the summer to poison the water? It rarely rains at that time of year, so the people would be forced to drink from the river. So, why now? Why poison the glacier?"

"And Borsea's forces were supposed to hold us until the first shoots of green," Petre said.

"I'll bet early crocuses have appeared," the captain said. "The snow is melting, and we've even had some rain."

I tapped my gloved fingers against my hilt. The upcoming battle weighed on me more and more with every passing hour. "Let's get to the base of the mountains, then. We have no time to lose."

We continued to the inn and stable and paid the innkeeper to care for the griffin, as well as horses for Petre and me.

"I'll be sendin' my boys out to hunt rodents," the innkeeper said. "Can't have the majestic animal goin' hungry, now."

"Save your energy," Petre said. "The beast is perfectly capable of killing her own dinner."

"Should the poor, tired creature not be rewarded for carryin' our Golden Protector so bravely 'cross the kingdom?" It was more of a statement than a question, and she sent her sons scrambling out the door. I admired this woman — she didn't seem to care a whit about the opinion of the strange, wealthy, foreign man in front of her. She turned to me. " 'Tis an honor to care for your griffin, majesty. I shall feed him rainwater, a'course. But when the rains stop, what's to be done?"

I wish I knew.

"The Healers will be our guides. But prepare yourself; your family may need to move south, away from the poison."

"My family has owned this inn and stable for generations... " She clucked her tongue, not finishing her thought.

I wanted to tell her that her land would be fine, that her family would be safe. But I wouldn't make any promises I might not live long enough to keep.

After paying the innkeeper, the three of us rode along the dirt road leading north. Our breath formed puffs in front of us. The captain pulled up his cloak, covering most of his face, but compared to the ride we'd just taken in the air, I felt fine. Arcidava well behind us, we took turns scanning the mountains with a spyglass.

"There." The mountain I pointed at wasn't as tall as the others, but I didn't need height. "Notice the steep grade on the bottom half of that mountain? There's little snow at that elevation. It's perfect for a rockslide from the mid-point to the ground."

The captain took his turn with the glass. "Where do you plan to hide your unit?"

"Just above the midpoint, where the snow meets the rocks. You'll have to bait the Norte so they'll follow you to that spot in the canyon," I said. "It'll be dangerous."

"You'll need an escape route," Petre added.

"I have an idea for that, but we'll have to start soon," I said. "I estimate it'll take the Norte another five days to march to this point."

"They'll be climbing mountains or going around them," the captain said. "That could take a moon."

"The Norte have been planning this a long time. Generations, perhaps." The Norte knew passages in Rupea Castle that even Jamil hadn't been aware of. "Let's not underestimate them the way they've underestimated us."

"It'll take us a day just to hike up that mountain," Petre said.

"Petre, listen carefully. I'll give you a list of things we need," I said before turning to the captain. "Find me someone who grew up in this valley. Someone who knows these mountains. We leave within the hour. It's time to get to work."

I NEVER PICTURED myself working with a bandit, especially after the fear they instilled in the people of Dacia had caused so much heartache. But Garipy knew these mountains. Not only had he grown up hunting on the edge of the Norte lands, but he was one of the spies Katalin had sent earlier. So, for the last three days, he'd overseen the digging of the snow tunnels for my Sonus unit.

The wind blew loose snow that stung my cheeks like angry wasps. Garipy, Petre, Seneca, and I stood on a flat expanse wide enough to fit twenty soldiers across in any direction. The valleys of the Rodnic lay out below us.

"How likely are the tunnels to collapse?" I wriggled my toes to keep the blood moving.

"Snow is heavier this time of year, so we took that into consideration," Garipy said. "But there's always a risk that your Sonus vibrations will collapse the tunnel and suffocate you all."

It was a risk we had to take, but I still wanted to do all I could to avoid putting my unit in a death-trap.

"Also, have you ever heard of an avalanche?" Garipy asked.

I shook my head, only vaguely remembering the term.

"This time of year, snow melts on sunny days, then re-freezes at night. It creates layers of unstable snow. One of your vibration-spells could jar the new snow on the slick base and send it crashing down on your heads. That would be far worse than a tunnel collapsing." Garipy pointed at the mountain of snow above us. "From up there, down onto your unit, possibly even crushing your fancy, hidden infirmary as well."

"What do you think the chances are of that?" Petre asked.

"Depends on the Sonus wielders' ability to control their magic." He folded his arms across his broad chest as if defying any argument I might make.

"I can try to strengthen the walls of the tunnels," Seneca offered. The Bonder glanced over to where Poppies from Arcidava were dragging buckets of snow. "Water is tricky, though. By its very nature, it's constantly moving. If we slightly melted the inside of the walls and let them re-freeze as a sheet of ice, that might stabilize it."

"A torch'd do the trick, if I can keep it lit. At least I'll be out of this infernal wind for a bit," the bandit said.

Garipy's face was set in a perpetual scowl, and he bristled whenever I gave him instructions though he did as I asked. He trudged across the somewhat flat area and around the growing wall of heavy snow that had been excavated from the tunnels.

"If your estimates are correct, the Norte will arrive in two days," Petre said. "We need to talk."

"I need to finish up the Bonding on the infirmary. Jalab is anxious to finish," Seneca said as I excused him.

Jalab, the Red Valley Protector who'd cared for the dome, had been one of the volunteers to come to our aid. The Protector had taken the concept of combining magic and invented a unique infirmary on the mountainside. Seneca, who was generally reserved, had been as close to enthusiastic as I'd ever seen him about a Bonder theory.

Petre and I walked to the edge of the packed snow where the ledge dropped away, revealing rocky cliffs below.

"I'm no good to you here," he began. "I'm going with the centuries assigned to bait the Norte."

"You'd leave me now?" I tried to sound like I was teasing, but in truth, I would miss Petre. He was a brother in every way but blood.

Earlier, we'd received word of a well-trodden path in the mountains. It stretched from east of Auripo to just north of where we now stood, which meant it lead to the Norte camps at the base of the glacier. We expected to hear from the spies soon, informing us the Norte army location on the trail. Once the Norte armies approached the new camps, we would lure the enemy to chase us down the canyon and into our trap. The best time to act was when the greater portion of the Norte army was still exhausted from their travel.

"I haven't practiced with Sonus magic," Petre continued. "But I can help your armies. You know they need more experienced soldiers among them."

"What will your brother say?" I asked, hesitating to send the prince straight into danger.

"Asander would be proud of his brother," Dyana's voice sounded behind us.

Petre and I spun to see the queen consort. Midnight was at her side. I put my hands to my mouth, tears welling.

Midnight bounded to me. I dropped to my knees, inspecting her, and she licked my face.

"How did you... ?" Petre said.

"We marched straight here, only sleeping when we had to," Dyana turned her attention to me. "That mother of yours, Rubia, she is wicked powerful. I'm not even tired."

"She didn't... " I couldn't believe Rubia would be so reckless with her magic. Well, maybe she would.

Dyana stepped forward, but Petre stopped her, despite knowing my dire wolf would have alerted us to an impostor.

"What did I spill on you the morning of your thirtieth birth-day?" he asked.

Dyana narrowed her eyes. "I'm not thirty for another two moons."

"Well, now you know you have something to look forward to," Petre smirked.

"Just remember, I'll be watching over you while you sleep," Dyana said, though I caught a hint of a smile tugging on her lips. She turned to me. "I spoke with the captain when we arrived. He said a contingency is moving deeper into the mountains, to the spot you've designated, to await your signal. The Auripoans are going with them."

"I can hardly believe you're here." I ran my fingers through Midnight's fur.

The three of us worked our way back down the mountain. Even without an enemy attacking, traversing the snow patches and rocks covered with invisible layers of ice was treacherous. Even Midnight struggled. I would have preferred to leave my dire wolf on the safer ledge, but she wouldn't leave my side. As we hiked down, I scanned our rows of tents between the mountain and the town. My stomach shriveled knowing that this field, if it became battleground, would be the last defense before the Norte descended upon the people of Dacia.

At the bottom of the mountain, I found the battalion that I'd sent along with half my unit and the Auripoans. One of the captains who'd been stationed in the Rodnic Valley jogged up to Dyana, Petre, and me.

"When we asked for Healers from Findava, several responded along with other magical Getaens. Bonders, Protectors... fifty new recruits of all ages. Seeing the nobles of the Rose Court returning to Findava, coordinating their personal guards with the city guards to defend Findava, well, I think it frightened them. Then, getting letters from loved ones in the armies, losing friends and family on the battlefields, it stirred them, prompted them to act."

I hoped my people hadn't waited too long to accept the seriousness of this war. The captain and I discussed necessary logistics. Arcidava was already strained, and Findava had supplies a day out — we'd have to make do.

As night fell, I reunited with my Sonus unit. Midnight sprawled half on me, threatening to crush my ribs. As comforted as I was to have her, I wriggled out from under her, breathing easier. Even with my dire wolf, I couldn't stop my mind from running through every possible scenario. How many Scythians had joined the Norte? How many Theracians? Were more marching north, or was the bulk amassing in the south?

Unable to sleep, I dressed and stepped out of my tent. The night was utterly still, the stars glittering dagger points of light hanging over our heads. I stared up at the dark mountains, listening for any sound. Beside me, Midnight stiffened then relaxed as Dyana approached.

"How are you holding up?" Dyana asked.

My grip was improving, but I knew that wasn't what she was referring to. "Fine, I think? I keep everything b-bottled up where I don't have to feel anything, which helps."

"You have to protect your mind, especially in war. Before one sees blood spilt, they are innocent. They don't know to be frightened. Not really. But now you know the ugliness and the horror. All the waiting, anticipation... it becomes worse than the fight itself."

Her words were raw and true. The bards sung of the glory of war, but I knew the truth: war was the stage Zalmoxis created to torture the living, and as an added benefit to him, it sent more souls for him to devour.

"Nicoleta," Dyana said, her voice softening. "When you come out on the other side of this battle—"

If I live.

"—afterward, when the world goes quiet. When you're alone and your mind starts to churn through all the things you've done, the missteps, the mistakes, you must... you *must* allow those feelings out. If you don't address them, examining everything you've buried, and make peace with your actions, there will be consequences. They weigh you down, the pressure growing until all those bottles boil, spilling out burning acid that will destroy you and everyone you care for. It's better to face them and deal with your past a little at a time—"

I stopped the queen. "What did you say about letting it out a little over time?"

"Your emotions — even if you let them out one drop at a time, it's easier."

"One drop at a time," I repeated, my mind suddenly whirling. "It makes it easier to *absorb*."

"That's a decent analogy, yes."

"That's why the Norte are using the glacier." I considered the new possibility.

"Glacier? What are you talking about?"

"That's why the Norte didn't put the poison in the river. They want it to be absorbed slowly."

"As the glacier melted, the poison would be slowly released?"

"The land can probably only absorb so much poison at once. A little poison over time would saturate the land better. Perhaps deeper into —"

Dyana held up a hand, dropping into a crouch. She drew her sword in one quick, silent motion. I followed her eye line. Ahead of us, the valley narrowed running up into the mountains. I tensed, the Canina Thorn in my grip.

We moved into the shadows outside the ring of light cast by

the fire. Then I saw it. A shadowed form moving toward us. Dyana tossed small Luminary pebbles out about twenty steps in front of us.

I didn't know when Dyana had gotten the stones, but apparently Saam wasn't the only one who made good use of his time in Dacia. The shadowed figure slowed as he walked through the lights, allowing us to see him. From his dark coloring and style of clothing, he was clearly a Theracian.

Dyana raised her sword, a growl deep in her throat.

"Wait." I grabbed her wrist, thinking of the message from Saam. "Be on guard, but don't attack. Not yet."

We held steady, letting the soldier come to us.

"I come on behalf of Emperor Saam Oeagrus," he said, keeping out of range of Dyana's sword. "If you wish to negotiate, come with me."

"How far?" I asked.

"You can't be seriously thinking about this." Dyana gripped my shoulder, her fingers pinching down. "You're walking straight into a trap."

Did Saam know the Norte would turn against him? Did he know the Illyrians wanted to? I wanted to find out.

"Give us a moment," I said to the soldier.

"This entire meeting was planned with exactness," the Theracian said. "We don't have ti —"

"I should end you right now," Dyana said.

"Come or stay, it's up to you." The soldier skulked away.

"I've taken precautions," I whispered to Dyana, thinking about the pocket I'd sewn into my shirt and the single black seed it held. "No one will find out Dacia's secrets from me."

"Mother earth and stars," Dyana cursed, guessing my intention. "If that's your escape plan, you shouldn't go."

"If I don't return by dawn, you are to take command."

"Your captains won't follow me," Dyana spat.

I stepped back, loosening her grip on my shoulder, rushing my words. "I've already told them to do so, in case I didn't return."

"You *knew* this would happen," she breathed.

"I didn't know for certain. The letter I showed you from the emperor at the Curat — it was a coded message. My papa worked it out."

Dyana started to argue, but I cut her off, slapping my forehead. "Oh, no. The letter."

"What?"

"The emperor said he would meet with me the *night before* the b-battle." I glanced over my shoulder at the retreating shadow.

Dyana's attention jerked to the soldier up ahead. "The Norte are here? I know you'd estimated mere days, but I honestly planned to camp in the mountains for weeks."

"I thought it was p-possible, but not p-probable. It's likely the Norte we fought at the Curat are the *last* of the enemy's army to arrive. They're ready to fight. They could be here at d-dawn, for all we know."

"I'll come with you," Dyana said.

"One of us must stay." I took a step to follow the Theracian. "B-besides, I have a feeling they'll kill anyone but me."

"I don't trust this situation, nor Emperor Saam," Dyana growled. "But you've been right about too many things for me to doubt you. So, go. You have a kraken to confront."

I HAD half-expected Saam to ambush me as soon as I entered the canyon. Instead, two horses waited. The Theracian soldier was already mounted and waiting to lead the way. The horses raced through the snowy pass. The farrier must have used special shoes because the horses managed the traitorous terrain with comparative ease. Though we rode quickly, I wasted no time in using my teeth to remove my left glove and dip my fingers in my Sonus powder. Then I replaced it, hiding any glint of Sonus magic.

The mountains soared above us, jagged pillars that shut out all the light except for the ribbon of stars overhead. With some trepidation, I rode past the very same mountainside I planned to collapse in a rush of rock and debris. Anyone in this same place tomorrow would meet a terrible demise.

After an hour of riding, the soldier pulled his horse to a halt. He dismounted and cinched the reigns of the horse to a stake that had been driven into the icy ground. I stayed mounted, one hand on my hilt, the other on the reins, ready to bolt at the first flash of metal. The soldier led me around a bend. I kneed my mount and trotted forward. A shallow cave came into view with a small fire inside.

The hair on the back of my neck prickled.

"Emperor?" the soldier whispered. Nearing the fire, he fell to his knees and let out a cry, his back arched. My horse reared. Two paces behind us, the soldier's horse struggled to free itself from where it was tethered to the ice. I eased my grip, trying to project calm though my own heart pounded. Orange flames reflected in a dagger buried in the soldier's back.

"Empress?" Emperor Saam's voice sounded. A soft blue Luminary ignited in the darkness, held in the air between me and the dying soldier, lighting up Saam's face.

"Stop," I commanded, not sure if I was about to face a Mirror or the emperor. "Prove your identity."

"Last time we spoke, I told you I looked forward to continuing our conversation. And just as I'd predicted, here we are." His oily words sent a shiver of terror throughout me.

I swallowed, pitying the poor soldier who had, unfortunately, been called on to fetch me. Clearly, the emperor wanted no record of this meeting.

"Any Sensitive could have learned about that conversation," I said flatly. But, if this was a Mirror, they were doing an excellent job of imitating the emperor. "But I believe you."

"I knew you would find my note," Saam spoke as he pulled his blade from the dead man's body. I winced. "I was concerned you would not arrive in time."

It was more than likely that Saam hadn't known how quickly

the Norte would march across the frozen expanse — a costly miscalculation.

"What do you want, Emperor?" I said, feigning annoyance to hide my trepidation. I tried to scan the darkness, but the fire made it impossible for my eyes to adjust.

The emperor cleaned off the bloody dagger and picked up a thick branch of burning wood from the fire. He wasn't wearing armor, nor was I. We were both conveying our willingness to nego-tiate — so far. Saam moved to the mouth of the cave and held up the flames to the overhanging lip of snow as he spoke. "You haven't witnessed the full power of the Theracian army falling upon you. Everyone you love will be slain. The Norte is nothing alone, but with me, we're unstoppable."

Plus the Scythians. I knew a lot more than Saam realized.

"I don't want to eradicate Dacia's armies." Saam continued to run the flames across the overhanging snow. "I want you to join me. But I won't offer again."

"Dacians want p-partnerships, not foreign rulers." I kept my retort simple.

The snow over the cave dripped. Then with a sudden *swoosh* and *crash*, the snow fell. My horse jerked back from the plume. After settling, all evidence of Saam's murder and our meeting were hidden.

I steadied my breathing, watching Saam in the dim Luminary light as I looked over his shoulder toward the Norte encampment. Without the flames, I closed my eyes for a heartbeat, letting them adjust to the darkness. Scanning the canyon again, I still couldn't see much, but there wasn't a third horse.

Saam was clever. He chose a section of mountain with a high ridge, allowing snow to collapse over the cave while keeping the rest intact. Underfoot, the ground was primarily ice and rock, leaving scant footprints and little evidence of our rendezvous. It was improbable that Saam had set foot here before today, meaning he'd selected it after a quick study. He was no fool, especially considering he lived in a desert.

I held the reigns still, alert for any sound or movement.

"My proposal has not changed," Saam whispered.

After all the gifts I'd seen for Borsea, I assumed he'd made her the same offer. Had she refused him? Or did he sense that she would?

"You wish for me to be your first wife?" I clarified. For a moment, I envisioned an end of the fighting. End of the bloodshed.

Except it wouldn't. The Norte would never stop coming for a land they'd coveted for years. We'd be a colony state to Theracia, unable to act on our own and *still* fighting the Norte. Not wanting to fuel his vengeance further against Dacia, I prepared to repeat that his offer was an honor, but I'd refuse. I clamped my mouth shut. Everything made sense. His letter. This meeting. Giving me a 'second chance' to join him. Furthermore, he'd offer to take a wife from a colony state for only one reason.

"You're afraid." Though I feared Saam's power, I sat up straighter on the horse. "You've *finally* come to realize that the Norte are stronger than all your armies combined."

Saam was silent.

I pressed harder. "You need us. You need the Getaen magic for even the slightest chance of defeating the Norte."

"Empress, that's where you're wrong," his voice was cold, laced with an unsaid threat. "I'm using them to get what I want: the Auripoans."

"Don't you see? The Norte are weakening you, stringing out your armies along the northern mountains. They don't need your armies to win the battle with Dacia. They've been manipulating you, your colony states, and the Scythians from the beginning. And you made it all too easy. They used your hatred of the Auripoans to blind you to their true intentions." I watched his hands, the Luminary making their outline plain, refusing to be surprised by a blade. "But something changed, didn't it? You saw something? Was it the Clarifiers stealing people's memories? Perhaps a Sensitive guessed at one of your secrets? Or the Bonders, commanding the leopards. Whatever it was, you knew... you *knew* you were outmatched."

Saam's breathing grew heavier as I spoke. If I was right or wrong, either way I hoped to rile him into making a mistake.

"The gods have chosen me to lead Theracia and rule Cornara." Saam took a step back, clenching the Luminary orb tighter. "You don't know what's beyond your western mountains. They're vast, but they do have an end, Empress. Don't you fear who will come charging over them one day? You *need* my protection."

"You're lying to yourself. You *know* that you've been tricked." I seethed at the tragedy of the situation playing out on our battlefields. "What will Borsea do when she finds out you left tonight? Will she even ask you before she blinds and then maims you? Kills you?"

Saam's eyes lit with fury, the Luminary casting his face into contorted shadows. In my periphery, I saw no movement, heard no unexpected noises. The emperor was truly fearful of Borsea discovering him if he was alone.

"She'd murder anyone for using a Luminary, filthy Getaen magic. Just imagine what she'll do when she figures out your intention to betray her by joining with those same Getaens." I slid off the horse and stood before Saam, feet planted. He didn't step back, but he kept the Luminary between us. I stepped toward him, closing the gap. "You're wise to try to defeat her before she turns on you."

Down in the canyon, it was difficult to determine when the sun would rise. I didn't mind detaining Saam. If he was caught, that could start a battle between my enemies. Or, if he never returned to the Norte camp, that might be even better. I slid my hand down to my hilt.

Saam stepped back, his eyes narrowing. "I had hoped you would see reason."

As I ripped my sword free, Saam kicked his foot, hard. The ground under me slid away. I fell onto the ice, rolled backward, coming up into a crouch with one hand braced against the ground, my short sword in my other outstretched hand. Before I could charge, Saam was poised with his curved blade at my neck.

I froze. The dropped orb illuminated a flat board sticking out from a patch of snow. I'd stepped into a trap. He'd kicked the board, and I'd lost my balance. Saam hadn't arrived with extra soldiers, but he'd prepared.

He studied me with cold calculation, his blade pressing against my skin. The cold bite against my neck should have frightened me, but instead, I was infuriated. I dug my gloved fingers into the crusty snow. If I was going to die, I would bring Saam down with me.

"Did you really believe Captain Kekad would betray me? I hold his family hostage? He played his part well and died in an attempt to gain your trust." Saam's voice was calm, his tone almost scientific as if he were studying a map instead of holding a blade to my neck. "Did it work?"

"Is that why you sent him to deliver your message at the Curat camp?" Kekad had been hardened by war, but after the events in the Norte camp, I'd trusted him.

"He was a brilliant battlefield tactician. That's why I allowed him to live and serve me. He knew an opportunity when he saw one."

As a conquered colony, the Illyrians would likely be placed at the front of the Norte army. I would have tried to allow them to walk right out of the canyon before sending down a wall of rocks. But that consideration blew away like ash in the wind.

"I could have made you into a goddess." Saam's voice hardened.

I wished I could have spit in his face, but my mouth was too dry. "You couldn't even make me your wife."

Saam's nostril's flared. I swung my blade, knowing I would die before it connected with his body but hoped the momentum would carry the swing. But Saam jumped back, avoiding my blade. I let myself spin, staying crouched, and threw the chunk of ice in my hand at the horse.

As I'd hoped, the horse bolted forward past Saam, providing a distraction. I jumped up, pushing my hand through the air toward the emperor.

"Skenai!"

The magic simultaneously shot the glove off my hand and knocked Saam back. Though my glove had muffled the magic, it was enough for me to lunge away from Saam's tricks and into the darkness. I sprinted for the staked horse, practically pitching into the beast. Fumbling with the rope, I found the stake and yanked it free. I slapped the horse's rump, and it charged into the darkness back toward my camp. The loud neighing and clomping covered my hasty footsteps as I moved past a boulder. An arrow sung through the air, followed quickly by a second down the canyon. The horse screamed, making my stomach curdle, though the animal kept running. As I'd feared, Saam was prepared to stop me from escaping. If he couldn't convince me to yield, he wanted me dead.

I crouched in the darkness, my heart beating so loud I could have sworn Saam would have heard it. His footsteps raced after the fleeing horse but only a few steps. I shrunk away from the blue light, clutching my sword with both hands. I didn't want to die hiding in the dark.

Saam cursed. Something ricocheted off the mountain — a thrown rock.

A well-trained horse would likely not bolt far. The horse I'd sent running back to the Norte camps earlier wouldn't be far up the canyon. Still, Saam would have to hurry to find it, hope to get back to the camp undetected, and make a perfect excuse as to why a horse was suddenly missing.

His footsteps retreated, much quieter this time. Perhaps he'd seen the horse's shadow well enough to know I wasn't riding it. Was he searching for me? Lying in wait?

I held my breath, straining for any sound. Part of me wanted to race after him and cut him down. But with the Luminary, he could see far better, and he'd hear me coming. I gripped my sword tighter, wanting to scream. I counted to a hundred. I pressed my hand against the thin trickle of warm blood dripping down my neck, and I counted to a hundred again, trying to calm my racing heart.

A sound overhead caught my attention: the flapping of Baise's wings. I clutched my chest, feeling like I could breathe. If Saam was still hunting me, let him come. I pushed away from the mountain and made my way back toward camp. With every step, I felt exposed. I constantly checked over my shoulder, looking for the dim blue light of Saam's orb.

I couldn't be in the canyon in the morning. I had to get on the mountainside with my troops.

My fears rose up, and I swallowed them down. I pulled out my Luminary orb. Then I ran.

The key the empress wears.

It is an amulet of power.

Residual magic is all the plague requires.

I See the warlock. I understand his meaning. Only one with a 'true heart' can control the plague. Stop it. Unleash it.

Will the true heart break?

Is this an ancient queen consort? Or a future empress? It could be both — my dreams are raindrops, mixing as they slam into the desert sands.

— ESME

THIRTY-FIVE

THE OCEAN CRIES OUT

What had taken an hour on horseback would take me hours on foot in the darkness. The cut on my neck wasn't terribly deep, but I pressed my one still-gloved hand against it to help stop the bleeding. Rubia would cluck in disapproval when she heard I'd needed her Healing even before the fighting began.

This battle is really starting off well for me.

Baise flapped overhead, a dark mass blotting out the stars, streaking across the sky. I was tempted to whistle and wave my Luminary to catch her attention. Though it was unlikely that Saam was tracking me, Baise was too valuable to the battle to lure into possible danger.

But the griffin swooped down, letting out a cry that set my teeth on edge. She landed well ahead of me in a wider portion of the canyon. Relief and joy spurred me toward my escape. I ran my hand across her feathers. I let out a sob and put my arms around her neck. She didn't try to peck at me, but her muscles tensed.

"You can't rescue me and not expect some tears." I grabbed Baise's harness and swung up onto her back. The griffin spread her wings and pushed into the air. I let freezing tears leak down my cheeks while I was alone, soaring up into the fading stars. From here, I could see the lightening gray skies in the east, indicating the sunrise was not far behind.

If Saam was still alive, he was back with his army by now. They'd march for us shortly, so I couldn't delay. My elbow brushed against the conch shell. Bitter embarrassment unfurled inside me. I unhooked the conch shell, ready to throw it down against the rocks below. But as I did, I remembered that this had come from the Illyrian people shortly after I'd been crowned. They wouldn't have had time to coordinate a grand scheme with the Theracians. Furthermore, Kekad couldn't have known I would show up at his feet in Borsea's cave. I felt the sincerity in his voice as he explained his situation. He'd been speaking the truth.

Saam was acting like he was in control, and maybe he thought he was. But he was no god. He was a human playing his own game.

I secured the shell again as I spotted the dim points of blue light moving through the canyon. Two of my century units were already marching toward the Norte camp. With a nudge, Baise turned and rode the wind to the bottom, tucking in her wings as we dove lower.

Baise landed, and soldiers ran to meet us. Dyana, Petre, and the captain's eyes were wide. I imagined that I looked like a windswept urchin with blood smeared across my neck. I quickly recounted what had happened while my captain held a Luminary and Dyana inspected the wound.

"You'll survive," Dyana said. "See a Healer as soon as you return, though."

"You escape death once again," Petre grinned.

I squeezed his shoulder, climbed up onto a boulder along the edge of the mountain, and dabbed Sonus powder on my lower lip in the pre-dawn light.

"Today, for the first time, we will take the fight to our enemies," I shouted to the soldiers. "They won't expect it. We will bring them after us, down this very canyon, where we will unleash our magic upon them. This enemy will see our might.

"Our enemies desire our land. They mean to rip apart our families and subjugate them. Today, we fight for more than our fields, our gold, and our ports. Fight to protect your families from having their homes burned and children enslaved. We will not replace one tyrant ruler for another!"

I paused as a chorus of cheers and war cries rose from my troops. I scanned the crowd of faces. How many would not live to see the night? And yet, they showed no fear. My heart swelled at their courage. I swallowed a lump in my throat and continued.

"At this moment, the Norte are poisoning our land. If we don't stop them, this will become a land of desolation. Families will be forced from their homes, others around the kingdom will suffer illness and death." I lifted the Canina Thorn over my head, the blade reflecting the sun. "We will not trade one plague for another. We will not lie down for death by the north's hand. And we will not be enslaved by the south. We will fight!"

The Auripoans banged the pommels of their swords against their shields, and the Dacian's joined them, shaking the ground, echoing through the pass. If the sound reached our enemies, even better.

I ran to Baise, mounting her in one motion. As we soared into the air, the deafening sound of our armies carried into the sky. I swung my sword over my head. Baise flew toward the Norte for a beat of her wings before dipping one wing down, making a wide circle in the sky. We headed south, back for my unit burrowed in the snow.

Tucking the griffin into a notched, protected spot on the mountain facing the Rodnic valley, I hiked up the mountain to where my unit lay in wait. The clouds were heavy, and a storm rumbled in the distance. The wind cut like a knife. I was almost to the flat expanse next to my tunnels when a red-headed woman seemed to rush out of nowhere. But I knew of the hidden infirmary mere steps away.

"Empress!" she shouted and rushed over. She was one of the Red Valley Healers dispatched from the Curat a week ago. "You're hurt!"

I shouted above the wind and pointed at my still oozing neck. "Just a scratch."

The Healer nodded and beckoned me to follow her. Wary, I wiggled my fingers, reassuring myself the Sonus powder was still there. I walked after her through the narrow slip of space between the snow and the mountain. After three steps, the space opened up. No ambush — just three Getaens.

Logically, standing on snow barely clinging to a cliffside with nothing below it but air, one would think our weight would send us falling through the floor to break our bodies against the mountain far below. Instead, it was an infirmary carved into the snow. Underfoot, encased in clear ice, a strip of black Sonus powder lined the perimeter of the space. Impressive. Protected from the wind, but allowing in diffused light, it felt almost welcoming.

Seneca fitfully slept on one of the five pallet beds.

The Healer grabbed a bowl and a jar of herbs from the shelf. "Seneca only just finished working with Jalab to put a Protection around the entrance to dissuade notice. And that's after your Bonder spent the last three days sealing the snow to the mountain so it could support our weight. Seneca reassured us that the magic will hold until the walls melt into slush, moons from now."

"Is Garipy with my unit?" I had expected the bandit to hide here.

The Healer stirred oils and herbs in the bowl, shoving in and frantically coating a strip of linen. "Garipy returned to Arcidava. He said he'd put in his dues and left."

I was a bit disappointed, but not surprised.

"A Clarifier took the bandit's memories of this infirmary and the tunnels." The Healer set the cloth to soak and grabbed a wet rag. Without warning, she pulled away my cloak, and I winced as some of the fur tore away the forming scab. With efficient scrubbing, she wiped the blood, leaving my neck stinging.

"Are the other Healers at the other infirmaries?" I distracted myself from her aggressive cleaning.

This one was the smallest of the three infirmaries in the Rodnic

Valley, an emergency retreat for my unit. It was also built in case of fighting on this mountain; transporting the injured to the valley would be incredibly difficult.

Garipy had identified a good location for the wounded on the opposite side of the pass. On the western mountain, near the base, the infirmary was hidden with rocks and a Protection. The last infirmary was the largest, sitting on the far edge of our camp, the side nearest to the town.

The Healer grabbed the linen strip and pressed it against my wound. "We brought our personal supplies, and scant more have arrived from Findava. The rest won't be here for several more days."

I frowned. We'd have to make the Healing herbs stretch. Even so, soldiers would die who might have lived if we'd had more magic. Even with the rockslide, I didn't know if we'd be able to hold back the Norte army another four days when the rest of our army and supplies arrived.

I glanced at Seneca. The Healer hadn't given him a sleeping draught because she was saving the ingredients for the battle.

"We can only do the best we can with what we have," I said.

The Healer lifted my bag from behind a pile of blankets.

"Liviana brought this. She asked Jalab to infuse Protection into your gorget, and I've added Healer magic in the mask. They're ready for you."

"Thank you. Last time I wore the collar, it saved my life."

"Looks like you could have used it last night."

"I went with intentions to negotiate. But I'll not have any such illusions today."

The Healer clasped the gorget over the newly-applied bandage.

"Thank you for gifting the Red Valley the warlock's ancient crown," the Healer said. "It's the reason many of us came."

I missed the *Crown of Lore* — the delicate, emerald dotted crown. Though, I didn't regret gifting it to the Red Valley clan to renew their Protective dome.

"It is my honor and my duty to protect my people."

The Healer handed me her own gloves. "You'll need these."

"I couldn't." I pushed her hands back and grabbed my mask and the spyglass from my bag.

"I know your grip was weakened. Please, at least take one to replace the one you're missing. You need it more than I do." She pressed the glove into my hand. The standard glove was fashioned for all the Thorns, not nearly as nice as the fur glove I'd lost. Still, I was grateful for it.

Tugging it on and securing the mask in my belt to reserve the magic, I gave my thanks before I hurried out and climbed up to the flat expanse.

Near the entrance tunnel, a towering mound of snow was evidence of the digging which proffered protection from anyone who might attack from below. But I was more worried about snow leopards surprising us from above.

On the other side of the wall of snow, a deep bowl had been dug with two tunnels cut into the far side. Inside a tunnel entrance, Liviana was waiting with Midnight. My dire wolf jumped up to greet me.

"You're alive." Liviana clasped at her chest. "We were beginning to worry."

"But you would have carried on," I assured her.

"We would have done as you'd instructed. Still, I'm glad to have you back. How long do we have?"

"It depends on how deep the Norte are in the mountains. It could be anywhere from now until this evening."

Liviana jumped back down into the pit, and I followed. Both tunnels were taller and wider than Midnight, but not tall enough for a human to stand upright.

"Give me a report as we move," I said.

"With you, seven of our unit are here," Liviana said as we walked, hunched awkwardly. "We have two soldiers from another unit stationed higher on the mountains, and another around the side, to the west, watching for the armies. Ahead the tunnels connect, widening enough for all of us. It's actually dug all the way to the rock. Your weapons are waiting near the exit: one shield, one spear, and three javelins. Remember, they're poison-tipped now, so be careful. We'll grab the arms after the rockslide, crest the mountain, and descend on any of the army that didn't get buried. Twenty archers are already in hiding, ready to strike as soon as you give the command."

"Well done." Everything was in place, yet my heart thumped in anticipation. "So, this tunnel does a loop? The exit is in a tunnel on our right?"

"Yes. Seneca strengthened the walls but said it's weakest between the two tunnels. The Bonder said to take care, but Garipy grouched that it was more than adequate for our needs."

Yet, the bandit fled before it's put to the test. Of course.

Liviana pointed above her head. "We punched metal rods up through the snow for light and air. They're not noticeable from above. And even a slender beam of light shines bright in the darkness."

We emerged into an enlarged space where my unit waited. They stood shoulder to shoulder, large Sonus pouches on their hips, their hands already white. The room was charged, coiled and ready to pounce. Past my unit, on the opposite wall of the tunnels, the floor dropped down and out of sight. That space had a low ceiling, not even high enough for Midnight to enter, extending all the way to the lip of the snow. There, the snow thinned. My unit would be poised directly above a steep drop, plenty of loose rocks ready to send crashing down the mountain. My unit would be placed like a lattice work of bodies, their fingers pressed against the thin crust of snow down toward the rocks of the mountain below their bellies. In that suffocating space, they would make their move.

Liviana reviewed our plan.

"We all know this mission is dangerous. The goal is to send the rocks and a few trees down the mountain." Liviana turned to me. "We've taken turns, practicing this technique on mountains a half-day's walk north. It's tricky because the magic has to pulse strong enough to trigger the fall. If the magic is too strong, it will reverberate up the mountain, causing an avalanche above."

The soldiers didn't balk at hearing Liviana's warning. Their courage strengthened me. I shouldn't have been surprised as most of them were the earliest recruits — the ones who responded, no matter how weak my call.

Liviana continued, "There's a strong possibility that this room will collapse, possibly go down the mountain. You all have your assignments. When it's your turn to retreat, grab your spear and get to the rendezvous point. You know the route."

I spoke up. "When you retreat, I will be waiting. Look to the skies."

"The greatest danger will be withdrawing after we initiate the rockslide. But we should all be able to escape in time." Liviana turned to me. "In the air, you'll be a target. Not even you can avoid an arrow's bite. Are you sure I shouldn't take your place?"

"I need you to oversee this attack while I watch the entire battle."

Liviana nodded then turned to the group. "Let's give the empress a boost then, shall we?"

The soldiers pressed back, making way for Liviana and me to the back of the icy space. With no room for the soldiers to bow or curtsy, they gave me nods like they would their Thorn captain. That suited me just fine. In the back of the room, a large hole had been cut into the roof, wide enough for someone twice my size to fit through. I commanded Midnight to stay as her dark fur would be a beacon. Though after the retreat, Midnight would be a valuable asset against any surviving snow leopards.

Two soldiers boosted me up through the hole and back into the biting wind. It was mid-morning. Thick clouds were rolling in, muting the sun. Beyond the ledge, the mountain was almost a sheer drop to the ground. Baise soared much higher in the sky when we'd flown, but I felt more precarious standing on this mountain than on her back. I checked that my short sword was securely in place on my left hip and the Sonus powder on my right, with the conch shell just behind it. I dreaded killing Illyrians and any soldiers from colony states. This wasn't their war. But in the end, they would cut us down if we let them.

I kept a wary eye on the path below and a listening ear for a warning cry from the soldier's higher on the mountain. I bounced up and down on my heels, rubbing my hands together, trying to keep warm. If a day could both gallop and crawl forward, this was it. I anxiously waited, constantly bringing my spyglass to my eye with every phantom shadow below. But while I could see the entire section of the canyon where the rocks and snow would fall, I couldn't see north where the armies would be appearing.

Snow crunched above me. I spun to see a Dacian soldier descending. He landed next to me with a thud. He wore a Patridavan uniform under his heavy cloak, indicating he'd been a Thorn long before this war. He was a decade older than me with probably as many years of experience. "Our soldiers are returning after baiting the enemy. They're moving fast. The Norte and Theracian forces won't be far behind."

"Go," I said. He scrambled back up the mountain to his lookout point.

I strained to hear Liviana's commands below. "To your places, group one."

I put the spyglass to my eye. Still nothing. Yet, my heart thumped in anticipation. I counted as I breathed, trying to calm my trembling hands. Figures appeared below. They were running, the green Dacian flag snapping in the wind. Not far behind was the red Auripoan flag. I had to wait until they were all cleared of the projected rockslide.

"Group two," Liviana commanded.

Hurry, hurry, I willed my too-small army below. The forward vanguard was drawing near the entrance to the canyon. My spirits soared. Would this actually work? It had to. I clutched my fingers tighter around the spyglass.

"Group three," Liviana said. Final group. I shifted so I could see her below. She was already looking up at me, waiting for my signal.

I lowered my spyglass, cautious of a glint despite the clouds. I could easily spot my armies against the white, icy surroundings. It wasn't until the first wave of my army moved further out into the fields that they blended in with the areas of mud.

A narrow space was visible between the group of Auripoans and the next group of soldiers. I couldn't tell if the Auripoans had split into two groups. Through the spyglass, I studied the moving figures. I found a purple flag — either Theracians or one of their colony states. Maybe even Scythians. I couldn't see much beyond their helmets. My stomach clenched. I had to let some of the enemy through or else risk the rocks hitting my own people.

The mountain quivered. I signaled to Liviana to wait. Her brow creased. "We haven't started."

With dawning trepidation, I realized the tremor was caused by the soldiers below. Their pounding feet caused echoes up the canyon. This could complicate our task. But it couldn't be their army alone causing this amount of tumult.

Making a snap decision, I spun and climbed the mountain, moving north so I could get a better prospect of their army. As I came upon the Patridavan again, he practically jumped out of his skin before he realized it was me.

"Empress!" he whispered. He offered me a hand and pulled me up next to him. His mouth opened and closed, seemingly at a loss for words. He pointed through a hole cut in the wall of snow that encircled him. Peeking through, the sight made my head spin. The enemy's army filled the canyon, continuing until the mountains curved, and they disappeared from view. We both watched, speechless. I knew the Theracians had an enormous army at their disposal, but *seeing* them marching, *feeling* the ground tremble, my heart nearly failed me.

"Stay and keep watch," I commanded before I slid back down to Liviana. My Dacian leathers were covered by my white cloak, so I didn't fear being spotted. With the spyglass, I watched the rear of the Auripoans. The Theracians were picking up speed, intending to intercept.

In a few breaths, my armies would be clear. I signaled to Liviana: the last warning.

I lifted the spyglass again, risking a longer view. As I suspected, Norte soldiers marched amongst the armies, their white furs standing out against the darker leather of the Theracians. Did the colony states agree to report to Norte captains? Saam had allowed it — he was likely still alive, or the enemy armies would have been delayed, fighting amongst themselves.

Bile rose in the back of my throat. Zalmoxis would make this a bloody battle. I sat up straighter, refusing to let fear drive me. The front of the enemy army passed through the canyon. I had to trust that my army could fend off a portion of the Theracians and Norte. All I hoped for was to win this battle. Force them to pause while I came up with another plan.

I had to make my unit's attack effective; we wouldn't be able to surprise our enemy like this again.

I signaled to Liviana

"Phase One!" Liviana called to my unit.

The ground began to rumble. If I hadn't been waiting for it, I might not have noticed. Liviana gave another command. I couldn't hear words, but I knew she'd dispatched someone to send Baise to this ledge. I silently began my countdown to ten. Then I gave another signal.

"Phase Two!" Liviana commanded. The rumble grew. I rocked back on my heels but kept my balance.

Tiny fissures formed in the snow around me. A chill ran down my spine. We didn't need to increase the magic to send the mountain falling. At this rate, the mountain would slide on its own.

A cough and a thump in the snow sounded above. I spun, scanning the path to the Patridavan Thorn I'd just left higher up the mountain. I gave a silent signal to Liviana to begin the evacuation. This mountain was about to crumble.

There was a groan, and I rushed up the hill, my sword in one hand, Sonus powder on the other. A Theracian soldier lay on his back in the snow, his face purpling. My Thorn's arm was wrapped around the invader's neck.

"He just appeared out of nowhere!" my Thorn said, his breathing hard. His eyes darted back up the slope and then across the mountain, scanning for more.

The Theracian soldier thrashed, his fingers clawing at the arm around his neck. But my soldier had him pinned down, his legs wrapped around his torso. Seeing me, the Theracian flipped up the edge of his sleeve, revealing a yellow band, just like Kekad had worn.

"Zalmoxis," I cursed. "Release him!"

"What?"

"Release him." I pried away my soldier's arm until he finally relaxed enough for the Theracian to cough.

I pointed my sword at the man's face. "Choose your words carefully."

The Theracian lifted up his hands, still heaving for air. "We are... we have... ready... throw off oppressors."

I gasped.

My soldier frowned, "Wha —"

I grabbed the front of the man's cloak, shaking him. "What kingdom are you loyal to? Who do you fight for?"

"Illyria," he squeaked.

"Where are your armies?" I demanded. "Are the Illyrians in the front?"

"Why?"

"We have little time. Where are your people?"

"Scattered through the front half of the armies," The man swallowed, rubbing his neck. "Our people are usually the expendable point to the spear driven through the heart of Dacia. But something changed while the Norte were at the Curat."

"Did you expect Captain Kekad to report?"

He blanched.

"Kekad is dead." Without another word, I slid back down the

hill. We couldn't bring down the mountain now. We'd wipe out our few allies and leave the majority of our enemy army in place. I scrambled to the edge of the hole where Liviana was instructing the next person to evacuate.

"Stop! Stop the rockslide. We have allies below," I shouted into the icy space. With the Illyrians, we could push back the invaders, hard, but only if we worked together before the Norte or Theracians figured out the ruse.

"Wait for my signal to begin again," I said.

"It might be too late. Everything's unstable!" Liviana shouted.

"We have to try!"

Baise cried out from around the mountain. I cringed and dropped onto my stomach, not wanting to be spotted by soldiers now alert to the griffin's general location. I counted to a hundred, giving the army below time to move. Then I shouted for the Illyrian. With a crunch of snow, he appeared at my side near the edge.

"When all your people are in the fields, how many of our enemies will be all around them?" I asked. "We can cut off the invaders right here, but if we let too many through, we cannot fight them off."

"You can with our help," he said.

This was either the most insane strategy on the part of the Theracians to destroy us in one day or a desperate gambit on the part of the Illyrians. I spun the Illyrian to face me and searched his face.

"Why do you want to fight at my side?"

"I've already risked everything just for this chance to plead with the Golden Protector." His chin trembled, but he lifted it higher, meeting my gaze. "I would gladly call myself a Dacian for the rest of my days if it means escaping Theracian tyranny."

His heartbreak was clear, but I had buried my compassion too deep today. Even though I believed his sincerity, I had to be strategic with my army. With every breath that passed, more of the enemy armies were bearing down on my own.

I thrust my spyglass into his hands. "Tell me when your army is through."

He twisted the scope around in his hand. "It's hard to tell for certain."

"If you want them to live, you better figure it out," I growled.

He gave me a frantic nod.

My army turned to fight the Theracians and Norte. And my captains were probably frustrated to see the mountain had not yet crushed their enemies. They had no idea how many were bearing down on them. Norte soldiers began multiplying on the field. Reflections.

We were out of time.

I signaled to Liviana to bring down the mountain. With the snow cracking, it wouldn't take much. I would have to be fast.

"There are still more in the canyon!" the Illyrian shouted.

"This way," I urged him as I jumped over the hole. Instead of explaining, I just ran across the snow to Baise who waited on the wide expanse beyond the snowy barricade. In the pit, I signaled to the two soldiers waiting. Then, I spun to the Illyrian, my sword pointed at him again. "I trust you're telling me the truth. But I can't have an unknown soldier on the loose right now." I turned to my soldiers. "Tie him up."

His chin sank, but he gave a resigned nod. I bounded to the griffin. With one hand, I grabbed the harness and swung up onto her back. Without a word, Baise's body flexed, and she pushed into the sky, her massive wings carrying us higher. After a wipe of Sonus powder on my lips, I guided her to the entrance of the canyon and lifted the conch to my lips.

My heart pounded in my ears, and I blew into the shell. The sound bounced off the walls of the canyon like music from the ocean crying out for her people. The deep, horn-like sound caused the snow to tremble. I held my breath. The armies below jumbled, stunned by my sudden appearance. Mighty shouts rose from the canyon floor; then the screaming began.

I am so tired of fighting my own mind. I cannot escape.

— ESME

THIRTY-SIX

UNSCATHED

The Sonus powder combined with the conch shell caused my insides to vibrate and my ears to ring. Skirmishes between our enemies' armies broke out. I afforded myself one tight circle above my army in the valley.

I cried out, "If you are with Dacia make it known or be cut down."

Fights raged, but my attention was drawn to skirmishes in the neck of the canyon. The soldiers were not clear of the impending collapse.

I dove forward. The mountain rumbled. If anyone doubted what was to happen, they'd learn the truth soon enough.

Several soldiers threw spears at us, but Baise seemed to flirt just beyond their range. The griffin dropped lower, her back paws knocking over a line of Theracians, making way for a cluster of Illyrians to escape the coming torrent.

"Run for the valley!" I yelled.

Deeper in the canyon, another group of yellow-banded soldiers were surrounded. I urged Baise forward. The mountain next to us seemed to sink.

Soldiers screamed, trying to climb over each other in a vain attempt to escape the wrath of the mountain. The griffin let out a cry that rent the sky. Dipping down, her talons dragged across the heads of the Theracian army.

"Higher!" I screamed as a wall of rocks, trees, and snow rolled toward us.

Baise pumped her wings, rising. I pulled on the harness, willing her to move faster as the mountain crashed down. The army below us disappeared, swallowed by the earth itself. Broken trees and boulders littered the valley, the land coughing as it smothered all those below.

We hadn't buried their entire army. Not by half. But this would force them to regroup before attacking again.

Screams sounded below us. Too near to be someone on the ground. I gripped the harness, my knees tightening against Baise's side. I couldn't see her talons from this angle, but I knew we had a passenger. And the passenger was sobbing.

I circled the griffin around to return to the fields but then veered her up the backside of the eastern mountain. Skittering across the face of the eastern mountain, we swooped by the nest of archers.

I signaled to them to retreat. I didn't want a single arrow to fly. Best to keep their position secret. I preferred to save the archer nest to battle another day.

We soared over my unit, and I signaled for them to stay. Over the valley, my army was a blur below. As we flew, flashes of yellow appeared in the crowded field. The Illyrians had identified them-selves with wide, yellow bands on their arms, indicating their alle-giance at a glance.

On the outskirts of the fighting, Baise swooped lower and slowed, dropping her passengers. Three bodies rolled away. One immediately curled up into a ball, but the other two jumped to their feet, their yellow bands already showing, diving into the fight.

Dissipating Reflections smoked on the ground, many of them likely separated from their controllers in the crush of snow and rock. But for every broken Reflection, three more fought. This battle alone was far greater than what we'd anticipated for today. Complicating matters, Norte Clarifiers and Healers were wreaking havoc with every touch. Not even Baise was immune to their magic. The Auripoans already had their spears out, singling out the greatest threats.

I urged Baise back to my unit. They'd evacuated up the mountain just below the summit. Midnight was at Liviana's side, and the Illyrian was kneeling in the snow behind them. Two Dacian soldiers were with them, the two spotters from the top of the mountain.

"I need spears below," I shouted.

The griffin beat her wings, sending bits of ice flying. She grabbed two of my soldiers. I was about to turn her back to the fight in the valley when Midnight's hackles rose. I furrowed my brow and cut Baise closer to the mountain. I drew her reigns, slowing her enough for me to grab the shield hooked to her harness, which I threw down as I jumped into the snow. I rolled to a stop, and Liviana grasped my wrist.

"Go and return for me," I ordered the griffin. The beast cried, and Liviana covered her ear. Baise dove for the field, two of my Sonuses in her talons. I ran my fingers through Midnight's scruff, but as I feared, she did not calm.

"What's wrong, girl?" I wanted her to point her nose at the Illyrian, but she gave a high pitch whine as she stared at the tip of the mountain. My archers?

I leveled my gaze at Liviana, and she gave me a stern nod. We had to investigate. I pulled my dagger from my boot. With a quick downward slash, I freed the Illyrian.

"Return his weapon," I said to Liviana. She tossed him a spear and shield.

I pointed from Liviana to the path that led higher, to where the single Patridavan Thorn was positioned. She nodded and led two Sonus wielders and a scout through the snow toward the lone remaining outlook. My last Sonus-wielder, a scout, and the Illyrian marched with Midnight and me up an almost parallel path, straight up the mountain. It was not terribly steep, and with the added thrum of energy, we climbed it quickly.

Besides Midnight's warning, I had other reasons to crest the mountain. I needed to know if the enemy was retreating or triaging their wounded and camping in place. Despite the cold, sweat dripped down my back. I wiped the powder from my lip, not wanting to broadcast my labored breathing to the entire mountain. Nearing the top, we crouched down, ready to crawl to the summit. We'd already scouted the area earlier. The summit had a number of craggy places where a person could hide.

The hairs on the back of my neck rose. Midnight's low growl carried on the wind. I lifted my short sword just as a snow leopard bounded over the summit. A javelin sung past me, sinking in the leopard's chest. The cat screeched its eerily human scream then stumbled. The Bonded clutched at his chest.

Another leopard appeared. I tensed. Galtis' brother. Seeing us, he bounded forward. Another javelin flew past me, sinking into the leopard's front shoulder. The leopard snarled but barely slowed. Another javelin flew, the last one in my soldier's bundle. This time, the Bonder was prepared, and he lowered his shield, turning the leopard just enough to deflect the projectile though it left a massive dent.

Behind Galtis' brother, another leopard cried. My heart pounded. The battle hadn't stopped; it hadn't even paused. The Norte and Theracians were still coming, and I still had not seen the entirety of their armies. I dug my hand into my Sonus pouch, swiping more Sonus powder across my lip.

"Snow leopards!" I couldn't let Liviana stumble into them, unaware.

A leopard cried out, further away. And yet another leopard appeared above us.

"How many of these blasted beasts are there?" the scout cursed from behind me.

We needed to retrieve the javelins before we were overrun. No matter how fast we retreated, the leopards would be faster. I bounded up the hill, toward Galtis' brother with Midnight at my side. The leopard limped, the poison taking affect. I sliced my sword across the leopard's other front leg. The beast collapsed, and I jumped away, narrowly dodging a nip.

I charged, leaving my soldiers to retrieve the javelins. Galtis' brother jumped down from the leopard's back and lumbered toward me. I spun in the snow, a clumsy move, but the Canina Thorn sliced perfectly across his chest. However, between the bulk of my glove and my weakened grip, I lacked the strength and control needed to pierce his metal armor. The Canina Thorn rebounded off him. Fortunately, the Bonder's weight carried him down the hill past me, and I was able to slam my shield into the side of his head as he passed. The clattering of spears and swords sounded behind me. A javelin sung past me, sinking into the shoulder of the leopard nearest me. The beast veered just enough that I wasn't crushed underfoot. Rolling to the side, I avoided them completely. Pulse racing, I sped toward the crest of the mountain, desperate to see what was happening.

Behind me, my scout cried out. I spun. Galtis' brother's leopard had kicked out, sending my Sonus and his spear sprawling. Galtis' brother unsteadily lifted his sword over my Sonus.

I yanked my black dagger from my boot and threw it. From this distance, it merely clattered against the Bonder's armor. But the distraction was enough for my Sonus to roll away. He grabbed his spear as another Norte Bonder attacked him, her leopard staggering not far behind.

Galtis' brother stepped on my dagger; his nostrils flared as he faced me. "You desecrated my sister's body, tainted her memory, brought dishonor on our family." He pointed his sword at me. "You've made a fool of me for the last time."

Midnight pounced on him, knocking him to his knees. I spun, leaving Midnight to finish him as the Illyrian moved to assist my Sonus. I bolted toward the top of the mountain. From this angle, I could see evidence of where leopards fought near the Patridavan's lookout.

Another leopard crested the mountain; I was too close to avoid it. I lifted my shield just as the Bonder leaned low, reaching their long sword out to slice me in half. The impact spun me; my feet slipped, the snow coming up to greet me. I rolled, my momentum carrying me back down the mountain. My attacker pivoted, leaping for me. With panicked energy, I dove as they passed near enough for me to throw myself at the leopard's hind legs, nicking the bottom of the leopard's paw. The creature didn't seem to notice the injury, pivoting with ease.

"Leave her to me!" Galtis' brother bellowed from below. The leopard I'd just cut, hissed, whiskers pulled back, its massive teeth and black gums a hand's width from my face. It leapt past me. I struggled to get to my feet before Galtis' brother was on top of me, but he was faster. His sword pressed into my neck just above my armor.

His leopard gave a sorrowful cry, and the Bonder's eyes tightened. "Usurper, I will happily go into death as long as I send you first."

Where's Midnight?

Galtis' brother slowly moved his sword up to my hood. With the tip, he tried to lift my cowl, but it was pinned down, covering my crown. His nostrils flared, and he yanked back my hood. My cloak choked me before the hood ripped free and fell back. His face twisted in disgust.

"Go. To the top of the mountain where everyone can see you die." As he spoke, spittle hit my cheek.

Gray streaks spiraled across the side of his face, slowly rising from his neck. Trying not to stare, I held my hands out to the sides, still clutching the Canina Thorn.

"Keep the sword. I want everyone to *know* I've ended the usurper."

The tip of the Bonder's sword pressed to my back as I trudged up the mountain. The slower I walked, the harder the blade pressed. I looked for an opportunity to tip the scales in my favor. I was outmatched in reach and weight. More cries sounded above and below. The leopards' screams sounded human, but this time I recognized my Sonus' voices. My chest tightened as I trudged through the snow.

As we neared the top, a flap of wings brought a gust of wind. The Norte didn't take his eyes off me, but I gambled that some part of him was distracted. I dropped and rolled away, somersaulting to my feet. I slid in the snow, but my sword was at the ready.

The Norte Bonder limped after me, his sword over his head, his icy-blue eyes so dilated they looked black. He jumped as Baise rose over the mountain; her massive talons grabbed my attacker and throw him to the side. I ran across a jutting boulder and launched myself into the air just as my griffin pulled her wing back, coming closer to the mountain. I landed on her back, gripping harness and feathers as she climbed higher in the sky with a triumphant cry.

I peered through my spyglass only to find it cracked. Even without it, I could see a dark line of soldiers in the canyon without an end. Even if we sacrificed our lives sending avalanches down every face of the mountain, it wouldn't be enough to stop the coming army.

I didn't spot a single one of my archers. I slammed my fist into my thigh, sickened. The moment the leopards had caught my archers' scents, they were doomed.

Another wave of leopards appeared at the base of the mountain, racing toward the summit. And another grouping, almost invisible, was on the far mountainside. We couldn't survive another unit of Bonders.

"Retreat," I screamed to my remaining unit. Below, where Liviana fought, there were still battle cries. The Illyrian and my scout were desperately fighting together to stave off a leopard. Baise dove, plucked a Norte Bonder in her beak and threw him off the cliff side of the mountain. His leopard screamed then leapt after him.

"More are coming!" I shouted. "Run!"

I circled to the viewpoint where my Patridavan Thorn had been lookout. A leopard lay lifeless, a Bonder nearby. Just beyond, crimson dots splattered around two of my Sonus' lying at broken angles. I jumped down as Baise swooped forward, attacking another Bonder further down the mountain. Liviana was already cold, her pulse gone. My vision blurred.

I hadn't been by her side when she'd died.

The Constantin family would never be the same.

Had she been frightened?

No family in the entire kingdom would be left unscathed.

The Patridavan moaned, his face pale. I didn't have time to assess him before the next wave of Bonders would be upon us.

I pulled my heavy body onto Baise. The griffin clasped both Liviana and the Patridavan. As we lifted higher, I searched for the remaining two soldiers. I spotted my Sonus dashing down the mountain as instructed. The last body was mangled beyond recognition, the other scout from the top of the mountain — he was the only one not accounted for.

Swallowing the acid in my throat, I guided Baise higher, dreading what I would find at the top.

Along the ridge, I slid off the griffin and rushed forward, frantically searching the mess of leopards and Bonders. I leapt over Galtis' dead brother. Even in my hurry, I noticed the strange texture of his face. Blisters covered his flesh from his nose to his ear.

Midnight whined. Spotting my Sonus and Midnight near each other, I ran to them. I checked my soldier for a pulse though, by the amount of blood seeping into the snow and the angle of his body, I already knew there wouldn't be one. Next, with a trembling hand, I ran my fingers through my dire wolf's fur. She didn't stir, but she was still warm.

I called to Baise. The fewer she transported, the more carefully she could deliver them.

"Bring Midnight and him." I touched the breathing soldier. My heart cracked at the thought of leaving Liviana behind. I would return for her.

I dashed to where I'd last seen my dagger. I pawed through the churned up and blood-spattered snow until I found it. I shoved it back into its sheath. The hidden infirmary wasn't far, but we had to be quick or risk a Bonder discovering us entering the sanctuary.

Moments after Baise secured the injured in her talons, she set them on the wide ledge outside the infirmary entrance. The only living thing above was the Illyrian, struggling down the mountain. He must have sent my scout ahead alone.

I shouted through the entrance for the Healer.

A roar of celebration sounded from the field below.

The Healer appeared, joy on her face. "The fighting is over. For now, at least."

Squires, cooks, and others from the camp rushed toward the field to celebrate and to tend the wounded.

Inside, I roiled, unable to comprehend the bloody mass of bodies and mist in field below. Some part of me, a part I couldn't access, wanted to weep. But I was too numb. I couldn't allow emotion to prick my heart. Not when I knew what my army did not.

"Get these two inside! Quickly!" I shouted as Seneca appeared.

People on the field were on their knees, weeping. Others dancing. None were watching the mountain. I jumped onto Baise's back, and she quickly moved to scoop up the lagging Illyrian. Hovering above the mountain, the injured soldier in the griffin's grasp, I screamed to the valley.

"Stop!" I lifted my hands in the air as my voice carried across the field. "Our enemies are still coming. The battle has only begun!"

❧

"ALL CAPTAINS," I shouted as I slid from Baise's back onto the field, the Sonus powder still smeared across my lips. "To me!"

Dyana pushed her way to the front, finding me. "How long do we have?"

I scanned the mountain, looking for the leopards. "Bonders should have come over that mountain already."

"One did. She didn't make it far." Dyana pointed near the base of the mountain.

The one I'd slashed on the paw, probably. "Six more are coming. Followed by more."

Dyana cursed as Petre, Ivan, other captains emerged.

"We need to press forward, closer to the mountain," I said. "I will search from the sky, determining where the armies will strike first."

Dyana wiped her sword with a cloth. "Let's assume they come over both the western and eastern mountains *and* over the rock pile at the bottom."

"Should we evacuate the mountain infirmaries?" Petre asked.

"They're spelled so people don't notice them, but it's only a distraction. The infirmary midway up the mountain is worth the risk. The one on the western base is more noticeable, depending on how many soldiers are nearby."

"There are more soldiers than ants at a picnic," Dyana said. "They'll detect both infirmaries soon enough."

Traversing the mountain under the best conditions was treacherous. Transporting injured soldiers from mid-way up would be even harder. They'd have to stay. We could move soldiers from the western infirmary if done quickly.

I rubbed my temple, the weight of the situation bearing down on me. Even Dyana had been naïve about the vast resources of the Theracians. Though they lacked the Norte's fierceness, the Theracians could crush us by their numbers alone.

"Split up the battalions. One on each mountain and two in the center." I turned to Ivan. "I have a feeling the Norte will march right through the middle. They likely lost most of their Mirrors, so be prepared for more Clarifiers, Healers, and Illuminators. Their captains are likely Protectors with essentially armor inside and out."

Many of my soldiers had swords rubbed with poison specifi-cally for Protectors though it was untested.

"Also, send a unit to start relocating the injured from the western infirmary," I said. Every moment counted. The captain nodded and sprinted into the camp.

I rushed to Baise, but Dyana grabbed my shoulder before I could mount. "Don't get yourself killed. Get the information. Return to report to the captains. Remember, you're a spy, not a shield."

Dyana's grip loosened, and she pulled me into a one-armed hug before releasing me. I wasn't sure what to think. Dyana was the least affectionate person I knew.

"My biggest regrets are always letting people I love die without me having a final *moment*," she said.

"This isn't —" I wanted to say it wasn't a good-bye, but Esme's vision of my future flashed into my mind.

I'd said good-bye to Mama — though it was a terrible thing that gutted me, I'd gotten some closure. But Mystic Marianna, Valentin, Liviana, and so many others had been ripped away without warning. I wrapped my arms around Dyana and poured all my regrets at never-spoken good-byes into that hug.

"Too much." Dyana coughed and wriggled free.

"I need your spyglass," I said.

She pressed her spyglass into my hand and then jogged to her century, leading Petre and the Auripoans to join the battalion at the western mountain.

I mounted Baise, and we soared over the reforming battalions. Healers and others scrambled to check for survivors. I could have stayed to help regroup those with fallen leaders, but I trusted my captains. Only one person in the valley could ride the griffin; I had to do what no one else could.

We flew higher than we ever had, the pass a wasteland below. It blurred past as Baise swept forward. The dark line of the armies wove through the canyon. We flew and flew as the army below stretched to an unimaginable length. I cursed under my breath.

Using the spyglass to search the mountains, I spotted groups of Bonders, and pairs of Norte scouts. I doubted they'd noticed me above, but I saw them well enough. Finally, the enemy army dwindled and ended. I calculated that the Norte Council was commanding the army from the rear, but I had no idea where Saam would station himself. A few wing flaps later, we were above their bustling camp deep in the mountain, at the base of the glacier.

We soared westward. Rivers from the glacier flowed underneath the rocks, reappearing in waterfalls and streams. As the glacier melted, the poison would be carried into the river. The river would roar in the spring, carrying poison like rot in the blood that would eventually kill.

Over the western mountain, I saw fewer spies. On a hunch, we flew further west and circled back toward the battlefield. Sure enough, Bonded leopards and a century were tucked into a high canyon not far back from the avalanche. In fact, they could climb across the mountain and straight down into the valley from their location. They probably had something special in store for us. Using the spyglass, I spotted several Norte.

While the Council would protect themselves, I knew Borsea would want to perform a noteworthy feat. She'd insist on being out front. Through all the battles in the Curat, she pulled her entire army back at the first sign of trouble. But this battle was different.

We circled lower, over the separated century below. With the spyglass, I could only see the tops of their heads. I wasn't going to act like a lone-shield, but I was the empress. I could very well approach and negotiate as the Theracian delegation had done in my camp.

Lowering, I estimated there were about a hundred soldiers below plus the six Bonded snow leopards. The majority of the Theracians carried spears, the Norte preferring swords. A few javelins. No archers. From this angle, I scanned the faces until I found the one I was looking for.

"Borsea," I called, the Sonus powder carrying my words. "I come to discuss the state of our peoples."

High up in the pass, they were cut off from the main contingency.

"You have seen our vast army and come to surrender?" Borsea smirked.

"You're p-probably wondering about the crashing noise." I spoke in low tones, letting the Sonus powder carry my voice.

She pursed her lips. "Here to gloat about your pathetic rock slide?"

"And the Illyrians who have broken from the Theracians to join us," I said.

Behind Borsea, a few Theracian soldiers eyed each other, but a Norte soldier spoke up. "We've known they were going to try and betray us for a moon."

Another Norte shouted, "Let that be a lesson to you, impostor. Illyria is like a mouse attacking a leopard. We'll hardly break a sweat as we crush them. Even so, it will be noted, and their families will suffer because of the soldiers' betrayal."

I kept my face a mask, though I believed their every word. Even with the Illyrians, we were roughly two thousand strong. In comparison, they easily marched ten thousand soldiers upon us. And they had dozens of leopards while I had a single griffin. By the time the rest of our army arrived from the Curat, it would be too late; the Norte would already be laying siege at Rupea.

"Did you know," I said, looking at the Theracians, "that when this battle is over, when the Norte have the throne, they mean to conquer you next?"

A Theracian spit on the ground. "Do not presume to fool us as easily as you have your own people."

A trumpet sounded over the mountain. Borsea licked her lips like a cat about to feast. My stomach twisted. I needed to return to the front to tell the captains what I'd learned. Though I had no positive news, the information needed to be shared.

"Don't turn your back on the Norte," I said to the Theracian.

"The Norte will betray your alliance. Even Emperor Saam understands, which is why he came to me last night."

Borsea glared at me.

The Theracian spat, "How dare y—"

"Did you have a soldier missing in the night? P-perhaps a horse?" Horses would be very difficult to transport through the mountains. If one went missing, it would cause a stir. "The *emperor's* horse?"

Borsea's nostrils flared. She knew about Saam.

Responding to the slight pressure in my heels, the griffin launched into the sky. I couldn't risk staying any longer. One well-placed throwing knife, and everything I'd learned would die with me. Borsea would be delighted to rip my crown right off my head and pry the Canina Thorn from my fingers. Sure enough, Borsea twirled her spear in an arc in front of her, an extension of her pent-up frustration.

"Ask B-Borsea yourself," I shouted to the Theracians.

I suspected that due to their experience with Sensitives, most Norte either carried their secrets deep or had a Clarifier remove them. But Borsea's pride would mean she didn't concern herself with the Theracians' opinions — and in her moment of surprise, her face revealed everything.

Theracian soldiers looked at Borsea. I didn't know what they saw, but there was a chance they'd seen through the Norte's mountain of lies.

Hearing a cry below, we circled higher, surging well out of javelin-range. But we hadn't needed to. The fighting was between the Theracians and Norte. I watched the efficient horrors that quickly ended the Theracian attack. The remaining soldiers started hiking the mountain: twelve Norte plus five leopards and their riders.

I rode the griffin straight down the path of the enemy armies. I screamed to them below. "The Norte will turn against you all. Scythians, Theracians, all colony states, rise and fight the Norte or you will *all* b-become a colony state of the north."

I shouted my message over and over as we flew toward the mouth of the canyon just in time to see the enemy armies flow over the expanse of rocks and trees between the jagged mountains. The eastern mountain was crawling with soldiers, and Borsea's unit would crest the western mountain soon enough.

In the valley, my captains were too far apart to explain and create a new strategy. I was too late; I had to speak to my entire army. I placed Baise above what was approximately the middle of the Dacians, Getaens, Auripoans, and Illyrians.

"Our enemy is vast."

Ten times our size.

"But they do not have our heart. They do not defend their own lands and families. We stop them here!"

The Auripoans slammed their swords against their shields and chests and cried out. And the Dacian's echoed their calls even more strongly. With the rush of energy, my army charged across a narrowing strip of muddy land between the two opposing forces.

I came to myself only to realize a year has passed. Mama claims I'm fifteen. After all the things I have Seen and experienced, I feel as if I'm a thousand years old.

— *ESME*

THIRTY-SEVEN

MY BLADE IN A THOUSAND HEARTS

The armies clashed with a sickening crunch of metal and flesh. I swallowed the bile that rose in the back of my throat, forcing myself to search for opportunities from above the field.

The base infirmary was still being evacuated, and already my army was being forced back. Norte Clarifiers fought with abandon, their fingers attacking *anyone* who wasn't Norte, creating a buffer around another Norte and them, a Mirror, before the pair pressed forward, ending anyone in their path.

I quickly discovered how dangerous the Healers could be. With every nick of their blades, even the Reflections poisoned my soldiers, causing them to seize on the field.

The griffin banked suddenly to the left. Something *whooshed* by. An arrow? Theracians with long-bows faced us from a ridge on the eastern mountain. I tried to guide Baise back to the field, but she shot straight up into the clouds, flying in a backward loop over the archers. I screamed, upside down, centrifugal force the only thing keeping me from falling from the sky. Baise completed her arc, coming down on top of the archers, crushing several.

I couldn't reach the Theracians with my sword from Baise's back. I ripped off my glove and shoved my hand into my Sonus pouch. Baise leapt back into the air. I sent a pulse of Sonus magic, but from this distance, it merely scattered the remaining archers and several soldiers.

Baise winged to the field. If I wanted to really fight, I'd have to dismount. Esme had said my sword was crucial, and I was useless with it when on a griffin's back.

I paused, a spark of hope igniting inside me. Esme had said we could win. That meant that there was a way. And it involved my sword.

My stomach dropped. Having grown up the daughter of the clan leader, the Seer was intimately aware of the complex magic of the dome. A notion that I hadn't considered until now. Her words tumbled in my mind.

Pierce the sky.

My attention whipped to the clouds rumbling overhead. Back at the base of the mountain, my troops were evacuating the infirmary. A Healer and Protector were inevitably still there, the last to leave. The Auripoans were holding off the enemy soldiers, but not for much longer.

I shifted so I could see the mid-mountain infirmary. The Norte and Theracian armies hurtled past the hidden entrance, surely thinking it was a snowdrift. The Healer still tended Seneca and my soldiers inside with her sparse supplies.

I didn't know much about a Protection shield, but if Esme's vision was true, somehow she'd Seen me figure it out. Which meant I *could* make it work. A massive amount of magic would need to be channeled through an ancient relic: the Canina Thorn. There was a way to win this battle; use the Protectors and Bonders as anchor points for a dome, my sword would be the keystone at the top. All it would cost is one life to try.

Mine.

Guiding the griffin forward, I wiped the Sonus powder from my lips. In case some powder remained, I whispered to Baise. "Drop me by Petre."

Baise cried her dislike for my plan but landed on the ground, easily the most dangerous place for a griffin. I rolled away as Baise pounced on several Theracian soldiers and re-took to the sky.

I signaled for Petre to follow me and slipped into the relative safety of the infirmary.

"What are you doing, Nikka?" Petre shouted, running in after me.

I looked around and found just the Protector I needed.

I grabbed the Jalab's shoulders. "We have to recreate the dome. Here. Now."

"What?" Jalab jerked back.

"Nikka!" Petre shouted. His broadsword clashed with someone behind us. "Whatever you are doing, hurry!"

"I have a relic. We have Protectors at three points in the camp."

"The spell over the city has dozens of layers of magic we don't understand," Jalab argued. "We don't know how to recreate the detractor spell, or—"

"What do we *absolutely* need to create a shield right now? I don't care about the extra layers."

My griffin cried out in the distance. The Protector chewed his lip. After what seemed like an hour, he nodded. "The only other thing we must have is a Bonder. And the words."

I snapped my fingers. "I have the perfect word. Salt!"

Jalab's eyes lit up. "Sura. In Getaen it has a layered meaning. Salt, family, protection — a powerful combination."

"I'm going to take you to the infirmary by the camp. You need to explain it to them." I hurried Jalab to the exit, which Petre blocked, fighting another attacker.

Jalab stopped. "There's no time to go back and forth. I'll stay here and wait for your signal. Find the Protector in the camp named Irena Redvalley. She's clever — won't need much explaining."

"Yes, I know Irena." Though I didn't know she'd arrived already.

"Good," Jalab said. "Hurry!"

"You can't stay here, the infirmary has been noticed. It'll be overrun," Petre shouted.

"Can you hold it for another half-hour?" I shouted.

"Do I have a choice?" Petre grunted, pushing someone back out of the doorway. "Go!"

I dodged past Petre. Baise shot down from the sky, grabbed me in her talons, and leapt back in the air as I shouted directions.

From the air, I watched the eastern mountain. Six Bonded leopards crossed the summit and descended along with several units of enemy soldiers. Once they were well past the infirmary, Baise swooped down behind an advancing party. Before the next century crested, I signaled Baise to drop me on the flat expanse near my collapsed tunnels. This time, when I landed, I held my shield in one hand, my Sonus-lined fingers extended.

I thought of Papa at the castle, a future Norte soldier descending upon him. I sent several pulses of magic down in front of me. Norte soldiers went tumbling to their deaths. Baise flew over the ridge, distracting the upcoming wave of soldiers, and I slipped unseen into the infirmary.

Inside, the Healer jumped back, clutching her chest. The injured Illyrian was awake along with my Sonus, the only survivor of Liviana's group. Both were being treated near the Patridavan guard lookout who lay unconscious on a pallet.

Near the back wall, Midnight was curled up. She lifted her head as I entered. I rushed to her side and ran my hands through her fur as I explained my plan to Seneca.

Soldiers' shouts sounded outside the door, passing very near. Seneca paled, but gave me an emphatic nod. "I'll help create the dome."

Midnight licked my hand, and I pressed my forehead to hers before turning to my Bonder.

"Watch for my signal in the sky." I didn't know what it would be, exactly, but he would know the sign when he saw it... I hoped. "I must find a Protector."

The Healer stopped me. "There's a Protector here."

My Sonus-wielder struggled to her feet, her hand heavy on the Healer's shoulder. I hesitated, unsure. With her dark hair, she clearly had Dacian blood. How strong could her magic be? Seeming to sense my unease, the Healer spoke up.

"She's the only reason your lookout survived." The Healer nodded to the Patridavan. "She's been working with me to treat him."

"You don't have time to bring another Protector here," my Sonus-wielder said. "I'm strong enough to do what is needed, I swear it."

Hearing screams just outside the door, I nodded. She was right. We were out of time. The base infirmary could already be overrun.

Seneca hurried to my side. "The sword."

I placed the blade in his hands. Seneca closed his eyes and whispered words of magic as sweat broke along his hairline. He spoke of the earth, of giving and receiving. Eternal rounds. Protection and safety for all hearts who were loyal to the one who wielded the sword — the Golden Empress.

When Seneca slipped the sword back into my hands, I could feel the magic thrumming through my fingertips, down to my core.

Baise screeched. It was my window of opportunity.

"Thank you," I whispered before dashing to the doorway. Not seeing any soldiers, I darted out, my Sonus-powdered hand at the ready.

Baise cried a warning before plucking me straight off the mountain just as more soldiers crested far above.

"To the infirmary in the valley, near camp," I shouted over the wind. Near the eastern base-infirmary, Auripoans were fighting back a wave of soldiers. Fortunately, one of my Sonus-wielders was with them along with other Getaens; otherwise, my plans would have been already ruined. I couldn't risk dropping lower to help, so we dove for the last infirmary.

As I was quite the spectacle, Irena and Rubia came running to my side. Irena asked few questions about the Protections, nodding, seeming to understand what was needed. She quickly named a Bonder who could assist her.

The battle raged, louder with every passing moment.

I pulled them both into a quick embrace, biting back my fears. I knew they'd object if I explained the Seer's prediction — insist on looking for a different way. But there was no other way. Not one that didn't involve moons or even years of war with victory only a dim possibility. I'd been willing to trade my life to save my people from the plague. I'd expected the sacrifice when I placed the True Key into the treasure. Every moment I breathed after that moment was a gift. Though I didn't want to suffer a painful death, I trusted the Seer's words. This was our *only* chance.

Rubia squeezed my hand, not letting go.

"I love you, Nikka," her voice cracked.

My voice stuck, unable to allay her fears. She knew my plans; she always could see through me.

I kissed her cheek and pulled away. I mounted Baise and launched into the air, allowing myself one last final look back at my mother, in all but blood.

Our army was dwindling. Borsea's troops were triumphantly marching down the hill, clearly planning to be the scythe that ended the war in a blaze of glory — an orchestration — so her future Theracian subjects would witness and learn to fear her majesty and might.

My bitterness burned away to pity at her blackened heart. My sympathy aside, the Norte's decision to conquer rather than seek partnership was absolute.

A river of soldiers flowed across the settled rockslide and into the field. My heart thumped. One way or another, this war would end soon.

Part of the group defending the base-infirmary must have noticed Borsea. They moved to intercept. My heart jumped into my throat. If the Norte breached the base infirmary, Jalab wouldn't last long. Nor would those who were attempting to stop Borsea.

Baise screamed in pain and fury. I didn't know where she'd been hit, but she wobbled.

"Climb," I begged her.

Her wings strained. We couldn't go as high as I'd wanted, well above the mountains in order to encase the sides facing the valley. Below, the Auripoans were nearing Borsea.

I guided Baise to where I estimated the center of the dome would be.

"Higher, girl! Let's create something they can't climb over today, or ever!" I dipped my finger in the Sonus powder, wiping it on my lip for the last time.

I had to trust that the three Protectors were watching.

"Sura mezenai," I screamed, thrusting my blade into the sky. Streams of light shot from my sword, brilliantly splitting into a hundred beams, illuminating the stormy sky. I shuddered as the light retracted *back* into the sword as if called home. With a jarring pulse, three wide, blue ribbons of vibrant light streamed across the sky like a rainbow, connecting to the Protectors below.

From the location of the base of one of the ribbons, I realized Jalab was at the rear of the Auripoans who had split off to intercept Borsea. By moving deeper into enemy territory, he was attempting to enlarge the dome. How far could he get, protected by the Auripoans in front of him?

They wouldn't realize they were about to collide with Borsea, the Commander. A giant beam of magical light connected to an approaching Getaen would definitely get her attention.

A surge of energy filled me, clogging my ears. My body trembled, magic coursing through me. Every time the Protectors moved, the magic strained inside me, trying to bond with the earth but unable to.

Jalab, hold still!

I focused my mind on the magic thrumming through my veins. Turning my attention inward was even harder than witnessing the carnage below. I had learned to sense magic, but this magic even separated into a thousand strands would still be the strongest magic I'd ever felt.

This was more than the warlock's curse, the True Key, the *Crown of Lore*, and The Canina Thorn combined. My original oath binding me as a Guardian to the True Key came back into my mind; all my experiences with magic.

A single word makes a difference. Intention strengthens spells.

I tried to shout the magic words, but only a mumbled whisper came, my lungs barely able to support even that.

Bind the sword with the Earth
Poltim o skalam met o griva
Protect the land while it protects you.
Mezenai to tautareshai mezenazi veshreshidi

The sword grew heavy. It took all my strength to keep the tip pointed skyward. Underneath me, Baise faltered, her wing movements jerking.

Strengthen of the curse, drive away our enemies
Balan apo to zalm, skenailo baidasori mishi

My mouth dried, and my mind blanked, unable to think of another coherent word. I sensed my Protectors. Jalab strained to move forward, but the spell had rooted him. The earth had its own magic. It reverberated back up to me. I gasped for breath; pain pierced me. I couldn't release the spell too soon, or it wouldn't properly connect the earth to the sword, the keystone relic.

I concentrated on the magic. It was ebbing in erratic directions. I pulled it back into the sword, into myself. The spell extended deep into the earth. I twisted the magic until it unfurled from the Protector's grasps.

Screams sounded below, and my heart ached to help them, but the magic consumed me. Tears flowed down my cheeks as I strained to hold the magic, the spell and the sword, blinded by pain. The magic clawed me from the inside, trying to escape. Baise waivered in the air. I wanted to steady her, but I couldn't speak.

Yet, I could feel. The magic soared, finding the anchor points. A steady pulse of magic reverberated down around me. Relief filled me. My shoulders slumped. Dizzy, I felt myself slipping.

A roar of noise sounded below me, a riot of screams and pain. Through my half-closed eyes, all I could see was a vibrant blue-green shimmer across the sky.

The magic worked independent of the Protectors, sliding past them like rain falling from the sky. But for me, the magic shot through me like lightning.

I squeeze my eyes shut. Darkness. Bright light. Dark. I was unable to protect myself from the blinding Illuminator's weapons.

My body sizzled, unable to move, transformed by the magic that emanated from the relic in my hand. I had chosen the magic words with care; the warlock's ancient and deadly curse still lived inside the Canina Thorn. While the crown killed anyone who touched it with greed, the Canina Thorn was far less discerning about its victims.

I didn't have insights on the relic that safeguarded the Red Valley, but the nature of the Canina Thorn was not one of passive protection. The sword was aggressive toward any who dared cross me, who dared make Dacia an enemy.

I felt victorious. Resolute. But not joyful. The spell settled. I sensed the Protectors moving away from the anchor points. The spell stayed in place, rooted to the earth for a millennium, perhaps longer. I tried to grip the sword tighter, but my fingers wouldn't move. No, the sword was gone.

I couldn't breathe. I was falling.

Forcing my eyes open, I caught a glimpse of what I'd created. A shimmering dome, a gold star at the apex. Lightning cut across the sky, quick as a viper's tongue yet slower than the moon crossing the sky. The walls reached from the mid-points of the mountains on either side of the pass, cutting down the mountains in an arc and meeting in the middle of the avalanched devastation. The dome had completed its circle, forming an impenetrable barrier.

My vision grayed at the edges. But what I saw crushed my soul. Bodies were scattered across the valley floor. No one moved. Not a single soul.

What had I done?

~

I DIDN'T REMEMBER how I landed, if I fell or if Baise lowered me, but I came to myself near the edge of the shimmering dome. I dragged myself to my feet. Around me, my soldiers pushed themselves, heaving, to their knees. Every enemy soldier, Norte or Theracian, lay motionless. Only the fur of their cloaks fluttered in the wind.

I fell forward, catching myself with my hands. I vomited into the trampled mud. Soldiers called out to each other. Above them all, a Sonus shouted, his words making my head throb. I put my hand to my temple. It took me a moment to realize the Sonus was giving commands on Borsea's behalf from outside the protective wall.

"Climb the mountains. Go around the dome," he yelled.

I yelled back, "Why can't I stop you?" But my words were just a whisper.

What had I done wrong? Esme had said I could defeat them, I could pierce the sky. Clearly, I hadn't done the spell well enough. My very survival was proof of that. I pounded my fist into the ground.

The soldiers around me were shaking off their bewilderment. All the enemy under the valley's dome was vanquished. But even at our height of vigor, we were still no match for the remaining army. Outside the dome, the fighting was blurred. But I recognized the Auripoans engaging with the Norte. I had to help them. If I could get them to safety, we could come up with another plan.

I wiped the putrid spittle from my lips. I could barely stand, but I could probably ride. I turned to find Baise. My stomach sunk. I half-crawled to the mass of muscled fur and feathers.

"Baise?" I croaked. I stroked her jagged beak.

She was gone. Someone had died to create the dome, but it hadn't been me. Enraged, I shoved my mask to my face, recoated my fingers in Sonus powder, and picked up my dented shield. Limping to the edge of the dome, I took a breath and stepped through the shimmering wall.

It sizzled in my ears, and the stench of burned hair filled my nostrils. My ears popped, and I was through. Instead of feeling further drained, the protections in the shield seemed to restore a drop of my depleted strength. Even without it, my rage propelled me up the hill.

I felt naked without the weight of the Canina Thorn, but wielding Sonus powder had become second-nature. Though my words were muffled, my heart's intention was clear as with a quick gesture, dozens of soldiers were thrown off their feet.

For the first time, the Norte looked concerned, and they were fighting harder than I'd ever seen. A Sonus shouted Borsea's commands. The ground shook. The only survivor of my Sonus unit still remaining in the valley was sparring with a Norte. Jalab was on the ground, injured. Ahead, Dyana was being pushed back by two more Norte. One of the leopards was down, two javelins protruding from its side. Another leopard was lunging at a cluster of soldiers.

Borsea spotted me. With a command, the leopard changed direction and bounded toward me. I pushed with both hands in front of me, snapping a spell that sent the leopard stumbling. I yanked my dagger from my boot and, using Sonus magic, threw the dagger at the beast's eye. I missed, but not by much. With a cry, the leopard fell, the Bonder cursing, holding his eye.

Giving the creature wide berth, I left it for the poison-edged swords of my fellow Dacians. I kept my focus on Borsea. She smiled broadly, taunting me closer.

"You've been holding out on us, Nikka," Petre said, grunting as he and another soldier finished a coordinated attack on what I guessed was a Healer or Clarifier. "Where have you been hiding that magic?"

"Nicoleta, the Imposter!" Borsea's voice rung out above the din. "I was hoping you'd return."

"You've already met her today? You're full of surprises," Petre said, his sword raised, ready to fight alongside me.

"End this, Borsea! Dacia was never your destiny. The Norte will lose." I didn't issue detailed threats knowing a Sensitive would immediately sense my bluff. "This is your last chance. Leave, or die here."

Borsea laughed. Without a word, without warning, her magic flared. It was like I was staring at the noonday sun.

I was blind. And without Luminary cream.

Only the Norte Illuminators would be able to see. Rough hands wiped my eyes.

I blinked, my vision spotty. I shot up my hands as Borsea lunged, thrusting her sword forward.

Petre cried out, crashing against me.

I screamed at the too familiar slush of a blade through flesh. I tried to grab Petre as he sunk to his knees. His eyes were bare — he'd put his Luminary cream on my eyes instead of his own.

Borsea advanced. I stuttered the magic words. With a pulse from my fingertips, Borsea flew back.

"End her!" Petre gasped.

I stormed forward, passing Dyana, who was furiously blinking.

"This was your plan? Blind your army so Illuminators can finally find some glory in defeating their enemies?" Of course, Borsea wanted to show that a low-Lit could crush them all. "Is this all to earn yourself a seat at the Council?"

Even with the Luminary cream, my vision was spotty. Even so, with another pulse of magic, I pushed Borsea back against the rocks before she could lift her sword.

"Finish this, Nikka!" Dyana yelled. Behind me, swords clashed again.

Already, the Illuminators were rising up to strike us down. Nearby, a Norte wiped Luminary cream across their eyes. I blinked, anger and sadness and disbelief crashing inside me.

The Norte claimed to want to lay waste to the Getaens and their dirty magic, but yet they used it when it suited them.

Borsea lunged. I jumped back, narrowly dodging her blade. She screamed, bearing down on me. My Sonus magic wasn't enough to kill her. I had no weapon. Stumbling back, my foot knocked my dagger from where it had fallen in the leopard's death throes.

I rolled across the thin snow and snatched up my blade. Half-blind, I waited a heartbeat until Borsea lifted her arm to slash. Shooting to my feet, I drove the dagger up under her ribs. Her sword dropped, her eyes wide. I pushed her off, letting her crumble to her knees.

She tried to grab at me, but I simply stepped back. Dyana and other Auripoans clashed with the rising Norte. I scrambled to Petre's side.

He was on his back, near the leopard I'd killed. I wasn't sure if the blood around him was the leopard's or his. By the volume, it was probably both. He was staring at the sky, breathing with short, rapid gasps.

"No, no, no!" I cried, fumbling for my emergency herbs. I couldn't lose him, too, not after Liviana.

Borsea stumbled closer. I pushed my hand out, shoving her back.

I ripped out the herbs I needed and turned Petre on his side, feeling with my fingers for the wound. Finding it, I pressed them deep inside, whispering words of magic. Part of me knew Borsea's blade had doomed him to a slow and painful death, but the greater part of me couldn't accept it.

Petre started to shake. I turned him back over in my arms. I ripped off my mask and pressed it to his face. Maybe the Healing magic could save him. It had to. It was all I had left.

Someone was muttering, "Please, please, please, please," and I realized it was me.

Borsea approached again, a hand pressed against her abdomen. I cursed, pushing her with my magic, and she stumbled to the ground.

"Petre!" I rocked him in my arms, crying. If only I'd been a proper Healer, perhaps I could have saved him.

Petre mumbled through the mask, his hand rising to bat it away. I set it aside, half-blind from tears and Borsea's magic.

"Sister... sister. I will see you... in the land beyond," Petre gasped, his words rasping. "Don't... don't cry. I'll be waiting with honey and... "

Petre's body jerked. I clutched him tight to my chest. "I'm here."

My body curled around his. I held in a silent cry so he wouldn't hear my mourning. His body finally relaxed, his head falling against my shoulder.

I sobbed. I couldn't catch my breath. Around me, fighting intensified, but I couldn't bring myself to move. My body was spent, my heart crushed. Snot and tears smeared across my face. I wanted to shut my eyes to all of this. To lie down.

Esme was right, I would die today. I already felt dead.

Dyana's voice cut through the fog in my head, her grip pulling me to my feet. "Mourn later. Retreat now!"

Despite her command, her voice was tight, her fingers bruising my shoulder as she pressed a gentle hand to Petre's chest, uttering solemn Auripoan words.

"My d-dagger." I could barely force out the words as I wrenched myself free. I needed a weapon. I scanned, my vision blurred, as my hands searched the ground around Borsea's still body. I froze. Borsea's face was a mottled gray with bumps on her neck.

My fingers brushed up against the dagger. I grabbed it and jumped away from Borsea. Dyana grabbed me. "Some of your soldiers have left the safety of the dome. Call the retreat!"

I nodded absently, my mind stuck on the markings on Borsea.

I'd seen them earlier today — on Galtis' brother. But I hadn't cut either of them with the Canina Thorn.

I gripped the orb at my chest. Somehow, I'd transferred the plague into two enemies. My legs weakened. I pressed my hands to my knees, propping myself up.

Dyana tugged at my arm. Her finger wiped gritty Sonus powder across my lips.

"Call the retreat!" She shook my shoulder.

I blinked, seeing only pieces of Dyana's face. I nodded again, more fervently.

"Retreat to the dome!" I screamed. "All those loyal to Dacia, retreat!" I pushed Dyana ahead, jogging down the mountain behind her just long enough for her to believe I was following her back to safety.

Near the dome, I spun and ran toward the center of the pass, littered with rocks and debris. I gripped the orb, pulling off the necklace, reconsidering the Seer's words.

The True Key wasn't just a key to the treasure; it was inextricably connected to the plague. Somehow the Lilac Plague lived inside of *me*. The Canina Thorn was literally an extension of me — of the curse I thought I'd ended when I opened the treasure. Instead. . .

I became *the weapon*.

Splaying my fingers in front of me, I pushed back two oncoming attackers. Facing the hordes of kingdoms and colony states still marching toward Dacia, I took a deep breath, concentrating on the *True Key*.

Something hitched inside me as if a hook had pierced through my stomach, extending out to my spine. I sucked in a breath as I fell to my knees. The Lilac Plague had awakened and was working its way through my body. Searching, prodding as I called it forth.

I struggled to breathe. I focused all my energy on connecting the key to the magic that had been inside me for moons. Blurry figures moved in my periphery. The enemy that hadn't been affected by Borsea's blinding light overtook those nearest me, moving to slay me.

Our enemies would merely split around my dome like a river, intending to converge on the castle and leave the poisoned valley to wither and die.

My lungs seemed to collapse, my body making a sucking noise, clawing for air. I shook, the exhaustion and pain from creating the dome melting me inside.

Magic sparked in my gut. A small pulse. I gritted my teeth, fanning it again, clutching the orb in both my trembling hands.

The magic pulsed faster, harder. My body melded with the gold orb. I couldn't release my grasp even if I'd wanted to. I shut my eyes tight, willing myself to push beyond the pain. The plague flared, blistering me from the inside, burning me to ash.

It blasted from my chest, a wind between my arms, my fingertips blazing. The plague rushed between my fingers like a fierce desert wind, scraping against my bones, threatening to shatter them. The sharp smell of the plague filled my nostrils; I breathed it out. The plague unleashed through my pores; my braid came loose, my hair snapping around me.

Even with my eyes closed, I could still see the plague in my mind, rushing forward, burrowing into every attacker — skipping over one, then another, sparing them. The rest, the plague filled their lungs, ripping their hearts.

The mountains and valley filled with pained screams. Yet the plague bubbled inside me, boiling. I called upon it to be my wrath, my blade in a thousand hearts. All the fear and turmoil I'd held so tight burst open, fueling my will. I cried out, but my voice was snatched by the wind, a vortex around me and the pelting storm within.

In a sudden *whoosh*, I was empty.

Without the magic, I was a vessel with no life. My face slammed against rocks and snow, my arms crushed underneath my own weight. Every fiber of my body screamed in pain even louder than the thousand souls now under siege by a plague they could not fight.

Petre, you will not have to wait long for me.

Darkness swooped in, and I welcomed it. The screams faded, and my senses began to float.

A PLEASANT BREEZE caressed my cheeks. My eyelids fluttered open. Distantly, I heard the Theracian and Norte soldiers screaming in agony. I pushed myself to my feet, my pain merely a dull echo.

Mists from Reflections rose around me. Snow began to fall on the dead and dying. Behind me, I felt the pulsing power of the dome. Down the mountain, past where Petre still lay, a lone, slender cloaked figure moved like a cloud.

Rubia?

The silver cloak billowed in the breeze as snow gently swirled around her. Drawing nearer, she lowered her cowl. Her honey-blond hair was pulled into a loose braid and draped over her shoulder. Her skin was healed of the pockmarks and blisters — whole.

"Mama?" I gasped. I rushed to embrace her, but she held out a hand, stopping me before I could reach her.

She smiled. There was a diffused glow about her.

"Our golden-eyed girl," she said. "I am so proud of you."

Tears filled my eyes, and my chin quivered. "Mama…"

She turned, and I followed, walking side-by-side across the fresh snow while more mists began rising.

"You protected your people, my sweet daughter." Her words were a balm cooling my wrath. She continued forward, as a wall of mist rose, blocking our way.

"The warlock, is his curse finally gone?" I asked.

Mama nodded. "You used the plague, the warlock's weapon, to secure the true heart on the throne and, in so doing, finally released the curse's last hold." She paused and looked at the undulating wall, snow flurrying around us. "The warlock had a strong hand in your fate — in mine and Rubia's as well. But you're free now.

I stared at my semi-translucent hands, not of this world anymore.

"I've come to give you a choice." Mama studied me. "The choice I robbed you of as did the warlock."

I wanted to follow Mama wherever she would go. My place was with her.

"If you cross to the other side with me, you can never come back," she said.

"B-but... I died. How can I go back?"

"You are young, and Rubia is already administering healing salves and wrapping your wounds. Even though your spirit has separated from your body, there is still time for you to return if you choose."

I turned to see Rubia pressing her hands to the mask on my face, her lips moving with her words of magic. Irena rushed to her side, sinking down next to my body. Part of me yearned to leave it all behind. But another part of me wasn't ready to let life go. There was still much I could do.

Mama's face was filled with kindness and so much love. Seeing her only increased my longing to be with her again. I'd missed her so incredibly much.

I felt torn between the mist ahead and my physical form behind. I had to choose.

"I'd do it all again, Mama. I'd take the path you gave me even knowing what I do now." Whatever guilt she carried, I wanted her to unburden herself.

She smiled, but her cheek twitched. She knew my decision. And I knew she knew.

"You have so much life left to live, our golden-eyed girl. Embrace the life you've always wanted. Go back to your papa, to Rubia, to him."

Mama reached a hand out from beyond the folds of her cloak, a long-stemmed canina rose between her fingertips. She placed it in my open palms, her eyes lingering on me. "I'll never be far, only just beyond, watching over you."

She stepped into the swirling mist. My heart swelled, wanting to hear her voice, just one more time. One more syllable. In a blink, she was gone.

I stared at the mist where Mama had gone. I could still follow.

Wind blew my too-thin cloak, slicing against my skin. My hair whipped across my face and my cloak dug into my neck.

I clutched the stem tight, closing my eyes, and stepped back.

As if drowning, my lungs screamed for air.

It has been a moon since Mama found a Ripper who dared to treat me, three moons since the Golden Empress died. I watched her die so many times, in so many different ways. It's almost unbelievable to know I witnessed her death though I was far away.

Ripper magic subdues my Seer ability. I honor the woman who showed Mama what was possible. Perhaps one day she will seek me out again, and I will be able to thank her myself.

I still dream, but I have far more control of it. I barely remember my dreams from before, but my journal entries help spark remembrances of what I saw, including how Empress Nicoleta used the key to unlock the treasure from the warlock, the treasure she had inside her.

A terrible way to die.

— ESME

CHAPTER
THIRTY-EIGHT
QUIET OF THE TOMB

A deep pain reverberated inside me. I wanted to retch, but I couldn't move — not even a finger.

Perfect. My plan was going as I'd hoped.

Rubia's voice sounded in the darkness, her tone low. She was talking to Jamil, his voice ragged. Rubia would tell Jamil and Papa the truth of what had happened to me after my funeral. But for now, she and I had to keep up pretenses.

My mind started to drift again, aching for sleep. It had been a little over a week since I'd died on the battlefield, and my body had slowly begun healing while Rubia's magic kept me deeply unconscious most of the time.

"I thought Nikka would survive in the end." Dyana's voice caught my attention. "A bitter disappointment, indeed." I hadn't ruled out the possibility of telling Dyana the truth someday.

"Nicoleta, Baise was yours more than she ever was mine, it seems," Asander's voice broke. "It brings me comfort to think of you riding her and harassing Petre. You saved me, and she saved everyone. Please take care of her. I know you will."

I'd heard the story of how I'd pierced the sky. Rubia had said that she saw Baise spiraling down from the top of the dome. The landing was rough, but Baise saved my life, cushioning my fall the

532

best she could. The magic had been too much for her, and the impact with the ground ended her.

Remembering the event, I struggled to breathe. My lungs began to ache for air. I felt trapped in my unmoving body. *Baise!*

"I'm still angry with you, you know," Dyana sniffed then cleared her throat. "I thought you were behind me as I rushed into the dome. I shall take this up with you next time we meet; don't you think you can get out of it." Her voice softened. "Safe passage, sister."

"The sun is setting," Rubia said. "Tradition holds that we must seal the tomb before dark or her soul will be trapped in here forever."

The Valley of the Emperors was a series of tunnels deep in the hillside, sealed with a stone that might as well have weighed as much as the castle itself. It would be an interesting escape.

The sound of rustling clothing indicated the Auripoans were complying. Rubia hurried them out, nervous they'd notice that I was breathing. Only slightly, but enough to reveal that I was decidedly *not* dead.

The footsteps faded outside my catacomb. The stone began scraping across the rocks, trapping me inside. I opened my eyes a slit, seeing only darkness. A weight fell on my chest, a momentary concern that I'd be trapped in this cave with the bodies of past royals. Pushing aside my fears, I focused on wiggling my fingers and toes.

Most people believed I died mere steps from the dome, which was true. What few knew was that I had revived long enough to squeeze Rubia's hand before slipping into unconsciousness. Rubia told me that a canina rose appeared in my grasp and the True Key vanished.

She let people mistake my unconsciousness for death. While the wagons traveled south to Rupea Castle after the war, when I awoke, she and I hatched a plan.

Rubia pointed out that someone with a goddess-like reputation could always "miraculously recover" if I chose. But I intended for Empress Nicoleta Aurelian to die. The Red Valley clan leader was right; it was time for a new leader. And I'd create a future of my own choosing, free of the bonds of the past.

Pinpricks in my extremities signaled progress. My breathing deepened. I blinked open my eyes to complete darkness. I eased myself up onto my elbows, the flowers slipping from my body and onto the floor.

I had no recollection of the ceremony, but as promised, Rubia had placed my Luminary orb next to me. With a brush of my hand, it illuminated the tall, narrow space. I stripped off the fine dress, worth more than everything I'd ever owned in Moesia. It was a pale green, which I couldn't believe Tulia had allowed. Then again, she had taken a position with the Agricultural Emissary, over-seeing his entire estate.

Underneath the dress, I wore plain clothes fit for a Poppy. I smeared my face with ash as a proper Getaen in mourning.

Dipping my fingers in the Sonus powder, I then pushed back the square, pale marble stones that blocked the doorway to the rest of the cave. My hands ached whenever I used magic. The dull pain was caused by either creating the dome or releasing the plague — Rubia wasn't sure; both times my hands grasped powerful relics. Only time would tell if the effects would fade.

I put out my hands to pulse the stones back into place, but I paused, my mind clearing.

Oh, yes, I nearly forgot.

It was almost eerie how quickly I'd forgotten to prepare for common things like gathering coins for food and lodging. The Rose Court likely found my burial dress quaint with a commoner tradi-tion of stitching coins into the apron. I returned to the gown with my black dagger, and I snapped the threads.

After shoving the bronze bits into my pocket, I lifted both hands to my crown, a simple circlet. For the last time, I lifted the weight from my brow. I set it on my dress and stepped back, a wistful last good-bye to the finery of my empress-self before leaving it in my now empty tomb.

But the accoutrements of the palace were never my true desire.

I pushed the stones back in place, closing the door, shedding my royal life like skin I'd outgrown. I limped past the column of white marble, passing the rest of the rough, natural cave. Rubia had been able to save my frostbitten toes, but I had other, lasting wounds.

The scar Borsea left on my cheek would never completely heal. The deaths I'd witnessed would always be imprinted on my heart.

At the entrance to my royal tomb in the Valley of the Emperors, a massive stone had already been rolled into place. I waited, wanting to be sure the crowd of mourners had dispersed though Rubia would have forcefully reminded them of the tradition.

I slipped the glowing orb into my rough cloak, snuffing the light and placed my fingers on the stone. Tilting the magic at just the right angle, it budged. I peeked through the crack. Only burning torches stood sentinel, fiery flames set against the black sky. As I pushed harder, the stone rolled away. The snow crunched under my thin boots as I pivoted and returned the stone into place.

Without a backward glance, I walked into the night.

The war ended. The invading armies were reduced by the Lilac Plague, but some survived, especially those furthest from the late Empress. Theracian colony states have risen up. I See many paths for each battle. Most importantly, Emperor Saam is too busy putting down rebellions to turn his attention to our people. Though Saam should be wary of his own court; several traitorous paths lead to his murder.

My brother, Cy, our new clan leader, is simply relieved to hear that the Theracians will not harass our clan.

The Norte have slunk home, licking their wounds. Most of their people were involved with the battle, in one form or another, so their population has shrunk considerably. Most of their slaves have escaped, and my brother sent word to the new empress to alert her to refugees in need of care.

In the future, the Norte paths diverge greatly. I am recording the ones that could impact Dacia in the upcoming generations as a warning and a guide.

It is a reminder of how the future depends on the decisions of those on the paths. Sometimes, people or events push one off the path they'd intended. But those times usually pale in comparison to the impact of each individual's decisions; they cause their paths to split and branches to disappear.

As Empress Nicoleta showed, we choose to be a hero.

I can no longer See every possibility, but I do not miss my power. I could not be more gloriously happy.

— *ESME*

THIRTY-NINE

A NEW REIGN

High in the mountains, far above the Rupea Castle's turrets, I sat on the rocky precipice from which I'd watched Mystic Marianna's funeral moons ago. The fields below were cut like spokes on a wheel, each section a different color: rich brown, shades of bright green, and deep emerald. In the fall, some would turn a grainy-gold as they completed their life-cycle in blazen glory.

Merchant wagons trundled across the road, kicking up dust on their way to the Capidavan markets, almost like the war had never happened.

Almost.

"I thought I'd find you here," Katalin said as she joined me. We watched the moving landscape in companionable silence, each lost in our thoughts. Or so I thought.

"Do you regret your choice?" she asked.

I considered her question and what I was ready to share. After a deep breath, I answered. "I regret many things. But I don't regret stopping the plague. I don't regret defending our people." I faced her and smiled. "And I don't regret handing over the crown."

What I couldn't tell her was how my heart ached. Even

knowing the decisions I'd made were for the greater good of the kingdom, they still stung.

"Black looks good on you," Katalin said, a gleam in her eye. "Are you ready to exchange aprons for something befitting one of the Empress' Own?"

I tucked up my knees to my chest, trying to hold in the hurt. "A year ago, I would've preferred death over becoming a Thorn."

"And now?"

"Now, I respect the Own. The honor of being one should be earned by coming up the ranks the proper way."

"Captain Lucius has already offered positions in the city guard to all those returning from the battle." Katalin stared at me, her eyes narrowing in her shrewd way of assessment. Then, she cocked her head to the side. "Walk with me."

I opened my mouth to protest, but she shook her head.

"I'm not sitting next to you and getting my gown dirty. Besides, you've done enough moping out here."

Grinning, I stood and followed her through the secret door and then down the winding stairs. She moved with grace while I gripped the railing with my good hand, limping down behind her. Ever the thoughtful friend, Katalin had an ironworker reinforce the railing when I'd returned to Rupea Castle. Otherwise, it would've broken under my weight on the first trip up.

"Rubia is coming today, correct?" Katalin asked.

"Yes, I'll use the Own's tunnels to meet her in Papa's room."

Katalin's silence indicated she was waiting for more, but my personal health was something I'd only share when I was ready. Not before.

My grip strength had returned to my left hand, but my right was still weak. My knees were generally fine, but after sitting so long on the mountain, they ached, my movement stiff. Rubia warned I might always have a bit of trouble when the weather was temperamental.

Initially, I feared I'd never wield a sword again. The Canina Thorn had been an extension of me, easy to control. Re-learning with other blades felt clumsy in comparison. However, I was making progress. And I was more than proficient with Sonus powder.

We approached the bottom of the newly-repaired stairs where one of the Empress' Own waited. Instinctively, I dropped my chin to my chest, my hair falling to obscure my face. Just as quickly, I reminded myself that all of my Own who'd survived had been sent on assignments in other areas of the kingdom, a necessity of circumstance. Furthermore, the newly-appointed Owns' minds were altered to remember a blurred version of the Golden Empress.

At first, I'd been nervous about my true identity being discovered in the castle. However, between Rubia coloring my hair chestnut brown, my plain clothing, and my new scar, no one seemed to notice an additional orphan of the war under the protection of Empress Katalin Vulpe.

I walked at Katalin's side, her Own flanking us as we walked through the secret, windowless passageway. She flashed a small Sonus stone, and I nodded my agreement. She placed it between her hand and my shoulder, making it look like she was merely pulling a confidant close. A pulse of magic signaled that our conversation was silenced even from her Own.

"What's the update on the poisoning of the Rodnic Valley?" I asked. Such questions might raise the suspicion of the Own, especially as I was now a lowly orphan Lilac.

"We think Irena's assumption is correct. The Protection in the dome is filtering out the poison as it passes through underground aquifers. It's acting like a net."

"So, the people didn't need to move?" I asked.

"The water from the glacier flows underground in sheets, and not all pass under the dome. So, some of the fields have significant poison deposits. Irena estimates two years to remove it all. Some of the northern families have relocated closer to the glass houses for work until they can return home."

Katalin gave me a small pat, reassuring me that I had done well. "Between the relocated farmers and the freed slaves, many workers are available to hire. And with the need to re-plant and grow crops, there's plenty of work to go around. The best part is that all the crown has done was facilitate the match-up of former slaves to new jobs. A little bit of work, and the kingdom will gain future taxes in the process. The nobles are a bit sore about their change in lifestyle, but I think the fear of losing their lives to the Norte softened the blow. At least for most of them."

I smiled ruefully. "There will always be a few who are resistant to change. You can never please everyone."

I hoped her lessons would be far milder than my own in this arena.

Katalin slowed as we neared the door that led to the main portion of the castle. "I'm glad you've rested here these last weeks. I've appreciated your compassionate ear as well as your wisdom. You're the only person I can fully trust and confide in."

I'd come to realize the Getaen clan leader tradition of passing the mantle of leadership was a wise and good pattern to curtail corruption and lead to more stability. Though I didn't know if Katalin would choose to hand over the crown before she died, all I could do was advise her, which suited me fine.

As we entered the stairwell, Katalin dropped her hand away, removing the silent barrier, and returned the stone into her pocket.

"I'll miss you while you're in the Red Valley," she lamented as we climbed up the stairs to the Hall of the Emperors. "I expect letters every week and a full report when you return."

"As the empress commands," I said with a hint of sarcasm and a deep curtsy.

In the protected corridor, I stood back as Katalin continued up to the main floor of the castle without me. We'd agreed not to be seen together often, publicly; favoritism would lead to suspicion and questions. I hurried down the Luminated corridor to the secret entrance to the Own's tunnels. I plunged inside the darkness. Controlling my fears had become easier though they never completely went away. I slowed in the cramped corridor as I approached the entrance to Katalin's chamber. I identified myself to the Own, and they escorted me into the room. Midnight jumped off the couch and bounded over to greet me, practically knocking me over with her enthusiasm.

"Hello, my beautiful girl," I scratched behind her ears.

Seeing Midnight's approval, the Own returned to his duty in the tunnels. On my knees, I wrapped my arms around Midnight. Giving her up was even more difficult than I'd imagined. Midnight had always been fond of Katalin, and an empress needed a protector. But more importantly, everyone knew Midnight was my near-constant companion.

Dogs and dire wolves were not easy to fool in regards to *true* identity.

I suspected that Marcus wouldn't be either.

I'd told Katalin I needed to cut ties to my former life, including Marcus and Midnight.

The truth was not quite so simple. I had a wagonload full of emotional baggage to sort through, much of which included my feelings for the farmer-boy-turned-emissary: from my guilt over not saving his sister's life, to pulling him close and letting him go.

Surprisingly, the person I'd confided in the most was Jamil. I might not have revealed that I was alive to my former Own, but as he and Rubia were nearly inseparable since his announced retirement, Katalin agreed that he should be informed. I was glad I had decided to include Jamil in my secret. Between Papa, Rubia, and Katalin, he was the only one who could understand the trauma of war and the sacrifices I'd made.

Marcus could have too, in some respects, but I was too late. Even I'd heard the gossip about the handsome Agricultural Emissary and the dark Lazican beauty who'd come to reside at the elegant Constantin estate.

Katalin entered the room, delivering a command to the guard, and then the door shut behind her.

"You sit in the mud and then on my couches, Ni —" she paused her teasing, flicking her gaze up to where the Own was stationed, hidden behind the wall. "Leila, I just keep getting you confused with another orphan." With her back to the viewing port, she gave me a grimace in apology.

"Well, understandable with all the orphans under your care." I'd taken Mama's name to honor her, but everyone was having a difficult time with the change, especially Papa.

I hadn't told anyone about my vision of Mama. It was my sacred experience, one I might never share. After I'd seen Mama, my nightmares of her had ended. I'd had plenty of other nightmares since, just not any that tainted my memory of her anymore.

I held out my Sonus stone, and Katalin pressed a finger against it, silencing our conversation. We sat with our backs to the Own, pretending to only play with Midnight as we spoke.

"You'll need to practice my name, *especially* if you want me to be one of your Own," I said.

"I would prefer to have you as an adviser. In a few years, no one will ever suspect who you really are. But, I know your heart is set on going through the ranks of the Thorns, spying and whatnot. I'm patient."

"We shall see." After my experiences, I knew I could become one of the elite Empress' Own, or a spy, a healer, a scholar, a royal adviser — anything felt possible. I was thrilled for a chance to pursue my own dreams. "Have you heard from the queen of Auripo?"

Dyana had only sent two letters since my death. She'd agreed to new foreign emissaries who would reside in either kingdom, keeping communication and ties strong. She'd already emphasized that they considered Dacia to be a sister-kingdom, in honor of Asander's blood sister, Empress Nicoleta. And as long as she or Asander were alive, our kingdom was considered their greatest ally.

After telling me the Auripoan news, Katalin retreated to the fireplace, staring at the glowing embers. I ran my fingers through Midnight's fur, finally breaking the silence.

"I miss him, too."

"Who?"

"Petre," I said softly. "I know he was special to you."

She stilled. "I don't know what you mean."

"He was a good man, Empress. And I know he cared about you, too. That's why he rode Baise, a creature he felt was vile beyond belief. He came to see you."

Katalin's fingers pinched the mantle, her chin dropping.

Before either of us could speak, someone knocked on the door. Our lunch had arrived. Not wanting servants to see me in her chambers, I scurried to the tunnel, practically shoving the Own stationed there out of my way before sliding the door back in place.

I peered through the viewing port in time to see Katalin wipe her eyes and smooth her apron. The Imperial Guard entered. Strange because they usually didn't officially announce the servants for lunch.

As the guard left, a man entered the room.

I gasped.

Despite his appearance, I drank him in. Marcus had grown a beard. Were those dark circles under his eyes? Was Katalin working him too hard?

Was he not happy?

My treacherous heart thundered against my ribs as if trying to escape. Trying to find its way to my love.

Marcus said something to Katalin, but his words were too muffled to be heard over the roaring of blood in my ears. A vice tightened over my chest, and I pounded a fist against the stone.

Why would Katalin parade him in front of me? Meddlesome friend—

I spun on my heel to flee, but guilt pricked my soul. If I ran now, what kind of person did that make me?

Marcus was mourning the loss of his sister. His family's farms had been poisoned, forcing them all to relocate, which I knew Otho and his eldest daughters would hate. If I turned away from Marcus, I was never worthy of his friendship; the least I could do was to listen to his pain. He'd earned that much. Steeling myself, I turned back to the port.

He was closer now, and I could hear their conversation.

"— guessed that your Lazican guest would fall in love with Lord Jovian." Katalin's voice was overly apologetic.

"Oh, you've heard the latest rumor about our family friend." Marcus sighed. "Lord Jovian is a bit too high-hat in my opinion, but she'll move on to some other lord and leave him with a broken heart. She has no intention of settling down anytime soon. She enjoys fine events and freedom more than a committed companion. Besides, she's wise enough to know that half of the men are after her beauty, and the other half want her coin."

"And you have no interest in her?" Katalin glanced at the viewing port, seeming to look right at me through the wall.

"I adore many things about her, but not in any romantic way." Marcus shook his head, his brow furrowed. "She's a childhood friend, nothing more. We already discussed this —"

"Indeed," Katalin replied. "I now recall you saying as much. I simply think at least one of us should be happy." Katalin spoke to Marcus, but she gazed straight at the viewing port, at me.

She moved to her desk, Marcus behind her, as she shot me a look of exasperation.

"There's something of Nikka's I thought you should have." She slid a box into the center of the desk, signaled to my Own to follow her, and then walked to the door.

"What? Empress, do you want me to wait here?" Marcus called after her.

Katalin snapped her fingers, and Midnight hurried out the door. "Oh, yes, Lord Constantin, please wait. I'll return shortly. I just need to step away. . ."

The door slammed before Marcus could reply. The Own next to me slipped away, following Katalin through the castle. Marcus threw up his hands and paced to the fireplace. He folded his arms across his chest and glared across the room at the box.

I chewed my lip. Katalin had orchestrated this private meeting.

She wouldn't force me to go to Marcus, but she gave me the oppor-tunity. The next step was mine.

I pressed my forehead against the port and closed my eyes.

What did I want?

I was stuck as time both crawled and flew by.

I'd spent countless, sleepless nights wishing for what I could never have. I'd gritted my teeth and sacrificed on behalf of everyone else — even the entire kingdom. I'd spent so long thinking about what I should do...

Blood rushed in my ears, and my mouth turned to cotton. The wound I'd believed healed bled with fresh agony.

If I said I didn't love him, I'd be a liar.

If I ran away now, I'd be a coward.

But if I stepped back into his life, it would turn his upside down yet again? What would that do to him?

I opened my eyes as Marcus slumped against the wall; the dying embers in the fireplace lit the hollows of his face. He continued to stare at the box, barely blinking.

Abruptly, he straightened and, squaring his shoulders, strode to the desk and jerked open the lid. His expression crumpled, and he swallowed, his neck bobbing up and down.

Reverently, he pulled out the leather lace that had once held my necklace, and his hand trembled.

Tears burned my eyes.

This man...

Marcus balled the lace up in his fist, slamming it against his chest. His shoulders shook as he unfurled it in his palm and pulled the lace over his head, tucking it under his camasa.

He lifted his chin, his eyes shut tight, pressing his hand to the leather against his skin.

I ran my finger across the scar above my cheekbone. He was so good. And a Lily now, with responsibilities. I was noth-ing. A ghost. A woman in the shadows. Officially, an orphan Lilac with no inheritance, no title, and no reputation of any kind.

If I let him go, Marcus could move on. He could have an honorable life with a wife appropriate for his station.

But if I let him go. . .

If I couldn't be honest... I'd never be worthy of him or trust myself.

All that I fought for, all that I believed in, culminated in this moment.

Because now it was my decision.

Marcus returned the lid to its place and straightened.

I pressed my hands against the wall, and my breaths grew shallow. Why was I so afraid?

He marched to the door, and my heart stopped.

Suddenly, my fear of rejection, unworthiness, and everything else fled. My only fear now was I'd lost my opportunity and would never have another.

I burst through the Own's entrance into Katalin's chambers and caught a glimpse of Marcus' back as he stepped out the door.

As the door shut, I could barely choke out a word.

"M-Marcus—"

The door clicked shut. The carvings in the wood blurred as tears welled in my eyes. I sucked in a breath, determined to rush past the guards just outside.

But the door slowly reopened, and Marcus stood in the doorway, staring. At me. He blinked, his shoulder slamming into the stone wall as he clutched at the leather under his camasa.

I tried to speak, but words refused to form.

His chest swelled as a smile lit his face. He rushed forward, sweeping me into his arms, and he buried his face in my neck.

Tears spilled down my cheeks, and I murmured his name, over and over — both a plea and a benediction.

"I'm sorry," I whispered. "I'm so sorry, Marcus."

"Nicoleta, my love, Nicoleta..." He pulled back, and his gaze caressed me as his words filled all the broken parts of my soul. "If you're a trick of my mind... I don't care," he said, keeping one arm firmly around my waist, the other trembling as he grazed my jawline. "I don't care," his voice cracked. "Just don't leave me again."

I'm real. The words caught in my throat. "I won't."

Marcus brushed his fingers over my neck and collarbone, sparks igniting under his touch. He pulled my hands up between us, gently caressing the flesh between each knuckle, first with his thumbs and then with his lips.

He pulled me closer and kissed the tears from my cheeks. And when he pressed his lips to mine, the salt of our tears was lost in the sweetness of his lips. My knees weakened, and his other arm wrapped securely around me, keeping me on my feet.

"I thought letting you believe I was dead would allow you to move on."

Marcus shook his head. "Don't you know, Nicoleta? There's no moving on from you."

My eyes welled with fresh tears, and he wiped them away. "You may be a Thorn or a Rose or a Lilac, but you'll always have my heart. Please don't leave again, my love."

"Remember when I was a scholar's d-daughter, and you asked if you could v-visit me?" I wet my lips. "The answer is 'yes,' but I'm hard to find. So, I came to you."

Marcus' hands pressed up my arms and then around my shoulders, enveloping me in his scents of warm hay and sharp mint. All the residual anguish melted into the background, but there were things he should know.

"Marcus," I said, stepping back, trying not to stare at his lips. "There are things I want to d-do."

He nodded. "Then we will do them together."

"And I have n-nightmares."

"Then I will hold you."

"No one can know who I am."

His laugh burst from his lips, and I stiffened.

Bending to look me in the eye, he said, "Then you will have to trust me to keep your secret, for I would know you anywhere." He picked up a lock of my dark hair. "Something from Rubia?"

When I nodded, he added, "Then perhaps she can do something more."

"There will be gossip," I warned. Tongues would wag about the esteemed Lily emissary entangled with a Lilac with a resemblance to the late empress.

Marcus shrugged. "Let them talk."

"And I want to become one of the Empress' Own."

He exhaled and pressed his forehead to mine. In a low voice that was strained with emotion, he said, "I would move all of Dacia if I need to, every grain of desert sand; I'll quail every rumor. I'll stand by your side and help you discover whatever your next steps should be. Nikka, I would do anything to make you happy."

How could he not see?

"You already have."

Marcus smiled, tension melting in his shoulders. "You know, my home is one of the oldest on the hill. It has a few secret passages. Whenever you're ready, we could explore them together."

"I look forward to it," I whispered.

Marcus stepped back and pulled something from his pocket, a mischievous glint in his eye. He took my hand and pressed something into my palm.

"I've been holding onto this for you."

In my hand was the Moesian gold that I'd given him moons ago. I clutched it to my chest.

Though my heart was still healing, my mind buzzed with the future, an elation I hadn't felt before. A smile blossomed on my lips. Marcus pulled me close again, and I rose to meet him. Our kiss was like home in the spring with flowers bursting with color and beauty and promise. I moved my hands to Marcus' beard, then squeezed his arms, making sure he was really next to me.

He was.

I actually looked forward to the rumors of the Rose Court. No matter what storms came our way, we would weather them. Together.

THANK you for joining Nicoleta on her epic journey. Please join me as I tell more fantastical stories!

Find me here:

Newsletter sign-up at Kristinjdawson.com

Instagram @KristinImagines

Facebook @KristinJLiterary

Amazon at Kristin J. Dawson

Bookbub at Kristin J. Dawson

AUTHOR'S NOTE

Thank you for going on this wild ride with Nicoleta! This was an amazing story to tell. I knew the beginning and the ending of this story before I started writing, but even so, getting Nikka to this point cost me more tears than I'd imagined. I hope you loved the emotion, the twists and turn, the magic, and the epic arcs of the characters in the Unchosen trilogy.

This story is about the rise and fall of power, but in the end, it was always about relationships and our genuine friendships and love for others.

ACKNOWLEDGMENTS

My fantastic editor, M.K. Martin, has been with me on this series for three years, from conception to fruition. She continued to develop the unique an linguistically correct 'language of magic,' and she lent her hardwon combat expertise to *The Canina Thorn.*

Several author friends helped with snippets of this story, but Raye Wagner spent many hours helping develop the romantic arc. Readers may not realize how many tears authors pour into each story, and when I ran out of tears to give, Raye gave some of hers, too.

My Beta Readers, Emily and Jessica, you ladies are amazing!

Extra big thank you to my critique partners, Polly Irving, Paul Tallman, Sarah Shipley, and M.K. Martin, who helped me form the initial story. Paul spent extra time helping me sort out the magic system early on so it could develop so epically beautiful in this last book.

Thank you Kathleen Gooch for the copy edits, to Dawn Yacovetta and Sue-Ellen Welfonder for the proofreads. Your notes in the margins are always a delight!

Biggest thank you to my husband who held down the family-fort so I could write this wild tale.

About the Author

K. J. Dawson loves lionhearted, tenacious characters who step into their own adventure! She also loves chocolate, forests, and staying up too late — night owls unite! Kristin writes high fantasy with political intrigue, a bit of romance, and of course, magic. When she's not writing, toting her kids around to sports practices, or cleaning out the chicken coop, she's probably curled up with a fuzzy blanket and a book. Find her at: www.kristinjdawson.com

Also by K. J. Dawson

The Unchosen

The Lilac Plague

The Rose Court

The Canina Thorn

Stand Alone Fairytale

The Poisoned Prince

Fae Illusions of Trinth

Elven House of Ivy

Elven Council in Ashes (coming 2025)

www.ingramcontent.com/pod-product-compliance
Lightning Source LLC
Chambersburg PA
CBHW020512110726
47899CB00004B/1094